Published by
Metapulp, Inc.
New York

Library of Congress Cataloguing-in-Publication
Data

salem, 1969-
Black Hole Butterfly / salem

p cm

ISBN 978-0-9894161-1-5

BLACK HOLE BUTTERFLY

BY SALEM

PART ONE: Detective Rook Black

CHAPTER ONE: Marco Polo

1: The Scent of Blood

Grass and blood, Rook thought. *Why?*

Papers spread around the lab like ornate white hand fans, scrawled with brittle, black-inked handwriting and chemical equations, revealed Dr. Chess's research was obsessive. The botanist, detective Rook Black quickly surmised, took pride in his ability to discern the scents of numerous species of grass. A framed photo showed the white haired doctor blindfolded, an assistant waving a small vial of oil borne grass extract under his nose. *Name that grass*, Rook thought, *name that blood.*

Dr. Chess, far beyond simply studying grass, was studying the relationship of grass to blood. The molecules of each, Rook noted from equations prominently and seemingly permanently displayed on a chalkboard, were quite similar: four atoms of nitrogen made a square and in the center was one atom of either magnesium or iron. The difference between a plant and an animal was an improbably simple jump from chlorophyll to hemoglobin, from green to red. *From go*, Rook thought, *to stop.* He observed animated screensaver footage of chloroplast cells squirming like green bubbles alongside footage of red blood cells flowing in an artery. Both: cellularly viscous in form, and sharp, acrid and metallic in scent. In grass, the metal was magnesium, and in blood, iron. The olfactory difference, Rook seized as he breathed in the scent of the laboratory's live grasses, was in the smell of the metal. *Grass and blood*, he realized, *one miraculous atom apart.*

Rook knew all too well the scent of blood, if it could be called a scent. When fresh, his own, a nick on the lip while shaving, it was not cannibalistic to lick it. It was strangely pleasing. Blood was the taste of iron, of red rusty oxidized iron, but when pooling in death, then coagulating, it was rust deflowering into rot.

It was an abhorrent stench he had first smelled when he had found his father in the bathtub, the man's wrists slit and the edges of iron rich red spatters, like the stain of dying leaves, blackening on the slick white tile.

The detectives investigating his father's apparent suicide eventually had burned pounds of oily roasted coffee beans to mask the stench. Cleared of patricide, released solo to the world, an ashen Rook struggled with the mental void of death, and he reeled against the overwhelming silence that took the place of what had been his father's immense genius. His father was the only person he had ever really spoken in depth with, and he ambled the dark New York City streets, his ears crashing with unanswered questions, seeking solace from the ugliness and voiceless noise. The streets reeked of sewage, haunting him with death.

In time, as Rook became accustomed to dead bodies, he became increasingly silent and comfortable with the void left behind from vanished lives. But he never became accustomed to the stench. Menthol under the nose was not strong enough. Away from the crime scene, Rook habitually sank his senses into a cup of black coffee thick, dank and bitter as mud. He was addicted to coffee and he was addicted to crime. He understood his addictions and accepted them in the same way he accepted the color of his eyes: coal black and simply there.

Weed. Blood. Grass. Chess. Hash. Assassin. The alliteration rolled over Rook's inner tongue and clattered into killer. *Hashkiller. Chesskiller.* That one dredged through him, opening a memory of his father's murder, and his next thoughts stretched over that grisly image of the naked man in the tub. *Chesskiller. Grasskiller. Weedkiller.*

Rook abandoned the memory and the lab with his forensic samples carefully arranged in a black leather case, his mind idling whether Dr. Chess was a pusher or being pushed. The hash oil seemed to be absolutely pure. The skanky jar, so innocently out in the open in the lab, could stone the city.

Back in his office Rook studied the samples. A piece of used chalk that cleanly held a set of bloody fingerprints, most notably the index, belonged he discovered to Dr. Chess.

The vomit proved to be paper pulp, black ink and gastric acid.

The blood samples proved to be animal. Rook wasn't sure which one.

Relaxing as his preliminary day of investigation came to a draw, Rook contemplated his desk, within which a chessboard was neatly inlaid, and he dipped a needle into the hash oil. He lit a match and held it under the needle. When the hash oil smoked, Rook sucked the smoke into his lungs through a glass tube. He coughed spastically on the harsh fumes for a long moment, and the stone hit him like an iron blanket. Reaching for his leather feedback mask, in which were sewn 113 nanoelectrodes, his mind rippled like the sea. He slipped the mask over his head, and as he buckled it, the nanoelectrodes mated with those embedded under his scalp. He sailed adrift in clues as the pungent stench of the hash jammed his lungs and tongue.

Rook Black the psychonaut closed his eyes, thinking, *Something smells*.

2: Black Market Reality

In the shadows under Pell Street in Chinatown, a man poured water into a tank of brilliant green papyrus reeds, and he said in a breath that stank like yellowed newsprint, "Reality has always been organic." With a dull razor clutched in blackened fingers he severed a reed at its base and slowly unrolled the fiber, holding it up to the other as a scroll. "Like plants, reality has cultivars. See here. I've grafted newspaper with papyrus."

The other man, a reality trader from Ningbo, Zhejiang province, leaned in and touched the dew beaded scroll. Chinese characters printed inside the fresh reed, seemingly leached from black organic residue, rubbed into his fingers.

"Careful. That's what I call black market ink. It's indelible. No soap will wash it out." The blackened fingers in the blackened hands rolled up the scroll quietly, absorbing black ink as it squeezed from the reed into his skin. He wrapped the reed in bright orange tissue paper as if it were a flower.

The reality trader watched the hands. "And have you grafted with the black market ink?"

His black pupils, set inside black corneas, stared at the reality trader. A knowing grunt issued as his answer, and his breath rushed forth, ill with the odor of old newspaper. "I have grafted with my shadow. I have grafted with *the* shadow."

The reality trader pulled back, his nose twitching under the paper mask he had been told to wear around the shadowy—and literally jet black—black market man, a man who had many nicknames but no real given birth name, at least not to anyone's knowledge.

At an antiquated gunmetal gray cash register, the blackened fingers tapped the sale button. The cash drawer shot open with a ding. "We invented paper money, and now we are known for what? Laundromats! Remember, it is birds and insects—but mostly the winds of change—that pollinate the reality weed."

Outside in the humid night, the reality trader glanced at a Chinatown laundromat. He laughed, knowing they had been using their laundromats as fronts for collecting DNA for over a decade. The Chinese gangs—tongs—had been suppressed, their products mocked as cheap and as knockoffs. *Knockoff DNA*, he thought, *good as the real thing.*

His tong had been enslaved to reality, and soon their new reality, carefully cultivated, would invade the city and then the world, returning control of it to his once dominant people. The Yellow Emperor, the father of China, was born to a thunderclap in a clear blue sky, and when he passed from the earth, he flew to heaven: half-man, half-dragon. The merchant from Ningbo had been present when they had dug up the Emperor's sacred grave on the mountaintop and sampled DNA from the petrified bones. *Half-man, half-dragon, so shall he return!*

Wind from a thunderstorm reached into Pell Street and grabbed at the fronds of the papyrus. The fronds quivered, and as gang gunfire peppered Chinatown, pale yellow pollen leapt into the air, suspended as a halo within raindrops dense as New Year's confetti.

3: Chinatown

Chinatown had always smelled bad. Fishy was the polite way to put it. The only thing that smelled worse than a dead body was, Rook thought, *Chinatown*. On morning two of his investigation, after his psychonaut session during which dream images loomed with noses, nostrils and snouts, Rook took his gut hunch and headed to the Chinese pocket of Manhattan. At street level in the morning, he observed as box trucks dropped off wooden crates of bitter greens and living blue crabs. Catfish flopped in buckets, and tilapia—claimed as fresh—thawed in cardboard boxes on the dirty sidewalk. He watched as an old woman attached seven small gray fish, their bellies slit, to a pink hanger by clothespins and hung the contraption on her clothesline. The fish dangled, their dead eyes staring at the squalor, next to her girdle and brassiere. The foul black air of Grand Street was her smoker. *Fresh rotting fish*, Rook thought, and it was a stench so dense he could almost bite it.

Angela had given him the lead to Dr. Chess, he decided, not just for the pun on game playing. Hash and blood pointed to an assassination, he believed, that either had or would take place. The epiphenomenon of Dr. Chess, he knew, was incidental—held inside the parentheses of whatever greater crime it was he had been hired to solve. The greater crime was as yet undefined. If he knew what it was from the beginning of his investigation, he would make inferences and mistakes. Rook preferred to solve crime in reverse: his assistant Angela gave him a lead far removed from the crime he was hired to solve, in this instance, the phone number of Dr. Chess. Through the process of discovering the crime he would inevitably find the guilty.

It was not uncommon during the course of an investigation for Rook to come across the dead. Crime begat crime, and the motion of guilt inevitably rippled into patterns that would, in time, direct Rook's investigation. Rook was still inclined to set aside the whole of Dr. Chess—his relevance would surface eventually—and focus on the man's unique powers of smell. He breathed in again the funky, fishy rot of Chinatown, thinking, *Somehow Angela wants me to understand the crime I'm solving literally stinks.*

He remembered the hash oil. The cultivation was another first the Chinese could lay claim to. Wandering Chinatown randomly he let his nose guide him, sniffing for the part of Chinatown that stank the most. He switched to method and walked the Chinatown grid, perusing its small and crowded streets one by one, window-shopping gold jewelry stores here and there in case anyone was watching him.

The stench found him before he found it, and the noxious urge to vomit queased through him. He calmed himself mentally and breathed in again. A curtain of large black flies dodged him and nipped at his bare flesh. He brushed them away and peered into a taxidermist tannery.

Inside, behind mosquito net tents that held back the flies, translucent skinned Chinese men in white coats spattered with blood hacked away at an eight-foot crocodile. They were seemingly oblivious to the stench, and the cheap white paper masks they wore strapped to their faces under their slashing black eyebrows were as useless as napkins. The crocodile had already been skinned. Splayed open for curing and tanning, the giant crocodile skin itself seemed marked like a city street map, and it dwarfed the men who tweaked it on a rack. Several other greenish skins were already splayed and well on their way to putrefying. The stench issued not from the dead crocodile but from the chemicals being used to prepare the skins: shit and piss. One of the workers urinated shamelessly into a large communal white ceramic chamber pot already foaming with bright yellow urine. Electrical wires dove from the lights in the ceiling, terminating in the pot. They were using the chamber pot for as many products as possible, Rook noted, *Even electricity*. Credit card sized batteries that jumped electrons from copper to magnesium through the electrolytes in urine had been the rage in Singapore and China but not here. Bioelectrolytes could not power the world, but they did power this tannery, *Keeping it*, Rook surmised, *off the solar empire grid. Why?*

Another worker used his bare feet to massage fecal matter into a putrefied skin. The very little of the dead crocodile the Chinese had no use for was the chemically decomposed, scraped skin mixed with the urine and feces. One worker sloughed the waste into a pit Rook assumed was filled with quick lime. The stench rollercoastered his stomach. He had to leave.

Further out on the street, his eyes stinging, Rook noticed the shop where the completed skins were sold. They were displayed and stacked like green Persian rugs. *If somebody wanted to get rid of a human body*, Rook thought, *this would be the place to do it.*

He bought a cup of coffee from a street vendor, rolled its bitter blackness in his mouth, then took photos of the tannery and sales shop through his digitized mirrored sunglasses. Parts of the signs were in English, and the rest were in Chinese. Back in his sedan he sipped the coffee as a computer entrained to the sunglasses translated the signs. Respectively, each sign read *Marco Polo Tannery* and *Marco Polo Taxidermy*.

Rook turned the ignition and slipped into the speeding traffic of Front Street. A small orange handball bounced into the intersection from the East River walkway, and his eyes jerked right to where a young Chinese boy, maybe five, burst from his mother after the ball. Rook hit the brakes, cranked the parking brake and leapt out into blurring, manic traffic. Amidst the rude rush of honking, Rook caught the ball on a long bounce off a yellow taxi hood and quickly tossed it to the boy.

Simultaneously traffic condensed around Rook's parked sedan, and chaos erupted: two yellow taxis collided, one flipped skyward, twirled like an acrobat just over Rook's head and rolled, crashing down roof to roof on top of Rook's sedan with startling metallic thunder. Shattered windshields spattered red.

Dozens of cars flooded past in panic, veering around the chaos. At its center Rook calmly waited and watched as the boy caught the ball by reflex, halted and teetered in the gutter, awed by the destruction in the street. The white stem of a lollipop poked innocently out of his lips under his widening eyes. His mother's harsh reprimands became lost in smearing squeals as a black towncar almost clipped the boy, and she jerked her son backwards to safety. The lollipop ejected from the boy's lips into the gutter. *Too young*, Rook thought, *for the void.* Rook turned to the metal crunching as the upside down yellow taxi flattened, threaded his way through traffic and pushed into the pedestrian crammed sidewalk before the boy and thankful mother could get a make on him. *I just saved his life*, he thought, *and he just saved mine.*

From under the brim of his black hat, a compact pea souper of overlaid, thin synthetic bands designed to keep the ever present humid rain off his brow and to further hide his dark, always searching eyes, he called Cosmo. "The sedan has been in an accident. I need a tow immediately."

Five minutes later a specialized tow truck extracted the sedan from the metal mess, and by the time Rook walked home to the Lower East Side, an identical sedan was parked in front of his door. He observed it, identical in every way to the other, down to the cracks in the upholstery. Like the tannery, his sedan was off-grid as well. Rook did not want his moves traced, and neither, he inferred, did the Marco Polo Taxidermy and Tannery. *There's something*, he thought, *they don't want the solar empire to know.*

***

Forty-five minutes later Cosmo Hamilton, a lanky, bald senior who favored three-piece tweeds and bright bow ties, received the wrecked sedan upstate, thinking, *All is going according to plan.* The tow-truck driver handed Cosmo a small plastic bag, which sealed the sticky stem of the boy's orange-flavored lollipop.

From the hard drives built into the sedan's computers, Cosmo extracted the past twenty-four hours of Rook's surveillance, and he copied the data before sending the drives to Rook by private courier. He felt a gnawing, that even though everything was going according to plan, something was amiss. He isolated the boy's saliva from the candy and therefrom derived his DNA. Cosmo's wrinkled and liver spotted hands placed the sample inside an atomic imager and momentarily generated an artful reproduction of the DNA. Within a monitor, which suspended wirelessly as a large tactile screen in his lab, the reproduction spread like wings of a butterfly. Cosmo touched the screen, and the alternating orange and blue colors rippled in response. He manipulated at the quantum level what he recognized as a DNA strain named Silk Road, and he let the reality storm —seemingly having intelligence of its own—do the rest.

***

Simultaneously in midtown on the east side of Manhattan, a plastic auction paddle with the number *113* emblazoned on it was held high for the last remaining collection of original Shakespeare Company flexible matchbooks. The man holding the paddle, his face crisscrossed in calcified scars, his golden eyes obscured behind lightly orange tinted eyeglasses, held his paddle aloft for one more moment while the auctioneer pestered the crowd for a higher bid. There was no longer any contest.

"Sold to 113!"

The man lowered his paddle, stood and headed toward the cashier to make immediate payment by quantum currency transfer.

After the sale made its way through the encrypted Federal Reserve servers, the matchbooks, a lot of one hundred, were carefully wrapped in a fireproof box and delivered directly to the representative of the buyer. The sinewy, bald man appeared to be in his sixties, and he was impeccably dressed in a shark swimming in dark waters gray suit and pale green, tieless shirt. He signed for the package, Mr. Jules Barbillon.

He read in the yellowed company brochure, now sheathed in a museum quality plastic sleeve, that the origin of the name of the Shakespeare Company was derived from the owner's fondness not for the works of Shakespeare but for his love of Shakespeare's neologisms. He read further, "*At the heart of everyday English speaking life, there thrives in and on the tongues of conversationalists a relay of phrasing lifted from the heart of the Bard's ink.*"

As much as two smokers might assist one another in the lighting of a cigarette, leaning in against the wind, hands cupped, manly faces brushing close for the inhale, so would they inevitably, the brochure boasted, exchange gratuities and conversation between exhaled blasts of smoke. And this language might contain keywords such as *arch-villain* or even *sanctimonious*. Not because these words were on their minds but because they had been planted into their minds via the inclusion of the word, its definition and Shakespearean origin, on the inside of the matchbook.

Only in America, he thought, *would a man try to spread the wealth of Shakespearean idiom through the pop culture of a matchbook.*

Safety matches, during the short-lived heyday of the Shakespeare Company, had not been invented yet, and from time to time the match-striker would find his or her fingers quite suddenly holding nothing but a flame, bursting like a rose from the hissing heads as the entire book blossomed into fire.

Only in New York City, he thought, *would these be wanted for the purpose of poetic arson.*

4: Ningbo

The reality trader recalled with some amusement the saying about his city Ningbo, named for the tranquil waters of the harbor: *Where there is a market, there are Ningbo merchants*. Ningbo was the only city anywhere in the region to be listed on a map drawn over 600 years hence by a council in Florence, Italy. Ningbo was the Pacific Ocean port of the ancient Silk Road, and the trader was privately thrilled to be eating rock sugar turtle in a small restaurant specializing in his city's cuisine. Around him the sounds of New York City pummeled his ears, and he watched as the men and women of Chinatown read copies of the *Zhi* newspaper, the indelible black market ink staining their fingers. After his meal he walked to the East River and gazed at the papyrus reeds clutching the industrial shoreline. They were growing thicker by the day, and as humid spring weather choked the city, the winds slammed the reeds and sent the pollen into every crack and crevice. *And every man, woman and child*, he relished, *is breathing it in*.

Later he went to a brothel, pushing his own personal seed between the white thighs of a prostitute. Black market ink seeped from under his fingernails into her skin, making her look dirty and gray, like newspaper mucked by rain. His own armpits had come to take on that odor, of old yellowed newsprint, and when —instead of ejaculating inside—her he vomited up yellow pulp, he was only mildly stunned.

About an hour passed before he regained his senses. Frantically realizing he was lying in a cart of paper pulp in what seemed to be a paper factory, he raised his head only in time to witness the mashing machine he was being dumped into. *Something*, he realized too late, *has gone terribly wrong*.

The metal rollers squeezed the blood out of him as it crushed his bones, and he did not even have time to scream.

About a dozen copies of the evening paper seemed a touch pink. Nothing more.

***

Jack the Butterfly, the shadow man of Pell Street, read the evening newspaper headline about a paper trader from Ningbo getting crushed to death during a visit to a paper mill in New Jersey. Somehow he knew the article had written itself, and within the *Zhi* newspaper offices, sure enough the editors wondered who had written it and placed it inside the copy. They questioned one another and none could understand. More and more over the past months, mysterious articles were appearing inside the copy and less and less of the paper could be accounted for. The editor in chief knew it had to be some kind of insider sabotage, and yet no matter whom she fired the mysterious articles continued to engulf the newspaper, mostly the evening edition.

Sooner or later the mainland Chinese will get the hint, Jack thought, *they have no business with the reality of New York City. What did they think, I would sell New York to them just like that?*

He imagined New York City with a price tag dangling from it. While no human had ever trekked further than the moon, it was easily inferred that since the city was the center of the world it was for all human intents and purposes also the center of the universe. The shadow man laughed, and his breath expelled a yellow cloud of dust as he imagined the center of the universe with a price tag dangling from it. As he did, he saw an eye at the center of a cosmic spiral, and it seemed to him it winked.

***

In the Naranja solar empire penthouse in Central Park, the doctor observed the brilliant blue of the night sky. Mastering the art of reality grafting was akin to playing god, and he knew it. He knew well also of the black market and the cheap, hallucinatory realities they concocted and sold, hyping the goods as real when they were only escapist reality forms.

But he knew more than that. Much more.

The solar empire had been managing reality for years, cultivating it like a precious flower, illuminating it at first, until the reality technology took on a mind of its own, rocking back and forth between warring reality gangs until reality itself became a storm. A woman, his daughter, held an antiquated copy of Shakespeare's tragedies in her hands. She opened it and the light pulsing in the room rushed into the pages like water swirling down a drain.

The doctor answered her unspoken thought, "We will graft an eye into the storm."

5: Aqua Vitae

Rook drove the duplicate sedan and spent the dusk investigating the crocodile operation in the field: the crocodiles were harvested from the East River at night by Chinese men dressed in black and manning small, fast black boats. That night they went out in the midst of a thunderstorm, when the Kings County Kong who policed the air would not fly. Brought back into Chinatown by truck, the crocodiles were not immediately killed. They were sported first at an underground crocodile wrestling club. The club was tucked at the end of Chrystie Street and was well illuminated by bright green lights arranged to look like a crocodile swallowing its own tail. Rook watched from the darkness of his sedan as fresh wild crocodiles were wrangled inside the back door and exchanged for others that apparently had fought, the bloody teeth their confessions.

After a stint at the club, they were killed in the taxidermy shop by a quick bullet to the large sinus vein at the base of the heart. From the *sinus venosus*, he learned, the crocodile's blood was drained. The leather goods were traded, the meat was sold to butchers, the bones and teeth to collectors and the blood to doctors. The blood, Rook discovered, had powerful properties that made it like gunpowder to bacteria. Crocodile blood detonated infection, and its immunization prowess was why a crocodile could lose a limb in a fight and survive. Specialists in Chinatown sold the blood as an *aqua vitae*.

Rook bought a liter of fresh crocodile blood. A test proved it matched the blood sample taken from Dr. Chess's office. Rook knew well of the Egyptian god Sobek, and he had discovered the crocodile-headed god, first mentioned in the Pyramid texts, as a youth. It was believed Sobek had arisen from the primordial black waters of Nun and that he formed the universe. It was also believed the universe would return to the chaotic waters at the end of the world.

To the void, Rook thought.

For many years Chinese and Indian doctors, he learned, had been transfusing crocodile blood into human patients to make them into immunological superhumans, and many of scientific mind expected that, similar to drinking a shot of wheatgrass juice, drinking the crocodile blood could produce a similar effect. Rook brushed it all off as nothing more than snake oil peddling when he sniffed the blood then allowed himself a quick taste. Like human blood, it tasted of iron. He washed the taste around his tongue and swallowed, then he drank more deeply as if approving a vintage. He did feel invigorated, but he was certain it was the intrigue of the crime, not thc blood.

If crocodile blood was the trail to follow, there was one place where it would readily be spilled.

Back in Chinatown at midnight Rook strode deliberately to the Marco Polo Crocodile Wrestling Club. He took a hard stare from the bulky Chinese bouncer, paid the entry fee of one hundred dollars and was allowed in. The tall, raven-haired detective, who sported his short hair in blunt spikes, saw his reflection bouncing off of glass. He descended a stairwell past the thick, aquarium grade walls, and within the massive aquarium, as if taxidermied and suspended in formaldehyde, he witnessed crocodiles hovering more than swimming. A twitch of a tail quickly convinced Rook otherwise. They were all alive, brooding, and quietly ready to kill.

6: The Pimp

Outside in the dark, swarming thunderstorm, Jules unpuckered his umbrella with the press of a small button. Its arms snapped and arched above his tall and sinewy body like his own personal cave. Inside his stainless steel clad and fireproof briefcase, he carried the matchbooks past solar powered black cars lined up outside to the nearest subway entrance two blocks away. The video feed transmitted by implants in his eyes sent images to his boss, who observed with great interest from his penthouse perch far above Central Park.

Mr. Jules Barbillon, his name embedded into his quantum currency card and bank accounts, folded his umbrella and slipped down the throat of a wet stairwell into the humid clutches of subway air to a Second Avenue T train. Within moments he found a vagrant looking to sell a swipe off of someone's stolen card. He could not exchange it for coin: there wasn't any anymore. But he was willing to sell an untraceable swipe for just about anything else that held appeal for him. Jules flicked a token from a Blue Room bar to the man, who nodded, swiped the card along the slit in the card reader and stood aside.

Jules pushed at the turnstile, cranking it once, lifted his briefcase and umbrella high and pushed into the damp crowd of people in transit.

Packed inside the train like, he thought, *Matchsticks*, Jules smiled inwardly knowing he was a *go-between* – itself a word coined by Shakespeare. His name was an ostentatious and obvious mutation of two words that meant in French, under the right circumstances, pimp. Only Jules did not deal in women and men. Mr. Jules Barbillon, known otherwise by his street name of The Pimp, hooked reality.

The earliest bound folio of Shakespeare's collected works, most importantly his tragedies, had been scheduled to go under auction at Sotheby's, and Jules had been under contract by the Naranja solar empire to purchase the folio at whatever price necessary. That he had also been contracted this week by the empire's arch-villain—the president of the Petroleum Club—to win the matches they would use to burn the folio, was to him a unique coincidence. It was a conspiracy only a god could author, and he gave thanks to his own personal god of choice, Sobek.

He transferred in Chinatown to the D train and stood towering over the mainly Chinese riders on the platform, their orange shopping bags billowing with greens and pale green apples, wrapped fish and dumplings. A woman dressed in a bright orange skintight suit and motorcycle helmet stood behind him, out of sight from his wired eyes. She placed an identical steel briefcase at his feet, adjacent to his. A wind pushed down the tunnel and lights from the approaching train smeared over the cracked white and blue tile. Around them people read electronic media, listened to electronic media or dozed. The two did not look at one another as they swapped briefcases at the Grand Street stop, she going her way and he going his.

Over the Manhattan Bridge the train shook and screeched, coming up from the dark underground into the low thunderclouds. With knockoff copies of the antique Shakespeare Company matches, Jules headed back into the hard weather at the Atlantic stop, into the borough known as Brooklyn and by those who controlled it as *Gasland.*

7: Bai Jiu

Crocodile wrestling had been a popular South Asian sport, a tropical monsoon culture sport. New York City, with its two seasons of swelter and freeze, had lacked the palm trees and fruity cocktail culture that welcomed it. The sandy Coney Island beach of Rook's father's youth was cut with broken glass not coconut oil, inspiring knife fights and gunfire but that was about it. When the hurricanes migrated north during his twenties, so did the hellish humidity and brackish waters the saltwater crocodiles favored. The Kings County Kong were to blame for the introduction of the species into the East River, and the Malaysian Chinese were to blame for the taming, if that is what the violent sport of crocodile wrestling could be called.

The bar in the club was also an aquarium, but it was gaily filled with flirtatious koi. Two severe looking Chinese men served the patrons, who were an all-male mixture of Chinese, tourists, thugs and some high rollers looking for a weird trip. Rook pretended to be one of the latter. Sealed inside an air-filled clear case floating in the aquarium over the koi, the Chinese-English menu offered crocodile blood, soup and steak. A Chinese woman, who Rook immediately took as a madam, sent him over a shot of clear alcohol. She cheered him across the bar with her own raised shot glass and a smile. He raised his shot, and in unison with her he knocked back the alcohol. His left eye twitched, but other than that he made no reflex to what tasted like liquid black powder vomit. It caught fire in his throat and rushed out across his lips. She laughed at him and showed him her shot glass was empty by holding it out, then upside down. She thunked it onto the glass bar. He mirrored her moves, proving his was empty too. When he set his glass down and turned toward the wrestling ring, instantly she was at his side.

"By Joe," she sang out and held up another shot for him.

"By Joe," he repeated in a voice chiseled by whiskey. He knew what it was. *Bai jiu*. Chinese hard liquor made out of a variety of grains.

Grains, Rook thought, *grass*. It did sort of taste like grass, like wintered black mildewy grass. She pushed the shot at him. She would try to get him drunk, sell him a woman, roll him, he figured. She was probably drinking water herself. He nodded his head, no thanks, and furrowed into the crowd, finding himself a table with a good view. The semicircular seating was made out of crocodile skin. The tables were opalescent. Below the seating was a dark black pool streaked with green and red accent lighting. Rook was reminded of chlorophyll and blood, and he thought as he folded himself onto the seat, *Ideal location for snuff.*

8: The Petroleum Club

In Gasland Mr. Jules Barbillon set the briefcase in front of the president of the Petroleum Club. The club was housed in a penthouse in downtown Brooklyn, not far from the Atlantic subway station, and it was furnished with the red leather couches and fine oak furnishings salvaged from the former club financial district club, when the last of the gasoline cronies were shouldered out by the gunfire friendly Naranja guards. Jules pressed his fingertips, all four from each hand and then his thumbs, into the biometric reader, and the case made an impressive, bassy horn sound then released the locks with a click. The president, Rocky Astor, lowered his eyes from the gruesome, ritualistic scars on Jules' face down to the case. Jules opened the case and rotated it so that Rocky could peer inside. Rocky made eye contact with Jules through the orange tinted eyeglasses, then dropped his own watery blue eyes under his sweeping black brows as he reached for the case set within. His fingernails were perfectly buffed and manicured. A large single stone diamond pinkie ring flashed, as he flicked a latch with a thick thumb, opening the inner case to its contents: another box, this one cardboard. Rocky put his hands squarely around it and stood in order to shake the lid free. The bottom dropped, heavy with a hundred matchbooks from the Shakespeare Company. He lifted one of the matchbooks out, observed the red, yellow and black cartoonish printing of the otherwise well-known portrait of Shakespeare included in the auctioned folio, a folio Rocky longed to burn as if it was the equivalent of virgin sex.

With a lop-sided smile half sneering, he shoved a box of cigars toward Jules. One thick cigar had been poking out of his mouth for a good hour as he waited the delivery of this obscure but precious investment. If it was only for the sake of irony that he wanted to use these particular matches to destroy a folio he knew for certain Dr. Naranja, his energy empire arch-rival, owned, then it was also for irony that he had employed Mr. Jules Barbillon to handle the matchbook auction. He motioned to the cigars with a gruff sweep then pried open a matchbook and, with great interest, read the phrase printed within, "*Investment.* Shakespeare coined the word *investment*? I love it!" He lit his cigar with great enthusiasm and read the rest of the fine print, which detailed the origin of the word, "*Hamlet. Not of the dye which their investments show.*" He coughed, "What the fuck does that mean?"

Jules winced. "Not money. Clothing, like a suit, as in a vest. A tuxedo, for example, might indicate that the man within it is noble, when in fact, he is a pimp. An in-vest-ment."

Rocky squinted, opened his mouth, his red lips like bicycle tire patches, and he laughed, "Pimp! Brilliant, Jules, brilliant." Then he was dismissive. "Condense the works of Shakespeare onto a matchbook, and I still can't read this fuckin' crap." He lit another match, stared at Jules for a long moment as he puffed out a cloud of smoke and said in a manner that was more of a threat, "Jules, doesn't it feel great to be alive!"

Jules smiled as he bit the tip off his cigar. "Yes," he finally answered, "it does feel great." He leaned forward and inhaled the flame from Rocky's outstretched hand, then as smoke billowed out his nostrils he turned to the brilliant night sky that could only be observed from a high-rise penthouse belonging to the ultra rich. Rocky and the Petroleum Club gang had threatened to kill him if he didn't cooperate, but they were to him like babies eager to suck gasoline instead of milk from the nipples of Nuit. Nuit was the great night sky goddess and mother of his god, the crocodile-headed Sobek. Jules revered her as well.

What the Petroleum Club thought was their plan to destroy Naranja was so easily manipulated by a reality pimp, into his.

***

The woman in the orange suit sat across from Jack the Butterfly, under Pell Street in Chinatown. Jack, his blackened skin increasingly transforming into a wireframe cross-hatching of shadow, observed a matchbook through a quantum magnifying glass. Within the matchbooks, the word *arch-villain* was printed. "Yes, it is carbon ink," he stated.

Through perforations in the helmet she always wore to conceal her identity she smelled the stench of Jack's breath. "Copy it."

9: Blunt

Rook had long practiced the means to observe without looking. There was one man amongst the spectators whom the madam and her female cohorts avoided. He was Asian with a European build, and he sat at his table drinking *bai jiu* and rolling a cigarette. He took out a small vial of oil and with a brush swabbed the rolling paper down. He neatly tucked the vial away, pushed in the tobacco and machine rolled the cigarette. Rook listened to the Chinese pop music, a flutter of synthesized strings and flutes, but he still heard the Asian-European man light a match. The lights came up in the pool with the change in music. A lithe Chinese woman was revealed lying on her stomach and on the back of a seven-foot long crocodile.

After the sulfuric bite of the match faded, Rook smelled the unmistakable odor of hash.

Rook tightened his focus on the female performer, who was encrusted in ornamental orange gems. *If those are real sapphires*, he thought, *then she's the most valuable woman in Chinatown*. Rook felt an immediate lust for her. Even her face was encrusted, even her lips. The gems adhered to her body in a pattern suggesting she was also a crocodile or a goddess of crocodiles. She and the unmoving crocodile lay on a small concrete island in the center of the pool. The music came to a lull, and the man smoking the hash blunt stood. The performer raised herself and flipped. She held up her right palm. Around her fingers was a series of white metal rings that looked not unlike brass knuckles minus the brass. A small metal cable as fine as fishing line shot from the rings like a firecracker. The hash smoker caught the cable end seemingly by magic, but probably, Rook inferred, by a kind of programmed magnet. The man whipped out a hundred dollar bill and attached it to the small wire cable that spanned from his hand down to the performer in the ring. He let the bill go, and it zoomed, retracting down into the pool, straight into the performer's palm.

She unclipped the money from the cable and waved it with a flourish. The crowd erupted into applause. She flexed the platinum knuckles, triggering an explosion of cables into the audience. Visually, as the metal smeared, it looked like a water fountain. Choreographed, the women working the audience caught the ends of the cables and wasted not a moment soliciting. The madam was one of them. Right away she was again tugging at Rook's sleeve. In one hand she held a cable, in the other a shot of *bai jiu*. She set the *bai jiu* on his table, and from her red gown she produced a paper one hundred dollar bill.

"Money for sale," she explained and waved to where the performer was now taking the initial hundred dollar bill into her mouth. Glancing around at the dozen women who had magnetically caught the fine cables, Rook thought, *They look like kites*. Down in the pool the orange encrusted goddess seemed to be flying the lady kites. Slowly she sank to her knees then erotically languished onto her belly. She was face to face with the green beast, whose daggery seventy-some teeth menaced behind slit pupils in golden eyes. She brushed at the nostrils of the crocodile with the first hundred dollar bill clenched in her teeth. Mesmerized, the crocodile yawned, revealing its thick white yellow tongue. Inching her face inside the clutch of the jaws, she gently blew the bill out of her mouth into its.

"Money for sale," the madam intoned, and Rook saw he was not the only one being urged to buy. The women were working the whole crowd. Rook watched as another man swiped his quantum currency through a slot on his table, buying an old cash hundred dollar bill. The man was already drunk, and his female saleslady had to clip the money onto the cable for him. He hooted as the bill shot down into the pool and landed in the performer's palm.

Rook removed his quantum currency from his wallet. He had cloned it with a dead man's history earlier in the day. If the Marco Polo Crocodile Wrestling Club wanted to know in the next few hours who had been sitting at table seven, they would find out he was twelve feet under, just a name on a tombstone.

It was hard to tell who wanted to know what and best to assume someone always wanted to know everything. During an investigation Rook left a manic trail behind every purchase, just in case someone suspected him of something.

He swiped his quantum currency through the slot in his table. The slot emitted a stream of photons, which made the plastic card flash briefly. Possessing quantum memory, a memory literally entangled with the holograph embedded in the card, the photons immediately transmitted to Federal Reserve servers.

The madam smiled knowing she had bagged a sale. The display in the opalescent table showed he was being charged exactly one hundred dollars for one hundred dollars. The madam handed him the paper money after the sale flashed an authorization. Rook peered at the hundred dollar bill. It looked real and felt real, like cotton. Out in the pool the performer inched her face into the crocodile's open mouth and dropped the second bill in. The audience responded with uniform bursts of laughter and applause. The performer stood up, and Rook noticed the madam gave a signal to her before prompting Rook to send the money down. Rook felt the eyes of the Asian-European man on him as he clipped the bill onto the cable, and he purposefully angled his body so the man would see at best his silhouette. He let it go, and the bill zoomed down into the ring where the performer deftly snatched it. At his side the madam cheered Rook on and pushed the *bai jiu* toward his lips. He chuckled, seemingly loosening up as he knocked the nasty liquor back. His face contorted as he exhaled the fumes, and he gave the madam a friendly squeeze. She giggled and spoke into his ear, "I find you girl, you want?"

It was at the very least an exit strategy. The Asian-European's eyes had shifted away from him to the next patron the moment the bill had left his hand, and Rook wanted to make sure this man, should he look this way again, saw only a shadow of whoever had been sitting at table seven. The madam indicated to him a girl would cost five hundred dollars and enticed him to swipe his currency again. Rook nodded to the performer in the ring, and the giggling haggle abruptly stopped then started again.

"No, no!" the madam exclaimed, "Not for sale!" And she pointed to the women working the crowd. Rook settled on a simple, sleight woman in green silk who was not too dolled up and swiped his currency again. The madam flickered away, and momentarily Rook's date sat down next to him, close. She put her hand on his thigh. *Too close*, Rook thought, to the hundred dollar bill he had just pinched from the madam's gown. More than the cold, routine sex he might have with this woman, he wanted to examine the hundred dollar bill and see if it was real. He looked deep into her eyes and saw, *Only the void.*

10: Snuff

Within ten minutes the crocodile had thirteen hundred dollars in its jaw. Thirteen was a lucky number to some Chinese. Chinese numerology was based on alliteration: whatever the names for numbers sounded like, rhymed with or tonally evoked, twisted that meaning in. *Thirteen* in Mandarin was *shisan*. It meant *definitely vibrant* or *assured growth.* The performer bowed to mighty applause, lowered herself again and teased the crocodile's tongue. Slowly she reached her arm in all the way to the elbow, around which the crocodile yawn appeared for a long moment like a nasty trap about to spring. She retrieved the cash achingly, one bill after another. As she jerked her arm out, the crocodile's mouth slammed shut like it was the end of the world. The placid crocodile looked like it was smiling. The lights dimmed to a roar of applause then went black, and the orange sapphire encrusted female performer and her placid crocodile, in an instant, were gone.

There came a thrashing sound in the water, and the music jerked to a bass drumming beat. As pale yellow lights flickered, Rook saw a much larger crocodile —and not one tamed for tricks—rolling in the waters. The crowd's applause shifted to hollering as drunken men stood, shrieking with vicious joy. There were no women other than the prostitutes in the audience. Yellow and red lights whirred like helicopter blades. Rook squinted as the scene evolved and a man rolled through the black water, beating his head against the crocodile's white belly.

Two young men trapezed across the pool, back and forth, over the wrestling. This was still simple entertainment Atlantic City style, beyond wild but not deadly. It was Chinatown glitz.

Later, in a small room above the wrestling club, Rook pushed the woman down and unzipped his pants. The orgasm would take his mind off the snuff that had come after the glitz. Two untamed and freshly snared crocodiles from the East River had been cut loose into the pool. Rook recognized the beasts: they were the ones caught fresh the night before. All music halted under a canopy of shrieking as a naked man was dropped from a platform high above. Rook heard at least one limb snap as the naked man hit the concrete, and instantly the numeral 4 was cast in light then strobed over him. Four was the most feared number for the Chinese because the word sounded like death, *si*. The crowd shouted the word at him, taunting him. The man was Chinese, and he lay helplessly screaming in a loud tonal language Rook did not understand. *Fukinese maybe*.

The numeral 4s strobed spastically, shifted, and the raging light show spattered images of crocodile eyes shedding tears. Light, sound and crowd mocked him as the audio ricocheted with multilayered sound effects issuing from his own desperately high-pitched crying. The screams were filled with fear and hatred and the shrill anxiety that comes only when ones know it really is the end, and it is going to be a violent one.

These crocodiles were hungry. The ones from the earlier performances, Rook believed, were well fed in advance. If they weren't hungry they wouldn't attack. They had been Shakespearean. Rook remembered the line from *Othello: If that the earth could teem with woman's tears, each drop she falls would prove a crocodile.*

The satisfied literary crocodiles were polite as poetry, but not these vicious beasts. It was only a matter of minutes before the man's hellish screaming fell to silence, and the silence frothed in the angry bloody waters. Rook's date was utterly emotionless. He wondered how many times she had seen this show.

The hash smoker savored the last section of an orange he was eating and promptly took his leave.

Rook knew by instinct he had made his man. *Weedkiller*.

Rook followed a quick minute later with his date. He asked her if the man who had delivered the first hundred dollar bill was part of the show.

"Mr. Millioni," she told him, "is the owner."

Rook didn't ask how to spell the name.

11: Mr. Millioni

Rook stepped outside with his date on the pretense he wanted a quick cigarette in fresh air. Rook didn't smoke, but he kept a pack with him as part of his cover. There was nothing fresh about the air. It was gummy with humidity and the tannery stench. He watched as Millioni seated himself into a limousine behind his driver. The license plate was boldly memorable: a sideways 8, the oroboros. Eight was the luckiest number to the Chinese, and for the personalized plate this man would have paid hundreds of thousands. Owning it meant Chinatown insiders knew exactly who was behind the wheel. Owning it meant, at least within Chinatown, the man had serious face, even though he was clearly not fully Chinese. Rook trailed the car virtually.

Millioni's limousine was a sunjuice vehicle, an electric car powered by solar. Even beyond the brute vanity of the metal license plate, which made it easy to track, the limousine was digitally encoded, and its global positioning system made it fully traceable. *On grid*, Rook thought, *why?* Rook's date, seemingly impatient, told him the half-hour was getting shorter. Rook drew on his cigarette and glanced at his custom wristwatch, pretending to glance at the time while pinging the vehicle with a remote hidden inside the watch. Also inside the watch was a miniature nanosilicon world that synchronized much more than time. Within moments he located the vehicle's internet protocol address. For the rest of the life of the vehicle, Rook would know exactly where it was—to some degree for both its past and for its future. *There's something he wants the solar empire to know.* He gave Millioni a fifteen minute lead, and in those fifteen minutes Rook knew exactly what he would do to kill the time. He kept his jacket on so she would not see his gun.

In the small room up above the wrestling club, Rook watched the woman's red tongue lick his cock. He slipped the tip of it into her mouth then pushed it in further and gently pulled out. Slowly he fucked her mouth, letting his mind quiet and listening only to the wet sounds of her tongue, mouth and lips. He closed his eyes and saw 8s. They rolled like the crocodiles and became crocodiles swallowing their own tails. He knew the image well.

She smiled at him when it was over, seemingly thankful he did not come on her. He washed his hands. Sex, no matter how sordid and brief, was a meditation. It had taken only ten minutes, but he was relaxed now and focused in a way that didn't require paying attention. He didn't need to see the chessboard to play the game.

"How long has the club been open?" he asked her. She was lighting a cigarette. *Probably to get the taste of me out of her mouth*, he thought.

"Forever," she said softly, exhaling smoke.

As he drove away he thought, *Bai jiu would do it. It could take the taste of death out of a mouth.* Maybe he would try that as a remedy after he came across the next dead body. That thought resonated. *Is Millioni getting the taste of something worse than bai jiu and hash out of his mouth? Is that his method for burning up the stench of murder?*

Rook had managed to keep the *bai jiu* down to just the two shots and was glad his date had not pushed any on him. The nasty flavor still irked his throat. Peripherally he had watched Millioni sip at a glass of *bai jiu* throughout the one hour show. That and the hash would gong just about anyone, but Millioni had maintained. Like Rook's date, Millioni was utterly emotionless during the snuff. He was a cold synchrony of titanium sheathed in silk.

12: Gasland

Jules wiped the raindrops from his waxed bald head, his fingertips lingering over the scars crisscrossing the skin taut over his skull. Through the pale orange lenses of his eyeglasses, which obscured the slit pupils in his golden eyes, he glanced at his reflection slanting off a mirrored storefront. He made haste toward the subway stairwell, its entry still marked by stencil-like, green-lit art deco lettering. His eyes had been grafted and embedded within them were nanocameras that sent digital images to the Naranja Empire regarding his infiltration into the Petroleum Club. Jules turned at the stairwell, focused through his grafted eyes to an interior display on his semi-permanent contact lenses and looked up to the high-rise he had just exited. A phone number came up in the display, and Jules blinked for dial.

Inside the Petroleum Club, inside the matchbook box, identical cell phone wiring was buried within each and every matchbook cover. The match heads—laced with pentaerythritol tetranitrate—ignited from the simultaneous cell phone signal shockwave, and there was an enormous detonation, a booming bellow accompanied by an explosion of penthouse window glass. It burst out from around the tower like a crystal sugar ring of Saturn before it dissipated, glittering as the glass slowly showered down.

Jules lowered his gaze and padded down the wet steps a little faster than his feet wanted to carry him. At the turnstile he glanced furtively for anyone wanting to sell a swipe. The moments stretched and activity at the street clogged the stairwell as pedestrians realized something warlike had taken place. "A bomb!" someone yelled, and the word echoed out of the mouths of many: *Bomb! Bomb! Bomb! Bomb!* In the mass frenzy collapsing into the subway system, Jules followed the man in front of him and simply jumped the turnstile. He blended in with the stampeding panic, and when a D train pulled in, he squeezed onto it, as anonymous as the rest. Word spread quickly through the car about a bomb, and Jules was relieved when the train dutifully lurched into motion, back toward Manhattan.

In his Lower East Side loft, Jules removed his gray sportcoat and slowly unbuttoned the pale green shirt. He hung both up neatly and made his way to the kitchen. Cool small lights washed across the calcified scars crisscrossing his back, chest, torso and the full length of his arms. He eyed the skyline, where he could see Gasland's biplanes buzzing like angry dragonflies around the devastated penthouse of the Petroleum Club. He opened the refrigerator door and removed a liter of crocodile blood. In a crocodile leather seat arched up like a throne—a crocodile skin from Marco Polo Tannery under his feet—he faced the small live crocodile he kept in a tank in his sanctuary. He clipped the blood bag to a medical rod attached to the throne and inserted a needle into a vein in the crook of his arm. Slowly the blood began to flow into his body. He inserted another needle into his other arm and his own blood transfused into an empty bag. He stared at the crocodile, its lithe length curling in the murky waters of the tank, its dark green body flinching with lighter greens, yellows and muscle.

He had been going about his business as Mr. Jules Barbillon, dealing his goods through his chain of Blue Room bars, where patrons gathered for synthetic sex, when the Petroleum Club had captured him. He did not believe Rocky Astor had been so naïve that he could not appreciate the wile of a double agent, but then the gasoline tycoons were not exactly known for pursuing the edges of the scientific future in the same way the solar empire did. Rocky had not at all seemed to notice his pale orange sunglasses: a transparent insignia of the orange colors the Naranja guards always wore. The Petroleum Club had, when they had first captured him and wrangled him into the backseat of a gas-guzzler, thoroughly examined him for surveillance, including an examination of the sunglasses.

And found nothing.

They had first spotted him at a Sotheby's auction, purchasing a Shakespearean folio, fourth edition, which Jules later identified to them as finding its way to the Central Library where it was placed inside the permanent Naranja collection. When they had brought him to the Petroleum Club that first time, they demanded he confess his relationship to Naranja. Rocky held his cigar up and sucked on it, making the end rush with a cherry glow, then he leaned in as if he was going to burn him right between the eyes.

"I'm a reality pimp," Jules told him, "I sell people what they want."

Rocky halted his advance and after a moment leaned back. "Blue rooms?"

"Naranja threatened to," he paused and selected his words with great consideration, "confiscate my operations if I didn't, you know, assist."

"But why books? Hell, matches are more valuable than books, right, fellas?" Rocky glanced around at the barrel chested gang who ran Gasland and puffed smoke out of his mouth like an old train.

It was well known that the Central Library had undergone a massive fireproofing renovation. It had also gone on the Sotheby's auction block and once sold it became privatized by the Naranja Empire. The Librarians—heavily armed guards dressed in black uniforms sporting the simple zodiacal sign for Libra, the scales—allowed visitors in two dozen at a time. The local fire department engine houses were handsomely paid to protect it at all costs, and subsequently their red trucks also sported the Libra scales insignia.

Jules knew immediately that the men of Gasland did not know that time was not, and in fact had never been, linear. It was concentric, like the rings of a tree, organically evolving around its once seeded core. There was no way to tell them, no way to get them to believe or even entertain the idea, that for the Naranja Empire and those close to it, there was but one week repeating itself over and over again, not really rewriting itself, but overwriting itself. There were always April showers and never any May flowers, but those not in the know just blamed it on global warming. In the city almost no one remembered what birdsong was anyway.

Jules at once lied and told the truth, shrugging, "He's a collector."

"But why you? I could send my shoe-shine boy to hold up a paddle at Sotheby's."

"I'm a collector as well, gentleman. An unknown face at Sotheby's buying some of the world's most expensive books would be unsettling. They might think your shoe-shine boy a fraud, an accumulator of objects, but not a collector. There is a vast difference."

Rocky pondered this. "What do you collect?"

Jules wanted to say, realities, but instead he curtly answered, "Anything crocodilian."

Jules watched his young crocodile become still in the tank. *The idiots of Gasland, their machine guns and gas-guzzling cars, couldn't burn a barrel of trash unless Naranja let them, let alone the Central Library.*

Or, unless the guards, the Naranja slaves as they considered themselves, in their intricate ways of communicating with one another, helped out. *Idiots*, he thought. He had been buying Shakespearean works over and over, always close to the same date: April 23rd—Shakespeare's birth and death day. This week, the anomalous and sudden appearance at Sotheby's of the antique matchbook collection, Jules witnessed as a sign. It was easy to forge the copies that were handed over to Rocky Astor, since the matchbooks were displayed in catalogues. And what they were doing with the original matches Rocky could never fathom though he would approve.

Paper news, like a dinosaur, had gone extinct, and digital news had been hacked by someone who called themself The Machete. The hacked code, named *Oroboros,* did not spit out junk; it deliberately generated and delivered news based on what it thought a reader wanted. The book collection of the Central Library housed what was left of public history, and Naranja guarded it in the same way he guarded his daughter's heart. Jules closed his eyes and dreamed of the night he would no longer be enslaved to guarding the folios, but would help set the Library on fire and serve only his god of choice, the crocodilian abyss, the end of time that was but one week away from swallowing them all.

He voice dialed Rocky Astor's number from a computer phone.

At the core of the blown out penthouse, his pants around his ankles, his head bleeding from where it had hit the urinal during the blast, his cigar turned shrapnel from the trace of the explosive chemical left on the end of it from when he had lit it, and his whole face peppered with tobacco, Rocky blinked to the sound of his ringtone and scrounged for his phone in his pants pockets. He answered slowly, "How did you know I'd still be alive?"

"I didn't," Jules stood and walked close to the crocodile tank, his eyes stealing out to the night sky, to Gasland. "But since you are, know this: you work for me now."

"The fuck I do!"

"Exactly. The fuck you do. The brothers will come and find you."

"The brothers? My men, my army will fight! And—"

"Your gang and their silly planes? No match, pardon the pun, for Naranja. Feels good to be alive, doesn't it, Rocky. Now, pull up your pants. They're on their way up." Rocky suddenly sensed his partial nudity, his penis pressed against the cold tile, urine splashed onto his trousers. Crammed into this vulnerability was awe for whatever surveillance Jules had on him, and he yanked himself up in a hurry as he heard the elevator bell indicate the car had arrived at his floor. *The bomb*, he realized, *detonated out but not in!* His hands were a flurry on his zipper as footsteps, even and doubled, clipped onto the tile floor, and he looked up to witness two men, identical twins in black suits, their black hair swept back from their brows, their eyes hidden behind dark sunglasses, their guns pointing at him.

Simultaneously they said, "Let's take a walk."

Jules hung up, reached into the tank and gave a loving stroke down the snout of the young crocodile. He bundled his scarred body into green crocodile leather pants, a shirt, boots and an overcoat. He turned to a hat rack, tucked his bald head under a green crocodile leather cap, and looking every part a pimp, he walked down the Bowery through the thick crowds, rain from the latest thunderstorm rolling off his water-proof crocodile skins. Jules entered his closest brothel, where men and women bought synthetic sex. The hard beats of dance music drummed the interior, and synthetic blue night sky, spattered with twinkling starlight, pushed like velvet into the folds of the crowd. He observed the crowd from behind the illuminated walls as he toweled his face and eyeglasses dry. He observed further as a program altered the lightscape—only for a flickering moment—and the night sky projections became in a blink the skin of a crocodile. Immediately they transformed back to peaceful sky. Reality for the human never changed cataclysmically. Parallel reality addiction, like heroin addiction, did. Jules knew by small turns and cranks, by minute flashes, human beings would come to accept, in the same way a junky chased addiction, revolution. *Half-dragon, half-man*, he thought, *so shall Sobek return.*

He stepped back into the humid night, his skin scintillating with beaded sweat, and he quickly padded down the wet concrete steps to the D train platform again. He never took a car or a taxi. It was utterly impossible to be traced by train as long as he took the necessary precautions. He felt the wind pick up down the tunnel, the way it always did when the train was arriving. It blurred, a hammered silver thing gunked with black dirt and graffiti. He almost smiled when he saw the car stopping before him tagged with the signature of the artist, in billowing yet boxy green letters, *Sobek!*

He stepped into the train, a revolution on his mind, and with a blatant intent to incite by means of subtle insider reality trading, he rode toward Gasland to meet with the brothers and the now kidnapped Rocky Astor.

***

The woman in orange sat in her office on the top floor of Orange Security in Times Square. The circular high-rise was made of glass, and each floor was comprised by an alternating band of either opaque white glass or opaque bright orange glass. At ground level a retail store covered what actually took place in the building. In its core was another high security building, and from here she commanded the Naranja guards. The Naranja Empire did not control news or any of the other big brotherly advantages it did in fact possess. On the contrary it carefully cultivated reality and maintained it so that it would not become a victim of itself.

The Naranja guards did not police New York City: they policed reality.

It was said the great Library of Alexandria had accidentally been burned down by a firestorm that had leapt from ships, down a dock to the library itself, but no one really knew. Thinking of this, the woman in orange—Agent Orange—sat at her desk and opened the case of original Shakespeare Company matchbooks. In many ways she was the most powerful woman in New York City, and in many ways, she was the weakest. Inside her helmet, she closed her eyelids over bright blue eyes and considered what it would be like to lose all printed history, for the city to sink into the anarchy of irreversible misinformation. She witnessed a terrifying darkness, a darkness that was calling her name.

***

Rook circled the midtown block where he had traced Millioni's vehicle. He inferred it was parked in a subterranean garage beneath a motel named Marco Polo. The topology of New York City was so complex, that for a detective who thought he knew its every nook, the sudden presence of yet another Marco Polo business with which he was unfamiliar was almost unnerving. But the topology of New York was always in flux. Businesses closed and others opened overnight. Streets that had run north to south for years suddenly ran in the opposite direction. The vertical topology seemed infinite, and the once remarkable Empire State Building was now a dwarf amongst pinnacles that stretched like twinkling harp strings into the thunderstorm clouds. The aesthetic of Times Square had long pulsated outward into the rest of the city, and the lower stories were all covered with electronic advertisements, making the city somewhat of a lagoon in which day-glo tropical advertisements, like flitting fish, swirled, blinked, stretched, snapped and winked with not a moment of peace for the eye. The Marco Polo Motel was an aberration from this gaudy display, and was both cool and serene in its silvered art deco prowess. The architecture belied construction from earlier years, and yet Rook could not place it in memory at all. Rook attenuated the surveillance feed in the sedan's windshield and zoomed through the glass façade of the main entry to peer into the interior lobby. He was immediately struck by the scintillating nature of emerald green wallpaper covering the high walls and echoed in the flooring. Rook zoomed further into the details and witnessed what seemed to be a raised and reiterative pattern in the wallpaper that struck him as looking like sheaves of wheat. *Or*, he thought, *weeds*.

12: Jackin' the Butterfly

Jack the Butterfly spent the next hour cultivating the ink in the matchbook. It seemed every day she was giving him something Shakespeare or another. He could not understand a single line of any of the works.

Fucking Shakespeare, he thought, *fuck him.*

First he cloned the ink passage, then he entered a black hole chamber and spliced the passage into a quantum space-time crotch. This was the equivalent of grafting a flowering fruit tree limb onto the trunk of a rooted parent tree. April 23rd, Shakespeare's birth and death day, was the axis of time in New York City, around which one week looped over and over—never repeating exactly but accumulating organically, just like the growth of a fruit tree—through quantum feedback. The citizens of New York for the most part did not sense it as they still believed in annual cycles.

April 23rd was the 113th day in the old annual calendar. Among its numerous unique properties, the number 113 was ominous in that it was both a natural prime number and a centered square figurate number, meaning it was the sum of two consecutive square numbers. When drawn as a lattice 113 made an elegant chessboard-like figure. It was upon this seemingly inorganic lattice that the Naranja solar empire had first discovered how to graft photons, but of this the shadow man knew nothing. He was content to be grafted with *the* shadow.

The quantum void.

Within the black hole chamber—a dark cylindrical room on the outside and an amorphous place with no hard boundaries on the inside—the air had a static charge. Black hole crotches, like tiny tree knots in space and time—what he called butterflies—fluttered, evoking a low buzzing sound. In the earliest days of his experiments, upon entering the chamber he would don a protective suit reminiscent of a beekeeper meets radiation suit. The butterflies would cling to him as he manipulated space and time like taffy, blending past and future into möbius strips shaped like little butterflies. These crotches, these pseudo-lepidopterans, were tiny by butterfly scale and to the casual eye might appear as gnats. In their quantum chrysalis stage they contained all potential change within.

Jack vaguely recalled his time in Ningbo, when he had himself been a merchant, cloning real butterflies for agriculture and entertainment. As agriculture became increasingly biosynthesized, it became necessary to generate insects that could tolerate and enhance the engineered species. It had also become popular to release butterflies at events like weddings and inaugurations, and Jack's pioneering butterfly-cloning business had easily made him a millionaire.

When Jack's business shifted away from biological cloning to quantum grafting, he experimented further, as far as science could take him, with the cosmic essence of the butterfly—a creature so unique in its ability to become, from a kind of wormy thing, something extraordinary and beautiful. It was during this time he grafted his first black hole butterfly. His grafting experiments failed frequently, but the few that succeeded took him to America, to New York City, to the Two Brothers Tong. In time his ability to manipulate and transform reality through nano-organic grafting—what became the origin of what he later called his black hole butterflies—gave him the power to take over Chinatown, New York City. And in time he no longer donned the suit. Jack the black hole keeper, a dense wireframe of cosmic darkness meets man, had evolved into a black hole butterfly.

Jack had grafted himself so many times, he could no longer recall exactly who he had been. No more than a butterfly would be disgraced by its emergence from the chrysalis, if instead of bursting with brilliant color, it turned out only to be a black moth of sorts, what he was becoming in Chinatown—a kind of cocoon of darkness—did not unsettle him.

Jack the shadow man, Jack the Butterfly, sampled the ink phrase *arch-villain* again from the matchbook. He set about grafting the phrase again, a task he would have to repeat 113 times that night. *113. Tedious but lucrative.* He donned quantum goggles, which magnified the quantum scale so that it seemed fully touchable by human hands. He took the body of a chrysalis by miniature forceps and placed it into a space-time crotch. In another box, which functioned as both a quantum sampler and regenerator, he placed the original matchbook.

Years earlier he found success developing a strain of papyrus in which lignin, a chemical compound found in all vascular plants and key to paper production—mostly newsprint and brown papers used for boxes and bags—could allow for the conduction of ink through a plant's cellular structure. Lignin, a so-called hydrophobe, was critical in allowing for the conductivity of water through the vascular system of a plant. Lignin provided, in essence, the vascularity, the veins, the tubing structure without which water would too easily pass from one cell to another. Jack had modified the lignin so that it became a graph-phobe—phobic of ink—and at the nano-organic level he injected his ink into the vascular structure of the living papyrus he maintained in an artificial wetlands of sorts in his lab. He had no idea then that the ink he sampled from a newspaper article would replicate itself and graft into a living organic pattern within the plant. What use he could possibly have for authoring actual language into plants he did not know. He simply monitored the experiments in which ink organically entrained, like the spots of the leopard moth or the ridges in an oak leaf, into the identifiable markings of a species. Further research with inks led him to realize that lignin, when burnt, provided the powder form of carbon black—used in anything from automobile tires to mascara. When he realized that the global leader in innovative lignin research and developments was located in New Jersey and not Ningbo, he left for New York City.

Years passed. When he discovered, unrolling his grafted papyrus scrolls, that the original news story he had sampled the ink from was transforming, as if an editor or journalist was actively typesetting into the vascular structure of the plant, he felt what was akin to hair standing up on his arms, prickling his entire body.

Plants, long thought to be responsive to human speech, he realized, were thinking. Or perhaps more ominously, the original authors of the texts were thinking through them.

He then wasted no time injecting ink into the quantum butterflies, and he discovered he could also transform the patterns in their wings. And he realized too the butterflies were thinking, or somehow, through the potential intelligence inherent in the sampled text inks, they had become vehicles for the author. Either dead authors had been brought to life or ink was writing itself. In any regard, it was too late when he realized the ink had the seductive power of heroin. He was already smitten then seduced by the ink ravaging his veins.

Jack sampled the phrase from the matchbook. The Orange Woman, as he called her, was paying him with his rival's DNA—and even more valuable to him—with the DNA lifted from the man's tattoo inked skin. That was worth everything to Jack or at least to what little he still cared about. Jack isolated the odd phrase about the arch-villain again, sampling it through a nanoscanner, boiling the ink to make it liquid and carefully injecting it into the chrysalis. The metamorphosis would take place within a week, and he could not guarantee what would emerge from the cocoon. He never could.

Once any ink had been sampled by Jack the Butterfly and copied at its quantum core, it gave him and his client access to the author's will. A novelty at the least and a dangerous weapon at the most.

For the Naranja Empire, which had also discovered how to sample the will of authors through ink, it was the will of Shakespeare himself that it coveted. If the Naranja Empire's collection of Shakespearean folios were to be destroyed, the elegant reality Naranja had cultivated would snarl into chaos.

For Jules Barbillon and Agent Orange, they cared only somewhat about the seemingly frivolous matchbook company owner's interest in Shakespearean neologism and very explicitly for his will to start fires. They believed each time Jack sampled the ink phrase *arch-villain,* a primordial quantum arson was, like quantum paper giving in to an inky villain, combusting.

***

Agent Orange peered at the Naranja tower in the Manhattan skyline from her Orange Security penthouse in Times Square. The city lights reflected in her shiny helmet, curving the skyline in miniature around it. *Naranja*, she thought, *you've met your match!*

13: Operation: Shakespeare

Dr. Naranja strode across the cold marble floor in black cashmere slacks and a gray silk shirt. He poured himself a mild scotch at the wet bar and took a sip through curiously full pink lips rimmed by salt and pepper stubble. Through amber eyes framed by heavy black glasses, the sixty year old man gazed down at the black clouds hugging his high-rise. His free hand petted the similar salt and pepper stubble on his large round head before dropping to his side and balling into a pensive fist. On a bank of monitors he observed feeds from cameras below the clouds. They revealed the city grid, long laid out in rectilinear fashion. It was many years hence, when time still flowed in years, that he had been staring down at the real city streets, contemplating what was called taxicab geometry, as it was inspired by the Manhattan grid. It was then he had watched a single taxi drive a rectilinear path down consecutive city blocks in an elaborate, angled loop that he imagined the taxi as a chess piece, a rook navigating the chessboard of the city. As opposed to how the crow flies, and like a taxicab, the rook could only move in straight lines and right angles. That night he had dreamed of light particles, of photons arranged in square patterns like brilliant orange wallpaper, multiplying organically and geometrically. When he woke the next day he set aside his experimental attempts to clone light.

He had a servant purchase a navel orange for him from a street vendor, and by nightfall he was well on his way toward implementing the process whereby he could graft light. He succeeded by multiplying light by itself.

By squaring it.

Within a week he had invented a nanolattice of light. One photon had become many. He called his invention *sunjuice.*

He did not know then that light had a shadow.

As his technology illuminated and powered at first New York City and then the world, so did it usher in a cosmic darkness. Reality warped, pulled into the funnel of darkness, and by the time he realized he had invented in miniature the big bang, he realized the unfortunate consequence of inventing the end of time simultaneously.

He sipped his scotch, rolling the mild alcohol slowly over his tongue, and observed a monitor feeding him close-ups of the explosion in Brooklyn his people had engineered. Gasland had needed a spanking, but the Petroleum Club bombing was itself a detonator of a much larger shock wave he had in mind. His mind turned to the eye of the reality storm. If reality derailed, it would collapse back into the black hole from which it had been birthed. If at the very least he could stabilize the reality week that looped around itself over and over again, there was a chance the universe he so loved like a daughter could survive into eternity.

Inside a giant glass terrarium that comprised one quarter of the tower floor black hole butterflies fluttered like television noise. A cool narrow beam from a small sunjuice flashlight deliberately positioned by the doctor excited the noise. As he moved the beam, the viscous butterflies spread like waves in black inky oil. Jules brought butterflies to him each week from Chinatown when, also each week, he returned the latest Shakespearean folio won at auction. The latest folio was now centered inside the terrarium, and the black hole butterflies emerged from the open pages, exponentiating the essence of the volume. The doctor understood that once a person came in contact with Jack's organic, black market ink, their lives would begin to transform as if an internal, subconscious ghostwriter was penning their reality. Those who sought out the experience were known as parallel reality addicts. What the doctor suspected was not just that they became addicted to self-authoring a more exciting and rewarding—ultimately an extremely selfish reality—but that reality itself was an addiction of the fundamental conscious nature of the universe. The universe was self-authoring, and for whatever reason, it was authoring itself through a persona not ubiquitously godly but at once humanly tragic and Buddhistically post-death.

The fundamental nature of the self-authoring universe was brilliant, elegant, eloquent, obtusely tragic and ultimately unknown.

Shakespearean.

CHAPTER TWO: Cycle of Seven

1: Memo

The week stitched into itself, renewing some semblance of the cycle of Seven.

Rook set his gun on his desk. It made a hard thunk. He observed the deadly hardware in the darkness of his office and rolled tension out of his shoulders. In his timeless black suit Rook Black was architectural, and just like the chess piece his father had named him after, he was solid and tall, a fortress in motion. Photographs, drawings and sketches of rookish castles smothered his walls in dense layers. His desk, inlaid with a chessboard, had been custom made for his father—the greatest chess champion the world had ever known—by his mother. Rook never knew her. She had died while giving birth to him during The Great Hurricane.

Rook clicked on a lamp. As the yellow light burst his shadow cast, brooding high against a wall as if it was watching him. And in the quantum world where even photons had shadows, in a sense it really was. Space and time were regenerating and overwriting the previous week, but Rook did not sense this acutely. Sensing an organic reality as tactile, as fully physically real, was not common in his culture, and just like the sensation of gravity, he appreciated the constant of spatiotemporal change only as a soft abstraction.

The detective glanced from his gun to where a small memo rested on the desk. The sight of the memo made his loins twitch. Rook, though profoundly cerebral, was a man physically ripe with lust, and he had hired his assistant Angela in part so he could look at her. She knew it. The memo was in her handwriting, and it looked like her: sinuous and soft. He in some ways looked like his gun, in his bluing hard jaw, of a metal meets testosterone. In his imagination, fetish illuminated the sight of the two of them together, limbs tangled, and made him hard. He reached for a fifth of whiskey and slowly poured himself a neat glass as he savored his sexual tension. It was a testimony of his selfish attraction to the sensuous aspects of living that allowed him, as it did for most others, to view life through the hard candy shell of classical reality. To let go of the illusion, to transcend the illusion into the stratosphere of the Buddha's enlightenment, would be, on the rare occasion he thought of it, an utter bore.

He lifted the memo under the lamp. Yellow light splashed over it.

It read, *Shadow* and gave the address of *160 Amherst, East Orange*.

A mere block away a dozen members of a gang thrust a bag over Angela's head, her cinnamon hair tufting from under the black vinyl as someone cinched it tight. She could not scream, and the silence did not reach his ears.

Somehow, still he heard it.

He looked up to the door as if expecting a knock. There was none.

Yesterday and tomorrow washed over each other like waves, and within this sea of feedback, crime was notoriously difficult to solve. As much as a man with a heart like a black tattoo could, he loved it. He unbuckled his belt, unzipped his pants and reached in to stroke the pleasant ache. Four minutes later, with a grunting sigh, he came into his bare hand, then he reached for his whiskey and drank it down.

2: Quantum

Outside his shadow slanted long and thin, a blackish transparency, touching the tattered trees of heaven, the sidewalk and his sedan. At his feet it joined him, following him. Rook, its driving force of pulse and muscle, opened his sedan door in silence. Voiced words were to him lackluster, and he prowled the streets during investigations alone in thought.

Rook obsessed about criminal shadows. He obsessed over what they left behind. Bullets. Blood. Semen. Fingerprints. Filaments. Deoxyribonucleic acid. Suicide notes. Hatred. He followed criminals like a shadow and forgot about his own.

Still, poetically, the deep black eternal night was to him the sun's shadow. Car key turning in hand, the ignition rumbling, he watched the mouth of impending night swallow the brash, glittering electronic towers of New York City. His black sedan lurked through the sudden dusk. The white sun looked orange to him, and the black sky looked ultramarine blue. *It's artificial*, he thought, *looks too surreal.*

He blinked: the sun became a bouncing orange handball, and Rook decided he was correct. The windshield had the appearance of normal tempered glass on the exterior, but it was in fact a window, a filter and a computer monitor. Within it a digital video replayed the earlier incident with the boy and his ball. Rook adjusted the monitor, attenuating the feed from the world outside by analog dials on the dash, dials that looked like they controlled the old AM radio. The bright blue faded from the windshield, and through it he saw blackish storm clouds brandishing lightning in the distance, smothering the ultramarine. *More like it*, he thought, but the windshield burst with orange again then alternated with blue. *East Orange is making me think of orange*, he realized, in turn leading his imagination, his memory and his windshield to complementary blue.

His brain was electronically entrained with all of his machines—his car, his watch, his computers—by the feedback nanoelectrodes long implanted under the surface of his skin. Camouflaging his advanced technology, his car and watch appeared from a distance merely antiquated and analog.

"Map. East Orange," he quietly commanded, "New Jersey."

A map of East Orange flashed into the windshield display. Rook did not use global positioning. The last thing he needed was a satellite tracking his every move.

He drove west from the city toward East Orange, and he squinted at the intermittently lurid sky before slipping on his lightly mirrored sunglasses. Through the sunglasses, if he wanted, he could make everything look black and white or he could tint and tune. It helped him reduce the complex visual world howling with feedback into a stark chess game. In feedback, reality was like AM radio fuzz meets the sea. His technology helped him focus and find the hard edges of reality, which in many ways was just like finding radio channels, using radar to locate a submarine or being talked down to an airstrip landing in a blackout—except he was doing all of this at the quantum level.

3: Feedback

He didn't know exactly what he would shadow that evening. It was a game he had taught Angela to play with him. If he didn't know, then move-by-move he discovered the crime he shadowed in the same way his father discovered and destroyed a gaming opponent. Rook had taught Angela when he hired her only to use the word *shadow* and to give him one lead at the start of a case. The lead was usually a name, a phone number or an address. The previous lead had been the phone number of the botanist who specialized in invasive species, and ultimately it led Rook to the assassin who went by the moniker *Weedkiller*.

Yesterday Rook had wrapped that case, or so he believed, and today he was onto what he believed was the next one. That Rook did not recall the solution to the Weedkiller crime did not plague him, nor did he realize even vaguely he had been solving it over and over again.

Not yet.

Tomorrow, April 23rd, would be his birthday. He almost smiled again, but when the bright orange sun blipped onto the windshield monitor then again transformed into the bouncing ball, he felt the lilting sensation of a seizure aura. He immediately sought to buckle his imagination down and stared hard through the sunglasses, forcing the visual world to simplify into black and white.

As a young man wandering the streets after his father's death, his thoughts jumbling and the city smelling only of death, he had slipped into a small coffee shop. By the time the smell was blacked out by the coffee taste from seven espresso shots, his body was shaking from the potent caffeine. The jitters kept him awake most of that night, and as his brain sought to turn itself down over and over again, Rook experienced his first seizure. With that onset of neural fire, Rook had believed he too was returning to the void, but within seconds the phenomenon rushed with godly hallucinations like, he thought later, the stained glass windows of mind. Next came the sensations and visuals, wrapped in a cosmic velvet, of free-falling in outer space. The initial seizure had terminated in a euphoric orgasm.

Many years later, he had experienced over 200 of them. Like coffee and crime, he was addicted to them.

Mindfuck yourself, he thought, *what do you expect.* He turned a knob on the dash and concentrated. Again, the vivid colors washed away, replaced by gray tones.

Overall Rook preferred to saturate what in crime was gray into black contrast with white. It turned crime into an airless moon with whites harsh as snow and blacks slick as India ink. He focused hard, and the gray tones in the sunglasses separated into hard black and white lines. The cameras in the sunglasses tracked focus with Rook's eyes, but they did much more than that. They helped him skirt the aura that was the onset of seizure. He absolutely could not afford to have one while driving. In addition to simplifying the visual input to his brain, nanoelectrodes in the sunglass temples sent cooling signals to his temporal lobes.

Rook calmed down, aware he had circumvented the neural fire of seizure, which he well understood was the howl of a brain looking, listening and touching itself—the brain in unchecked feedback.

New Jersey, moonlike in black and white, came into view.

If Rook paused his stare for a long moment then blinked, a single high contrast image became transferred to an encrypted database from the sunglasses. When he reviewed the images later, those keyed images were prioritized. He printed them onto plastic cards, shuffled them and played a kind of solitaire chess with them—over and over—until a pattern emerged. The idea was to treat crime like a game he had discovered but didn't know how to play. If he were to come across a chessboard with the pieces suddenly in halt, would he be able to infer the opening of the game? Probably. Card games were different. So many different games could be played with the same fifty-two cards, and the patterns in the abandoned deck would definitively suggest benign *Go Fish* or perhaps hazardous *Blackjack*. If a detective had never played these games, the detective would have to design a game that would repeat the patterns of the card game in halt.

With these things in mind, Rook shuffled his clue cards until the pattern formed in his imagination a specific crime. By the time he figured out what the crime was, he had enough evidence to nail the guilty. Blood did not mean murder. Semen did not mean rape. DNA did not mean death. A smoking gun may not even have been fired.

Especially in a world where reality changed hands on the black market with an incalculable velocity.

Especially in a world rippling with quantum feedback.

Most people only understood feedback as comments posted about their buying and selling on the web. Some knew it as the squeal from amplifiers when stuck in an audio loop with a microphone. A few knew it as an optical phenomenon as well—a flashing of digital light as a camera and monitor looped input and output. Others knew feedback as scientific oscillations within economics and biology, but only the elite knew reality itself was a closed feedback loop. Within it every possible variation of reality, a multiverse more concentric than parallel, conjoined at the quantum level.

Quantum reality was akin to a constantly evolving weather system that had become increasingly stormy, and inside this dense storm Rook Black was the rare man who could chase it. He knew well as he chased the eye of the reality storm through its wild hunting oscillations, it chased him.

Reality, he knew, was conscious. It was a conscious mirror reflecting itself. Science fiction had become science fact. Quantum reality wasn't just magical, it was magic.

Still, he was a human being, and taking quantum reality to its full conclusion was not anything he was capable of.

Not yet.

***

The kidnappers removed Angela's lingerie. Agent Orange used a small swab to collect DNA samples from the lining in the panties. She knew, bitterly, the sample would contain not just Angela's but also Rook's.

Rook's quantum DNA, like his shadow, like his signature, did remember solving the Weedkiller crime, and Agent Orange more than knew it.

4: Masculiner

Desolate streets rolled under the tires. The black rubber bounced through potholes and shuddered across rocks in a landscape that was lunar minus the romance. Rook scanned for addresses that no longer existed, and he slowed and stopped: there it was, a minimalist industrial storefront with mirrored glass strained by time. The mailbox carried the address of black plastic numerals nailed to rust. He blinked twice in a row rapidly, and the accelerometer buried within the acetate sunglass frames sensed the change. Black and white washed away, and Rook observed the world in color. The air was dense with thunderstorm. Fickle pink lighting veined the dark gray sky.

There was a beauty to the warehouse he appreciated, as if the aged mirror was silver leaf peeling while time brushed past it. It looked like a painting scratching the surface of East Orange, his own black sedan a dented reflection within it. He sweated, scanning as he breathed in and smelled it: *Decay*. East Orange never thrived. *From the beginning*, he thought, *it was dying*. Clouds cleaved, and for a moment he saw again an ultramarine blue sky and the sinking orange sun above the weathered walls of the warehouse mirror. It was a brief split-lip of calm sky otherwise punched by storm.

He stroked at his shoulder holster and stepped out of the sedan, surveying the emptiness around him. He seemed to be the only soul in it. He scanned the dust filming the street, looking for tire tracks and finding one other set leading to the mailbox but going no further.

He stepped toward the mailbox while snapping on latex gloves, and he thought, *Mailman*. The Postal Service, like the police and fire departments, had been well on its way to corruption before the great storm. Local police had no authority over it, and it policed itself from within through the mysteriously anonymous Postal Inspector. The Postal Service was just another gang. Mail had become completely electronic, and the postal workers, already notorious for murdering each other in public assaults, became heavily armed private couriers. If Rook ever found anything in his mailbox, it had been delivered by one of them. The Postal Service gang still maintained all city mailbox keys, though they rarely used them, and any sign of them was a sign of potential trouble.

He took a photo of the tire tracks before he pried the mailbox open. Inside was yellowed mail, one envelope. He pulled it out. Illuminating it with a small flashlight he noted: the mail was incoming and thirty-seven years dated, the lettering was childlike, the stamp's image showed dinosaurs and read, *The Age of Reptiles*. The envelope was addressed to *Masculiner Co.*

He flipped it for the return address.

It was his own.

His adrenaline surging, Rook carefully slit the envelope with a penknife and tugged out an advertisement torn from a mottled beige page. *Not from a magazine*, he thought, *comic book*. It sold fake mustaches, sideburns and a goatee mustache combo called the Van Dyke. The hair, the advertisement boasted, was not to disguise but to impress women. The would-be bearded had checked the box for a black deluxe Van Dyke and enclosed a five dollar bill. Rook examined the address the fake facial hair would have been sent to.

Again, it was his own.

And it was written in his own handwriting. He thought, *Angela Van Dyke*.

5: The Aura

One bullet. The lock shattered. One kick. The door blew open. He kept his gun high and level. The fact that his own address was on a thirty-seven year old piece of mail bothered him, and he was wondering, *Who in the hell would buy fake facial hair?*

He stalked through the voluminous warehouse. Soaked in shifting layers of abandoned night, in turn his shadow stalked him. He rotated abruptly, and it followed, twisting behind him as if it was clever. He peered hard, spying only one interior door, an office door. As he approached it, the door marked A-165 breathed open on its own as if the warehouse was just waking up. Rook was a man who did not know fear, and yet something licked his spine, chilling him. Each step he took closer to the door churned like butter made of lead, and as the warehouse darkness shimmered he heard the sound of electricity. His neuroelectricity. It was just like the buzz of high power lines under which a handheld bulb would glow with light.

It was an aura closing in. He knew well the experience of the aura, of the precursor to the seizures that haunted him before taking him to the edges of black hole event horizons: the quantum cores of feedback.

It took every muscle from quadriceps to abdominals and the full focus of his mind to enter the office, but when he did it seemed suddenly as if he could fly. The aura parachuted, and he was adrift in the event horizon. What was considered classical reality, he had begun to notice, had become increasingly irresponsive to linear time. *It's slipping*, he thought. He dared not slip with it. Rook braced himself, tuning his vision, hardening it, fighting the power of the aura.

The shimmering darkness and electrical sounds thinned, and he saw in hard reality a body lying down. His nostrils jerked, but there was no stench. *Alive*, he wondered, *or newly dead?* It was not moving or breathing. Rook's stomach fluttered in his chest as he pushed through the muddy darkness toward it. Light glinted through a window and struck a bright chord across the stiff body. It wore an immaculate white suit and, Rook noted, no blood stained it.

He relaxed. It was a mannequin. Rook circled it. It was a mannequin sporting a black deluxe Van Dyke. Looking exactly like him, it stared back at him like a mirror: black hair cropped close, hard jaw, about six foot two. It was dressed exactly like him also, except Rook's suit was the inverse in black, and it even wore photographic sunglasses. Rook touched his clean-shaven jaw, and the air shimmered again with the aura.

He thought, *This is going to be one hell of a night.*

Outside a man hidden in darkness touched buttons on a remote transmitter.

The light outside smeared, forcing Rook's shadow into an arch. Simultaneously, as the man in darkness worked the transmitter, the nanoelectrodes under Rook's scalp raged with electrical interference and jumped into a seizure. The light jerked, and Rook's shadow slammed down. The quantum blow to his head was internal, but it knocked him flat. Even though he was instantly unconscious and his ears bled, his gut reaction to fire his weapon prolonged. As his body madly shivered and twitched, five shots automatically, involuntarily reported from the barrel.

His shadow stretched away from him, seemingly more conscious than he, as it bounced in tandem with his shivering.

Within the warehouse appeared the man, and he was carrying a black doctor's bag. Pale light stroked the calcified scars on his aging weathered face, scars inset into his dark bluish black skin, scars that bespoke the cult of Sobek. He quietly walked straight to Rook, pulled a small console from his bag and attached it to the nanoelectrodes in Rook's head with metallic threads. A small screen surged to life, and spiking lines recorded Rook's brainwaves. As the man who had renamed himself after a major waterway turned a small knob, Rook stopped shivering. With a voice like a gravel road Dr. Kill van Kull said into a small wire, "Got him. Give me ten minutes to cool him."

***

On Coney Island a clothed, gagged and bound Angela Van Dyke was rolled behind the steering wheel of a black sedan. An orange vinyl gloved hand yanked the gag out of her mouth and pressed a fake plastic beard and mustache onto her face.

Agent Orange, her voice smooth and cool like vinyl, leaned back from the sedan and said into the wire built into her helmet, "I copy."

6: Angela Van Dyke

Angela Van Dyke first met Rook in the Central Library six years prior.

They were both there looking for the same book, an early pictorial study of blood spatter patterns. He made the gentlemanly offer, "Ladies first."

He didn't tell her what he did for a living, still it only took her a minute to guess. She said in a voice like acacia honey, flowery on the vowels and tangy on the consonants, "You're a detective, aren't you?"

Books by then were heavily protected by the Naranja Empire and could no longer be removed from libraries. Over drinks at the library bar, surveillance and security guards sporting the Libra scales insignia ensured books were not tampered with. Here their first game emerged with a life of its own. They challenged one another's knowledge of detective literature and true crime, utilizing the blood book's cold cases to advance theories.

"Your style is sexy," she said, and she wasted no time, "I want to assist."

He had been suspicious when they had first crossed paths, but then he was always suspicious. "Who do you work for?" he asked her.

She answered hopefully with a tease, "You?"

He did not believe her. But he hired her anyway.

Without her knowing it, he had photographed her brilliant blue irises with his sunglasses during their first conversation. A quick background check revealed she was who she had said she was. She had a Ph.D. in criminology and was a forensics expert with a penchant for literature. She was beautiful, a blondish redhead poured into a black blouse and skirt. And she was, she told him, "Bored."

Through his sunglasses he reduced her to black and white, to a sexual geometry of curves.

When Angela first joined Rook, he asked her to make his life more difficult. Under an arched brow, she shot him a look of inquiry.

He answered the look. "Solving crime is too easy for me. When the broker gives you a lead, find a way to keep it hidden from me. If the broker gives you a name, turn it into an anagram for something else. If the broker gives you an address, give me the same address but in a different city. If the broker gives you a telephone number, find a dead distant anybody related to the person who has the number. Give me their name instead. Be creative." It made her weak for him.

Angela had proven very adept at taking the principles of game theory and injecting them into his sleuthing.

It had not been long before they had begun having sex. Her bright blue eyes shone from across the office. Her cinnamon hair was alive with light, and her full lips, enviably not artificial, begged. She pushed them together in a hint of a smile, like a coral colored parasol about to expand under brilliant sunlight. It seemed also as if through them, just like her eyes, sunlight shone.

"You look like you want me to kiss you," he said to her the very day she started working for him.

"How long did it take you to figure that out?" she answered.

"May I?"

"You don't need to ask."

They kissed, and he ran his hands all over her body, searching her sexually.

"You're armed." He pulled back, his hand on one of her breasts, over her concealed weapon. Her clothes were tight, but he hadn't noticed the gun. It was his habit visually to frisk everyone he met. It was a good exercise, and in his line of business he never really knew who anybody might be. Somehow she had more cleverly concealed her weapon than most.

"So are you." She reached under his jacket and pulled his weapon out from his shoulder holster.

He slowly unbuttoned her blouse. There in her bosom was the exact same gun, a snub automatic, a downsized hybrid version of a pistol and a machine gun that could be fed a magazine with twenty rounds: a Z-9. His first thought was that she had been spying on him, had known his weapon and had copied him.

What she said was, "Looks like we were made for each other, Rook Black."

As time passed, Angela picked more and more difficult leads.

She had come to him out of the blue. Now she had thrust him into the orange.

7: Slipping

His eyes opened, squinting from a pain like a vise clamping his head, and it tightened as he awakened. Sticky blood pooled around him. *I will die here in lawless East Orange*, he thought, *with no good detective left to solve the crime*. He tried to move, but he was pinned by a nothingness that had the weight of his own car, some invisible two ton Detroit steel demon. The unforgiving force pushed down on his chest, and he realized he could not breathe in or out. His lungs starved for oxygen, his jaw was a sprung trap and thirst choked his tongue. His gun was still locked in his hand, as if *rigor mortis* had set in. *Maybe*, he thought, *it has*.

Something moved. He peered and saw only blackness, only shadows: they seethed and flicked like sharks in the quantum murk of dusk. They consolidated into one, and as the shadow rose up off his chest, towering over him, the weight released. Pale light flooded.

He gasped, and his head rushed with colors. He thought, *I slipped back*.

The drive from the city had been blue and orange—a parallel reality of a sky. He had switched it off to black and white. He had been focused like his father, warring chess, warring black and white pieces on black and white squares. Now his vision raged, as if he had never seen the world before. His vision became a feedback thunderstorm, and he could barely differentiate foreground from background—if there was such a thing. All he witnessed was lustrous, as if the world was beaded, as if reality was brocaded from neuroelectricity and gem, and he knew somehow it was—the stained glass of mind. The feedback world ripped open like a ripe fig, like Angela's thighs, and he submissively closed his eyes.

He felt his body and mind slipping into the delta brainwaves of eternal sleep. He fought it, and with a mental crowbar, he pried his eyelids open one again.

8: Effect Preceding Cause

The warehouse came into focus, like an old metal nurse, hanging over him. Numb with sleepiness, he fumbled his way to his knees and used a table to help him rise to his feet. As Rook's vision stabilized so did his legs, and he hobbled over to the mannequin. He touched his head where the blood was dry and mucky in his black hair and a nanoelectrode was exposed. When he touched it, his body jolted in response and his vision improved. The blood pattern on the concrete floor suggested, he decided, not an impact wound from his head hitting the concrete but a determined blunt blow from directly above.

He looked up and heard the wrench of failing steel just as a beam hurled toward him. He jumped aside as it angrily clanged the concrete floor and was suddenly still. There was no evidence of another that would have fallen ten minutes earlier.

Effect, he thought, *preceding cause*. It was happening more and more.

He reloaded his gun before slipping it into his holster, and he retrieved from the concrete floor his photographic sunglasses, one lens crushed. Another metal bang followed by a sonic metal crunch jolted his ears, and he realized instantly the whole building was coming down.

With the mannequin under his arm he sprinted, and it looked more like it was the wounded one who had been knocked out cold. Rook blasted out the warehouse door and dragged the plastic body toward his sedan, leaving behind two steady trails from its feet in the dust. The warehouse lurched improvisationally. Rook spun toward the steel on steel thundering as the building shuddered, and the artful painting of East Orange decline collapsed. An explosive wind rushed and pelted him with mirrored glass and grit. Within seconds only the mailbox was left standing. Rook looked at the tire tracks leading up to it, and intuitively he knew they tracked back—as the yellowed mail in his pocket strongly suggested—to his own address.

Around the collapsed building a wind lifted grit into a dust devil.

Rook quickly seated the mannequin, and as he did he tucked its plastic limbs and gave it a pat down. His fingers found a bulge, and he opened up the jacket. From its shoulder holster he retrieved a gun, and he examined it carefully. It was another Z-9. From the indentations and scratches he recognized it as Angela's. Rook smelled the Z-9 as if he were seeking the scent of the woman and the scent of her death. The gun definitely had been fired recently. Rook examined the chamber: there was one bullet left.

Dept. A-165 was a chess move, he decided as he hopped into the driver's seat. The windshield flared to life, entraining with his imagination, and it generated a digital chessboard. The white rook was positioned on the black square named A-1. If it were to move in a straight line along the A squares through rows 5 and 6, it would be one square away from direct confrontation with the black rook. *Who or what just confronted me*, he thought, *another Rook? Or is Angela playing a dangerous game with me?*

The idea made him want her even more.

As he drove away from East Orange, glass dust twinkling on the dried blood on his skin, he glanced at the mannequin on the passenger seat. "Maybe over a drink you'll tell me a little about yourself," he said in his whiskied voice, and he laughed darkly as he reached to the glove box for his flask.

9: Echo

Rook parked near his front door and examined his apartment as if he was casing it. The street was strangely quiet, too quiet, as he got out and carried the mannequin in. In his office he positioned the mannequin onto the seat opposite him at his desk. On its surface Angela had left another memo. This was not supposed to happen. He solved one crime at a time, never two simultaneously; otherwise in feedback the clues could overlap, entangle and garble evidence. During the investigation Angela also went away, so Rook could dig in solitude through the shadowy world for classical reality, the reality that most people agreed on was tangible. Rook's technology was not available to the masses: it was his alone, developed in the upstate Tuxedo Park lab specifically for him, so that he could shift at will between the overlapped quantum frequencies.

Rook carefully picked up the new memo by the edges and read it. It said simply, *Shadow, lingerie.* It was not in Angela's feminine handwriting. It was in metalloid ink struck by hard, clean architectural lettering. It looked like his.

When he had first become intrigued by detective work, it was because chess wasn't enough for him the way it had been for his father. Rook needed a lifestyle that was like a game. If Angela had wanted to work for him because she wanted him, she wanted him because she wanted to play his game. Sex was part of their game, a mutual fantasy in which he dominated physically, and she did everything she could to master him intellectually. Before he had met her he typically just paid for it. He didn't have the interest to cultivate a real relationship, and the last thing he wanted was a wife.

The mannequin stared at him through the lightly mirrored sunglasses. Rook removed them. "Let's see what you have been looking at," he said to the mannequin, "other than me. ECHO, on."

His voice turned on the ECHO, his computer. The wall-sized monitor, suspended as a dense tactile screen, flashed on in front of him. The blank screen requested a biometric, and Rook stared at the blinking question mark. It registered his eyes, scanned his dark black irises and confirmed his identification.

The camera in the mannequin's sunglasses transmitted the images, and the screen flooded with color. The latest image revealed Rook observing the mannequin in the warehouse just prior to taking the seizure hit, and behind him in the image, he could see only his own dark shadow. *Who could have been so silent?* he thought.

The previous image revealed Angela, almost naked in the sheer orange lingerie, her mouth filled with a ball gag, and her eyes covered with an orange eyeshade. Her arms and legs appeared bound, and someone, their hand in an orange vinyl glove, was holding Angela's own gun—the Z-9—to her head. He did not infer that she had been truly kidnapped, as she could have easily staged this photo herself, but he also did not dismiss it.

Rook searched for more photos, but there were none. He printed up the two, into the acetate plastic clue cards. Digital paper had been around for years, but it was volatile. The acetate he had developed at his lab, like the vinyl of old albums, had grooved analog memory that could not be overwritten by the self-destructive code rampant in the wired world.

The images synced with his archived ECHO database, and the ECHO powered through tireless computations, searching for similarities—the kind of mental muscle work only a computer could endure. There was no guarantee that the next time he looked at the digital images, they would not have changed. Like the self-destructive warehouse, almost everything had built in expiration dates and viral coding that ate itself. Even film that looked like 35mm was a hoax. Just as soon as people thought they knew what reality was, it was gone. Regardless they could buy whatever version of it they wanted on the black market.

Rook sent another image, of the blue sky and setting sun, from his broken sunglasses to his monitor. It filled the room, pouring into it some vestigial memory of placid nature. In contrast outside, there was no pristine sky to be seen. The tall city buildings were awash in electrified advertisements and propaganda. The omnipresent Times Square provided most of the light on a dark island otherwise engulfed by a dungeon dark sky.

Rook poured himself a glass of whiskey neat under the glow of the projected blue sky, which he understood was essentially a quantum parallel sky, like a gorgeous butterfly wing, plucked from a multiversal reality. It pleased him and took him back to his youth, to when he and his father knew such skies as real, before the butterfly effect of an accelerating reality looped into the howling tunnel of chaos. He drained the whiskey as he held up with tweezers the yellowed envelope and dinosaur stamp under an old school ultraviolet light. *Mail*, he thought, *mailman, male man, masculine, mannequin*. He did not find any prints using this method.

From a cabinet he pulled out a small box. He set Angela's gun inside, and he hit a button. The box illuminated with laser lightwaves, splashing interference patterns, and in turn these patterns reiterated on Rook's monitor, replacing the mellow sunset with an image of the gun. The box scanned small evidence for fingerprints by shining lasers, which in turn made the residue in latent prints fluoresce. Within moments six partial prints were isolated. Rook hit another button, and the print samples scrolled against an ECHO database. Two matches were found: Rook's and Angela's. There were no third party prints on this gun.

Rook scanned the new memo and found only his own fingerprints on the face, which he knew he had not touched. He removed the memo and was about to set the yellowed envelope within the box when he decided upon another method.

10: Psychonaut

Rook opened the door to another room. Unlike his office it was simple: exposed ruddy clay brick and gray mortar, buckling plaster and a bare bulb dangling from old cloth clad wiring. It was dark. Rook ignored the light switch and sat down on a buttery black leather psychologist style couch that had belonged to his father, upon which the man had lain while playing blind chess.

Rook snapped his feedback mask over his face, lay down and relaxed his mind, giving himself ten minutes. He had taught himself how to dream while awake many years ago. It had taken months of practice, extreme concentration, and even drugs at first—hallucinogens. The process was tedious, like climbing a mountain, tedious like becoming a mountain range, tedious like being. The tedium had become a lightyear-long journey into his own head that resulted eventually in lucid dreaming. The lucid dreams seemed tangible, and within them the world of quantum feedback had first opened up to him. The human brain was the penultimate quantum tuner, and as Rook's mind learned to reach for reality, so did reality literally reach for him.

But not, he thought, *like this. Could it really reach into hard reality?*

He knew that it did, but its reach was subtle. *This phenomenon*, he thought, *subtle as a baseball bat.*

That was pretty much what the crack to his head had felt like.

Rook relaxed. He had taught himself to envision his hands as if they were real, so that within the lucid dreams he could touch and feel the texture of his mind. Eventually it came to him, the ability even to see himself clearly in a dream mirror. Reality, he had come to realize, though external, was in many cases all in the head. He was one of the elite who knew how to tune into it, and his feedback mask—mechanically joined to the nanoelectrodes under his skin on an atomic scale—was the product of intensive top secret Tuxedo Park brainwave research. The nanographite ribbons in the mask had properties that led quantum scientists to label them either zigzagged or bearded. As Rook prepared to dip into a feedback session, he touched the hard bristles of black beard growing on his jaw, and he knew exactly what it was that told a boy he had become a man, and a man he had become a psychonaut.

Rook Black was not just any detective, he was a psychonaut, a mind navigator. Tuning to the quantum mind, he slipped into the collective unconscious deliberately, at will, with the knowledge that as he navigated he also created. But this crime was already garbled, like a hand drawing itself, and he would have to navigate this crime by its own accord.

The night had been free-associating around him. He needed to get inside its pulse, to have his heart beat with it and to have his dream hands hold his beating heart. He needed a session of controlled slipping, one with a mental anchor by which he could pull himself out of the quantum sea.

He breathed meditatively and pulled a black throw over his legs. His inner vision shimmered as if it could not wait to come out and play.

He slipped easily into hypnagogia, the early onset of dreaming, and while still awake he focused on the mail and the fake beard, seeking its quantum essence via the equivalent of mental radar. An image of a generic mailman emerged, a man clothed in blue-gray wielding a gun, and as the imagery became dense and colorful, Rook dreamed the faceless mailman held an orange fruit in his left hand. With his gun the mailman was spinning a globe. A sun rose over the globe's horizon, looking like a peeled navel orange.

Rook's mind merged and mulled, *Why are cities named Orange, after the fruit?* He twitched with the odd thought, *There are no cities named pink.*

Where the citrus sun did not shine in his dream, the dream globe immersed into dream shadow. The mailman became Rook, the sun became Rook's navel, and his navel became an envelope.

His mind slipped slower into sleep, into theta brainwaves and finally shoved him down hard, smothering him. In the adjacent room the ECHO computer faithfully recorded the dream images to an ecrypted database, and when his mind was overwhelmed by quantum static, the ECHO screen mirrored it with dark gray digital snow.

Just like the pounding waters of the world's most terrifying waterfall, the quantum mist pummeled him. He was at the event horizon, at the black hole, at the devil's mouth of feedback. His eyes opened, and he clutched for the throw, but his hands did not respond. He panicked. The couch was not flat side down, horizontal: it was vertical just like a waterfall. He looked down at his feet, knowing fully he would at any moment plummet, that he would slip, but a shadowy weight, some kind of mental g-force, kept him pinned.

The black throw writhed, wrapping him and spinning him. He had no control, and he could no longer tell up from down. He knew the experience well: it was the antigravitational experience that accompanied his entry into the directionless, nonlocal quantum world. The black throw became alive, transforming into a wraith, into a nebulous demon. It coiled around him and squeezed him, and it took everything he had to move. He wrestled it and momentarily he backed it off. He also knew this phenomenon well: the demon was the event horizon guard, his own primordial shadow mind, his anchor providing him with the mental acuity and strength needed to avoid quantum riptide.

The shadowy guard transformed into Angela, and she was wearing the orange lingerie. She forcefully rolled on top of him, and the translucent orange fibers flashed into lightning.

The imagery jumped, billowing into night sky. He plunged into endless milky way. It was orgasmic.

11: Pushing the Envelope

And barely a block away, in unison, the hard metal shutters to the Majestic lingerie store, crimped with rust and spastic graffiti, rolled up for the first time in years. A long brown rat darted out from the doorway to the gutter in a panic. In the quantum mist Rook heard the clatter.

Rook's body jerked up through theta into alpha brainwaves as he heard a sharper sound. He sat up and pulled off his mask. His wakening attention jumped focus to a subsequent knock at his front door, a knock he knew he had already heard. On a small security monitor he stared at a dark shape transformed into a blur behind the beaded glass of his front door. Rook watched as the small black blur rose over a black rook stenciled onto the glass and became another knock. Rook witnessed a machine gun armed mailman holding a package. The gigantic muscled mailman, his face hidden in shadow, gave the door another desultory rap, this time with the end of his gun.

Rook inferred if he did not accept the package, the mailman would, as the mailman gang was feared for, find his way to deliver it with a bullet. Rook untangled himself from the throw and crept into his office, knuckled his gun and slid toward a window where he fought to find aim past the curtains edge.

The mailman said into the intercom, "Angela Van Dyke?"

Rook choked on his silence.

The mailman turned, took three strides from the front door and spoke into his radio, "No answer."

"Leave it," Agent Orange's voice responded.

Rook now had a shot at the man's heart through his back, but he was certain the bulky man wore bulletproof armor. The mailman rotated and glanced over the windows. Rook pulled in quickly, his mouth dry from more than the whiskey. He waited a long moment before sliding on the floor to get a look at the door monitor. The mailman seemingly was gone and on the doorstep sat a small package.

The mailman strode toward his truck, sneaking words into his radio as he did, "Delivered."

Agent Orange heard him. In the Majestic glass storefront not far away, its grimy windows being wiped by an opportunistic street vendor window washer, she flipped a closed sign to open and said, "I copy."

Rook had no way to ping the mailman's truck: it was analog and untraceable. He waited for him to drive away before quickly pulling the package inside.

The package was from the lingerie company named *Majestic*. Rook set the package onto his desk, adjusting the lamp over it, and as he did it kicked his shadow into an arch over him. He bent his ear over the package and listened, and as he did his shadow leaned over him as if eavesdropping on him.

The package made no sound. He opened it carefully, like he was dissecting it, and he parted orange tissue paper. Inside was sheer orange lingerie in Angela's sizes and a brochure advertising the line of lingerie. He slowly examined each page: women modeled fishnets and brassieres; some wore masks, some playfully wielded paddles. He flipped to the last page. It featured models sporting fake mustaches and beards.

Van Dykes, he thought, *role playing*.

His lips drew back into an almost grin, and he thought, *Angela is outdoing herself this time*. He raised the lace, noting that inside the brassiere a holster was sewn, and as he smelled a chemical he wondered with a jolt of dread, *Or is she?*

He held the orange lingerie just under his nose and smelled it: it held not the scent of a woman, but the harsh smell of a common weedkiller. *Atrazine.* He recalled the smell with the immediacy of olfactory memory, the strange ability to recall intensely over great periods of time specific odors. He knew the odor of atrazine as a boy, smelling it for the first time at Tuxedo Park when the maintenance gardeners sprayed it to keep the weeds from erupting in the laboratory greenhouses.

He wrestled with pleated memories for the solution to the Weedkiller crime, but he could not locate it. The thought haunted him, *Perhaps the solution is nonlocal.*

12: Local Nonlocal

There had never been anything majestic about the Majestic lingerie store. It had sold cheap panties in the underwear district around the corner from where Rook lived until one day its shutters closed for good. *Close, too close*, he thought as he took a one minute shower, *local*. He was becoming less certain that this new crime was a game Angela had drummed up, especially as his memories of the Weedkiller crime shredded the further he pondered them. He stepped into narrow city streets in fresh clothing, in his standard black suit, jacket, white shirt and black tie, and felt a foreboding for a street name he had long taken for granted.

Orchard Street. It was only seven and a half blocks long, and there was but one tall and scabby gray-barked tree of heaven hanging over it. It was springtime, and the tree's small oval leaves were forcing the tiny yellow-green clusters of pollen off the limbs into the air. With them issued a smell not unlike cat urine. Rook breathed in the towering tree that was also called the stinking sumac, and he thought again, *Something smells, something stinks.*

New Yorkers and tourists crowded the upscale boutiques on Orchard Street, and Rook slipped through and around them. He found it, the old Majestic store spontaneously turned exotic lingerie boutique, and he was not really surprised to find it open. The eyes of New York City blinked, and things changed. The mannequins in the windows were dolled up in lingerie, just like the real models in the advertisement, and there they were under cool splashing white spotlights: the ones wearing the Masculiners, the Van Dykes.

A saleswoman poured into a slick orange vinyl jumpsuit, her face concealed in a motorcycle helmet, appeared to look at him through the clean clear glass. She was sexy in a cold way, and he wondered what the helmet concealed.

When he had woken from the feedback session, the black throw had tangled him, and Rook was sticky from the event horizon experience that always ended in a wet dream. *What is it about lingerie that's so sexy?* he wondered, and he answered, *The woman in it, a woman whose sexuality is veiled. But what turns the veil into a fetish?*

It was rare that he took off all of Angela's clothes. He was not gentle with her. He took her in whatever way he wanted, wherever he wanted, whenever he wanted, and yet even if she was on her knees before him, he knew it was she who controlled him. There was nothing more powerful in the world than a woman.

He entered the store.

"How may I help you?" the saleswoman wanted to know, her smooth voice broadcasting through a microphone in the helmet.

"Do you have anything," he emphasized darkly, "*in orange*?"

She thought about it, "We did. Last fall. October. If we have anything left of the orange line, it's in the back room."

"Show me."

She led him to the door, her vinyl orange pumps seamless with her jumpsuit, clicking an orange epoxy floor. She felt his heat behind her as she paused to unlock the door. He leaned in close, so close she felt his stubble against her ear. "Who do you work for?" he whispered.

The lock clicked. They were in.

"Who do you work for?" he insisted, pressing up against her. She tried to walk away, but he took her hands gently, seductively, and his eyes burned into her.

"Who do you want me to work for?" she teased. She watched him and purred, "Do you want me to work for you?"

He pushed her away and surveyed the mannequins. They were contorted, missing limbs and scarcely dressed. His focus hit a box stamped with the brand *Masculiner,* and he intrusively opened it: inside were several Van Dyke goatee and mustache kits. *They could not have come from East Orange*, he thought. He tore the packing slip showing a Brooklyn address from the carton. *Reality is slipping*.

He demanded in a blunt tone that meant the business of crime as he

turned to face her,
"Where's the orange lingerie?"

"Right here," she answered. Slowly she unbuttoned her top, revealing her bosom. She was wearing it, an orange semi-transparent brassiere. Her dark nipples seized his attention and in between them, in a holster, sat her bright orange metal gun.

That sensation rushed his spine, a trepidation bordering on fear. He reached for his gun.

And she reached for hers.

There were a dozen of them. They darted from the shadows: all women, all dressed in skintight orange jumpsuits and wearing motorcycle helmets. Rook was surrounded by potential gunfire like clockwork. His hand was still inside his jacket, and his gun was still not drawn. There was no way out.

She smiled innocently inside her helmet as she raised her weapon and placed his head in the gun sight behind her hidden bright blue eyes. She joshed him viciously, "I'm Agent Orange. I'm newly self-employed."

"Agent Orange, what do you want from me?"

"Let's be real, Rook. You're making it very difficult for me—to be real," she answered matter-of-factly, "or at least to get away with being real. I thought I'd give you an attractive—"

Her dozen stepped in closer.

"—Retirement opportunity. Face reality, Rook. My reality. Now, undress. Start with the gun."

Rook stood frozen. *Exfoliation,* he thought, *war.*

Like choreographed dancers, the twelve clipped silencers onto their automatics.

"Only one problem," he said as he slowly dragged his gun out, "You're in the crossfire."

"Not really, Rook Black," she responded, "I'm firing the first bullet."

He lunged for her, catching the gunshot in his shoulder. He fell with her.

She was slippery. He lost her.

Gunfire exploded everywhere. He rolled, tucked, spun and wielded a mannequin as he made for the fire exit. The head blasted off, an arm, a leg. They were ace shots, close-up assassins. *So, why*, he wondered, *are they missing me?*

As he crashed onto the city street he knew he had been hit only once, by Agent Orange's promised first shot. It was just a graze.

He pounded toward Ludlow Street and spotted his sedan. It was tagged with orange spray paint that looked like an anarchy sign: an *A* surrounded by an *O*.

Agent Orange.

He pivoted toward Grand Street, shoved his way through pedestrians and took the subway stairs three at a time, his thoughts an orange blizzard. He leapt onto a train just as its doors slid shut. The train lurched forth.

He was the only one in the car.

His eyes shot from one end of the car to the other, momentarily pausing and focusing on the train letter. It was the D to Brooklyn. The sign was colored orange, indicating he was on the orange line. The thought jolted him, *The orange line.*

He shunted himself up against the metal wall, peering into the next car. It looked empty too. He peered as far as he could forward and backward. They were all empty.

The train hurtled, and the faces of the predominantly Chinese women and men waiting on the platform blurred like lantern light on water.

Rook's mind blasted, *How is this happening?* He knew he would need to reach the motorman car to stop the train, and he pushed at the door between train cars. It refused to budge. He rattled the handle. It did not move. He darted to the end of the car and tried the same.

He was locked in.

Rook popped open an emergency window. It smashed against the dark wall of the tunnel and blasted into splinters of ill light behind the rushing train. Gray light bathed the car as the train emerged onto the new, much taller Manhattan

Bridge. It was a skeleton of gothic spires built after the Brooklyn bombings of his youth.

13: Hunting Oscillations

Rook contorted the top half of his body out of the window opening. He clung to the side of the train, gritted his teeth and gripped a metal lip running the top length of the car. The lip was only about half an inch high, a riveted joint between the metal side and the metal roof. It only took a few pounds of pressure to climb vertical faces—as long as he had that half-inch fingerhold. Rook counted to one, grunted and swung a leg up. With two hands and the back of one foot hanging on the metal lip his body had to intuitively decide how to get the rest of him up. It was the strength of his leg that kicked in and pulled him into a higher position. He slapped his hand out, finding the next joint in the rivets running along the top of the train. It was just enough for a fingerhold. He rolled on top in one final burst and found himself lying on his back, his limbs spread. Around him the bridge's accordion steel cables flickered like strings on a giant gothic harp. Pink lightning erupted and connected the pinnacle of a steel beam to the low thunderstorm clouds. The telltale gusting wind announcing the impending rain rushed over him. The sky spit.

Briefly he thought, *It is angelic, a visual choir of my doom.* His mind jumped from angels to Angela. *Where is she?* he thought, as he flipped up and over. He stood poised, facing Brooklyn, and he spied a Kings County Kong biplane sweeping the shore. *Pushing the envelope*, he thought, *old aviation slang*, and he knew now more than ever he needed aerodynamics on his side.

***

Angela choked on the ball gag as she came to. In her mouth was the vile taste of the weedkiller. She blinked under the blindfold and felt the weight of something sticky on her face. She wriggled and felt her arms bound to something in front of her. Overhead, she heard the sound of helicopter blades.

***

The shadow man, Jack the Butterfly, turned his black eyes to the latest merchant arriving from Ningbo. The merchant was a DNA fusion specialist. He held a reed of the grafted papyrus invading the city waters in his hand like a weapon. "We paid you to graft the reed with the wisdom of our dynasty. Instead you grafted it with atrazine! How can a weedkiller be a weed?"

He chucked the reed down.

Yellow paper dust issued like a halo around the increasingly inscrutable dark features of the shadow man. "The technology of reality grafting, if it was so simple, would be in the hands of the merchants of Ningbo by now, don't you think?" Jack's black eyes, voided hollows, rotated and fixed on the merchant. His words popped and sputtered like grease on water, "I did not graft papyrus with weedkiller!"

"What went wrong!"

Jack scratched his head, and from his darkness the yellow dust bloomed, a mix of old paper, pollen and flaking skin. "The growth of reality is accelerating. It is pitching back and forth in what is called the hunting oscillation. What comes to life in the graft contains its own death. Life oscillates to death. Death oscillates to life."

"You mean it is self-correcting?"

"Yes. The reed will not make the quantum jump we seek until the oscillations are strong enough. You can't simply expect to overwhelm the reality long grafted by the Naranja Empire here overnight. Their reality is a very hardy species, and it is more than inclined to survive."

The merchant from Ningbo reeled back from the shadow man's stench. "There is a botanist here in New York City I've been following, a specialist in invasive species—"

"Dr. Chess."

"You know him?"

Jack walked to a mirror. His reflection was increasingly vague, a wireframe of overlapping shadowy waves. "I know of every prominent botanist. I grafted myself into all of them to one degree or another."

The merchant from Ningbo's narrow eyes folded into flat slits, "But he is not Chinese!"

"His DNA reveals Silk Road heritage. You see we are all Chinese in the end."

That brought a smile to the tight lips of the reality trader. "The merchants of Ningbo believe Dr. Chess may have the botany we need! We must push the oscillation!"

Jack thought of The Pimp and had the curious sensation that he could not really tell who he was working for anymore. Like a pimp, Jack knew he was an equal opportunity bad man. He lied to everyone and worked for everyone. It was with an ultimate sense of grace that he realized he did not even care. His longing to merge with the great shadow of the void, to be released from the bondage of space and time, was overwhelming. Like a junky, he nodded off for a moment and dreamed neither of light nor darkness.

The merchant from Ningbo, simultaneously disgusted and delighted, left immediately for Dr. Chess's laboratory.

***

Jules Barbillon observed the ruddy lips of Rocky Astor as he chewed on the end of a lit cigar. He was handcuffed and leg-cuffed to a welded steel contraption that visually was both dungeonesque and thronelike. The identical brothers, in their black suits, sat on either side of him, their seats backwards, their long legs pitched at angles and their arms resting on the chair back, their guns loose in their fingertips.

Jules grunted, "Gasland has agreed to the ransom."

Rocky's cigar spat from his mouth in protest. "They wouldn't dare!"

Jules chuckled, "Oh, Rocky, but they would and they did." He adjusted his orange tinted eyeglasses. "When we threatened to kill them all. The Naranja Empire has been very tolerant of Gasland. But when the doctor learned you had intent to burn down his precious library, let's just say you burned that bridge of tolerance."

Jules knew that Dr. Naranja was listening and watching through his own eyes, and he was humbly thankful the man could not, at least to his knowledge, read his thoughts as well. But just in case, he framed his sole thought vaguely: *Bastard!*

***

Agent Orange watched the runaway train from security cameras placed along the bridge and throughout the metropolitan subway system—the same system used by the engineers to control train traffic, and the same system she used to monitor the city for the Naranja Empire. The security cameras fed into her motorcycle helmet into a one-inch screen. The feed transmitting to Dr. Naranja's penthouse she had hacked. He was watching an edited version, a comprehensibly realistic view of similar events.

She watched the train rocking harder and harder back and forth, its oscillations hunting enough to throw the train sideways. *Soon, she thought, I will be free, forever.* She smiled, thinking, *Life's been but a walking shadow, until now.*

***

Rook had four cars to run before the train slid underground again. He had to make it. The wind shoved him backwards as lightning tickled Brooklyn, and the train rocked violently. Raindrops huddled as a mist, and it would only be moments to the downpour. Lights from driving cars bled past him as he ran against the howling wind and leapt. For a long moment, he swam in the air until he slammed down onto the roof of the next car. He slipped and rolled across the wet steel hull, his knee caught, stopping him, and he jumped up. He was back on his feet, running with one car down and three to go. The train roared, drowning out the thunder, and it was already halfway over the bridge. He thought of relativity, of the speed of light. He leapt again, making it to the third car and running the moment his feet touched down. He made it to the front of the car in twelve long dubious strides, and he leapt again just as the clouds vented their fury. He was soaked instantly as he hit the second car, each footstep becoming a slippery dance with death.

The train was a hundred feet from going underground. He paused for a long moment and reloaded his gun. He faced the yawning tunnel. His lips formed into his almost smile as he witnessed orange spray painted horns and eyes glowing on the concrete wall around the black tunnel entrance, making it look like a mouth of a devil. Rook ran, drenched, and he leapt...

He hit the roof of the motorman's car and bounced on a soft spot. Airborne, he lost his slick gun. It dropped to the metal roof and shot along the central metal lip. He slammed down on his belly and slid forwards. *I'm frantic*, he thought, *I'm losing control, I'm slipping*.

He was falling. On this lawless orange line, he realized, he was finally going to die. He scrambled for a finger hold just as gravity took him over the front of the conductor car, just as the Brooklyn tunnel swallowed the train, just as he smacked against the front glass window. He got a toehold on a windshield wiper, and something bumped into his fingertips: his gun.

Through the glass he saw the motorman, a plastic mannequin that looked like him.

He fumbled for his gun on the lip up above. Clinging with one hand, he reached the extra inch and got it. He squinted as he fired at the window. The glass fractured but did not break, and he frantically banged at it with the butt of his gun. He twisted and slipped, one foot landing on the windshield wiper again. He placed his gun in his mouth, took hold of the lip on the roof with both hands and gave a furious kick. The window started to give. He kicked and kicked and kicked, a man fighting for his life in the dark entrails of the subway abyss. Ahead there was the bleak light of a station. With one final kick his body crashed through the window.

14: Coney Island

The train hurtled through the station. A single waiting passenger was asleep on a bench as the nearly empty train shot by, its lone passengers the man furiously working the conductor controls at the front and a mannequin. The controls were not obeying.

He pulled what looked like a brake, and the train seemed to shift to warp speed. Darkness rolled alongside the windows, then cold white light burst as the train shot through the next station, immediately plunging again into shadow. Rook realized the controls were useless. If the train was going about 120 miles per hour, as it certainly seemed to be, it would make it to the end of the line at Coney Island in less than five minutes. That is, if it did not jump the tracks before then. Rook slid sideways as the car rocked hard, and he slammed against a metal handle. He grabbed for it.

The end of the line, Rook thought, *that's what Agent Orange said.* Rook observed the mannequin, thinking momentarily, *Fake*, and he decided she had her hands on some kind of black market reality that was invading his.

The train would derail. It was rocking like a boat tossed in a storm, and he could not stop it. It was its fate, and if he had any chance of surviving, he had to go back out the way he had come in.

The train's wheels rimmed with glowing red heat. Sparks shot from the metal wheels like Roman candles and reflected off the dirty windows in blinding, neon white smears. Rook looked out to the tracks and saw the proverbial light at the end of the tunnel.

He wriggled back through the broken window and clung to the front of the train. As the train shoved out of the tunnel and up above ground again, he flipped back onto the top of the car, and for a long moment he crouched at the front of the train like a masthead.

The conductor car shot out toward the end of the tracks, the spitting spark of wheel on rail a deadly wedding train of fire. He did not see the orange graffiti marking the concrete around the tunnel opening as it receded behind the train. It was a simple spiral, like a curled tail. Rook stood up fully, swaying with the car, and he watched the dead night shuttle past him.

He leapt...

And thc conductor car shot off thc tracks.

The train cars derailed, slammed and flipped like beaching whales possessed by iron decibels and the crashing chorus of a demon quantum sea.

Rook hit the hard dirt and ran like hell.

At street level he heard the sound of an engine. It was a familiar sound, and it was roaring toward him at top speed. It was his own sedan, and inside was Angela Van Dyke. He thought, as he focused his high-definition corneas, *She's wearing sunglasses*. He squinted, drew his weapon and shot out a tire, but it kept coming. He shot out another tire. Still, it drove.

It was a hundred feet away, and he could almost see her. *I could*, he thought, *kill her, but is she trying to kill me?* The black rubber ripped off the rims, and echoing the train, the sedan rims sparked and squealed furiously as he shot another tire. She was fifty feet away, and he saw not sunglasses but that she was blindfolded, handcuffed to the wheel and wearing a Van Dyke. He shot out the fourth tire, but it made no difference. The sedan shrieked toward him, the Agent Orange anarchy sign mocking him. He shot at the passenger side, and the windshield shattered into spiderwebbing. He leapt, rolled onto the hood and kicked at the windshield. It buckled.

The sedan was headed for a brick wall. He slipped inside.

"Angela!" He took close dead aim on the steering wheel and fired. Plastic and steel bit into his face. He pulled her free from the wheel and opened the passenger door. He embraced her as they fell. The door smacked his head, hitting his wound, opening it. They hit the asphalt and rolled hard. He kept his hands around the back of her head, his knuckles scraping to the bone, and his bruised head smacking a curb. Behind Rook and Angela the mannequins in a storefront stared out.

As unconsciousness befell him, Rook's only question: *When did I become so predictable?*

The sedan hit the wall with a wrenching boom.

The orange fire, an undulating blossom of flame roiling soot, implicitly popped a pattern—a special effect from orchestrated fireworks: Agent Orange's signature.

***

Striding toward her motorcycle, viewing her signature in fire through a screen woven into her helmet, she smiled. Her long legs pitched like a capital A around her motorcycle. *It's my time*, she thought, *now!*

CHAPTER THREE: The Broker

1: The Broker

If the world had a face, it would be slackened by a thousand-yard stare. A ball of lava, rock, ocean and atmosphere, the world once so organically promising sung the dirge of impending human demise. Even if there were a million Rooks on the beat, there would only be one detective for every one thousand crimes. But there was only one Rook, and crime wasn't a number that could be rounded down to zeros. Crime could not be reduced to statistics, and like galactic stardust or dandelion seeds, its kin to beauty, violent crime spiraled. The world seethed crime. It always had.

Rook solved *per diem* for clients he didn't know and didn't want to know. He had ceased non-critical communication with his crime broker, the man named Cosmo Hamilton. That was part of his game. Angela took the hard leads, the ones specifying the exact crimes he was to solve, from Cosmo, who was a specialized class of topfeeder. Brokers were people who knew people. *Broker:* the word stemmed from the French *brocour*, possibly related to the Latin roots of *procure*—meaning, to see to it for someone else. Brokers saw to it. Brokers were go-betweens who picked up where the police had dropped off, and the police ultimately had become gone-betweens. They had long ago gone corrupt along with the police detectives who had conspired with them under the guise of an official badge. At first they had simply taken small fees to say who was guilty, but eventually paying off these detectives became irrelevant. Police detectives had become extinct. They were dinosaurs.

The concept of justice as implicit to democracy was as short-lived as a fly and just as annoying as the life of a fly to the human. Briefly, when Rook's father had been young, democracy had lulled the human impulse to conquer, but as Rook's father matured, so did the impulse. In its maturity the impulse returned to its infancy, and in the infantile world Rook knew, accused men and women were tried not by blind justice but by blind luck. Judges had the freedom to do anything they wanted to try an accused, from flipping a coin if they were in a hurry to stamina tests such as forcing the accused to swim across the East River in a thunderstorm. A person was guilty if they were unlucky or weak, and swimming to Brooklyn, thwarting the tidal straight crocodiles that had come to inhabit it, did not guarantee new life on the other side.

Not at all.

The wealthy still committed crimes against one another, as they always had, and if they wanted a crime solved, they had to hire a real detective. Detective was a polite term for mercenary. Rook was not a man of morals. He solved crimes for the thrill of the game and for payment of the specially manufactured, untraceable and programmable money invented by his father. His *per diem* compensation was the equivalent of a hundred thousand dollars, yet when he spent his money he left no visual trace. The currency code traded by the ultra rich, unlike the currency for the masses, was not quantum.

Quantum currency emitted photon streams that were immediately, eternally tagged by the currency sensors, which could backtrack through the entire lifecycle of an individual's transactions. The photon stream emitted during Rook's transactions was artificial and ephemeral. It self-destructed immediately after currency sensors processed it. For more than one reason Rook needed this financial invisibility. Rook Black, for all intents, did not exist.

Rook was intelligent enough to frame anyone and then collect his *per diem*, but that game would be too simple. Instead he collected the evidence, had Angela deliver the package of clues to Cosmo, and Cosmo in turn delivered the clues and verdict to the patron. Rook's untraceable payment always showed up in a box from the low-end, defunct lingerie company named Majestic.

Rook's untraceable currency was the same money the rich used amongst themselves. It looked like standard quantum currency. It was a quarter of the size of old credit cards and was even minted by the Federal Reserve, but only the elite few knew about it. The card held an internal monetary charge that depleted as Rook made transactions, and it contained no personal information about him whatsoever. In contrast, the holographs embedded in the clear acetate cards the average citizen used contained their complete biometrics: fingerprints, iris scans and even a voice imprint. Stealing currency had been made impossible, and even Chinese piracy was ultimately abandoned. When Rook absolutely wanted to leave a trace, a cold trail of an identity, he cloned.

If the Majestic box payment came to Rook with *The Bonus*, another million in untraceable currency, Rook executed. This put him in the vulnerable position of being guilty of many crimes himself, but Rook thought of crime as something that only existed if defined, and he held no high regard for words. Better, he thought, to go down corrupt than to fall as an innocent bystander. At any rate he had not met his match. Or so he had thought.

***

North of New York City, in his Tuxedo Park headquarters, Cosmo sat in his beige tweed suit in the midst of his massive clock collection. It contained the tiny cogs and wheels of thousands of timepieces. His warm dark chocolate brown eyes glowed under thin arching eyebrows, and he squeezed his eyelids tight, wondering if he had made the right decision. The clocks chimed, gonged, whistled and clicked in symphonic unison to 10:30 p.m., and Cosmo stood. *I'll find out in an hour and a half*, he surmised, *too late now*.

Cosmo's long lean frame looked like an hour hand, leaning along with the hands pointing toward eleven on the round-faced clocks. He made his way to the elevator, then upstairs to his private chamber. From his walk-in closet he produced a brilliant vintage white shirt and black tuxedo. He began to undress.

2: Pulpdom

The real estate kingpins had burned the Brooklyn waterfront to the ground during Rook's youth, and they had destroyed the bridges, then they had built everything back up, way up. Rimming the fast and dirty river were new, otherworldly sky rises that made the Empire State Building look like a toy. The gasoline wealthy lived there in penthouses they called *blue rooms*, not because they offered the sinful comfort of synthetic sex—because they towered above the filthy black smog and sudden storms. In these blue rooms the rich could still see the sky the way poets down below could only pine away for. They could watch the rarified sky blush and darken from cerulean to royal blue to the velvety darkness of cosmic night. Rumor had it the experience was orgasmic.

Stars were a myth to the many poor and the youth below the real blue rooms. Many of them had never left the city, and they could not conceive of reality beyond the confines of its towers. In the cruel world down below, so hungry were the masses for starlight, even bad poetry about the once great sky could get someone killed. Wax about sky blue on The Bowery and an agitated starfucker—as night sky deprived urbanites were called—might force a guy to bite a bullet. Subsequently The Bowery Poetry Club romantic series was driven underground.

Pulp had breathed itself into the casualty that had become American culture. The Brooklyn blue room guards were known collectively as Kings County Kong, and they flew small old Navy biplanes like those used to shoot King Kong down from the Empire State Building. The biplanes were rigged with Vickers-style machine gun turrets and retrofitted with rocket-powered ejection seats. They were also painted with black and gray razzle-dazzle camouflage: angular lines that confused the eye and made it difficult to see if the planes were coming or going. The airfield they commandeered was on Governor's Island, a sniper shot from their sworn enemy—the Manhattan solar energy empire.

The Manhattan guards—the Royal Rainmakers—flew sleek jets protecting the island's premiere blue room that was widely rumored by the masses to be owned by the mysterious solar philanthropist named Dr. Naranja. These jets flew at supersonic speed, and their mirrored bodies reflected whatever surrounded them. No one had ever really seemed to see one beyond a reflective blur, and the press wrote about them as if they were on par with UFOs. The Kong knew they were real: whenever they ventured too close to the Manhattan side of the river they lost a plane to a fury of fire. No one could argue either with the hammering decibels that followed the jet flight patterns like heavy metal.

The East River was their standoff.

Reality shows had simply become reality. Life imitated low art. Only the poor got charged with crime, and the judges had turned more and more toward television for trial broadcast. Subsequently both the poor and rich alike became addicted to snuff television. It was almost politely called Alpha TV, and it had its origins in legal off track betting houses that peppered the city, where gamblers gathered to bask in the broadcast glow of races and games. Much more vicious than the pitbull was man versus man, and on Alpha TV the accused battled it out with bare knuckles. Whoever survived was eventually released. Television spectators bet from home or at the betting houses on who would live and who would die as if they were betting on a dogfight. They watched the carnage on wall-sized monitors so realistic they could smell the fear and the blood as if they were in the ring. It had become too difficult to know who had done what. Eventually no one cared.

Reality was whatever they could get away with, sell or buy.

***

Cosmo stared at his shiny black shoes, indecision gnawing at him. *It's too soon*, he thought, *too soon.* On impulse, nervous, he dialed Dr. Kill van Kull.

One half ring. "Yes?"

"Something is not right," Cosmo whispered as if Rook would overhear. He knew in fact that, tuned to the multiverse, Rook almost could. "There is no way Rook hasn't caught on. He forgave me for my first betrayals because he wanted what you had to offer. But this! He will never forgive me for this!"

Inside the small black helicopter hovering over Brooklyn, the scarred man's bright green eyes—eyes like emeralds lit from within—pierced the darkness, and he responded, "Something has not been right for a long time, Cosmo. And it is not Rook's forgiveness that will redeem you. Tonight, we'll make things right. Tomorrow, forgiveness will start anew!"

The line went dead, and Cosmo buried his face in his withered hands. They peeked out from the bright white cuffs of his tuxedo shirt and pressed hard into his shiny bald head. He was old enough to remember the hard edges of things like chess pieces, glorious humid summers following the blossoming and greening of springs that coiled out of winters and the brilliant orange and red turnings of fall. He remembered his father's experiments with time, all of the joy he had had as a boy watching his brilliant father manipulating the edge of scientific discoveries as if space and time were just wind up toys. He remembered studying the history of the clock and its relationship to civilization, innocently unaware the invention of atomic clocks would fade into oblivion in comparison with the invention of synthetic black holes.

When they had discovered the beginning of time, they had discovered its ending. How he longed to return to classical, linear time, to a world filled with men's laughter, cigar smoke, chess and pleasure flying. To the world in which the man he loved as a son solved hard crime. Instead he was stuck in the cycle of what was called *Seven,* or more simply, *Jail.* Cosmo kneaded at his gummy scalp, and inside the imprisonment of space and time, he wept.

3: Lucky Dead Pawn

Outside the Lucky Dead Pawn shop in Chinatown, just blocks southwest from Majestic lingerie and adjacent to the Two Brothers Tong headquarters, Agent Orange parked her motorcycle. Her gang circled behind in Chinatown, protecting her. Under the vibrant flashing signs of narrow Pell Street, the orange almost blended in with the reds and golds of a Buddhist temple, out of which dense incense smoked. The Two Brothers Tong had been the dominant gang in Chinatown, and as the reality storm engulfed the city they had become increasingly powerful. For the current Two Brothers Tong boss and owner of the Lucky Dead Pawn, it had created the opportunity to trade in reality itself.

Agent Orange pressed a buzzer, and the shadow man blinked his way out of his exotic sleep. Momentarily he hit the intercom, and through it his voice squawked, "Yes?"

She coldly demanded, "Got it?"

There was a pause and his voice deepened with accusation, "*You got it*?"

"Yes," she said quickly, in deference.

There came the buzzing sound of the door lock releasing, and she shoved at the solid metal door. She waited for the lock to click behind her before she moved down the dark entrails of the hallway. In the dark store, lit only by tiny lights inside glass display cases, she observed the standard array of pawnshop booty: abandoned wedding rings, gold chains, power tools, guitars and the illegal assortment of guns.

The man swathed in darkness shifted behind the display cases, and she tried hard to focus on the face she had never seen. She set a small vial of a skin sample onto the counter and retreated a step. Jack retrieved the vial, opened it and viewed the grotesque flake of skin blackened by tattoo ink with a pleasure that in no way could register on his shadowy face. He placed the skin onto a swab inside a small machine. The machine hummed and immediately a male DNA strand was isolated and digitally duplicated on a screen. Jack nodded to himself in satisfaction. "And?"

She handed him a second vial, "This contains a woman's and a man's."

He nodded, knowing what the trade was. He placed in exchange a small black vial on the counter, and she now saw, his hand seemed only to be multi-layered shadow.

Inside the vial, inset into a dot of ink, was a microscopic reality seed custom manufactured in the lab below his shop with pirated nanotechnology from China. She pocketed it, turned on her heel and in moments was awash in the wild glow of Pell Street. The shadow man, Jack the Butterfly of the Lucky Dead Pawn shop watched on a surveillance monitor as she jumped onto her motorcycle. With her gang following like a school of goldfish, she sped away.

Stupid goldfish, he thought, as he separated the male DNA from the female. He cooked the other ink and DNA from the first vial into a quantum ink syrup, sucked it into a needle and injected it into a nanoelectrode terminal sewn into a shadowy black vein. The nanoelectrodes were sewn at regular intervals along the ancient acupuncture meridians and described essentially the circuitry of *chi*, the body's cosmic energy: what Western science had ultimately deemed quantum neuroelectricity.

He lay down on his antique opium den couch—a glossy black lohan. In moments the ornate mother-of-pearl couch carvings, licking like tongues, flames and talons, flowed into him, becoming inky iridescent tattoos. The tattoos swam on the surface of his darkness as he vividly dreamed he was Weedkiller himself. He loved the rush.

Was addicted to it.

Behind Mahjong fronts that once housed opium dens underground chambers were filled with addicts taking wild rides on other people's realities. After a Nobel Prize winner had discovered that DNA could imprint itself in water —seemingly teleporting itself across test tubes connected only by a simple copper coil—Jack set up his lab to duplicate the results. Only he placed himself into a man-sized tube of water connected to samplings of his cloned butterflies. The early experiments resulted mostly in withered skin at first and the taste of copper on his tongue. But once nanoelectrodes were introduced into the black market and he had them surgically implanted throughout his body, the experiments took on a completely different turn. Once suspended in the tube, with sinuous copper threads lining the entire tube like chain mail, Jack found himself able to lull into a dream state. When he first fully experienced the dream of becoming a butterfly—complete with vivid sound, touch, vision and smell—he felt like he never needed to experience anything else again. The ecstasy rebounded him to the experience until he became addicted to his own goods. He experimented with other conductive materials, and with time, he abandoned water for another liquid with paramount conductivity—even in a dried state: ink.

In his underground dens, addicts jacked into his butterflies through similar methods. They paid Jack by turning over their quantum bank accounts. When they ran out of money, Jack's den workers rolled them back into the street, where they typically died within a week. Their grotesque deformations spooked many to shy away from the shadow man's exotic goods, but the word was otherwise out: it was a most excellent way to die. Soon the parallel reality junkies called their habit, *jackin' the butterfly.*

Word reached Agent Orange about both his skills and his ambitions. When The Orange Woman, as he thought of her, first appeared at his door he had not let her in. On his suspended tactile computer he caressed her image with a black finger, tracing the tight outline of her lean body up to her motorcycle helmet. It looked to him like a shiny orange and black pupa. Months went by as she persisted, and when she eventually slipped a sample of her own goods under the door, he was very pleased to discover she had access to his number one tong's rival DNA, access to the man known as Marco Millioni.

She told him through a microphone in her helmet, "It's not just his DNA. It's a tattoo ink sample."

Jack was thrilled. He could care less about the new empire ambitions of the merchants from Ningbo. Within New York City itself, Jack ached to control at the very least the reality of Chinatown.

When she came back the next day with another DNA meets tattoo ink sample, he let her in. Oranges, after all, meant good luck to the Chinese.

4: Scion

The Great Hurricane struck the day Rook was born, pummeling Coney Island before raping Brooklyn and slamming the Hudson and East Rivers onto Manhattan. Weather was forever spectacularly transformed.

Wave after wave of sympathetic change transformed the reality of the city itself. Quantum technology overthrew every monomaniacal ideal, especially value, as the city's already jaded youth, hooked on video gaming, easily acclimated to a world at once magical and newly, gamishly technical. Wall Street filed for Chapter 11. Money became meaningless. Bank robbers became jobless. Entertainment became farmed with junk, and it took on the punky nerve of anarchy. Young Rook observed closely as reality suicidally jumped off a bridge.

In the double coincidence of wants problem, also known as barter, survival became the basis of exchange. If someone had a way of helping someone else survive, their commodity went up. Mathematical geniuses like Rook's father became called upon by the new Wall Street and Federal Reserve to help protect the vulnerable quantum world. It was, scientists had long known, mysteriously coherent, entangled and nonlocal, meaning things seemingly separated in space and time were not at all separate but unified as if they shared the same center.

Rook became a scion of this new world.

Over time, tired of roaring at itself, the corrupt American world quieted down to a quasi humane hum. During this period technocrats tried to patent the quantum world, a world magically entrained with itself at all points, a world sticky with feedback. If one so much as looked at it, even thought about it, the quantum world forever maintained the imprint of that contact. How to control the magical quantum world without affecting it became tantamount to technology. And people like Jack the Butterfly became its principal, accidental centrifugal forces.

The Chinese had always been ace shameless copycats, pirating everything from designer purses to designer DNA. And the Chinese, whose culture had never really separated science from magic, were far ahead on the technology curve. Currency, which for years was so unstable as to be utterly devalued, had been reinvented by Rook's father and his team as purely photonic, quantum and therefore purely traceable. Within days of its invention, the Chinese had counterfeited it. Again, Rook's father was called in by the Federal Reserve to straightjacket quantum currency, and ultimately he did. But he invented a second, hierarchical currency at the same time—one that few knew about.

Still, for the Chinese, their interest in hijacking currency faded against their interest in monopolizing power to be gained by synthesizing quantum DNA. As reality accelerated out of the butterfly loop of feedback into chaos, pioneering genome hackers realized that all DNA was also coherent, entangled and nonlocal. There was only one quantum DNA, and every seemingly unique human being was a variation of it.

A quantum calendar developed as the eccentric elite reconsidered the function of time itself. Replacing the 365-day earth cycle was a seven-day, Sunday through Saturday cycle inspired by the simple markings seen on prison walls to manage the counting of days. Some of the more existentialist elite started calling the calendar *Seven* and others *Jail.*

Agent Orange, the week's principal guard, had every intention of breaking out of it.

***

At the Lucky Dead Pawn shop, Agent Orange held high commodity, even though the shadow man barely had any life left to live for. His addiction to Millioni's inked DNA was killing him, but Jack the Butterfly thought of the quantum shadow that clothed him in darkness as a beatific metamorphosis. As their personalities became increasingly nonlocal and enfolded into the cosmic darkness of the collective unconscious, most addicts did. Jack looked at himself in a mirror and saw a transparent darkness, shaped somewhat like Millioni and somewhat like the detective man they had showed him photos of, the man named Rook. He turned sideways and briefly glimpsed what he considered his soul: a crocodile. *Jack the Crocodile*, he thought, and the vision faded into a dark mist.

***

A gate opened to a garage in the Lower East Side, and the thirteen motorcycles, helmed by Agent Orange, purred inside. The gate dropped quickly as the gang parked in a formation around Agent Orange. The first phase of her operation completed, she smiled, knowing at long last her employer would take the bait. She pulled her leg over the seat and marched to a metal arsenal painted bright orange. They had forced her to wear orange, had made all of them wear orange, and it was nearly hysterical to her that it allowed them to do all of her covert work in blatant brazen bright orange. She laughed deeply, the laughter bursting from her stomach and chest. As she tossed each of the women a box of bullets, she said in between laughs, "That truly was majestic."

Each of them smiled back and laughed.

Retreating to a small room, she watched a bank of surveillance monitors and observed Rook and Angela lying on the Coney Island street. Both were coming to. She glanced at a clock, noting that seventeen minutes had passed since her confrontation with Rook. She pulled a Shakespeare Company matchbook from a pocket, opened it to the phrase *arch-villain* and yanked out a match. She pondered it for a long moment. Inside it was a relay switch. She struck it and lifted her eyes to a surveillance channel focused on Orchard Street.

One moment later, as the relay signal located its home detonator, a bomb exploded in the lingerie store. The building imploded, its shiny windows webbing into shards and mists of glass, funneling into a tunnel of brick and dust. Flames erupted and shot out of the debris like snake tongues. She admired especially the orange in the fire.

It was her first arson, and she had indeed autographed it. Small strings of fireworks planted around the building laced a configuration of an A surrounded by an O. As the snaky fire licked through the debris, it spread outward and ignited the fireworks. She smiled as her insignia exploded in spasms of bright orange, jumping out of the orange flames like glitter and instantly, anonymously swallowing back into them.

A red fire engine painted with the white scales of a dragon, the cab its gaping maw, raced to the scene with sirens blaring. She observed as the Chinatown firemen, known as the Dragonfighters, protected the fire while the evidence safely burned. The gold she had bribed them with weighed heavily in their pockets.

Operation: Push the Envelope has just been shoved down your throat in more ways than one, Rook Black.

She opened up a black satchel and pulled out a black envelope. From it she slipped out a four-panel photo strip, the kind taken in a Coney Island photo booth. It showed her, smiling, her bright blue eyes shining, her cinnamon hair alive with light, and Rook grinning and kissing her.

You bastard. How could you? How could you forget!

Agent Orange tossed the photos down and opened a small vial in which the microscopic reality seed—also known as a *black market butterfly*, *ink* or *Othello*—floated in an ink syrup like the dot on an i. She sucked the seed into a syringe, tightened a rubber tube around her upper arm and injected the seed through a nanoelectrode terminal embedded under her skin into a vein. She closed her eyes and basked in the rush, kissing the quantum mist as once she had kissed Rook.

"Wake up, Rook. Wake up and remember!"

***

Overhead in Brooklyn, Dr. Kill van Kull peered at the neuroelectrical console and tweaked it, tuning into unconscious Rook's brainwaves, gently reviving him. A bright green line, as bright as the old doctor's eyes, flashed onto the dark screen.

5: Waking Up

As the fire raged on Orchard Street, a dead limb snapped from the lonely tree of heaven living there, and in tandem Rook's jaw snapped shut. Rook and Angela lay on the dirty street, his hands still around her head. She was on top of him—stunned but very alive. Seemingly unaffected by the feedback energy consuming him, she blinked and pulled up, shouting, "Rook!"

Inside the helicopter the doctor manipulated the console, calming the spastic green line, cooling it to an icy pale and looping blue. Angela heard the rapid pounding of helicopter blades against the night and craned her head. In tandem with the heavy mechanical ripple in the sky, a vibration issued from deep within Rook as he slipped into the event horizon. "Rook!" she shouted again as if she were begging the sky.

At first the vibration was like an old building shivering as a heavy truck drove by, except it sustained, rising into a sort of bodyquake. Angela placed a palm on his face, and she felt his muscles vibrating just beneath the skin. They were both sweaty from the humid night, but sweat became for Rook his own East River. The black hole event horizon externalized in unison with a thunderstorm, and his escalating heartbeat externalized as the rat-tat-tat of a Vickers machine gun in the distance.

The helicopter swooped low.

"Rook?" She touched his jaw. The vibration mounted and his eyes swarmed with grotesque rapid eye movement. "Rook," she whispered in a soothing voice, trying to talk him down before the onset of seizure, and she touched the exposed electrode.

His body's will was frozen, but the one thing he did feel was the vibration. He knew semiconsciously the vibration was external: it was the quantum feedback world internalized. It was as if he had swallowed the river and all its wild crocodiles, and mutually, it was as if the quantum world had swallowed him.

He heard the high voltage sound, like power lines meets cicadas. The sound amped louder and louder. The neuroelectric symphony coursed through him, seizing his body, and in his temporal lobe, in time with the black clouds above them, lightning struck.

Inside the helicopter the doctor glanced at an enemy Kings County Kong biplane approaching, and his fingers moved swiftly on the console. The pilot braced for a sudden backwards and upwards tilt, and a machine gunner sitting beside him aimed at the biplane. As a vertical hail of bullets ripped through the sky over Coney Island, Rook's internal symphony became visual and rushed from black to a deep blue punctuated with starlight. The shadowy event horizon guard rose effortlessly over him, elongating until it towered, then rip curled down onto him.

Rook understood vaguely that he was slipping to the other side, into the quantum sea, and at that moment the weight rushed away from him. He was deliciously fading, and he was mesmerized by an emerald light pouring from his chest. It was his internal Eden, his heart chakra. He had never felt, heard or seen anything like this. It was blissful. *No*, he managed to think, *it is bliss*.

The Kings County Kong biplane, shredding with bullets, twirled like a broken ballerina and slammed to the ground in an explosive instant.

With it, Rook's vision wiped to black.

The vibration halted, and Angela startled as he breathed hard and deep, filling his lungs. His eyes flicked wide open like switchblades, and his coal black eyes stabbed with life.

She kissed him tenderly and ran her fingers through his spiky hair, thinking, *Thank god!*

The helicopter swayed above them and pushed away toward the safety of the ocean. More biplanes were already en route, and the helicopter would have to sneak to the safety of Manhattan over the Atlantic and then New Jersey. Naranja's jets were positioned a mile off shore, and together they would make their return. Inside the helicopter the pilot and machine gunner, stiff from racing adrenaline, made eye contact that implied a mission accomplished. The calm doctor's bluish black fingers patiently turned the console's virtual knobs, cooling Rook's brain. Dr. Kill van Kull sighed with relief, and into his wire through his plump purple lips, he said, "We've got alpha."

***

"Can you walk?" Angela asked. Rook nodded, rose slowly and leaned hard against her. He blinked at a world that he had wanted to be black and white only twenty-four hours before. Again, as it swelled with color, it made him strangely happy, dizzy, and dumb, and to him, oxygen tasted like Coney Island cotton candy.

In an awkward dance, the two stumbled one step together.

We've become easy targets, he realized. As the seizure delirium washed through him, he thought, *Bulls-eyes*. He took one more step, but his peripheral vision screamed, and he fumbled, a confused dancer pivoting toward the alarm. Rook and Angela faced grated shutters. Behind them mannequins in a glass display window lifelessly looked back. *Storefront, costume shop*. Rook dug into his pocket and pulled out the Masculiner packing slip: it was imprinted with the name of the self-same store. *Coney Island Fantasy*.

Agent Orange is manipulating my every move, he feebly remembered, *shoving my face in it. Is that the joke about facing reality?*

Running from Agent Orange had led him straight into the heart of her game. *Maybe by running straight into it, I'll induce its cardiac arrest.* He knew himself well enough though to know he was, like an idiot savant, enjoying it.

Rook bent slowly, achingly, and reaching into an ankle holster, he pulled out Angela's Z-9. He had been carrying it so that no one else could. *Especially not a lifeless plastic copy of myself.* It was instinctual to hand it to her, but he hesitated for a moment. *Just who is she really?*

She sensed his reserve. "What now?"

After a moment he decided to trust her, even if he was only pretending to trust her. "Where did you find it?"

The look he gave her said he was not going to tell her. The bruised dancers stepped away from each other and sized each other up.

With a rapid jerk, he pulled out his own Z-9 and shot out the lock on the shuttered door to Coney Island Fantasy. In the next second Angela spotted a security camera. One more bullet destroyed it. One man, one woman, two guns. A tango of gunfire. Bang. Bang.

***

Observing from her hideout in the garage, Agent Orange's surveillance feed from the store went black, and she simply switched to another channel, to one aimed at Rook's Manhattan apartment. She stood and for a long moment waited to ensure she was not dizzy. She had been taking small doses, insisting to herself she would not become an addict. *I'm fine*, she thought, and she stepped into the waiting room where the gang was resting.

"Let's go," she commanded in her icy voice, and moments later the women were all on their motorcycles, speeding toward Rook's apartment on Ludlow Street.

6: Facing Reality

Every morning Rook played chess against his computer, and he always let it win. He wasn't interested in the winning. The computer contained an algorithmic encyclopedia of chess moves, from hippopotamus openers to rook endgames, and it was programmed with ten to the power of fifty known heuristic strategies. Rook analyzed the moves, and though Rook let the computer win, he manipulated the win: the computer was predictable. The pattern that remained on the digital chessboard when the computer announced *checkmate* was the pattern Rook had led it to. Rook was all about manipulating the endgame.

In the darkness of Coney Island Fantasy, he thought, *So is Agent Orange.*

Like computer chess, criminals were predictable too. Crimes manifested similarly and were like what physics called strange attractors. Like thunderstorm weather patterns they magnetically hugged the coastlines of human culture, grooving into it over and over again. Quantum crime patterns never exactly repeated but, just like chess games, they overlapped strongly. Quantum crime, like everything else Rook had philosophically considered in life, was a game. Even as it broke them, quantum crime had rules.

Rook could not infer the quantum rules governing Agent Orange, and the challenge gave him a dark pleasure. He scanned the shadows inside the strange costume shop, and his thoughts turned to his broker.

Cosmo had never handed him easy crimes, but in the very first year solving even the hard ones had become boring, just like playing chess against a computer. To make the computer fall for his moves was his way of winning.

Now, Rook realized, *I've slipped. I've fallen for my own moves. Agent Orange has been studying me in the same way I've studied chess. She's probably even watched me playing and manipulating my own losses in chess.*

Just like the stupid computer tirelessly winning one stupid game after another, Rook had been studied, analyzed. *Played.* Rook convinced himself as he pushed further into the darkness of Coney Island Fantasy, *She knows me better than I know myself.* She had had multiple opportunities to take him out, but she had let him live. And now she was making the clues to her game easier and easier to match up, he thought, *Like the silhouette nature of lingerie matching up to a naked woman.*

Inside Coney Island Fantasy, Rook observed the mannequins.

Angela grabbed at his arm, "What's happening, Rook?"

He didn't know. Reflexively, he pulled her in tight.

***

Agent Orange witnessed the embrace through the small monitor in her motorcycle helmet, and she hated it.

In the Lower East Side, she easily made her way into Rook's apartment with keys while her blatantly orange dozen guarded the street and rooftop. With a euphoric satisfaction she planted quantum seeds—and what would become within the next hour—the root of her escape from her enslavement. She had bought the seeds on the black market for what was the equivalent of the price of her heart, but she knew she would rather be heartless than not possess her own liberty. Sowing seeds was easy. All anyone had to do, Jack had instructed her, was think. Thoughts had lives of their own. But an even better method, he had taught her, was to reiterate the sowing through physical gestures, then let the quantum universe take it from there. Exactly what the seeds would grow was not easy to control but that did not stop anyone from trying to perform what essentially were acts of magic.

***

Marco Millioni himself had been brought into existence by quantum necessity, like a susurration chanting itself into reality, like the raging hurricane that manifested the day Rook was born.

Millioni sat in his black silk suit, his long black hair swept back from his olive skin, his folded eyelids and long black lashes blinking over his titanium gray eyes. He had snapshot memories of his childhood—enough to make him feel like he had been alive for many years—but not much in the way of continuity. He enjoyed the best of what any alpha adult male could crave: power, wealth and women. That his childhood could not play like a movie in his memories, he understood, was a normal human experience. That he was human but his latest variation had come about as part of an intervention in the past seven days and nights had empowered him even further.

Until he too discovered he was a reality slave stitched into the cycle of Seven.

He beheld the orange he ate each night for dessert and ate a section of the one Agent Orange had grafted for him. It was a blend of crocodile blood, mandarin and navel citrus orange. She had also had Jack the Butterfly graft the quantum seed of this curious fruit into the tree of heaven on Orchard Street earlier. The Majestic fire, he knew, by plan had almost fully consumed the tree. He knew also, as did Agent Orange, that the roots of the tree spread all the way under the city, into the cracks of reality itself. He also willingly allowed himself to be grafted with Jack the Butterfly, and he ate of the fruit that was an antidote to the shadowy quantum consumption he would otherwise succumb to. He thought, *Soon, both the city and reality will be ours.*

Dr. Naranja, we are so much cleverer than you think!

***

Dr. Naranja observed the surveillance feed coming through Jules Barbillon's eyes. He observed as the identical brothers in their black suits escorted Rocky Astor to a warehoused pier, the location of which he had come to understand hid a submarine named Leviathan. The men of Gasland used it for secret meetings. *Now*, he thought, *it will become your prison.*

***

Jules knew well that Dr. Naranja was watching his every move closely through his own eyes, and he knew also that as soon as they submerged into the murky waters of the East River, the transmission would be lost. He had been commanded by Dr. Naranja not to go under with the identical brothers but to transmit from the pier only. Just as Rocky was lowering into the submarine hatch the two brothers turned slowly and trained their guns on Jules. Simultaneously they said, "Welcome to Gasland."

The last thing Jules saw and transmitted to Dr. Naranja was the wide gape on Rocky's rubbery lips and the spastic explosions of gunfire. There was the sound of a body falling and an electronic shriek before the transmission went blank.

***

Sipping scotch in his tower blue room, Dr. Navaja Naranja, a man who had seen more than everything, was emotionlessly composed and utterly unfazed. He sucked scotch from an ice cube pensively, then radioed Agent Orange. In his nasal voice he said, "Please see to it that Jules gets a transfusion immediately."

Agent Orange did not respond.

7: Slipknotting

Inside Coney Island Fantasy, Rook was waking up, remembering with olfactory clarity details about Weedkiller and wondering if he had been wrong, dead wrong, if he had solved the wrong crime or collared the wrong man. *Agent Orange*, he thought, *a kind of weedkiller*. His gut clamped hard.

He whispered a question that was a statement, "Who doesn't commit crimes in this godforsaken city."

"We're being avenged." Angela's words were soft, a whisper and an admission.

Rook clutched for the memories that were coming back to him like flotsam from a train wreck on the quantum sea.

"Who's avenging us, Rook?" Angela insisted.

"Give me a minute," he responded. Rook shut his eyes and vividly tuned his imagination to the symposium he had attended. As if it were the actual present, he tuned internally into quantum space and time until he saw he was at the actual symposium, and it was just underway.

***

Six days prior: in the shadowy back of the Parks Conservancy hall, Rook huddled under his black hat that made his presence a fog.

Like a madman talking to a wall, Dr. Chess ranted on and on about the depletion of native grasses and trees to a scant audience, finally shouting in conclusion, "The trees of heaven must be stopped!"

Back on the street, Rook scoured the late-night city, where he discovered there was indeed an assassin about going by the moniker *Weedkiller*. The name had to be a joke, Rook thought then, about assassins being hashish smokers, people who got themselves so stoned they'd do anything—especially kill by command. However, nobody knew what this Weedkiller looked like or who he had killed. It was one of many murmuring rumors in the babbling belly of the clichéd underworld.

Rook asked a thuggish informant just how many people this Weedkiller had hit, and the thug had uttered, "Millions."

***

"What did you see?" she asked.

Rook opened his eyes with a gut gnawing he had not in fact solved the Weedkiller crime. He blinked away visuals of green fronds. "Weeds," he said, "weeds."

He did not want to tell her about his confrontation with Agent Orange.

He glanced at his wristwatch: instead of two hands there were four. Two were spinning clockwise, and two were spinning counterclockwise. Smaller dials moving in opposite directions indicated the greater wheels of time: days, weeks, months, years, centuries and millennia.

It was a special timepiece he had invented for himself to help keep track of the classical present, the only time most people experienced, but what Rook knew was the center point where future and past overlapped. The present was the navel of quantum feedback, and he spontaneously remembered he knew well the mathematics of how quantum reality literally pushed the envelope of space and time.

Reality, he remembered with a jolt, *is whatever reality can get away with!*

Rook's watch indicated it was almost his birthday, a day he was certain had just passed and was just about to come.

Angela touched him tenderly, and she said as she always did when she wanted him to open the doorway to his thoughts, "Rook, knock knock?"

***

With those two words, Dr. Kill van Kull watched two icy blue waves ripple across the console. "Good," he said quietly, "Good."

***

On cue Agent Orange fired two bullets, stepped back out into the night and shut Rook's door.

***

The submarine sank to the bed of the East River channel. A perplexed Rocky Astor was once again handcuffed and his face burned as red as his lips. The rest of the Petroleum Club surrounded him, and all of the men were handcuffed and legcuffed together.

He screamed, "Who the fuck are you people?"

One of the brothers eyed Rocky with a glance that told him to shut up while the other transfused crocodile blood into Jules' median basilic vein. They had aimed carefully and missed vital organs. While the blood slowly transfused, Jules coughed, spattering the face of one of the brothers with blood colored spittle. The man winced and wiped his face with a black handkerchief on which the initials M.P.M. were embroidered in black silk. Slowly Jules' eyes opened, and when he focused on the brother leaning over him, he smiled and chortled up more crimson spittle. The brother eased him into a sitting position.

Rocky's words twisted over his tongue, "What the fuck is going on?"

Jules breathed in deeply, feeling robust as the crocodile blood circulated. "I've been held hostage by Naranja for years. The whole city has been held hostage by Naranja for years, you dumb bastard. *Reality* has been held hostage." Jules removed the orange tinted sunglasses and stared at Rocky with his golden pupils and slit corneas. "Gasoline is our ransom. Burning the Central Library and the Shakespearean folio collection is our only way out!"

Rocky scanned the stony faces of the men with the initials M.P.M., "You mean, you really are with Gasland?"

Jules grinned and blood rimmed his lips, "You are looking at the new Gasland. Your plan to burn the library would have been foiled before a match was struck in Manhattan! You need us to get the gasoline in."

Rocky rolled his shoulders, uncertain and unwilling to believe in these men. "If you are my allies, why are we in handcuffs! Why did you blow up my building!"

Jules leaned in and kissed him on the lips. Rocky's mouth quavered, and he grimaced in hatred of the grotesque gesture. Jules fingers slipped into Rocky’s pocket and found a large bullet.

Jules whispered, his lips brushing Rocky's, "We are not your allies. For now, while we engineer the means to get the gasoline into the city, you will remain submerged and imprisoned.”

He held the bullet in front of Rocky’s eyes, “Is this your lucky bullet? Yes, it is. So you won’t have the chance to fuck up our plan with your lucky bullet or any other bullshit, you will remain submerged until you learn how Gasland must become *our* ally."

"In the name of what?"

"Operation: Push the Envelope."

"What does that stand for?"

Jules leaned back and smiled. "Reality revolution."

CHAPTER FOUR: Weedkiller

1: Weedkiller

Last week, when time seemingly flowed like a river, Rook found Mr. Millioni in the dark aquatic underground of the Marco Polo Crocodile Wrestling Club. As Mr. Millioni smoked his machine-rolled cigarette, the cuff on his black shirt shifted up the length of his forearm, revealing embroidered initials. With his high definition corneas, Rook zoomed the details: M.P.M., a titanium watchband and the edges of sleeve tattoos. His eyes, Rook later noted, also seemed titanium: dull would-be mirrors like those installed at truck stop gas stations back in the days of gas, dull would-be mirrors hung there just to make someone think maybe they could see their reflection. But they never could.

In the evenings Mr. Millioni retired to the Marco Polo Motel where he resided. Mr. Marco Millioni, unlike the dull warp of truck stop mirrors, had made the trail to himself remarkably reflective and simple to follow. If there was a business in the city bearing the name Marco Polo, Mr. Marco Millioni was a patron or owner—or both. Rook found Mr. Marco Millioni's reflection everywhere—except in a classical reality mirror that would nail him as an assassin nicknamed Weedkiller. Still, Rook knew this was the man.

In the analog black market on Canal Street, Rook sourced a paperback copy of the original Marco Polo's travel narrative and scanned through it. He already knew the original Marco Polo—a Venetian who had ushered Asia to Europe—had been one of the first to travel the legendary Silk Road. As he read the battered black market copy, he learned the Venetian had also been the first to reference the existence of Eastern tattoos and hash-smoking assassins. Rook noted on day two of his investigation—day two, as in, *what seemed like linear time*—the man he was shadowing had a fetish bond with anything Marco Polo. The man seemed peaceably eccentric, nothing more.

Inside the dark aquatic Marco Polo Crocodile Wrestling Club, where green-skinned beasts entertained, and inside the swirling emerald green wallpaperings of the Marco Polo Motel lounge—and everywhere Marco Polo in between—Rook witnessed Millioni openly rolling hash into his cigarettes and sipping warm *bai jiu. Hash and bai jiu*: both, Rook realized, had skanky, grassy flavors. Gasoline meets barn. Both were intoxicants, one a dried grass and the other a distilled grass. Both, Rook also noted, were either tastes passed on by the man's Chinese forebears or self-referential symbolic jests to his assassin moniker.

2: Tattoos

On days three and four of his investigation, Rook shadowed Mr. Millioni's unremarkable daily and nightly routine. He was a staunch regular at the same establishments, and he paid with traceable, quantum currency. Rook saw the predictability as a ruse, as a phony alibi grooved over and over into classical reality.

Without trying very hard, almost anyone could figure out where the man was or predict where he would be next. Rook tapped into the Federal Reserve tracing system through his office computer and queried the identity of the man who had eaten ragout at 9:00 p.m. at the Marco Polo Lounge. From there he quickly brought up the past seventeen years of the man's transactions. Marco Millioni's life and activities were so transparent, it was as if the man were made of tracing paper. And yet, after following the man around for a few days, Rook came to know he also owned a precious metal trading firm. That meant he relied on the underworld gold standard for whatever his real transactions were. Just like the taxidermy location, some aspects of the Millioni world were off grid. There was much he was flourishing to the Naranja Empire through his Sunjuice vehicle and his bold routines, but something else, some quirk, the man wanted hidden.

And yet, Rook thought, *he does his hiding in plain sight.*

On night five of what had seemed to be a linear investigation, Rook decided to steer away from the man's peculiarly predictable pattern and take a walk down St. Mark's Place in the East Village to investigate Marco Polo Tattoo for the second time. He had been past it earlier but had not gone in, and for whatever reason, just like all of the other Marco Polo businesses he kept discovering, it seemed at once woven into the fabric of the city and spontaneously brand new.

Alien.

Agent Orange's dozen, anti-camouflaged in orange, easily observed him from behind the hat racks cluttering the street. It was well known publicly the Naranja guards wore orange, and spotting them on the street was just as common as it had once been to see a New York City police officer on a subway platform or walking the beat.

They had been watching Rook, through the looping week, for the equivalent of six years.

***

Rook went inside, and he was inside, glancing over the numerous samples of Chinese art inspired tattoos inked onto rice paper and framed in displays, when the phone rang. The sole tattoo artist, a young attractive Chinese woman in a pink frilly Lolita skirt and towering black heels that pushed her height to maybe 5' 4", answered and chatted briefly in Mandarin before hanging up.

She said, "I have to close the shop for an hour or so since the owner is coming for an inking session." She turned to him, and from under shocks of orange and pink bangs, her eyes met his. One was blue and the other amber. *Contacts*, he realized. Around her eyes, down her cheeks and bridging her nose were tiny, fake gems—the kind sold up and down St. Mark's. Asian gothic. She noted Rook's attention, took it as flattery and explained quietly, "The owner does not like to be inked with public around."

"Okay," Rook responded as he quickly observed the tattooing chair. It was a hybrid vintage dental exam chair meets massage table with glittery, emerald green upholstery, and it was located in the back of the room next to the inking needles. Her back turned to Rook, the tattoo artist lowered the chair into full recline. Rook noted the upholstery pattern was the same as that of the upholstery and wallpaper in the Marco Polo Motel. He deftly dropped his photographic sunglasses onto a shelf, making certain the small security camera he had spotted above the door did not witness this move. When he left the tattoo parlor, the sunglasses were programmed for motion detect recording and transmission.

Remotely Agent Orange intercepted the transmission, as she had been paid to do for six years.

Across the street at a vendor rack exploding with cheap hats and sunglasses, Rook did see the guards, and he gave them no thought. Naranja guards were everywhere in Manhattan, policing the concerns of the solar energy empire, principally combating infiltration by Gasland. With no idea whatsoever he was within feet of a spy, Rook pretended to browse while waiting to see who would show. He turned toward the tattoo parlor while trying on smoky black lenses, and through them he found the owner entering the tattoo parlor. He was not so much surprised it was Millioni himself as irritated this strange timing would come on a day when he was not following the man. The irritation flashed with paranoia. He wondered if he had blown his cover, and if in fact Millioni was now shadowing him.

The door shut behind Millioni, and the emerald green curtains were abruptly drawn. The curtains, Rook realized, were of the same emerald green that made the Marco Polo Motel lounge a weedy garden in and of itself.

The inking session, Rook knew, was an aberration from Millioni's rigid routine, from the strange attractor groove that lent him a magnetized alibi. The inking was a novelty, and as Rook's paranoia softened, he decided it meant one of two things: since tattoos were rites of passage, the assassin had either just made a hit or was about to.

3: Precious Paper

Rook purchased the cheap dark sunglasses from the St. Mark’s vendor and made his way back across the street. Up above the tattoo parlor was a small bar, and inside Rook ordered a whiskey neat. When the bartender turned his back, Rook snapped a remote viewer onto the inner lens in the new sunglasses. He stoically stared out at the night through them, a man seemingly newly hip to the touristy bustle of St. Mark's. The dark lenses obscured his device, and after a few flickering moments the signal from his surveillance sunglasses was received—a signal Agent Orange had already been watching. Millioni, both saw, was unbuttoning his black shirt. The tattoo artist received it from him and hung it up neatly. "How are you?" he asked in a deep, even voice free of any accent other than American.

"I'm good," she answered, "You?"

"Content," he said. Millioni handed her a rice paper drawing, but from the oblique angle of his camera, Rook was unable to decipher it.

Millioni's back was a riddle of ink, and around his neck was a fine precious metal chain. He slid onto his belly like a white lizard, his skin brocaded in bright green, red and blue. The artist pressed the ink transfer onto his back, apparently already knowing exactly where to place it—and implying to Rook she had deeper knowledge of his body and tattoos—then she started scratching with the buzzing needle.

***

Orange lights blazed from the windows of Orange Security in Times Square. On a large monitor in her guard headquarters—Agent Orange zoomed the images coming from the tattoo parlor's security camera feed.

***

The tattoos on Millioni's back remained oblique and obscured in Rook's viewer, and he could make out only the general theme. The scrolling ink looked like an antique world map bursting with vivid neon. Like Agent Orange, he zoomed in on the pattern as the tattoo artist gently inked tiny scrolls across, around and within existing inked scrolls.

Not figurative, Rook thought, *decorative*. Millioni's heavily, infinitesimally tattooed body was pure decor—just like the patterns in the emerald green lounge wallpaper, just like the patterns in the emerald green curtains. Tattoos were supposed to have meaning for many enthusiasts, and yet Millioni's fashioned as muscled wallpaper. They were like paper money guilloche—hypotrochoidal, spirographical—and they were, Rook thought, *Meaningless*. They looked like antique maps but more like money, very much like the nearly impossible to counterfeit patterns in bank notes back in the day of paper money. Rook placed these thoughts on top of one another and pushed them back in his mind, letting them weave themselves together like grass into a net.

Just who, Rook thought, as he watched the man being tattooed, *did Weedkiller kill*?

4: The Color of Money

Not really realizing he only had seven days—not realizing he too was in *Jail*—Rook gave himself no more than one week per broker hire for the solution of crime. He thought fast, sideways, backwards and inside out—taunting quantum feedback until it yielded its mysterious clues to him.

It's too easy to track Millioni, he thought, *just as impossible to figure out who he's killing, and of these impossibilities which one I've been hired to solve.*

The obituaries and daily blotter could not be trusted as accurate or even real. All news was hyperbolic, infected by the hacker named The Machete and his self-destructive Oroboros code. News, like all information, ate itself as it spat itself back out. And the Oroboros code was intelligent: it did not generate random noise but built solid, believable content daily until it liquidated, recycled and regenerated nightly.

Only currency, no longer green, had been universally stabilized in the sea of parallel reality disinformation.

While Rook watched the tattooing session, he intermittently pondered Dr. Chess. Rook's mind hummed, germinating into a greenhouse of invasive species, rushing green with the grasses and weeds and trees that had historically overrun soils, fields and riverbanks. Rook's internal greenhouse cracked, citified, and he turned his thoughts to the weeds that could survive in concrete. There were plenty of those in the city. *Alpha grasses. Alpha weeds.*

The Parks Conservancy, which had maintained what little of the city was green to begin with back in the naive days of democracy, had submerged into oblivion when the climate changed. The thunderstorms of Dr. Chess's youth had evolved, flirting into tropical storms and low-class hurricanes, mostly licking the southern edge of Long Island as the globe warmed. Eventually the first major hurricane—The Great Hurricane—did take Manhattan, and a violently humid sky and winds pummeled the city during the sixty-seven-hour storm. The city had been building walls and dunes to restrict the sea, but politics had gotten in the way. The walls proved too low, the dunes too late, and eight percent of the island submerged under the Hudson and East rivers the very day Rook was born, April 23rd. The mucky edges of the island went reedy with papyrus a few years later, and the snout of the migrating and invasive crocodile emerged as the new face of the brackish waters.

Dr. Chess, a hater of stinking sumacs, Rook thought, *a myopic quacky bastion of what the city had been and would never be again.*

Historically, the man did not seem to be up to anything other than futilely addressing a bored group of botanists that something must be done about the non-native weeds and trees choking the city. It was a problem only an herbicide manufacturer could care about, and the few that existed post-storm only concocted poison meant for war.

The new weather bloated the parks, and the stray sycamores that survived were warriors. The bastardly stinking sumacs, the trees of heaven, thrived, hookcrooking out of any crack and towering high—even between train tracks. Other invasive weeds like the papyrus ransacked and shocked out of the city like copper green nails, and Rook in his way thought the weeds had returned the city by some minor degree to its wild roots, to its tenacious grit. Weeds were like old New York gangs. Human beings, to Rook, were the true species that had invaded the island and forged upon its wilderness unnatural towers of brick and glass and steel. *Human beings*, Rook thought as he watched the tattooing, *are weeds*. Rook contemplated then the word herbicide. Immediately it summoned suicide, homicide.

-cide: the Latin root for *to kill.*

5: Chess Grass

In the evening hours after the symposium, upon spying Dr. Chess exiting his Upper West Side brownstone, Rook had made his way into the man's home—which was much more laboratory than domicile. Just as Rook's own office walls were a collage of rook imagery, Dr. Chess's lab looked to him like a weed collage. Many living cultivars thrived under bright greenhouse lamps. A variety of poisons used to kill them pooled in glass jars. Rook glanced over at the jar labeled *atrazine.* He read in the doctor's notes adjacent to the jar: *Atrazine is teratogenic, meaning it can make something monstrous, as in birth defects. Atrazine kills testosterone, and it lowers testosterone levels in some male amphibians even below the natural level found in females. Some became hermaphrodites altogether.*

The word hermaphrodite was underlined several times hard.

Rook observed a small, dissected, hermaphroditic crocodile splayed in formaldehyde, its male and female organs suspended and labeled with identification tags.

***

At the time Agent Orange knew well Rook was inside Dr. Chess's lab. Simultaneously she entered the Chinatown reality black market, and she placed an order with Jack the Butterfly for a very special case of synthetic modacrylic mustaches and beards. "Van Dykes, they're called," she told Jack. "I want you to graft the acrylic hair follicles with carbon nanotubes."

"You want conductive plastic?"

"Yes. If someone is wearing one, when they speak it will transmit the audio."

She opened a satchel and showed him designs for mannequins that looked just like Rook. "I'll need some of these as well."

Jack's talent with reality grafting and plasticity was not in any way well known, but for those in the know, it was understood his work was dangerously unstable. Agent Orange wanted to procure samples of his work not because it would necessarily succeed.

But because, like his papyrus reeds for the merchants of Ningbo, it could catastrophically fail. He was not so much a grafter as a butcher.

“What you want this for?”

“A fantasy I have.”

"Synthetic sex? Like Blue Room?”

“Perhaps.”

“Huh. I don’t care why. Give me one week," Jack said.

She insisted darkly, "Not seven. Five days," and she taunted him by holding up a vial filled with fresh biological samples from Millioni's inked body.

***

Inside Dr. Chess's office at that moment, Rook did sense a *deja vu*, as if he had been in Dr. Chess’s lab before, but he brushed it off. It happened to him all the time, and he made certain not to be distracted by it.

Several other jars in Dr. Chess’s lab brimmed with solvents like acetone and petroleum ethanol. That last one struck Rook: gas was dangerously expensive to come by, especially in such a pure form. Other jars labeled a broad variety of dried grasses as their contents, and one of them in particular, Rook made note, was named *chess grass.* Another jar was glowing with at least a liter of golden green hash resin. *Hash oil*, Rook thought. He snapped on his latex gloves, carefully opened the jar and siphoned off a milliliter into an eyedropper. The skanky stench of the resin chafed his nostrils.

In a backyard greenhouse numerous live grasses flourished. The damp earthy smell of the greenhouse entered Rook's lungs as he stepped inside. He witnessed by their labels pigweed, ragweed and broom. A nomenclatured tree of heaven sucker—called out as *Ailanthus altissima*—was curiously hermetically sealed inside a glass chamber in which electricity, like a miniature scape of lightning, tackled the miniature tree.

Electricity, a weedkiller? Rook wondered.

Past this spectacle, amidst a large cluster of Dr. Chess's namesake grass —the stalks of which split into golden green brushes—huddled some suspicious nine-leaved *Cannabis sinsemilla* plants. Rook collected samples. When he exited the greenhouse and made his way into the cellar, he became interested in a color quite opposite to green.

Inside a stainless steel cooler—in bright crimson contrast to all the greenery—Rook found one four-liter plastic bag. It was medical grade and filled with blood. Rook contemplated it for a long moment, wondering, *Human?* He siphoned a milliliter of the blood as well.

He needed to look no further than a chalkboard to discern why the man's office was a sanctuary for both grass and blood. Chalked onto it in the doctor's crooked handwriting were various notations and molecular diagrams of various grasses in comparison to blood. Staged under each chalking was a microscope slide containing a chlorophyll sample from each grass. The notations, amongst scientific observations, made empirical and rather poetic remarks about the scent of each grass. *My namesake grass*, the doctor's note read, *is the scent of the dead pawn.*

Dead pawn. What the hell does that mean? Rook wondered.

Dr. Chess's molecular drawings were ordered as a series of logical variations. Concluding the series was the jump from the molecular structure of ordinary lawn grass—which no longer existed as common—to blood. Rook opened the vial of chess grass oil and took a whiff. It was the smell of freshly mown tall grasses, such as he had not smelled since he was a child at Tuxedo Park. With that olfactory memory popped another.

Tuxedo Park. Where synthetic reality was invented.

***

Simultaneously, below the Lucky Dead Pawn shop, Jack paused to water a small greenhouse in which he was growing a hybrid of plastic lawn and real grass. The water was not water but a grayish inky liquid—a quantum graphite lubricant. He moved to another area of his lab and parted a plastic curtain to a medical-style lab beyond. Here plastic mannequin limbs were hybridized, transforming into realistic body parts. He peeked into a human-sized glass aquarium filled with conductive quantum nanographite lubricant. Inside it was a naked hybrid human—a clone of Millioni, complete with tattoos. Soon he believed he could fully graft himself into his rival and by this process rebuild his shadow body into a human-esque form. This would also allow him to replace his rival, and not even Millioni nor anyone in the Two Brothers Tong, he was convinced, would be the wiser. As he contemplated the fresh vial of DNA brought to him by The Orange Woman, he was momentarily tempted to jack into Millioni. But he set aside the temptation. He had more work for her he had to complete.

Soon, Chinatown will be mine, all mine!

Such were the thoughts of an addict.

From a batch of other DNA samples given to him by The Orange Woman, he extracted black facial hair, and utilizing a host of three-dimensional images of Rook she had supplied him with, he began compositing a semi-artificial version of the man.

Getting high would have to wait.

6: The Present

The present is a river, an atmospheric river as long as cosmic memory and as wide as a quantum pinhole punched from the prickling essence that is Sobek, Jules Barbillon recited to himself. As for the atmospheric rivers that circled the earth's sky, inundating it with waters longer, deeper and more powerful than the Amazon, he understood them also to be manifestations of the cosmic Nile that had birthed Sobek. He stood in the submarine and watched through submerged monitors as a school of fish spasmed around a diver welding a pipeline, the pipeline they would use to bring gasoline into Manhattan, the gasoline they would use to burn Naranja's reality down.

***

Simultaneously inside Coney Island Fantasy, where space and time were closing in on themselves, it flashed to Rook: maybe Millioni's routines were actual rituals. What old school cults called black magic rituals but what the black market called planting seeds.

Reality seeds.

"Remember?" Angela whispered lovingly as he began to vibrate, and when his eyes closed and a new seizure overwhelmed him, she knew he had slipped into the past.

He could do it physically almost at will, and he did it frequently when he was trying to remember. When he did, the hands on his watch slowed then timelessly paused.

***

Outside, high above, the helicopter hovered. Inside it, the doctor monitored Rook's brainwaves on his console, and he manipulated them. Into his wire in his gravelly voice, Dr. Kill van Kull said, "Give me ten more minutes."

***

Inside Coney Island Fantasy, Rook's body jerked as he dreamed wildly of emerald green weeds and emerald green eyes. Angela held him closely, watching his eyelids twitch with rapid eye movement as Rook dreamed the past.

***

While the doctor cooled Rook's brain, while Agent Orange and her gang circled the burning debris of Majestic lingerie, the flames reflected in their helmets, a black limousine pulled up to the Marco Polo Motel in midtown. The limousine driver moved around to the passenger door to open it, revealing the flashy green silk upholstery and the brocaded design of foliage within. Millioni stepped out of the revolving front doors into the night in his characteristic black silk suit and slipped inside the limousine. As the vehicle purred into southbound traffic, he spoke Mandarin into a small two-way radio, "Coney Island Fantasy. Ten minutes."

A dispatcher squawked back, "Yes, boss!"

***

Dr. Kill van Kull tweaked the console. "One minute," he said into his wire as he made a final adjustment. He sat back with a sense of completion and observed as moments counted down on a digital timer. He gave a thumbs up to the pilot, and the helicopter tilted then rushed out over the Atlantic ocean, evading the Kings County Kong.

Inside Coney Island Fantasy, the shadows cast by the mannequins shifted, elongated and rose, washing over themselves like black, gray and silver watercolors. Water droplets dappled the exterior windows from a spitting rainstorm, casting cold golden halos. Rook's eyes opened and jumped focus as if no time at all had passed. Shadows were caused by light, but he saw no light source. He quickly slipped away from Angela and pressed behind a mannequin. Peering through the windows, he realized the source of light was his still blazing sedan, and he wondered gently why he had forgotten about it. The cozy endorphin rush of post-seizure stripped down to Rook's usual metallic emotion and quickly became replaced by something uncommon to him: a lewd cold anger at the loss of his earthly machine. As the endorphin rush faded, so did the lull in time. The hands on his watch began to move with the normal persistent ticking of seconds.

Angela explored the store.

There would be no Atlantic Hose Company No. 1 response. Just like the Postal Service, the New York City fire department, a fraternity loosely comprised of individual firehouses, had become a privatized gang. The fire department had literalized as a department of fire, and it started as many fires as it put out. In Brooklyn the firehouses were mostly allied with the Kong. In Manhattan they were alternately mercenaries of immolation or vigilantes of water—depending on whose side they happened to be on. Even Rook tipped them a gold coin from time to time to ensure his apartment was protected.

Inside the Fantasy shop, Rook's cold anger smoldered with the sedan, now a gasoline accordion, the chrome grill lost in brick and the hood snarled. Rook breathed in, smelling the harsh stench of burning rubber tires, and he flicked his eyes to Angela. She was wasted and scathed from the tumble in the street grit, the glass from the broken windshield and the brittle garbage of Brooklyn. She was massaging her wrists, which were still jailed in metal handcuffs, where only the chain binding them was broken from Rook's earlier precision bullet.

Rook, paranoid, glanced over to two mannequins, one wearing a stock, realistic fireman costume and the other a policeman costume. *That's all uniforms are anymore, just costumes*. Next to the two was a mannequin in a prisoner costume: a neon green jumpsuit. That was accurate. Imprisoned contestants on Alpha TV were cut loose into the East River in the neon glow in the dark jumpsuits, and it made it even easier for the Kong to spot them. They got lucky if they got gunned down instead of eaten alive by vicious saltwater crocodiles.

"Rook?" Angela called out softly, spying something.

The unanticipated sound of her voice sent a small jolt of nervous energy through him. The druggish bewildering anger he tucked under a brooding detective facade. He made his way to her, briskly moving in and out of the mannequin shadows as if he were a shadow himself. It was his way.

She peered hard, losing sight of him in the dark shop.

He snuck close, startling her and hushing her with a finger to her lips. A wildness in his eyes suggested they were being eavesdropped on.

She nodded to a mannequin dressed and appearing exactly like Rook.

It sported a black suit, white shirt and black tie. Rook slowly approached it as if it were a real human, and he gave it a patdown. He felt a bulge. With one finger, he lifted back the lapel, revealing the black leather shoulder holster. Inside was a Z-9. He peered closer, and when Angela's hand reached past his face, he snatched her wrist, squeezing the handcuff into her flesh. She winced.

"Don't touch it," he hissed.

She blinked, rattled at first, then she softened. "It's mine," she said, "I just put it there."

He stared hard at her for a moment, felt dizzy looking into her blue eyes, and he scattered his gaze as he let go of her. "Why?" he demanded.

She rubbed at her wrists again before taking the gun into her fingers, weighing the body of it and balancing her finger on the trigger.

"To see if it would fit," she answered simply. "I also found this in a pocket," she said. She held up a matchbook by its edges, the tactile method she knew well, to leave little trace of her fingerprints and so not to smudge traces left by others.

7: Perfect Match

She lured him with the warm and even sound of her voice, "It's a *perfect* match."

The matchbook was from the Marco Polo Car Service. The field was black, and the service emblem, of a crocodile swallowing its own tail, was emerald. The figure was not horizontal, like an infinity symbol, it was vertical, like a lucky eight.

Rook visually scouted the rest of the odd costumes, the facial hair options, the wigs, all the fakery, and his eyes settled on the masks. *Why did Agent Orange force us here?* he thought.

Rook played the words over his tongue internally, *Coney Island Fantasy.*

What is it in human nature that makes people fantasize? Why is reality not good enough? It was a question he had asked himself many times over the years.

Rook made eye contact with Angela again and was almost sympathetic. Under his breath he stated, "We're inside someone's fantasy."

She was deadpan, "Yours?"

He did not answer.

The sexual fantasy, he had long thought, was the only one worth having. Even the brute reality of sex was the reality of fantasy. Sex transported the mind away from the sun to the dark side of imagination. Pornography was nothing more than a prompt.

But this was not sex. Rook received the matchbook from her and carefully opened it. Inside was written a phone number he recognized as Dr. Chess's. It was written also, in some minor variation of his own handwriting.

Rook scanned an aisle of animal costumes. Animals were playful but they did not try to escape reality by playing they were something else. His eyes returned to the mannequin dressed like him.

Angela touched the suit, "Copy?"

He answered, "*That.*"

Rook and Angela were loners, yet both had contrived in imagination the other. Even when they were together, they were not real enough for each other's appetites. There was a sadomasochistic filminess, a translucent suspension that silver screened their sex, and sex had to be macrocosmic for them to get off. Rook grit his teeth as he spied a crocodile costume. *A crocodile does not have sexual fantasies*, he thought, and he wondered, *what kind of fantasy would that be?*

He could have sworn he had solved the assassin's crime, but the light of the memory dimmed, a flame snuffed. He dared not ask Angela about the past days. *It will come back to me*, he thought, as he glanced at his watch again. Time seemed to be closing in on his birthday, and yet it seemed now that it always was almost his birthday. Yesterday and tomorrow crashed over each other like shore and tidal wave. Sleuthing in this dense quantum feedback had never been this rough, and he felt like a child born suddenly into the body of a man.

The human child was alone amongst animals in desperately wanting to be anything other than a human child. These children must also have toys, and even if they had many, they would still get bored. Just like adults.

"To copy is to duplicate but also," Angela offered quietly, "to understand."

Rook uttered, "In radio."

Rook busied himself picking the rest of the mannequin's pockets but found not even lint. He examined the suit threads hard. The threading was an exact reproduction of his tailor's style. All of his clothing was bespoken, so it meant Agent Orange had found his tailor, and if she had found his tailor, it meant possibly she had found everything—even the wormhole science Rook implemented to sleuth in feedback.

It meant she had found Tuxedo Park.

Angela cautiously wandered down an aisle, observing the naughty costumes: the naughty nurse, the naughty secretary, the naughty female detective. *Put any profession into a short skirt and garters*, she thought, *and the fantasy becomes fuckable.*

Rook made eye contact with Angela as she fondled a plastic gun. Without talking Rook and Angela shared thoughts, their thinking mirroring like remote control, quantum stars.

He said quietly, "I'm not just being avenged. They could have easily killed me. I'm being toyed with."

***

In Manhattan Agent Orange revved her motorcycle and rolled away into the night. She placed a call to the Marco Polo Car Service on a phone inside her black helmet.

Millioni answered and said, "Marco."

The helicopter escorting the doctor flew safely north over the Hudson, and he listened in through his wire as Agent Orange answered, "Polo. Take him home."

8: **Think Inside the Box**

A counter featuring a sign for custom orders drew Angela in. Rook shivered, the thunderstorm and sweat finding its way into his bones. He quickly unbuttoned and unzipped the mannequin, exchanging his foul damp suit for the fresh clothes. He briefly examined the bullet graze to his shoulder. It was still bleeding, and as he slipped into the fresh white shirt, the sleeve stained crimson. He covered it with the black jacket and had the odd craving for crocodile blood.

Angela nodded to Rook that she had found something more. He quietly approached, paranoia flaring because Angela weirdly seemed to know her way around. She was finding clues before he was, as if she knew Agent Orange's plot.

An orange box, about a cubic foot in size, sat on the counter and was addressed to Rook, to his office and home address. Rook's black tattoo heart beat like a bass drum. He rolled up several sheets of costume order forms, and he leaned his paper stethoscope to the box. His ear strained, but he heard no sound coming from within. The box was taped tight, ready to go out for delivery. Rook leaned away. The postage was highly ornamental, checkered—a flattery of an antique chessboard stomping with tiny rooks.

Another wave of light, the cool wash of car headlights, stretched into the Fantasy shop, forking shadows into long slants. Simultaneously, reflexively, Rook and Angela ducked. They peered through mannequin legs and hands, watching the driver get out of a black towncar as he placidly walked to the front door and hit the intercom buzzer outside. A few moments wasted, and he hit it again.

"Hello?" the man asked loudly into the intercom, "Here to pick up a package?" His harsh accent frothed through the old intercom system. The burning sedan at the end of the street in this broken vertex of Brooklyn meant nothing to the driver. He wore a cheap black suit and white shirt common to drivers, and he chattered away in Chinese with his dispatcher. He looked down, and in the craggy darkness he realized the lock had been shot out. He took an awkward retreating step.

With a swatting hand, Rook gestured for Angela to cover him. Behind the police-uniformed mannequin, Angela hunkered. In a sleek second she swiped the toy gun out of its plastic clutch and aimed her snubby Z-9 from its wrist. Rook stood upright and snapped a clear plastic mask off a mannequin. The plastic featured rosy cheeks and frosty blue eye shadow, and as he slipped it over his head, it obscured his face completely. He walked to the door, the Z-9 in his pocket unobtrusively aimed down as if he were just balling his fist. She watched as Rook pushed open the door and exchanged words with the pale driver.

"Where are you taking the package?"

"The city," the driver said as he looked over a dispatch sheet, "Lower East

Side. Ludlow." If the driver was nervous, he swallowed it. "Two passengers also?"

"That's us," Rook answered as he whipped out his Z-9 and trained it on the driver. With his left hand he gestured for Angela to come forth.

The driver tensed but called the bluff, "Come on, man! I got no money!" It was a standard code for distress that would have already reached his dispatcher's ears. Rook snatched the man's phonepiece and crushed it underfoot.

The driver reached for his pockets as if to prove his wallet was empty. Rook shoved his gun at the man's jowl, swatted the man's hands away and patted him down. Rook fished out a small .22 and pocketed it. He fished more deeply as Angela, in a twinned plastic mask, joined him at his side, and he found the man's keys.

9: A Bearded Woman

Rook dragged the driver into the shop. While Angela stood guard over the driver, who was keeping face and street credibility by staying mum, Rook ransacked a display. He gnashed at the plastic packages containing cheap soft alloy handcuffs, breaking all seventeen pairs loose in a frenzy. Simple toy skeleton keys secured the play cuffs. Rook cuffed the man's wrists three times and his ankles three times, then cuffed him to the mannequin dressed in Rook's soiled clothing. In succession Rook cuffed several other mannequins together, turning the driver into an impossible tangle of plastic and nickel.

Rook checked his watch: twelve linear minutes had passed since they had broken into the store. When they exited, toting the orange box with them, anxiously zippering eyes up and down the street, they spotted another car parked down the block. Black smoke idled from a tailpipe: it was a carbon copy of Rook's sedan. *Cosmo!* Rook thought, wondering if his broker was safe—and then—*Unsafe*!

Rook and Angela hopped into the towncar and pulled away from the curb. The mocking dark sedan followed like an internal combustion shadow in a black velvetized night.

Rook kept his gun in his hand as he drove. Another fierce thunderstorm attacked the skyline. Black clouds mugged the skyscrapers and rain etched the windshield. Between Rook and Angela sat the blatantly quiet bright orange box.

The now immobilized driver's stoic style made Rook assume the driver worked directly for Agent Orange. Rook assumed everyone worked for Agent Orange. *Even me*. Rook slammed on the gas pedal and jerked the towncar toward the boardwalk, where the nonstop ragtag carnival reality of Coney Island glutted the beach. Unequivocally, the dark sedan easily followed, rumbling into the slow traffic comprised of clunky two-story cars, three-story motorbikes, motorized unicycles and the odd clutter of sideshow circus.

Rook veered through the beach crowd and glanced at the many bonfires dotting the sand. Near one a bearded woman juggled oranges. Angela pointed to her, saying, "The bearded woman."

"Masculiner," he said, "What does it mean to you?" He glanced at the fake beard she wore prickling behind the plastic mask, made even more grotesque by it.

"Nothing."

"It's something that's supposed to make you masculine even though it's fake as plastic fruit," he added.

"This is making me a Coney Island freak," she responded as she tilted the mask and touched the fake hair. She tried to tug a corner of the beard free, but the adhesive was like superglue. "A hermaphrodite."

"It's a Van Dyke," he said.

She glanced at him, was momentarily pensive and said, "I'm being mocked."

Rook thought, *Freaks dwell inside the skin of cheap fantasy. A way of life*. To a large degree, as a reinvented man, so did he. He said, "You're being implicated."

She repeated his words, "I'm being implicated, and we're both being copied." She licked her lips, touching the fake mustache, savoring the night, though her wrists, her back, her very bones and marrow ached. She kept her gun trained on the rear window, on the trailing sedan, and ignored the fake facial hair stuck to her soft cheeks.

***

Through a radio comprised of carbon nanotubes technology grafted into the fake beard, Agent Orange listened in.

***

Stuck in the thickening beach crowd the trailing sedan had fallen behind a block. When a parading chain of elephants lumbered into traffic, visually shielding the towncar, Rook turned off the head and taillights and nudged out toward the sand. The tires were sluggish, whipping a gritty spray several feet above the towncar as it pulled behind a row of tents and meekly worked its way up the beach toward a crumbling road. A saltwater crocodile edged out of the low frothing break and seemed to stare at them before backtracking into the filthy waters.

Agent Orange was raping his world, and Rook was secretly thrilled. *Agent Orange*, Rook thought, *is an overtone of Weedkiller*. Somehow they were copies but not identical: they were like personality frequencies, and he wondered indeed if they were synthetic personalities.

10: The Machete

Rook had traced Millioni's license-plated limousine in a database and discovered that Millioni kept a punctual schedule, snaking around the city as if he were tracing a giant figure eight out in the streets. The figure eight, Rook had noted in his photos from the club, also comprised an infinite eight in the oroboros: the beast swallowing its own tail. The club's emerald green crocodile sign swallowed itself infinitely.

Rook witnessed the Oroboros code, which had surfaced in classical reality, as a tangible reiteration of the seemingly intelligent quantum substrate—what Jung had coined the collective unconscious. When he had been hired to crack the Oroboros code, Rook dove into brainwave feedback sessions and self-induced seizures, seeking the most resonant forms of the Oroboros. When, upon surfacing from these feedback sessions, he mapped the resonant forms, he decided to coin them *quantum roots*. Further he inferred that at their greatest resonance, the roots hardened into the trunk of classical reality. It was during feedback and self-induced seizures that Rook the psychonaut navigated the quantum sea and separated resonant stereotypes and archetypes from actual living people—people who had unique irises, fingerprints and voices. As space and time condensed at event horizon edges, the separation thinned.

Millioni, Rook remembered, always ate an orange for dessert. Oranges and tangerines were good luck in China. The word for tangerine, *ju*, sounded like *ji,* the literal word for *good luck.*

But Agent Orange was bad luck. *Did she want to kill the assassin?* Rook wondered. *Did the assassin want to kill her?*

During his Weedkiller investigation, Rook remembered in a flash, he had printed out a satellite map of the city and collected real-time feeds from city cameras with coding he had long breached. These were not meant to be security cameras. They were mapping cameras installed by a private internet company, and all of these cameras ran on dynamic digital protocols, meaning the code to access them changed every minute. What the average duped citizen did not know was that the ever-changing, randomly generated codes were dictated by the internet company's central intelligence system. There was nothing random about these random codes. In an earlier version of the cycle of Seven, Rook had cracked a case for the internet company, and he had been given access to their code generator. It enabled him to ping any camera remotely any time he wanted. It gave him a god's eye view of the city.

As much as concrete remained concrete, something to ground the feet in New York City, information was a mashup and played havoc with the head. The digital encyclopedias the foolish world had come to rely upon, and all the third-party software that seemed to give human cultures limitless opportunities to know exactly what was up, had been mercilessly hacked by The Machete. Digital reality subsequently became a pastiche and a parody. Rook knew all about The Machete and his code because he had been hired by the pirated internet monopoly named The Wire to find him. Rook knew after the arrival of The Machete's corrupt code that reality had changed hands forever. Reality wasn't stranger than fiction: it was fiction.

It just wasn't authored by people.

It was authored by feedback code, by output slowly morphed into input.

Rook maintained access to all of The Wire's cameras, and through these Rook had spied medium close-up footage of Millioni's limousine as it ferried its passenger in a pattern. Therefrom, mapping his every public move, Rook deduced Millioni always enjoyed his dessert orange directly after dinner.

Rook had no idea Agent Orange had been watching this pattern with him all along.

***

Agent Orange shared the current view, and from a feed inside her motorcycle helmet she watched the towncar wade sluggishly in the Coney Island sand.

On a monitor inside his limousine, so did Millioni.

She called him again and commanded, "Send one car to Coney Island Fantasy. Send another to Ludlow."

Millioni called his dispatcher and watched the bright lights of Chinatown glaze the city as they drove toward the crocodile wrestling club. The night was closing in to when he made his nightly appearance and started the show with the hundred dollar bill. His thoughts turned briefly away from Rook and toward the orange sapphire-encrusted crocodile goddess.

He always had sex with her before the show.

11: Oroboros

After Rook had brought The Machete to "justice," The Wire did not request the execution. Instead, they let The Machete's mashup virus thrive and forced The Machete, imprisoned in their corporate headquarters, to work for them.

The same free-associative path that helped him solve all his crimes had helped Rook crack The Machete's mashup worm, the virus known as *Oroboros*.

The Oroboros virus forced most electronic media to continuously overwrite and rewrite but intelligently: the content made sense. The electronic advertisements gaudily flaunting Times Square became hydras of scrolling Oroboros change, and the change was a slow moving evolution undetectable by blinking eyes. Paper libraries, which could have so easily gone up in smoke, were vigilantly protected by the fire department on the payroll of some ultra wealthy history buffs and ultimately as a whole by Dr. Naranja. The daily newspapers, long slanted, slid off the abyss of bias in some egoistic attempt to compete with the Oroboros infected, day-glo electronic news sources. The Oroboros knew all internet addresses, could track every internet search and custom fabricate news for groups it had defined. Serious paper news survived as an underground phenomenon, and paper pirates substituted their own paper mockups of mashup. Digging through the obscene dirt of information, Rook needed a spade the size of Texas to find the hacker.

But unearthing The Machete had given him his shovel. With it ultimately he had spied on Millioni up close through The Wire's cameras and had opened up Millioni's precious tower tanks.

That memory popped for Rook: *The tanks!*

Now Rook and Angela had become traceable, momentarily trapped inside a sunjuice-powered towncar with gps. Rook pulled the car up onto the road, pinged the gps internet protocol address with his watch and hacked it with the Oroboros code. Instead of transmitting latitude and longitude, it suddenly spat out junk. He jerked open the driver door with the car keys in hand and stormed to the rear. In the trunk he found the bar for the tire jack, and he grabbed it. He pushed the tip under the back license plate and, with three rough, tugs pried it free. He did the same to the plate on the front.

Rook tossed the busted and bent plates, along with the seventeen handcuff skeleton keys, into the beachgrass. He jumped back into the towncar, saying, "We're now, as much as we can be—"

"Anonymous," Angela finished his sentence.

***

But even the beachgrass, tangled now with plastic keys and Jack's papyrus, sent quantum memory everywhere at once. Even under water inside the submarine, Jules Barbillon felt it tickling his skin.

***

Inside the Marco Polo Car Service office, the dispatcher yanked his headphones off when the transmission signal ripped from a logical hum to a painful squeal: the squeal of audio feedback. In front of him a screen showed the location of each of his towncars, all eighty-eight of them. The screen went black, then splintered back to life like an abstract digital painting. He slammed his fist down. His dispatch system, so carefully encrypted by his boss Mr. Millioni, had just been swallowed by the Oroboros.

***

Mr. Millioni, aka Weedkiller, stepped into the dressing room below the club, pulled the woman close and kissed her. Under his fingertips the orange sapphires were cool to the touch. As he pushed inside her, she gasped and ran her hands under his shirt. He grunted when her fingers stroked the raised, scabbing skin from the fresh tattoo on his back.

The look on her face, one of pure ecstasy, flashed with guilt. "Sorry," she whispered.

"No matter what happens," he responded, "Never forget, you are the one I love."

Blood seeped from the tattoo and made its way under her sapphire encrusted fingernails. She closed her eyes and kissed him, tasting again the hash that always lingered on his lips.

It would be the first night since the grand opening—a grand opening stitched into the fabric of the city by endless reiterations—he would miss the show.

Space-time would feel the missing link and fold over itself in search of him.

But there were two more of him, his triplets, and one was always available to take the place of another.

Even Agent Orange, he thought, *does not know.*

At that moment his brothers rose from the depths of the East River in a small three-person submarine, leaving Jules down below to supervise the Petroleum Club while they, up above, pushed to the extreme the envelope of reality.

CHAPTER FIVE: Postal Ictal

1: Penmanship

The letter in the East Orange warehouse mailbox had been addressed from Rook in his own penmanship. It was a realistic mockup, looking as though it had been sent around the day Rook was born, the day of the great storm. The return address, Rook's home address, was his original home, the one he had inherited from his father. He maintained the old address from afar, but he almost never visited it. Who Rook had been, an international chess star, he kept a secret. For nineteen years he had been underground, untraceable, and somehow Agent Orange had found out everything about him.

Rook drove tensely along a murky side street, craning his head at cross streets and otherwise ignoring the red lights. Angela flicked her eyes right and left in search of suddenly oncoming cars or the dark sedan. Nobody paid any attention to traffic lights anymore. The reds and greens still alternately blinked throughout all streets, percolating the slick night asphalt with an upbeat lightshow utterly ignored. Nobody enforced the trifles of traffic. At an upcoming intersection, one light blinked yellow, and on instinct, Rook slammed the gas. Angela's eyes flicked right, and she pointed to another car careening in. Rook corrected, jarring the steering wheel left. Side by side, inches from broadside collision, the two cars spun, then broke away from each other. The driver of the other car cursed profoundly, hacking his language with *fuck you*, his mouth silenced by the glass, as the quarreling honking bled quiet in the distance.

The near collision, so common, had forced Rook into an inadvertent u-turn. Prowling toward them was the sedan that had been following them. Rook stared hard, trying to make out a face through the dark windows, but he saw nothing other than the cold glass windshield beaded with raindrops.

The brooding, trailing sedan drifted slowly ahead of them, driving in the direction they had been going. Rook quickly spun the towncar into a one-eighty. Angela hit the windshield, then bounced back. Rook shot her an apologetic look before nailing his eyes to the rear of the sedan in front of them. Now they were the trailers. The windshield wipers of the towncar ached against the glass as rain misted then gushed. The sedan slowed as a torrential micro-thunderstorm pounded, then the sedan drifted again, slowing to an almost stall and deftly blocking them. Angela leveled her gun.

Rook cranked the wheel, lurching the towncar onto a side street. He hit the gas pedal and shot through a barricade, jamming the towncar into the shadows of an underpass, making a questionable turn across railroad tracks and bouncing the car back toward the Beltway.

2: Post

He glanced down at the bright orange box. Again, his penmanship had been acutely copied: it looked dead ringer for his own. If Agent Orange had not known who he was, she would have had to take samples directly from his current home and office. If she did know, public samples were easy to come by on the internet. Before the invasion of the Oroboros virus, they were even more easily found in his chess notations back from his gaming days. His originals had been donated to the Central Library, scanned and uploaded. Rook had also played correspondence chess with his Tuxedo Park friend Cosmo, sending cryptic single move postcards back and forth one by one. Postcard mail, before the fall of the Postal Service, had been their means of playing a long-distance game only they knew about. Later it became a common strategy toward circumventing traceability. Those postcards, he remembered through a lethargy at once liquid and gummy, were locked away at Tuxedo Park.

Driving in the clear plastic mask and sitting next to the mute orange box, Rook kept his Z-9 knuckled at the steering wheel. He looked a little cleaned up within the fresh suit and, at the same time, weirdly sterile behind the plastic mask. Angela was haggard, and she did not ask him where he was driving them. In the somber night, green and red streetlights flashing off the edges of the eternally unlit beltway, she knew just the same.

She glanced at his raw profile sleeked by the plastic mask.

This was the first time crime had been directed at Rook. Realistically there was no way what he did for a living would not come under scrutiny. The bounty was now out on him, on them. He thought, *Birthday gift. It's about time.*

The towncar jumped a meridian and plowed onto the Gowanus Expressway. There was no sign of the brooding sedan, but Rook inferred it knew exactly where they were going. If Rook was going to triumph over Agent Orange, he thought, *I have to think inside her box.*

Rook glanced down at the Pandoran orange box.

"Open the box. Please."

He yielded his penknife to Angela, and she slit open the tape promptly. She pulled open the flaps slowly and looked down into it. The abyss of the Coney Island Fantasy box looked back at her through a mask, another synthetic Van Dyke and in clear vials, two pairs of bulls-eye contact lenses. "Costumes. For two."

3: **After**

"She's playing with post," Rook thought aloud, "Playing with the multiple definitions of post. For example, post also means *after*."

"She?"

Rook eyed Angela, concerned about letting her know the details. "A woman. She found me, confronted me, just prior to me coming to find you." He kept the concept loose in his mind and rolled around the idea of linearity, of a hard tomorrow after a hard today, but as the night veered toward his birthday, tangibility seemed thin as paper.

"She is after—not just you and me," Rook voiced. "After something much bigger. She wants me to retire and yet she lets me live."

Angela mused, "Perhaps this bigger thing comes after something smaller. And she is keeping *us* alive to extort something from us."

Rook had too much information and way too much technology, and he hoped, darkly, Agent Orange did not want all of it.

The Age of Reptiles stamp. He knew it. An envelope in his storage—an old manila one—featured the same stamp. The envelope had been mailed from the hospital he was born in, and inside it had been the first copy of his birth certificate mailed to his childhood address. Father's occupation: *chess master*. Mother's: *deceased*.

The towncar took the ascent of the Manhattan Bridge over the roiling, inky East River. On the Manhattan side, Rook shot the towncar into a nefarious parking lane. He motioned to Angela, and as he leapt out so did she. He grabbed the box as eyes in the shadows watched. The location was a standard dumping ground for hot cars, and it would be less than an hour before most of this one would be stripped, leaving little evidence behind for the Marco Polo Car Service.

He tilted back the plastic mask and threw it onto a pile of trash.

From a street vendor Rook bought black umbrellas. Hidden under the arched fabric the two stepped briskly through heavy raindrops bouncing off the streets like dimes. They headed toward Ludlow Street in thinning rain, deeper into the smell of a large fire. They paused as they witnessed a long leaping flame unquenched by the rain. The streets were choked with fire engines and firemen.

A Marco Polo towncar was loitering, waiting. Rook spotted it. Abruptly he held Angela back. At the tenement on the corner, he surveyed the fire escape. He knew it well. He handed her the orange box, and in the shadows he jumped for the fire escape ladder. He hoisted himself up, removed an iron pin and quietly lowered the ladder for her. She kicked off her high heels, and in moments both were not visible, silently ascending as if they were darkness itself.

Peering over a parapet wall that hid him, Rook's focus twitched. Straight down below he witnessed the sedan: it had beaten him home and was parked near his front door. Above him soot billowed from adjacent Orchard Street, and Rook could now see the orange flames leaping above the flat tenement roofs on the other side of the street. He knew without fully being able to see that it was the Majestic lingerie store burning.

Nearby a Marco Polo Car Service driver sat in another towncar and casually smoked a cigarette. He scanned the smoky street. Over his radio, he heard in barking Mandarin, the handcuffed driver was just being rescued from Coney Island Fantasy.

Holding the black umbrella low over his head and blending in with the night, Rook hopped from the sixth story roof, down twelve feet, to a fifth story roof. He turned, caught the package from Angela and had barely put it down when she leaped for his arms. They scampered quickly, picking the path he had trained on over and over in case he ever needed another entry. The towncar driver focused hard on Rook's apartment but turned toward the sound of another car passing by: a mail truck. Rook leapt, crouched and rolled onto his own roof. Angela followed. He opened a hatch with a key, listened intently, said, "Wait," and dropped inside.

Rook swept the rest of his home, courting curtains and corners with his drawn gun in a brisk *allegro vivace*, each sweep and point sewn into the next move. It was the dangerous, almost silent music of a potentially deadly hide and seek.

One minute later he was down by his front door and confident his home was not otherwise occupied. A quick drum of footsteps: back at the roof he motioned Angela in.

***

Surveillance was transmitted to Agent Orange and both seen and heard inside her helmet as she and her gang drove north, weaving their motorcycles in and out of traffic on the West Side Highway en route to Tuxedo Park. She said into a wire, "He's home. Make the delivery."

***

Inside Rook's dark apartment Angela turned toward Rook, asking "What's next?"

"Are you able to leave for the week?"

Her face was a stone. "Rook! No! I just tried to leave!"

Rook peered past the edge of the closed shades. As the mail truck parked, Rook’s eyes followed it then shifted his stare to the twinned sedan. It seemed to be staring back at him through its silvery headlights, the chrome grille a sinister smirk.

He turned back to Angela, quietly stating, "The rules—"

She interrupted, "They've been more than broken," and in a barbing tone, "Are you worried about sharing the spotlight?"

Her words kicked his ego.

She was right. Together they had been forced into a violent game with an unknown threshold. He had been playing his crime games by himself before he had met her. Now, playing them with her, she was no bookend: she was brilliant, a racetrack of intellect and his unequal only because her ego was not his. He looked at her, a woman whose beauty could not be defeated by the absurd fake facial hair, and he said, "This beard, this Van Dyke, is not meant to disguise. This plastic one is meant to *impress* women."

She repeated with concern, "Van Dyke."

Rook asked, "What kind of woman would be impressed by a fake beard?"

She paused and said, "Impress?" After some consideration she offered, "Perhaps a fake woman."

Angela swallowed as Rook stroked the fake beard on her face, and he said, "We need to find this synthetic woman. Her name is Agent Orange."

***

Overhearing through the nanotube beard, Agent Orange smiled.

***

Dr. Chess opened the door to Dr. Cheng, the DNA fusion specialist from Ningbo. They had drunk coffee together once before, after the last symposium. "What if," Dr. Cheng proposed with excitement, "the weedkiller was organic, was itself a weed! Could we control weeds with weeds?"

Reeling the man in by the shoulder, Dr. Chess answered, "Yes!" He shut the door behind them quietly and brought the man deeper into his lab. He showed him his secret pride, a red-celled plant, dark as a beet. "See here, I have grafted hemoglobin with chlorophyll."

"Blood with grass!"

"Almost. Crocodile blood with grass—with butterfly! I'm going to plant it everywhere in this city!"

Dr. Cheng was more than pleased. "There is someone I'd like you to meet." And he handed him a card to the Lucky Dead Pawn shop.

***

Jack the Butterfly hovered over the body of the synthetic Millioni, tattooing black market conductive ink into it over and over again. It would allow Jack to control it through quantum interference, thereby allowing him in theory to control Millioni.

Oh, Marco Millioni, he thought, *I am so much more clever than you think!*

***

Upstate at Tuxedo Park, through his warm brown eyes Cosmo examined the laboratory collection of Silk Road DNA. He marveled at how he and then the reality storm had cultivated Marco Millioni inside out in space and time, grafting the sweet innocence of the lollipop boy into him, overnight. New York City had for the past several overlapping and reiterating weeks accepted Millioni's presence as a Chinatown boss as if he had always been there, and in a million ways he had.

Jack the Butterfly, so high on a million different realities, had utterly fallen for the idea that Millioni had long been his gang rival. *Jack the Butterfly*, Cosmo thought, *finally has something to live for.*

People like Cosmo, so close to the core of reality, knew that time looped in cycles of Seven, overwriting itself in space, grafting into itself via space, over and over and over. If addicts like Jack, too powerful and dangerously close to the quantum core of reality, gave in, reality could cave in with them. He thought of how he had staged the incident with the hand ball, had manipulated what was called taxicab geometry to initiate the crash, and about how thrilled they had all been to watch as Rook instinctively sought to save the boy. In a world ripe with darkness, any goodness at all gave them hope that space and time, light and darkness, would not completely twin and cancel each other out.

Cosmo heard the sound of the helicopter blades overhead.

Reality itself, Cosmo thought, *needs a reason to live.*

***

Inside the helicopter, lights from the console washed over the calcified scars in the withered leathery skin of Dr. Kill van Kull's black face. He almost heard Cosmo's thoughts. Those closest to the core of reality frequently could. Echoing Cosmo's sentiment, he thought, *The eye of the storm must want to see!*

4: The Hunted

Squeezed between lanky tenements stood the brick building where Rook had lived for many adult years. Next to the front door hung his mailbox. Out of the misty rain and seemingly sculpted from it, the burly mailman appeared. He brusquely passed by the attentive towncar driver down the block. The mailman was dressed in the standard old uniform's blues and grays, and in his satchel, it was widely known, he was carrying his small machine gun along with his letters. Tattooed on his hands was the phrase attributed to Herodotus: *Neither snow nor rain nor heat nor gloom of night stays these couriers from the swift completion of their appointed rounds.*

Feeling the eyes of the driver on him and committed to the safe and confidential delivery of his mail, the mailman turned, retrieved his machine gun and glared. Within seconds, sputtering in Chinese to the dispatcher, the driver rolled up his window and motored down the street, away from a member of the most brutal gang known in the city. The brutal mailmen made the firemen in their red trucks look like pale pink ribbons of men. Even Chinatown car service gang members wanted to go home safely to a bowl of noodles and a wife. Making a mailman go postal meant certain death.

Satisfied he was not under watch, the mailman continued his delivery. At Rook's mailbox he inserted a small brass key, gave it a hard turn and popped open the small metal box.

Rook's ears jumped, and he motioned Angela to the floor. He slid to a window and watched through a sliver of glass.

The mailman deposited an envelope with a gloved hand. The mail slid through a small chute into Rook's apartment. The mailman locked the box promptly, turned back to the street, and lumbered to his mail truck, atop which machine guns were mounted. A twist to the ignition, a brief firing of engine, and the man simply drove away.

Rook watched him depart then motioned to the interior side of the mailbox with a compromising nod. Angela pulled it open carefully. Inside was one black envelope, the size of which indicated it sealed a card. She removed it, holding it at the edges with bent fingertips. The addressee was, *Shadow*. It was in Angela's penmanship, in white ink. She turned her blue eyes up to his.

There was no stamp.

Rook gestured swiftly. Together they moved deeper into his apartment toward his office, he carrying the orange box and she bearing the envelope. The darkness etched into dense charcoal strokes, and within it Rook and Angela crept as if they had broken into some place unknown. Rook *hunted*—that was what he called his detective work—and he had long considered the detective a breed of human hunter. In the darkness, as his eyes adjusted, he hunted the office for clues, for anything missing, moved or new.

The mannequin still sat at the desk, but the head had been removed, and in front of the headless body were clue cards placed on the chessboard desk exactly in the manner Rook would play with them.

Though he had not created these.

Angela spotted it first, over the fireplace, mounted like a game trophy: the Masculiner mannequin head. It was wearing the sunglasses again. Rook set the box down on a table and scanned for anything else amiss.

Again, Rook searched each room intensely, frantically. He was not looking for people; he was searching for what they had left behind. Angela twirled behind him, covering his back as he jerked open each cabinet and closet door in methodical succession. In the kitchen the refrigerator light cast over a clean full liter of blood. Angela eyed him, but he shook his head.

"It's crocodile."

When he yanked open his bedroom closet door he jerked back defensively. A white figure loomed toward him. Angela immediately fired once, chest high, at the whiteness.

The whiteness shocked and swung violently on a hanger before easing to a simple sway like a wind chime. Instead of sounding with pleasant soft metal pulses, the disturbed wire hanger scratched meanly on the closet pole. The whiteness was a dress, a formal gown. The quiet white gown pleaded guilty to intruding as it slowed to a stop. Rook quickly forked through the clothing and suits with the muzzle of his gun and found nothing more other than the woman's garment that had not been there before. It hung next to his tuxedo, and together the two items made a lavish pair.

Angela's bullet had pierced the heart of the dress.

"Nice shot," he whispered.

She glanced up and spotted something else, a Majestic lingerie box. She pointed. Rook reached up for it, slid it down and felt its weight. It was full of something. He placed it on the bed and slowly pried the box open. Bundles of what looked like hundred dollar bills were neatly rubberbanded together. Rook took a bundle out and held it under light pulsing in from a streetlamp. They were newspaper clippings. He flipped through the bundle quickly. Each clipping, many of them duplicates, contained a story about his days as a chess master.

Rook glanced at Angela, then pressing a hand on her face, his gun held to her cheek, he kissed her. She wrapped her arms around him, her gun held in the small of his back.

They were definitely in this together.

5: Voodoo Doll

Rook returned paranoid and defeated to his office, to the black envelope.

He had already been directly confronted and allowed to live. *It would be a boring denouement*, he thought, *to strike me down in my own home*.

Angela poured him a drink, "She knows we are here, right?" then she poured one for herself. She was bruised, scraped and silent as she stared at the mannequin head. The murdered gown and her own heart were on her mind. She studied the lifeless mannequin head and mirrored sunglasses. "The gown too," she said, "is headless."

Rook hauled over a chair and stood on it to access the mounted head. He saw briefly his reflection in the convex mirrored lenses and behind him Angela withdrawing a few feet. As his own face filled the mirror, he plucked the sunglasses free. The mannequin's eyes had been painted with concentric orange and white bulls-eye rings just like the contact lenses in the box, and the pupils were now holes: bullet holes. Rook pulled the mounted head from the wall and stepped down.

"It's Agent Orange's way of getting inside my head." He set the head on the table next to the orange box, and when he spoke again he seemed to address the head, not Angela, "Am I going to be beheaded?"

"They are making us hunt ourselves in your own apartment." Angela cautioned quietly, "They are, they're telling us, right under our own nose."

"They?" Rook tossed back, thinking, *Something stinks*.

"No sooner than I left the last memo, walked out the apartment door and headed to the train, they had me. More than one. How did you find me?"

Rook's coal black eyes hardened. He dared not look at her, afraid they would spark and betray the story he did not want to tell. Not even an hour had passed since he had received the lingerie package leading him to Agent Orange. The train had hurtled for ten minutes maximum, and he had been unconscious for less, he figured, than a minute. The time spent inside Coney Island Fantasy was under fifteen minutes, and the drive back had taken around twenty. He had been inside his house now for about five. In her toying, Agent Orange insinuated whatever crime Rook was sleuthing was indeed close to home—perhaps even being committed in his own home—or one of his homes.

Rook skipped a direct answer, "Kidnappers never make it too far from their own front door. Though there was no ransom."

"And you rescued me nonetheless."

Rook shifted his attention to the mannequin head now sitting on his desk. He aimed his loaded gun at it, thought for a needling moment, then returned his thoughts to the headless mannequin seated at his desk. He had himself brought it back from East Orange. He could have left it behind, but it would have been almost like leaving a fallen comrade behind. It was his silent plastic twin. "Agent Orange took out on the mannequin what she could have taken out on me."

"It's a life-size voodoo doll," Angela concluded.

The bullets shot through the mannequin's pupils had been fired at close range. Rook seated himself across from the headless mannequin and aimed his gun where its head had been. In the darkness he spotted them: two entry bullet holes in the wall behind it.

Whoever shot the mannequin had done so from his own chair. Rook rose and fiercely, forensically examined the wall behind the mannequin. He squinted. The dim light was forcing his shadow to paint the wall, and he closed in, scrutinizing the wall through the darkness of his own shadow. Angela, gazing into the orange box, did not witness his shadow writhe with a life of its own.

While Rook pulled the two bullets free from the wall she approached the mannequin head. She peered through the two holes and found she was just able to see through the pupils, clear through the back of the plastic-haired head. She took a small flashlight and shined it into the empty cavity.

"Rook?"

He pulled the second bullet free and turned to her.

"There's something else."

He let her unbolt the ring that mounted the head to the trophy board while he sized up the bullets. They were .22 caliber close-up assassin bullets, just like Agent Orange's dozen had been firing. The graze in his arm throbbed as he remembered it.

When Angela lifted the head free, a paper clipping fluttered down from the neck and twirled like a butterfly until it landed gently on the beaten oak floor.

Not like a butterfly, he thought, *it is a butterfly*. It flew to the light streaming from the flashlight. Its wings trembled momentarily then it pacified.

Rook picked it up with the tweezers, and Angela kept the flashlight on it. The insect, its wings glossy, seemed torn from a magazine page. Its wings were organic, living, crenelated glossy paper. The printed phrase along its outstretched wings was clearly visible.

Rook read the phrase aloud, "'As an orange is final. As an orange is something nature has made just right.'" No sooner than he read it, did the phrase fold over itself like TV snow and fade into an ambiguous pattern on the insect's wings. From a drawer Angela procured a small, clear plastic box, the kind Rook used for storing evidence. She opened it and offered it to him. He set the strange insect inside gently, and she placed the lid on it with an opening, so the insect would get air. They looked one another in the eye.

Rook grumbled, "What the hell is this thing?"

"I used to collect butterflies when I was a child."

"This is not a butterfly."

"It is, somehow. An indicator of a metamorphosis."

"Indicating something final."

"Butterflies pollinate."

"Do they pollinate orange blossoms?"

"I imagine."

Rook walked to the window. The towncar driver, spooked by the mailman, had not returned. But the sedan remained.

Through a sliver of shade and window he saw a street corner vendor dragging his fruit cart by hand back to storage for the night. Thunderstorm through thunderstorm, the vendor sold his produce. Fruits in the summer: cherries, plums, melons, bananas, pears. Oranges. Rook sipped at his whiskey. *Why orange?*

6: Off on a Tangent

Rook spoke suddenly, hammering his words, "ECHO, on. Offline encyclopedia. Look up orange." The computer's tactile screen surged to life, illuminating the darkness with its cold electronics. In turn it probed immediately into an old offline electronic encyclopedia. The online encyclopedias could not be trusted due to the Oroboros virus.

The top entries blipped onto the screen and referred to the citrus fruit and the color. *The color orange*, he thought, *is bright, used in safety*. Blaze orange, that was a poetic way of talking about fluorescent orange, of hunter orange. He finally realized Angela was seemingly waiting for authorization to brainstorm with him.

"Hunter orange," he told her, "Hunter orange. A color worn by hunters so as not to be mistaken for game by other hunters." He took another sip of whiskey, rolling it on his tongue. The encyclopedia flashed with stock photos of hunter orange clothing.

Rook pushed his fingers into her cinnamon hair as he dictated to the computer, "'As an orange is final. As an orange is something nature has made just right.'"

The encyclopedia offered a prattling array of misses and no direct hits for the quotation.

Angela became rigid with an unearthly knowing. She faltered, "It is another way of making me complicit. The phrase is taken from a literary magazine. I know it well. And bullets, they also come from a magazine. It's... Listen Rook, this Agent Orange is playing with words and meanings, multiple meanings. She is making a reference to perfect fiction."

"Perfect fiction?"

"Yes, fiction is perfect when it is like an orange—organic, natural, complete in and of itself—final."

The office phone rang.

***

Inside her orange helmet, Agent Orange abruptly laughed, a mocking laugh full with knowledge of Rook. She edged between cars snarled in traffic and sped between them, her gang following behind like an orange snake. Through Rook's own sunglasses set on the desk, she heard his phone ringing.

***

The vintage phone with rotary dial—simple and black—rang for the fourth time. The vintage answering machine picked up, scrolling the cassette tape through Rook's voice, "Investigations. Leave a message."

"Finally! Now, open the envelope, Rook Black. *Then push it*!" It was Agent Orange. Click.

Clashing suspicion drove his eyes to the envelope and box. "That was her."

Rook slit the envelope with his penknife and gently, with forensic tweezers, pulled out the card. It was crisp, clean and black. The card itself proposed an invitation to something calling itself *The Black and White Ball.*

Place: *Tuxedo Park, The Glass House*. Time: *Midnight.*

Rook glanced at his watch. "We don't have much time."

"We're going?"

"I don't think we have a choice." Boldly, he turned on a lamp and he scanned for anything that could be surveillance. His focus landed on the sunglasses.

7: The Stamp

"Damn it," Rook glanced at his watch, "Damn it." It was almost 11:00 p.m., and the city was just starting to wake up.

Angela scrutinized the invitation. "It's a birthday ball," she said, "Your birthday party."

"If hell could be called a party," he muttered, thinking, *Agent Orange is impressive as hell.*

From his desk Rook quickly retrieved the laser fingerprint machine. He set the invitation inside, releasing it from the tweezers, and he closed the lid, sealing the box. Rook turned the machine on, and it hummed to life. A static field suspended the invitation inside the clear walls of the box while the red lasers searched it.

Paper, untouched, would yield nothing. Paper touched, in the old school days of silver nitrate and ultraviolet fingerprint lifting, could still yield next to nothing. If there was so much as a trace of any residue or anything else, the laser would elicit it.

The fingerprint box hummed to a whine, searching, and a database scrolled and blinked, *Failed Report*.

Rook and Angela's attention shifted from each other to the fingerprint machine.

Rook turned it off, opened the lid and scrutinized the invitation before turning his attention to the envelope. He used the tweezers to set it inside the box, closed the lid and hit the on button. The envelope hovered as the laser danced over it, and immediately a hologram projected from what seemed to be not a fingerprint but a stamp. Rook had not expected this. Gummed paper stamps and their replacement holographs and holograms, like paper money, were ancient history, collector's items from legitimate Postal Service days. *Dinosaurs*, he thought, *dinosaurs*.

He thought about the dinosaur stamp on the envelope addressed to Masculiner, and he thought about the five dollar bill. That was a dinosaur too. Stamps also had initially been replaced by holography for several years, before postal legitimacy went out of business. The mostly automated, internet-based postal system embedded a holograph into electro-glass fibered paper. As the technology improved, a person wanting to mail something would purchase the postage online and use their own holograph printer to generate the stamp.

The old holograph stamps were two-dimensional and could not fully be appreciated by the naked eye. The three-dimensional projected hologram could be witnessed only through an optical lens popular with collectors and philatelists. The new, robotic postal boxes found on street corners accepted delivery payment in gold coin only, then scanned for postage. A signal was immediately sent to the nearest mailman, who right away would retrieve the mail and deliver it.

Prior to the invention of an international synthetic currency, pseudo-holograms—shiny and iridescent—appeared embedded in credit cards as logos. For a while, before photonic transmission, the magnetic strips in money cards became replaced by radio frequency embedment. Merely by holding the card near a reader, the radio signal could be discerned. The fingertap fad popular during Rook's teens consisted of a radio frequency identification chip embedded under the skin, allowing one merely to wave one's hand near a frequency reader for payment. While the reader processed the signal, a biometric—the fingerprint—was also scanned for a database match. The intention behind the technology was to ensure the radio frequencies could not be stolen. However fingertap had gone out of fashion when amputation found the loophole, and the credit card became reintroduced because the human hand desired its biological evolution. For those who had lost a digit or full hand to the fingertap bank robber gang, it was no consolation that the same entrepreneurs who had invented the fingertap went into the business of manufacturing replacement limbs.

In a world where the human population had bust the ozone, an economy of space became vital to manufacturing. Smaller had reduced to smallest in the material world, and in the millennia since it had taken five-thousand fallen oaks to build a ship, the world had become vastly deforested. Money, insiders at the Federal Reserve joked, did grow on trees. There just weren't any more trees.

8: Philately

Rook peered hard at the black and white ball envelope. The hologram stamp pattern cleanly and seemingly fully planted in the upper right corner of the envelope was similar to the random whorls of biometrics. It was an ornamental pattern, like those found on paper currency to keep them from being copied and counterfeited, combined with the asymmetry of a fingerprint.

Rook commented, "A guilloche."

Angela remarked, "Spirographical."

Rook flinched, thinking again of Millioni, and wondering why she had chosen that word. He said instead, "Exactly. Inexactly."

Angela responded, "On the money, but not on the money." She smiled. Rook gazed at her, concerned about her ability to delight in humor despite their ill circumstance. It was the spontaneous gunshot that kept him trusting her only by a thread, the gunshot to the gown that prevented him from shoving her down and demanding, *Who do you work for*? Rook stared at her, and her smile faded.

Rook zoomed the fingerprint machine controls until the pattern displayed a foot wide on the ECHO screen.

The hologram spastically reiterated in three-dimensional detail. The iridescent whorls and scrolls stabilized, becoming a shady reproduction of *The Age of Reptiles* stamp. Rook zoomed in further and further until the fine lines filled the wall-sized display. A philatelist would be looking for detail such as the production plate number, but Rook was looking for anything. The woven light pattern, viewed from all sides as he increased magnification, finally became not ornamental scrolls, but the reiterated word, *Shadow*.

In Angela's penmanship.

Angela sucked in her breath. Her blue eyes filled with a curious light as his coal eyes searched them.

"A stamp," she said, "is an *impression*. Stamps are imprints. I take it I'm your prime suspect, Rook," Angela said, "Ask me any question you want."

The look he gave her told her he would not.

"Please!" she pleaded, "Maybe I know something."

His words dragged, "Maybe you do."

Angela was a strong woman, a brilliant woman, and a hard woman who softened only inside the brutality of sex. She scanned him. He was not scared. *He's never scared*, she thought, *in front of me*. She took another sip of the raw amber alcohol, and it emboldened her. She said, "If you truly think I have been up to something, it is best for you to keep an eye on me at all times." She traded an accusatory look before shifting her focus to the mannequin head. "Unless you think this Rook would be better at it."

9: Silencing Imagination

Rook made a decision. He had to. "We've been inside the apartment for thirteen minutes, and time is burning." He stood and unlocked a safe stocked with guns and ammunition. He paused, considered a box, then turned to Angela, handing her the box of lethal cartridges as if it were an invitation to kill him. Or herself. Slowly, obediently, she loaded her gun.

-cide: to cut. *Decide:* to cut in two and thereby make a mental split. To cut was to kill. Rook needed to slash a mental sword to divide Agent Orange's knot. He watched Angela's hands, noting the awkward cuffs around her wrists. From a drawer he produced a small electronic tool, and with it he set to cutting through the metal handcuffs still heavy on her wrists. The handcuffs broke off, and Angela thanked him with a glance, then her face fell to his and she tasted the whiskey on his lips. She pulled back, slipped the last bullet into the Z-9 cartridge and slid the cartridge into the grip: it made a satisfying solid click.

"We need to clean up quickly before we go to Tuxedo Park," he said.

"We," she answered gratefully.

He tore her clothes from her in the bathroom. She removed his jacket and unbuttoned his shirt, touching the strange scars that crisscrossed his body at one-inch intervals, within which nanoelectrodes were sewn. He eased her into the clawfoot tub, under frothing hot water.

"You're head," she mused again, touching his blood mucky hair.

"It's nothing," he lied, and he thought of the healing powers of crocodile blood. He glanced at his watch again, glad that time was behaving in a linear fashion. "Five minutes," he admonished her, not trusting her but wanting her sexually just the same.

Agent Orange did not want him to trust her. So, to thwart Agent Orange, by that one thread he felt he still had to.

At the medicine cabinet he jerked out isopropyl rubbing alcohol and cotton, and he momentarily stared at his straight razor. After carefully cleaning his head wound and bullet graze with alcohol, he doused a cotton ball with crocodile blood from the kitchen and dressed his wounds with it. He did not let Angela see this, and he was uncertain as to why he felt so compelled to try it.

He returned to the bathroom, to the open medicine cabinet and to the straight razor. An image surfaced in his mind, of the blade slitting his father's veins, and of the handle in his own hand.

He turned to Angela and found her watching him. "They know about the razor," she said, "and they know about the man who murdered your father as a birthday present, a man who wanted to *impress* you." Her words were etched with fear.

There she was in the tub just as his father had been, and bearded, the fake beard a mockery of the real Van Dyke his father had been sporting when he had been murdered. Rook got onto his knee as if he were going to propose, and with the alcohol and his straight razor, he gently scraped the grotesque fake beard from her chin. The thread of trust vanished, and he trusted nothing, not even himself, as he lifted the razor to her upper lip.

My god, he wondered, *does Agent Orange want me to kill Angela*?

***

All around the apartment then, from the Majestic box, behind the curtains, from open pages of a massive dictionary, from inside the closet—from everywhere—butterflies awoke and fluttered into the air. Across their glossy black and white magazine meets newspaper pulpy page wings emerged the phrase: END GAME!

One alighted on Rook's shoulder without him knowing it. Angela read it with concern and almost alarm as the excruciatingly honed blade scraped the fake hair from her lip.

And as the room filled with butterflies, the phone began to ring again. After three rings it stopped, not making it to the answering machine. After a moment's pause, again it started to ring.

For a brief moment as she watched Rook, Angela imagined him as an actual Rook, as a custom chiseled Rook made out of a synthesis. This synthesis was part human energy, the plasticity of life—and part rock. Silicone meets silica. Rubber meets glass. She imagined his gun organically sewn between his thighs. The first time she had seen him in person she had thought, gunlike. His muscles were like pinstripes, his arms gunstock, his tongue the trigger and the few words he spoke bullets hushed under a silencer. Sex with him was a firing range, and when they went to the firing range together, it was like sex. Gunfire, just like sex, silenced her imagination. Nothing else could.

The phone was ringing and ringing. "Who is this woman?"

Rook was wired on adrenaline, and the approaching midnight timed with his birthday seemed a million years away. Still, he said, "Soon, we will find out."

Pink lightning flashed through the shades, and the celestial boom of thunder crashed. There was no birdsong announcing dawn or dusk in the city hunkered under eternally black clouds, no raven to sing midnight.

CHAPTER SIX: The Big Orange

1: Timing

Rocky Astor contemplated his uncomfortable position, handcuffed and legcuffed inside the submarine now helmed by a man who seemingly had recovered from a gunshot as if it was just a mosquito bite. All of his comrade's mouths had been duct-taped and only eye contact communicated what they otherwise could not. They were not having this.

"And yet you've all been had, haven't you now," Jules Barbillon purred. He scanned the captured men with his golden eyes. "However, by now Dr. Navaja Naranja will have already begun to suspect he has been had as well. Easy enough for him to locate this submarine by sonar and to have his jets blast us. But he won't do it."

Rocky was sick of Jules, but he was the only one still allowed to speak. "Why? Why would he spare us?"

"Because if I die, his world dies with me."

"What's that supposed to mean?"

Jules stared him down, "You are puppets, gentlemen, inside his theater of reality. And I am one of his, you could say, principal directors. Without the directors, reality cannot go on."

"Enough! Enough of your bullshit!" Rocky blasted. "Speak in plain English or don't speak at all!"

"I am speaking in plain English, that is, if you are well versed in Shakespeare. And since your only brush with the Bard is some neologisms on some matchbooks, I expect this to be way over your head."

Jules stepped onto a desk, stared down at his audience, and delivered his lines like a true actor: "'*Sometimes we see a cloud that's dragonish, a vapor like a bear or lion, a towered citadel, a pendant rock, a forked mountain or blue promontory with trees upon't that nod unto the world and mock our eyes with air. Thou hast seen these signs. They are black vesper's pageants. That which is now a horse, even with a thought, the rack dislimms, and makes it indistinct,'"* he paused dramatically and lowered his voice to a growl, *"as water is in water."*

Rocky became pensive, his rubbery lips folding. "I fucking hate Shakespeare."

"Pity."

***

Dr. Naranja was not so much suspicious as anxious that the drama unfolding was too strong a bifurcation from the reiterative drama that kept reality going. "Agent Orange?" he spoke calmly into his wire. Nothing. From the gps tracking chips implanted in his people, he could see the location of Jules under the surface of the river and the location of Agent Orange as she drove north.

Agent Orange was still ignoring him, and he had not heard from Jules. They had both been his guardians and directors of reality, taming it, constraining it —as if it was a pitbull they hoped to domesticate. But he knew at any moment reality could lash out, turn on its own likeness and destroy itself. He whispered a thought, *Just as you turn on me now, reality may turn on you.*

He knew well that Rocky had long intended to destroy his Shakespeare collection, and it was not because he adored the Bard's work that he did everything in his power to keep it from going up in flames. Long ago in the cycle of Seven, those closest to the core of reality understood authors lived on through quantum ink. Years back in the cycles of Seven, he finally confided in Jules—after a long period of cultivating him—it was Shakespeare himself they were keeping alive.

"Shakespeare is our god," he had told Jules.

Jules indignantly responded, "He may be yours but Sobek is mine."

"You will come to understand all gods are one in the same. Shakespeare is Sobek at his most human. As the crocodile within us all, his authoring human self is the most eloquent."

Remembering that conversation, Dr. Navaja Naranja observed the black hole butterflies fluttering from the pages of the folio inside the giant terrarium. *If the only person still with me is my daughter*, he thought, *that may be enough!*

But then he thought of royal rain and librarians. *Ah, yes,* he thought, *as water is in water!*

He pressed a button, opening up a locked space-time shield, exposing a spiral staircase. From here he walked down a flight into his laboratory-library. The shelves were packed with seemingly endless copies of the Bard's work. He took a quantum scalpel to a yellowed paperback, copying the ink, cloning it, until he had a vial of ink just large enough to pen a short phrase. He did not exercise this power of imagination frequently. Anything he authored automatically, quantumly, somewhat uncontrollably, came to life.

He wrote the phrase he had written hundreds of times, pushing down hard and impressing the ink into the paper: *black hole butterfly.*

2: The Thinker

Cosmo Hamilton, Rook's broker, came from a family deeply involved in accurate time measurement. Located on his broker's estate at Tuxedo Park was a literal museum housing his extensive collection of timepieces. There, men who had played chess with Rook's father were the fathers of time and clock research and development. Early on they discerned even gravity's effect on time and employed clockmakers throughout the world to improve their mechanisms. Cosmo's family courted prominent scientists, romancing them with the park's sprawling acres and access to the unlimited funding at their private lab. Cosmo's family also courted Rook's father, who had once played chess even with Einstein at the upstate lab. Afterwards they had smoked cigars, sipped cognac and discussed the Einstein-Rosen bridge, which later was coined a space-time *wormhole*. During Rook's adult life the wormhole theory evolved into fantastic quantum theories about the nature of space-time, and it was concluded that the universe was a veritable junkyard of black holes. The black holes were omnipresent mouths, just like the Oroboros virus code, swallowing the universe in an imperceptible feedback loop. It was all theory, and no one involved in its complex mathematics was remotely interested in figuring out how to make a buck out of it.

Eventually of course the force of capitalism did.

***

Cosmos stared at the black hole chamber in the center of his lab and regretted his role in developing Rook's wristwatch. *We have been playing God*, he thought, *and we are merely bastards*. On an old record player he positioned a waltz album. As the entire horn assembly rotated with a needle around the disc, *The Blue Danube* gently lilted through the room, smothering the ticking of clocks and the beating of his heart.

***

Rook and Angela fucked for a quick and hard minute after bathing, the white sheets staining with blood speckles from both of them. He rocked meanly in and out of her as if it could be the last time, and afterward they lay like sleepy slashes for another minute. Angela, exhausted, shut her eyes, and Rook, reaching for his gun, allowed himself momentarily to refresh by dipping into an alpha state bordering on theta. Their bodies seemed imprisoned by the bars of light and shadow filtering in from the decorative iron window gates beyond the shades. Around them the newspaper butterflies quietly fluttered, casting their shadows down on the two as well. The shadow patterns shifted and stretched across their nude bodies, consolidating into a figure. When Rook lifted his head to a sound, he thought he saw a shadow on his chest posed like Rodin's *The Thinker*. He snapped his neck and gave the room a hard look. *No*, he thought, *just a hypnogogic dream*—a light trace of dream into reality. He stared at a single butterfly that flew in a delicate arc over him, and somehow it seemed to him that reality was becoming more and more like a hypnogogic dream and a butterfly. *Evolution*, he thought. *Can reality evolve?*

On the wall opposite the bed was a print of the painting *The Nightmare* by Fuseli. Within it a sleeping woman's chest was burdened by a small diabolical beast, posed somewhat Rook had thought like *The Thinker*.

Rook thought further, *Can reality think?*

***

Through the beast's eyes in the painting, Agent Orange watched in her helmet monitor as Rook raised himself, scratched an itch on his jaw with the butt of his gun and walked carefully through the airborne butterflies toward a phone. Traffic had thinned. She revved her motorcycle speed up to 160 miles per hour. The night blurred into gray and black stripes around her just like the synthetic reality rushing through her veins. She had introduced Rook's reality into her own body in small doses. The biomimetic nanoacids—nanoDNA—contained quantum memory. When they bonded to the nanoelectrodes embedded in her body, she took a ghostly ride on Rook. She never injected a heavy dose, one that would allow her to visit his reality in a druggy, dreamy jackin' the butterfly state. She injected his reality only to entrain with him. In the quantum realm, they were literally joined at the hip.

She could feel their quantum connection intensifying. As she observed in her mini monitors Rook walking to a phone, she knew in her hips—where the bones joined to her vertebrae, spinal cord and brain—he was starting to figure it out.

The gentle blonde beard she grew, like peach fuzz, was the hermaphroditic affect of the testosterone latent in his DNA. If Operation: Push the Envelope was to succeed, she would finally have to succumb to a massive dose of his DNA, and she could not get it by spilling his blood. She would have to get it the way Angela got it—or almost got it. The condom would have to go away.

They too were cosmically entrained. If he died, so would she. But if she could keep him alive inside her, she believed—as did Dr. Naranja—she could save their world.

And she wanted more than anything to live. To achieve this, she needed his semen.

She needed to become, this very night, pregnant.

She arched lower on her motorcycle, the orange leather seat sliding between her thighs a pleasurable foreplay of the acutely engineered, sexually charged, Black and White Ball.

3: Forgery

Rook placed a call to Cosmo. It barely rang once.

"Yes?"

"Are you alright, Cosmo?"

"Yes."

Rook swallowed, "Ramp up security."

"Why?"

"Because…" Rook struggled for the right answer, "Because I am coming to see you. Now. Somebody has found out."

"I understand."

"I'll see you soon." Rook gently hung up. He glanced back to Angela, who leaned up on an elbow and said to him, "Knock knock?" She lifted herself, walked to the closet and pulled out the white gown. "You're not going to say?"

He answered slowly, "The clue cards laid out in front of the headless dummy feature these images: a photo of me just prior to taking a blow in a warehouse in East Orange, a Van Dyke beard, the reptile stamp, the mannequin, the lingerie, the Agent Orange graffiti insignia, the ball invitation and the phrase *shadow* in your handwriting. Handwriting is biometric—a unique a shadow of the writing hand. It could be used to identify an individual. And yet your handwriting is forged, correct?"

She unzipped the gown, "To forge is to copy. The dummy is a copy. The beard is a copy." Butterflies flittered around her, and she focused on them, "The newspaper butterflies are copies." She turned to him, "What else is being forged?"

"Aside from the obvious association to money, forgery is also smith work. Blacksmithery. We can't leave that out."

Rook licked at his knuckles, tasting the iron metal of his blood. *Blood and grass are being forged by Dr. Chess,* he thought, *blood and grass are metallic!* He definitely did not want to share this particular thought. He thought again of Dr.

Chess and Weedkiller, his memory blanking the further he receded down the path. If it was the strange blow to his head that was numbing him, he decided he would, through sheer willpower, recover. *Are space and time*, he thought, *being forged?*

Rook hated this lull toward midnight. He expanded his watchband and slipped the watch onto his left wrist, adjusting it. In the illuminated face comprised of miniature red light emitting diodes, he watched the hands tick and tock and listened to the sound: *tick tock*. His mind echoed, *Knock knock.*

Rook murmured, "Why are magazines both periodicals and bullets?" He inferred with her background in literature and her extensive knowledge of etymology, she would know.

She turned to him again, "They are both chambers. Rooms. Storerooms, originally, for a variety of ammunition. Analogously, a periodical provides a variety of material."

"Both can be explosive," he responded.

She nodded, and said as she witnessed a butterfly landing on his shoulder, "Headlines."

Rook remembered with a startle the paper pulp vomit he had found in Dr. Chess's lab, and he thought of the headline screaming about his father's murder that had been issued nineteen years prior. *Did I conflate the two?*

Like the magazine clipping and bullets from a gun magazine inside the mannequin head, Rook knew he was in on Agent Orange's crime somehow. *The crime is inside my own head, and even mentally I'm somehow in on Agent Orange's impeccable timing*. Rook touched a nanoelectrode terminal under his scalp, and he thought of the surgical scars crisscrossing his skin under his hair. *Headlines*, he thought, *head-lines*.

He thought about the warehouse and the neuroelectricity that had slammed him into a seizure. He thought about the storehouse for Van Dykes, Coney Island Fantasy and of the Majestic store. He thought about comic books, and through all of these thoughts blazed one vivid color: hunter orange.

The city originally had been nicknamed The Big Apple under mysterious histories. *The Big Apple*, he thought, *really has become The Big Orange*. He imagined a wormhole in an orange, like the navel of a child umbilically attached to a mother universe, like the navel orange he had dreamed about during his meditation session after his return from East Orange. Rook let his mind drift, creating nonsensical rebus phrases from the clues. It was another way to jar discovery and make quantum leaps of thought. Quantum leaps: that was what he called the moment of surprise, when two seemingly unconnected clues connected. That was when lateral thinking bridged from one side of the universe to another through some kind of mental wormhole.

In his watch the second hands ticked and pushed the minute hands back and forth, emitting red flashes as it did. It was April 22nd, and Rook's birthday was less than an hour away.

***

Cosmo listened as the sound of motorcycle engines hummed their way into his ears within the lulling *Blue Danube*. He felt lightheaded, and he smelled a sweet odor.

Then he smiled, laughed and began to dance.

4: Shaving

As he lathered up shaving cream in a black porcelain mug, Rook contemplated his father's murder. He brushed the lather onto his face with a badger-hair brush, and for a pensive minute he stropped the pearl-handled straight blade against a fat leather ribbon. The leather was attached by one end to a towel bar. Rook held one end of the leather in his left hand and stropped, stroking the razor back and forth with his right. His whole body was a registry of the meticulous exercise of shaving with a straight blade. The razor blade was ornamented with meaningless antique frill, hearkening to times when people had time, time to engrave blades and time to shave. There were laser shavers on the market and had been for years, but for Rook the practice of honing and refining the dangerous razor edge was a meditation. One slip, and he could cut his own throat.

After the emulsified cream had softened his nascent stubble he dabbed more onto his face and, with the very same straight blade used to murder his father, Rook neatly shaved. The blade stroked his cheeks, leaving behind a shadowy Van Dyke. He rinsed the remaining lather from his face and rubbed the faint beard in satisfaction.

Rook rinsed the blade clean and carefully closed it before austerely setting it back in the medicine cabinet. Around him jittery newspaper butterflies wafted.

Agent Orange presumably knew the full details of his father's sensational murder and probably knew Rook still coveted both the straight blade and the ritual of shaving.

The edgy evening itself seemed sliced by stillness. When he stepped back into the bedroom, he witnessed Angela, naked, contemplating the Majestic box that had been delivered earlier, the one holding her lingerie. "This was the lingerie I was wearing when I was kidnapped. Agent Orange would have been able to get my exact measurements for the gown from these. The gown is custom." She added in a falter, "I wasn't raped. They were women, I could tell somehow by the feel of their hands. I was blindfolded the whole time, and I never saw anyone."

5: Tuxedo

Rook examined the suits hanging in his closet. They all looked exactly the same except they were now covered with butterflies. Rook Black was his own brand of man, and all of his clothing was bespoken. He had only the one tuxedo, and though it was not quite bespoken it had been tailor made. Rook took the tuxedo by the hanger and lifted it out of the closet, unsettling the several butterflies that had come to rest on it. Accompanying, tucked inside the jacket, was a shiny vest woven of alternating black and dark gray harlequin diamonds. Rook stood naked, and he contemplated briefly the natural history of the formal suit.

At a spring ball 129 years prior, the tuxedo suit had been tailored, derived from shortening the long tailcoat. The complete suit eventually became the signature formal evening wear of the exclusive Tuxedo Club members, and eventually it took its name therefrom. The club's men who first wore the black suits enjoyed blind chess and idly invented the atomic bomb. They were the gentlemen of war. Rook's father had been a member of the club.

The members had huddled together upstate from the city in the Village of Tuxedo Park, where an eccentric billionaire—a Wall Street tycoon—had built his own formidable and private science lab. A fan of Rook's father, the eccentric billionaire had invited him to play blind chess with him frequently and thus had indoctrinated him into his curious and powerful world. The billionaire had invented the electroencephalograph, had fabricated numerous clocks and radar machines and even godfathered cyclotrons. All of the machinery had laid the foundation for proving and disproving esoteric cosmic quantum theories. Rook's broker retained the original electroencephalograph machine in his Tuxedo Park glass house, which formerly had been the residence of the inventor. As a young man Rook and his father had experimented with the brainwave machine while playing blind chess—it was where he had first studied his own brainwaves.

He understood Agent Orange wanted him to revisit his past, his broker and his tuxedo. She was breaking the rules of his game and forcing him into hers.

While Angela fluffed into the white dress he stepped into his tuxedo. It was simple, black. The white shirt was classic with ribs and black buttons, and it was only the shiny vest that flashed. Angela assisted with his cuff links: two small hand-carved ivory rooks.

"Let's go," he said.

6: Knock Knock

Rook made his way to the office and poured himself a quick whiskey. The drive to Tuxedo Park, he knew, would take approximately forty-five minutes. He glimpsed through the window, spotting the twin sedan still parked silently out on the street. He inferred it would be their way up north. Rook tasted the whiskey and turned his attention to the Coney Island Fantasy box. Inside was the Masculiner Deluxe Van Dyke kit, the black rubber mask crowned with the gun turret characteristic of a rook and the two pairs of bulls-eye contact lenses.

"These are custom also," he said. He lifted out the contact lenses and stared at them hard. There was something organic about them, as if they were made of iris tissue.

As the whiskey taste thinned, Rook's nostrils drew open, and he froze. He turned and his eyes swept the antiquated hardcopy books kept on a shelf. He exhaled and slowly breathed in a dank smell that seemed to be intensifying by the second, just like the butterflies. He drew closer to the books, focusing on the old book smell and spotting one thing amiss: a thick volume of Shakespearean tragedies was now plowed between forensic blood spatter studies. He glanced over it closely but did not touch it. Rook was not a casual reader. His knowledge was a mishmash of tangential curiosities gleaned during his investigations, and the words he read were embedded in research. The rustle of Angela's dress pushed into the room. She was zipped tight into it, the bullet hole mocking her heart. It was 11:09 p.m.

"This book was not here before," he told her in a clipped whisper.

She narrowed her eyes and puzzled. "I know," she said under her breath, "in fact," she took it from the shelf by its edges, opened up the cover and glanced over the title page, "it's mine."

The odor of yellowed paper wafted around them and both reeled.

Rook observed the title page, on which was scripted her signature and dated April 23rd, six years prior. Rook grabbed his shoulder holster and rapidly cinched it in place. He jammed his gun into it and began filling his inner jacket pockets with ammunition.

Briefly, reading his paranoia, Angela seemed to pale into her dress.

"Knock knock jokes have their origin," she told him in a hushed confession, "in Shakespeare's *Macbeth*."

Rook placed a palm over her mouth and leaned into her ear, "Quiet."

"It would seem to me," Angela quickly whispered into his ear, "I am the one being framed. They are pitting me against you."

She flipped slowly through pages and leaned in again to whisper, "I haven't seen this in years. I had donated it to the Central Library, and I was looking for it the day I met you."

"Then why were you in the forensics section?"

"When the librarians couldn't find the book, I simply continued with my other research."

Rook observed her darkly, "Why were you looking for your own book?"

She wagged her head indecisively. "It was just a flash of nostalgia, that's all." She looked into his eyes, regarded his suspicion, and explained further, "I donated most of my books. I wanted them protected."

“From what?”

Angela regarded him again. “From the ravages of time. What else?”

Rook had read some of Shakespeare's plays when he was young, and he remembered suddenly the reference to crocodile tears in *Othello*. The language was impressive to him but the plays dull. Now looking at a play he thought he must have read many years prior, he was impressed by the fact no one really knew who the author was. Only six accounts of Shakespeare's signature had been found, and each one was different. *Signatures*, he thought. Angela's signature was now a recurring theme, as if she too were a ghostwriter—a shadow writer. *From this book Agent Orange could have plotted her handwriting.*

But how did she know about it?

He glanced over at the orange box addressed in his forged handwriting.

The phone began ringing and again the answering machine picked up. Agent Orange's voice pushed into the room, "It's time to go, Rook. And have her bring the book, won't you?" Click.

Rook and Angela locked eyes. His jacket heavy with surplus ammunition, he slipped into it then grabbed the orange box and invitation. He peered through the peephole. Seeing no sign of any Marco Polo drivers, mailmen or anyone else suspicious, he opened the door.

Out in the night they were far less than two well-kempt, attractive people en route to a ball. Their bruises and scratches were pink and puffy, and Angela's cheeks were raw from the removal of the fake facial hair. But the average pedestrians still ignored them. In New York City, anything went.

Rook's keys easily opened the sedan doors as if it really was the original. He tossed the box in, his anger brittle. Angela slipped in, the bullet hole in the breast remarking the poignant state of her heart.

And her heart of all things was something Rook, with his internal black tattoo cardiovascular muscle, gave no thought.

"Look," she pointed up at a streetlamp, its ornate metal scrolling into the illuminated globe. It was covered with the butterflies. She glanced down the street. "They are everywhere!"

***

Cosmo opened the glass door to Agent Orange and her dozen. He said, “I have to admit, I have an uneasy feeling something is going to go awry.”

“You’re right.”

The gang shot past her and wrestled him inside.

7: Dr. Chess

Dr. William Shakespeare Chess, his hoary plume like the smoke from a just extinguished match, removed his white lab coat and rolled up the sleeve of his white shirt. He tapped the vein in the crook of his arm and did not wince as he slipped the point of the needle in. The clear tube running down from the liter of crimson crocodile blood rushed red, and the doctor patiently sat in silence as he transfused the blood into his system. He inserted another needle into the vein in his right arm, fumbling with his left hand only momentarily. His human blood slipped into an empty bag hanging adjacent to the crocodile blood.

His colleagues had for the most part given up on the man, writing him off as a loon. Only one had paid any recent attention to him, the Ningbo, Zhejiang affiliate named Dr. Cheng, and it was Dr. Cheng who had surreptitiously placed a business card for the Lucky Dead Pawn shop in his palm the week prior. "The solution to the invasive weeds can be found here," Dr. Cheng had said.

As was his habit, Dr. Chess had lifted the card to his large, long nose scarred with tight blue veins, and he had sniffed about it in search of its essence. It smelled vaguely of a meat and a citrus, by which he inferred Dr. Cheng had eaten lunch in Chinatown and washed his hands with citrus scented antibacterial soap. And still the card had smelled of something else, of a decay. How a pawnshop could help him, he could not fathom, but the Chinese were both crafty and legendary for using common businesses as fronts. He decided to find out.

On his way to Pell Street, he had passed a tiny restaurant named Ningbo, and on the menu he discovered a dish named rock sugar turtle. He thought perhaps that was the suspicious meat and made a mental note to order some to go after he investigated the pawnshop.

When he found the Lucky Dead Pawn, he sniffed the air and catalogued the street in his olfactory memory. He hit the intercom buzzer and was surprised to hear Dr. Cheng's familiar voice crackle through the intercom, "Welcome." The door lock buzzer sounded, and he pushed into the dark hallway. He made four uncertain steps down when the door quickly groaned and slammed shut behind him. He felt the butt of a gun in his back.

Dr. Cheng said, "Keep moving."

Inside the dim pawnshop Dr. Chess blinked at the muted gray displays. A small warm light flooded on, and he was pushed toward it by the gun. "What is the meaning of this?" he demanded as if someone was merely asking for a cup of sugar at two in the morning.

As he breathed in, cataloging the essence of the shop, he smelled with some certainty the yellowing of paper—of oxidized lignin: a chemical compound found in all vascular plants.

A shadow moved into the space, and it spoke, "Come closer." As the words filled the stale air, it became even more rank with the old paper smell, and Dr. Chess realized it was the odor of the shadow man's breath. He stepped closer at the insistence of the gun and gazed down at a large antique volume, a collection of Shakespearean tragedies, encased under a large bell glass. The shadow man's dark, vague hand reached down and lifted the lid. A foul odor, like a corpse made of pulp, blasted Dr. Chess's hypersensitive nostrils. The man gasped.

"You are on the verge of discovering that reality is a weed, Dr. Chess," Dr. Cheng said in his pinched, high-toned but perfect English, "and we can't have that."

An hour later Dr. Chess was an addict, lying on his back on the shadow man's opium den lohan couch, vividly hallucinating he was Shakespeare, vividly inking onto parchment a passage from *Macbeth*.

The stinking shadow man hovered over him, lacing his body with nanoelectrodes and injecting his own dark essence into him. Dr. Chess, in the aftermath, vomited vascular pulp all over his white shirt. When they dropped the dazed man back off at his lab he could barely crawl.

Like a grafted ghost yet to give up, in the quantum murk of space and time, Dr. Chess opened his laboratory fridge and retrieved a bagged liter of blood. He had named the synthetic crocodile blood he had invented *The Assassin* because it could kill just about anything. Transfusing it into his own circulatory system now was a near desperate attempt to kill the addiction plaguing him. As the vomiting ceased, he prayed, *Dear Lord, please deliver me soon from this wormy evil and forgive me this sin. I have played God, but I am not even a man.*

***

At the Marco Polo Lounge the waiter delivered dessert to Mr. Millioni. The blood orange was cut in half, and its juices were as red as freshly spilled blood. Millioni licked it, tasted the metallic flavor and thought, *Delicious.* Unexpected shouting issued from the entry as the maître d' relented and backed down from a large mailman. Millioni observed the intrusion quietly.

The brusque machine gun armed mailman spotted him sitting in a red leather booth. He stomped over, and in a voice like a dungeon reverberating with bass he stated, "Mr. Millioni."

On the table he set a black envelope, identical to the invitation delivered to Rook, except it bore an orange wax seal of an A surrounded by an O.

Millioni nodded in acceptance. The mailman set down one other small package: a clear box encasing a lollipop. Millioni nodded again. As the mailman retreated, Millioni rose and walked through stainless steel swinging doors into the kitchen. Through an underground chamber he made his way to an exit. Now risen from the depths of the East River one of his triplets strode toward him. The two stopped, embracing with a quick brotherly arm around one another's back. Each brother shared the same legal name on his New York City identification card. This had always kept things simple for any work requiring only facial recognition. Each otherwise played a very different role in their operations and substituted for one another only when necessary. Aside from the formal legal name, each held a unique moniker reflecting his role.

Weedkiller's distinct role would make an abrupt bifurcation this night. While he slipped into an untraceable gas-guzzler, his brother, nicknamed The Accountant, took his seat at the table in the lounge. He began to eat the orange.

The other brother, nicknamed Tank, watched surveillance feeds of Tuxedo Park from his office.

It was not that they had come into existence overnight by any means, rather that through the accelerating quantum cycles of Seven, by a power of three, their realities were maturing such as to make their appearances in New York City seem overnightly. Their Silk Road DNA, now woven with a youthful sample from the lollipop boy, was literally weaving a silken net into the black hole butterfly transforming their universe.

There was no means as yet that would allow them to articulate this.

In its own way, wanting to be heard, their universe was becoming not just a swallowing mouth, but one that would soon, if initially only though ink, make itself read.

Then heard.

The rain lashing the city, quietly, began to murmur the word: ink.

The murmur enfolded in clanking city sounds: radiator pipes, jangling keys, a rap on a metal door. In the perpetual ticking of clocks and watches it synchronized the pulse of its Shakespearean rebirth.

8: Shakespeare's Birthday

Rook surveyed the vinyl interior of the sedan. It was a perfect duplicate, down to the cracks in the dash. *Cosmo could not have sent this*, he thought, *there's no way he could be involved. Unless... Unless he too is kidnapped.* That made sense. *The other duplicate sedan, the one that crashed in Brooklyn, perhaps that one was the fake.*

Rook had not had any time to observe that sedan's details, especially not through a shattering windshield.

On the ill-lamped street, the light choked off by the clustering butterflies, Rook fired up the engine. They pulled off into the night, two chess pieces in search of a chess ball. It was 11:14 p.m.

"You and Shakespeare have the same birthday," Angela said.

Rook was instantly irritated. "That's the only thing we have in common. I'm a man of few words. He's is a man of—a million."

A million. Rook's mind halted over the world million, remembering Mr. Millioni, the exaggerated man. He knew that Shakespeare had also allegedly died on the same day he was born, on an April 23rd. Rook wondered if the omen was also his fate to share, but the gas in the tank needled high, enough for a round trip. It seemed there was a possibility of coming back home, though Rook knew there was no going back to the life he had enjoyed.

Angela located the knocking texts and read them aloud to him.

> *"'Here's a knocking indeed! If a man were porter of hell-gate, he should have old turning the key. Knock Knock, knock, knock, knock! Who's there, i' the name of*

Belzebub? Here's a farmer that hanged himself on th' expectation of plenty. Come in time! Have napkins enow about you; here you'll sweat for't. Knock
Knock, knock! Who's there, in th' other devil's name? Faith, here's an equivocator that could swear in both the scales against either scale, who committed treason enough for God's sake, yet could not equivocate to heaven. O, come in, equivocator. Knock
Knock, knock, knock! Who's there? Faith, here's an English tailor come hither, for stealing out of a French hose. Come in, tailor; here you may roast your goose. Knock
Knock, knock! Never at quiet! What are you? But this place is too cold for hell. I'll devil-porter it no further. I had thought to have let in some of all professions, that go the primrose way to the everlasting bonfire. Knock
Anon, anon! I pray you, remember the porter.'"

The sedan slid down an avenue into the neon wash of towering, skyscraper-high advertisements, into the Times Square glitz that had engulfed the entire city for years. Angela watched him closely, awaiting his response, but he did not share.

Five words had jumped at Rook like dogs: *porter, hell-gate, equivocator, farmer* and *tailor*. Knock knock jokes were equivocative, using words to give them a dual sense even when they did not explicitly contain that duality within them. *Orange* slurred into *tangent* for Rook. A tangent was something that merely touched on a curve, and the word tangent included all of the letters for *agent,* only missing the letters o and r from *orange*. Rook free-associated further: the letter *o*, he knew, most likely came from a hieroglyph representing the eye, and the letter *r* from the head. That, he realized, was symbolically encrypted in the bulls-eye markings on the mannequin's eyes and within the bulls-eye contact lenses. The hell-gate that had been graffitied onto the tunnel and the Van Dyke, both were essentially hell-gates also: mouths of an oroboros.

Tangentially, it meant to him that the black and white ball invitation was an invitation to a black hole, to an event horizon.

Blackmail, he thought.

It was at Tuxedo Park that Rook and Cosmo had first discovered how to replicate black holes. *And now*, he realized with a dull mental ache, *Agent Orange knows this*. He knew the Chinese had replicated the technology, but he also knew their replicates were unstable as hell.

If Agent Orange has infiltrated Tuxedo Park, she has the real deal in her hands. And with it she can bend, shapeshift and cultivate reality.

The sedan slipped west, toward the Hudson. *Am I really driving us of my own free will to Tuxedo Park, or is reality driving us there?* He felt the desire to pull his hands off the wheel just to see what could happen.

Lit walls of information from the sky rises splashed down onto the sedan's black glossy hood, spastically shifting from one rainbow-colored electric string of Oroboros code to another. For a slanting second, Rook saw mirrored in the sedan's paint the phrase, *knock knock.* It snarled and dissipated. His glance shot upwards, searching the illuminated city signs, but already the phrase had faded.

He glanced at Angela, who did not seem to have noticed.

"Read the passage again," he requested quietly.

She swallowed, nodded and bent her face over the page. This time, as she read, Rook kept his eyes on the miles of signs walling the city. As she spoke the very words of the passage began spattering into the illuminated signage across the city for as far as his eye could see. *The sedan's bugged*, he realized. Everything they said was being broadcast and looped into a now quickly evolving Oroboros code.

The same, he realized, *would have been true back at the apartment, at Coney Island Fantasy and everywhere else I go. It's elemental to how Agent Orange is timing everything.*

Via quantum feedback.

Means Agent Orange has also cracked the Oroboros code. She's hacking it with analog information extracted from me.

Rook's nerves slit to an edgy fire in honor of the anarchic beauty of it.

Somehow Agent Orange has forged a super Oroboros code.

Rook requested, "Read the passage again, more loudly."

This time when she did she followed his intense scrutiny. She paused, stunned, witnessing the Shakespearean text manifesting, sized dozens of stories high and shimmering throughout the city walls.

"'*English tailor come hither*,'" she recited, watching in amazement as the phrase exploded in light and reiterated, dazzling the entire island into stitches of text and light.

Along with this came a smell, infusing the entire island as if a gas main had broken, except it was the odor of yellowed paper.

Rook remembered, *Something smells!*

He hit the gas, pushing the sedan further north along the West Side Highway. He inferred Angela was the porter, as it was she who was opening the door to this tangential crime. He savored the words of the passage in his imagination, remembering his graffitied car, the hell-gate graffitied tunnel, and inside the word graffiti he saw the word *graft*. Grafting was used in horticulture but it was also a form of corruption, of political insider trading.

Agent Orange is the opposite of a farmer, of a Dr. Chess, Rook thought, *of a Dr. William Shakespeare Chess.*

"Graft," Rook uttered, and the word burst in brilliant orange light seven miles long, erupting like the fire that had condemned the sedan in Brooklyn. It dazzled golden and drifted down the city skyscraper screens like bewildered fireworks sputtering toward earth.

He remembered somehow, in a memory ripe with darkness, Agent Orange was tied at the spine to Weedkiller. Their crimes were somehow entwined.

Angela watched the golden lights shunt to darkness and regenerate back into the flow of more stable Oroboros information that decorated the city like a macrocosmic candy store. She desperately wanted to know what he was thinking, why he had said that word, but she knew there should be no more words between them for the duration of the ride. She smelled the musty odor of the book and the city, and she held back the desire to gag.

Rook was thinking about thinking. He remembered the illusion of *The Thinker* sitting on his chest. Rodin's *Thinker* was a sculpture of Dante at the gates of hell and originally had been named *The Poet*. The piece had been commissioned by the Musée des Arts Décoratifs in Paris to create a monumental portal for the entry to the museum—a museum that housed around 30,000 costumes. Rook knew. He had been there.

What was he thinking? He squinted and rolled the steering wheel, switching lanes. The city signs washed into an almost mirage as another thunderstorm slammed the island.

Rook was thinking about the wallpaper in the Marco Polo Motel. He was just remembering it.

And inside the motel room desk, instead of a copy of the Bible, there had been a copy of the travels of Marco Polo. The book had smelled, he remembered, of old paper.

Rook's investigations had made his internal library of social cross-references so profound that he knew well the identities of the world's most powerful players. As the years had passed, in a way, he had become a serious player of global human nature. It was almost as if he could predict who would commit a crime within a time frame, and the more he learned about how to navigate event horizons, the more he really could. Strangely neither Weedkiller nor Agent Orange had been on his mental radar at all, yet both now became the only people he could think about as he desperately tried to place them. *Agent Orange could simply default to destroying me, but she isn't. Is the invitation to the ball an invitation to graft within her operation or a demand from her that she graft within mine?*

He formed another lateral puzzle in his mind: *A detective finds an invitation to a black and white ball in his mailbox, signed by forged handwriting. Inside his office a dummy head has its eyes decorated as bulls-eyes with a bullet shot through each. The head is mounted on a wall like a trophy, and in his library is a copy of a Shakespearean tragedy. What crime does Agent Orange want to commit?*

This time even his thoughts attuned to the city lights. They rushed with pulsating orange light, and the entire city, for a long moment, erupted into a beacon of bright orange.

Good god, Rook thought, as he realized Agent Orange had even invaded the nanoelectrodes embedded under his skin. For a lengthy moment stretched like balloon skin, he was afraid to think.

Around the city pedestrians were awed by the walls of uniform orange light washing over them. They had never seen anything like it. Every screen—everywhere—was awash with orange. The surface of the Hudson, gyrating toward the Atlantic, reflected and twisted the phenomenon. Rook and Angela observed the transfixed pedestrians as they uniformly looked up, as if they expected to herald a long-forgotten sunrise.

Are Agent Orange and Weedkiller working to kill the Oroboros? Rook wondered quickly as if the thought was a hurdle. *Are they using me to do it?*

The Oroboros did grow like a weed. It was invasive.

Or did it invade me?

"Knock?" Rook uttered, prompting again the feedback phenomenon. The letters literally rapped at the hell-gate that was the city, smashing in Courier font across the screens, replacing all of the orange with simple black on white. Slowly Rook echoed, "*Knock.*" The way he emphasized the word the second time suggested it was the answer.

The gigantic letters of the word *knock* spontaneously doubled, one layered over the other. The second tilted as a shadow stretching ten miles long down the buildings on the West Side Highway. Citizens everywhere puzzled over the phenomenon. Angela drew in her breath with wonder.

Huddled in the sedan, Rook and Angela passed by a utility truck parked at an intersection and manned by workers dressed in reflective safety orange. From out of a manhole they tugged a writhing, four-foot long saltwater crocodile, one of the many that had escaped into the underground utility system. Rook turned an eye to Angela. He was not certain yet that she would not knock him off nor that he would have any other option but to take her life. That was not anything he wanted to consider.

Rook answered his puzzle under a silent tongue: *knockoff.*

The crime is a forged code, a knockoff.

It's brilliant!

And with that thought, the word *knock*, now stretching across the city, folded into itself, reiterating into a gigantic, inky digital and infinitely looping butterfly.

***

In Dr. Chess's lab, the man rested as the synthetic crocodile blood circulated through his body. He believed he felt much better and was convinced the gnawing desire to vividly fantasize he was in fact William Shakespeare the great Bard was over. As his heart pumped and the antibodies in the new blood attacked the DNA the shadow man had injected into him, he slowly found the obsession replaced with a new one: to transfuse even more blood.

He walked slowly to his cooler, opened it, thought for a moment about the choice he was making, and he reached in for another liter of synthetic blood.

***

Inside his gas-guzzling limousine, Millioni aka Weedkiller observed a freshly wrapped lollipop. He removed the wrapper, absorbed the commands and slipped a single bullet into his .22.

CHAPTER SEVEN: Tuxedo Park

1: Tuxedo Park

Black and white balls had been around seemingly as long as the urge to dance had become formalized in the masquerade. In the crisp clash of shadow against hue, black and white clothing reduced a world of fancy to simple contrast. The first color photograph, curiously enough, had captured as its subject a Tartan ribbon necktie. Prior to that there had been only black and white photos of a world not black and white. Woodcuts, etches and prints were comprised of black and white. Color was simply too grand, grotesque and lurid in anything except reality.

And so in suits tailored from cloth made of midnight and noon, the immanent power of the tuxedo was born.

The word *tuxedo* was Native American in origin, and over the years it had morphed itself into an aristocratic noun. There was something about the sound of the word, of the way the *tux* slid into the torp*edo* ending. The word tuxedo became an English firecracker sizzling when the tongue hit the consonant *x*. Linguists battled over what the word had meant in the language of the native Lenape—*lake* or *wolf*—or perhaps even unspectacularly: *round footed.* Regardless the word had shed its mundane origin and taken on the life of the moneyed. Lake Tuxedo itself conjured images not of wolves but of men in black suits and white shirts informally discussing split-second timing and quantum physics.

Rook's broker had always lived in Tuxedo Park, and Rook had come to Cosmo's profound attention when he was only seventeen and sleuthing his first crime: the murder of his own father.

Rook's father had died at the young age of forty-eight. A suicide note had been left behind. It had read, "Enough of this world, so black, so white. I tire of being Number One."

2: Number One

Young Rook had noticed right away—beyond the absurdity of the suicide refrain—there was something alien about the note. His father had dabbled in writing what he admitted was bad poetry, a vain attempt to water the garden of his mind in which grew mostly only mathematical equations. The suicide note was in his father's handwriting, but somehow it wasn't. It was as if someone had been holding his father's hand when it was penned—or a gun to his head. The handwriting was sending a message, and a Morse code of urgency tapped within the angled lettering. Whoever had murdered his father had not been smart enough to examine closely a writing sample. Just as Rook's own chess notations were publicly cataloged, his father's were publicly celebrated in displays at the National Chess Society Library, and they were reprinted widely in numerous books. Rook's father's writing angled to the right, as is symptomatic of right-handers. In the suicide note the lettering angled upright. It was a clear signal to Rook the note had been written under duress or by a poor copycat. The autopsy however did not reveal any drugs or poisons in his father's system.

At Rook's insistence it could not be a suicide, the police department focused the possible murder investigation.

On him.

Rook had no strong alibi. He had been sitting by himself in a dark room in the very same house, in fact meditating a murder, though he had told them instead he was playing blind chess by himself. They did not have a clue, they insisted, as to what blind chess was.

"Sure you weren't masturbating, kid?"

"Mentally, yes. Physically, no."

When he was done with his blind chess game, he told them, he heard the shower water running. Not wanting to disturb his father, he left without saying anything and took the train to the Manhattan Chess Club where he gamed throughout the night, admittedly drank, admittedly spent the night with a woman twice his age who worked at the club—she confirmed—and returned late the following day.

His birthday.

Again, he heard the water running, and he assumed his father was simply back in the bath for his daily washing. He took a nap, and when he awoke, he understood something was very wrong.

In the dense humidity of the bathroom, the corpse was already bloating and gassy.

"Why would he commit suicide the day before your birthday?" They wanted to know.

Rook didn't know. Couldn't believe it.

A detective theorized the old man must have been suffering from an inferiority complex. After all, his son was expected to succeed him as chess champion.

Pondering a murderer's motive, the first question Rook asked himself was, *Why?* Chess was viciously competitive, and whoever had chosen physically to destroy his father had chosen to destroy the competition. Without the competition, there would be no more games. Behind his world champion father, Rook was the primary grandmaster in the world of chess, and with his father's death Rook vaulted to number one. While the police considered him the prime suspect, exploring the possibility of rivalry, Rook explored the personality of the chess master who had been rated number three. The man, a Polish recluse, having miraculously made a public appearance at a concerto during the murder, had a tight alibi, and Rook quickly dismissed various other chess-related suspects. There had to be more to it.

Rook, apprenticing under his father, had extensively studied the Federal Reserve, the Treasury and the technology behind the new synthetic currency. The Federal Reserve had access at that time only to a minor database consisting of paper transaction history. The database tracked the history of bill serial numbers voluntarily entered by consumers into a non-government website. Eventually the government seized the information, and Rook's father had pored through it, studying velocity patterns and paying close attention to abrupt bifurcations to indicate fraud. The data was too meager, and Rook's father had suggested to the

Federal Reserve that synthetic currency start from scratch.

During the currency revolution, as it then was called, when value had to be reinvented, it was thought the ability to trace all commerce would contribute to literal definitions of money. It was information that chiefs at the Federal Reserve had thought would be valuable in predicting trade, but Rook knew the massive proliferation of data had simply contributed to misinformation.

Economists were always after the minds of the poker players and the chess geniuses who had come of age playing games in public parks around the city. Like-minded economists knew Rook's father from Tuxedo Park and had asked him to step in and work side by side with quantum physicists to generate the new synthetic international currency. During this brief period when global society was still taking a stab at legitimacy, the new completely traceable currency became utilized as evidence tantamount to DNA for solving crime. Eventually this explicit information only became available to the inside trader or for someone who wanted to leave a false trace—someone like Rook.

And Rook alone, upon his father's death, held the full set of encryption keys to synthetic quantum currency. Only he knew his own father had created it from an algorithm based on a blind chess game they had played together.

His father's ties to the Federal Reserve provided him with many powerful friends and their enemies, and these ultra upper class people chose their social interests by their pedigree in life, such as sailing, aeronautics, golf, drinking, cigar smoking, chess.

And blind chess.

This profound secret algorithm young Rook initially believed was the motive for his father's murder.

He was stunned to find it was not. He needed another motive.

***

His father had been found in the tub wearing a blindfold, the one he had used when he was deep in chess thought. It blacked out the light as he played chess in his imagination, either against others, Rook or himself. It was a simple blue bandana, and it had been found soaked with blue blood.

As a young boy Rook had watched his remarkable father play blind chess. While blindfolded the man could play seven games at once and remember every move. During each game Rook took notes, and later at night, he would replay the game alone in his imagination and thereby embed into memory his father's strategy. This catalog of chess became Rook's inner playmate. While other children were playing with plastic guns, Rook played chess with seven imaginary blindfolded friends.

3: The Fruiterer

After his father's death Rook quit competition chess altogether, and subsequently the police scrutiny he had come under faded. In fact Rook had been bored with chess for years. Playing the game was like, he imagined, having sex in the same position night after night after night. Chess was purely technical—it was missionary sex with a black and white board, and he could no longer get excited about it. Rook had had another boyhood passion: detective stories. As an avid collector of literature that referenced chess, his father had long owned a copy of Poe's short story *The Murders in the Rue Morgue*. Given its brevity and its quick attack on the "elaborate frivolity of chess," Rook took an early interest in this particular story. Though the story itself was burdened with heavy-handed antiquated language, quirking with words like *bizarrerie, stereotomy* and *fruiterer*, it was charged with lateral thinking. The fruiterer, Rook had thought, is a very minor character who trips into the narrator thus causing a haphazard yet logical lateral succession.

Early on Rook had thought of the Rue Morgue's narrator and his sleuthing mentor as simply homoerotic, then later as the masturbatory imaginary friends of Poe himself. Rook could relate. Long before his father's murder, Rook had become obsessed with detective stories and true crime and was increasingly interested in forensics. Over time he found himself daydreaming crimes much more complex than anything the average dumb criminal committed for real. He would blindfold himself, imagine the murder or the robbery or the rape, the exit path of the guilty, the details of the crime scene then contemplate in meditation the time lapse before the crime was discovered. Crime, unlike chess, had sexual energy to it. As Rook became a young man he also became aware he could not separate the two. From his shoes to his tie, Rook cultivated the classic look of a classic detective cut out of the cloth of shadow sculpted by fact. Noir was Rook's fetish.

He had tailored for himself a custom blindfold, one that could completely kill the light. He had it fashioned in the Lower East Side at a sex shop that only unlocked its doors if one had an appointment and a committed sadomasochistic air. The shop specialized in leather, rubber and latex. Midnight spilled from young Rook, and the tailor, sizing him up, appreciatively let him in. The tailor asked no questions as he measured Rook's head, but Rook knew the man wanted to ask at least one.

Without it being asked, Rook had finally answered, "I'm sixteen."

Rook also knew what the next question would be as the tailor gently wrapped his tape around Rook's brow and pushed at his temples, looking back tenderly at both of them in a mirror. Before the proposition dropped from the tailor's lips, Rook halted him. "The blindfold is for blind chess," Rook said, "not for sex."

4: Blind Chess

The tailor, whose lean and gnarled body was stretched inside tight black rubber asked, "What is blind chess?"

Rook answered, "Playing chess without the game or board. The game is in your head only."

The tailor laughed heartily. "If the game isn't there to see, you don't need to be blindfolded not to see it."

Rook had nothing more to say to the tailor. He handed the tailor a sketch of the blindfold he had designed. Standard blindfolds had the tendency to let light in under the cheeks. His design dropped the blindfold down below the nose, over the upper lip, and wrapped completely around the head, buckling in the back. There was an inverted V cut out of it for breathing through the nose. The ears were covered and doubly insulated for silence.

The mask was a black straightjacket for the mind.

Rook wasn't going to tell the tailor he had come to the conclusion that playing blind chess wasn't about memory but about visualization. He wasn't going to elaborate that he had come to the conclusion light existed in the inner mind as much as it seemed to source from the sun. He had begun to notice while blindfolded he could see, dimly, the chessboard as if it were tangible.

Phosphenes burned a pattern behind his closed eyelids. Eventually he could also see his imaginary murdered bodies and their spilled blood. When he wanted to entertain a sexual fantasy, he found that the clearer he could imagine the woman and her sexual body the more he became excited. In the fluidity of the imagination accompanying sexual desire, he found it difficult to imagine a play by play of advances. Of course chess, being so sexless, was easy to imagine as a game, but to turn sex into a similar succession of strategic moves seemed impossible. Sex, unlike chess, was best when real and blended with fantasy. *The reality of sex*, Rook had thought as he left the tailor and passed by a butcher shop, *is the reality of the meat market. Body parts.*

A year later his father was dead. The police detectives finally admitted when Rook insisted, the blood spatter patterns did not suggest suicide. It almost seemed as if an action artist had painted the suicide by flicking blood-soaked bristles, and his father's blued body had been the canvas.

Why is blood red? Rook had wondered, and subsequently he learned the hemoglobin protein dominating blood bent crimson out of the light spectrum. Further, he learned that oxygenated blood turned bluish blood into bright red blood. *What*, Rook had wondered, *makes an aristocrat's blood blue?* The phrase stemmed from a Spanish idiom, *Sangre azul*, and like the word *tuxedo*, no one really knew the origin.

5: Blue Blood

In the Tuxedo years later, en route to the black and white ball, Rook observed the charcoal sky tucked around the city lights. He veered the sedan toward the bridge, toward Orange County, and as he imagined blue blood, the city lights rushed with the ultramarine color he had witnessed prior to driving to East Orange a few hours ago. Angela's brow was tight. She too was laterally spinning. Rook drove faster, inferring or at least hoping the signals from his electrodes would fade as they entered rural upstate. He made his mind go silent and behind them the city light puzzled and darkened then plunged into a blackout. Citizens clutched for light sources, and a rogue thug lifted a garbage can in preparation to break storefront glass.

***

Inside the Zodiac laboratory at Tuxedo Park, Agent Orange manipulated a quantum radio remote attuned to Rook's nanoelectrodes. She dropped the signal to zero, and the city lights spasmed, returning the city to a normalcy of bright pulsations and the nearly sensible glow of digital Oroboros information.

***

The thug weighed the garbage can in his arms and caught the stares of those around him. He set the can down and gave them the finger. In moments the blackout was mere gossip.

***

Blue blood, Rook thought, and in the rearview he saw his thought did not affect the city's electronic shell. He let his mind wander as an experiment, but the phenomenon for the time had quelled.

***

Hovering just outside of Tuxedo Park, unaware of the electrical interference Agent Orange had just applied to entrain Rook's nanoneuroelectricity with Manhattan, Dr. Kill van Kull tuned the virtual knobs on his brain-cooling console. It was his mission to wait for Rook and to perform the intervention's final cooling, and wait he did. But now like Cosmo, he felt something was not right. The taut folds of his Asian-African eyelids narrowed over his brilliant green eyes.

With his gravelly, baritone voice he quietly called into his radio, “Cosmo?” There was no answer. "Agent Orange?"

"Copy."

"Where is Cosmo?"

"Zodiac lab."

He looked down to the tree canopies through the darkness and witnessed light blooming inside the glass house. The glass was obscured, sandblasted on one side, and through it he could only see soft shadowy outlines. Cloaked inside it and under it was the formidable Zodiac laboratory, a place charged with powerful equipment capable of bending reality like light through a prism—or crushing it like a bottle under a wheel.

"I see."

***

Inside the glass house Agent Orange and her gang made haste assembling a mannequin from parts removed from their motorcycle bags. Each wore a small oxygen tank on her back that fed into helmets. Cosmo danced and laughed hysterically at them, clapping with a foolish laughing-gassed joy.

She had her orders to lure Rook to Tuxedo Park. It was to be the final segment in the intervention. Dr. Naranja had made her rich and had empowered her in a way she never would have imagined, but in exchange he had stolen from her what she loved most. In the interstices of space and time, she had forged her plan and now she would need only minutes, but precious and dangerous minutes, to take back what she had long thought she owned.

In the Zodiac laboratory adjacent, the gang unloaded two orange cases and assembled the contents: synthetic limbs, torso, head and other Rookish body parts. They dressed the mannequin in a tuxedo and arranged the synthetic knockoff Rook onto a simple foldout chair. Like a figure in a wax museum, he would be realistic enough for the purposes of a digital image feed to the helicopter, though it had other purposes. Cosmo, high on laughing gas, clapped his hands in joy at the marvel and spun around it. "Rook, my boy! So good to see you at long last!"

Agent Orange ignored him and prepared to enter the lab's central chamber, into which light rushed like liquid glitter. She witnessed the spectacular void of the synthetic black hole. No electronic frequencies could escape it. It was here some six years prior that Cosmo had been forced to graft Rook's reality into a quantum space-time crotch, and it would be here that Agent Orange would graft Rook's reality into her. *You were mine in the beginning, and you will be mine in the end! Come hither!*

***

In Manhattan Dr. Naranja balled his right fist against his black cashmere slacks. He made another attempt to connect, this time through a quantum feed that flashed inside Dr. Kill van Kull's eyes and inside his ears. It was a private security feed only his most trusted ally could participate in. Unlike the guards or Jules Barbillon, Dr. Kill van Kull was not an employee. He was an advisor ten years Dr. Naranja's senior.

Kull?

As the helicopter landed in a mowed plot surrounded by billowing green grass adjacent to the glass house, Dr. Kill van Kull heard the quiet plea inside his head as if it were his own thought. In thought he responded, *Yes?*

When you return, instruct the pilot to land at the heliport platform on level 113.

He understood right away the serious implications, and he thought, *Copy. Level 113.*

6: Come Hither

If there was anywhere socially inbred in the world, it was Tuxedo Park, where the blue-blooded inhabitants gated out the lesser world and assuredly anointed themselves a social royalty. After news of Rook's father's death broke, Cosmo invited Rook to convalesce at his ten-room house on Lake Tuxedo. Cosmo had inherited his wealth, the estate, the laboratories and an encyclopedic scope of patents from his own billionaire father.

Rook had accepted the offer and had driven his father's sedan forty-five minutes upstate to Tuxedo Park. Cosmo had been ten years older than his father's age then, a tall and lean man who looked like an exclamation point. Avuncular, he told Rook to help himself to everything in his house, anything to ease his suffering —from library to laboratory to airplane. At Cosmo's private airfield Rook accepted the final instrument lessons necessary for mastering piloting. He had taken many lessons—a rich boy's fancy—and had put more than ninety hours into the pale blue skies as a young teenager.

Soaring over Orange County on a landmark solo flight, young Rook glanced at the tufting tree crowns below, pulled a hood over his head and closed his eyes to master the technique of flying and landing in a dark storm—what was called blind landing or ground-controlled approach.

Cosmo talked him down to landing over the radio using the radar his father had invented. He smiled when the wheels of the small plane touched the ground, and through the plane glass he observed the hooded Rook roll by. When Rook removed the hood and emerged from the plane, Cosmo was surprised to find a grim and brooding young man who revealed no physical sign of triumph.

"My boy! Congratulations are in order!"

Rook wordlessly brushed past him, rudely immersed in thoughts of blindfolds. H took a few more rash steps, then realized his attitude was in poor taste. He turned and looked at the kind man through his coal black eyes. "I'm sorry. Something's come to me during the flight. I need some time. I'm, really, so very sorry. You've been nothing but kind to me."

Cosmo nodded that he understood and waved Rook on.

Rook immediately retreated for a meditation, and the room he chose for his meditation was the old electroencephalography lab. It was a bedroom with walls meshed in copper to keep electrical noise interference at a minimum such that the delicate phenomenon of neuroelectricity could be quietly explored. In the bedroom's early years, when the billionaire had first built it into a lab for brainwave experimentation, even his then-young son Cosmo had been a subject. Young Cosmo had gladly endured his father's passions and had slept in the laboratory bed while attached to crude neuroelectrodes. As an adult Cosmo later employed modern equipment in the room and indulged in blind chess against Rook's father while both were attached to improved neuroelectrodes, the precursors to nanoelectrodes. Each practiced shifting their mind from beta to alpha brainwaves during these special games. Afterward they compared their brainwave activity records with the closely timed and accounted for gaming moves.

Eventually Rook himself played against his father in this lab. After numerous sessions, each gained an acute scientific understanding of their individual brainwave patterns arising during chess strategy. In turn each honed his ability to outthink their competitors by manipulating their own waves during actual gaming competitions. Beta was employed for hard strategy and alpha worked best for intuitive gaming. Each could also infer what brainwave state their competitors were in and bluff just as well. Unnerving the opponent was key in chess, and the Tuxedo Park insiders became masters of making other people sweat. Cosmo, as both an invested chess and science enthusiast, patted himself on the back for employing neuroelectrical feedback as a means to improve Rook and his father's immense gaming talents. It was Cosmo's way of becoming chess royalty with them.

***

After the blind landing, a concerned Cosmo quietly followed Rook into his house. When Cosmo found young Rook sitting quietly in the dark lab under the odd, insinuatingly sadistic black leather and rubber blindfold mask, he backed away ashamed, as if he had witnessed a man having sex.

Later at dinner the stoic Rook ignored his plate. “My apologies again, Cosmo. I’m just not hungry.”

Cosmo asked quietly, "Who were you playing blind chess with?" Cosmo was certain the answer was the ghost of his father.

To his surprise Rook informed him, "Not blind chess." Rook's dark lashes tightened over his eyes as he contemplated elaborating. He opened his eyes and met Cosmo's warm brown gaze. "I am solving my father's murder."

8: Cosmo's Library

"A murder," Cosmo pondered. "Why do you think it is a murder?"

"Well, by deduction, I know I didn't do it." Rook skewed his logic and made reference to the fictive killer of the Rue Morgue, "I'm also excluding orangutans because that theory is preposterous." Rook motioned as if he was moving a chess piece. "However, someone killed him just to see if I could solve it."

"Now that," answered Cosmo, "is preposterous."

"No," Rook responded, "it's paranoid."

In order to console a young man he witnessed as grieving and in denial, Cosmo offered his financial support behind the sleuthing and did it by way of surprise. The next day Rook received a large shipment of forensic tools—all the latest technology had to offer such as 3D scanners and gunpowder sensors—all from ties Cosmo retained through his inventor father. It was equipment the police detectives had already employed in his father's brownstone but was utterly new to Rook.

The forensic evidence had been locked away in a police vault in the city, and Cosmo used his influence to have the evidence packed up and delivered to them at Tuxedo Park as well. It was his hope the young man would eventually conclude the unfortunate reality of the suicide.

Rook soon discovered the police had been clumsy and had hog-handled everything from fingerprint samples to Rook's massive collection of sinister true crime books.

It took Rook only one week to prove it was murder and to nail the suspcct.

During another quiet hour—this one spent in Cosmo's library—Rook daydreamed the scenario unlocking the crime. His thoughts had turned toward the art of bookbinding, and he was examining the ornamented leathers of older books on which the leather skin was etched, stamped and scored. The old hand art of bookbinding, by the time of Rook's youth, had been replaced by laser technology. Rook at first wondered if his father's wrists had been slit by some special laser, but he had discarded the notion when Cosmo proved to him that lasers cut only by burning. There was no laser on the market with an edge like a straight razor. Rook's father's veins had been slit from the wrist all the way to inner elbow, and Rook knew it would have been nearly impossible for the murderer to have cut both the right and left veins so cleanly with anything other than a razor.

The tailor who had stitched Rook's blind chess mask had etched by hand the design Rook had given him. It was pebbly, organic—crocodilian meets machine—and very much like the ornamental leather of the old books. The design was what Rook imagined his skin would look like if he were indeed architectural. The tailor could have used the laser-etching machine he kept in his shop, but Rook had insisted it be made by the hands of a man. Beyond tattooing, scarring by laser had become a body art fad in the sadomasochistic community, and the tailor's own hands, Rook recalled as he looked at the leather bound books, were highly decorative and laser etched. The patterned scars on them were white: the calcified edges of burned skin.

In the library Rook closed his eyes and could not get the sight of the tailor stitching his blindfold out of his mind. When he opened them he went directly to the lab, pulled open a stainless forensic case marked *Exhibit B: Blindfold,* and he withdrew the bloodied blue handkerchief his father had been wearing.

8: Iron Blue

Rook subsequently reopened the digital files containing the blood spatter pattern surrounding his father's body. He had already applied basic trigonometry to locate the central point of death, and he had decided already that the antique straight razor found in the tub had been in fact the instrument used to cut his father's wrists. This time he wondered if his father had been killed prior to the slitting, that the slitting was not the actual cause of death but a grotesque cover up of something much subtler. The slitting could only have been possible, he thought, if his father were already dead and dead quickly, since blood stopped flowing at the moment of death and drained to the lowest gravitational points of the body. The white porcelain walls in his father's bathroom had been spattered with an unnaturally unoxygenated purplish blue. Making investigation even more difficult was the fact the water in the tub had been running and draining, washing away evidence for almost two days before Rook had found him. And the water would not have remained hot had his father not invested in a commercial-grade water heater to replace their ailing heater in the months prior.

In Cosmo's lab Rook researched blue dyes. There was, he found, the very common natural indigo and common synthetic Prussian blue. The latter immediately interested Rook, as it was a cyanide, the iron hexacyanoferrate. *Cyan*: Greek for blue. The synthetic Prussian or iron blue dye could be converted to toxic and deadly hydrogen cyanide if exposed to an acid, Rook discovered. The walls of Nazi gas chambers, Rook also learned, were long stained with blue residue from hydrogenated ferric ferrocyanide.

Once acidized the iron blue was not readily absorbed through the skin, but it rapidly entered the blood if exposed to a membrane. The acid choked respiration, immediately withdrawing oxygen from the brain and paralyzing cardiac ganglia.

Death took mere minutes.

Rook knew the eye was the brain externalized, and he considered the means by which an iron blue dyed handkerchief could sweat poison into the corneal membranes.

The police detectives had virtually ignored the blindfold after Rook told them his father wore it while playing blind chess. The detectives simply had theorized his father had donned the blindfold so he did not have to witness the gore of his own death.

Rook snapped on a rubber respirator and rubber gloves. A simple test with organic oxalic acid applied by an eyedropper converted the bandanna dye to deadly cyanide inside a glass cylinder and proved that the dye in the cloth was indeed iron blue, not indigo. As Rook examined the bandanna threads under a microscope, through the darkened blood stains the awesome brilliant blue of the iron shone. Rook compared the samples to those from a new bandana purchased at the store where his father shopped in Manhattan. He discovered quickly the threads of the typical bandannas his father wore were indeed indigo, not iron blue.

The bandana his murdered father had worn in the tub had been specially dyed, printed and stressed to look almost exactly like his father's original blindfold—except there was something different: in the antique Navy paisley stylings, cleverly blended in as ornamentation, a name scrolled. It looked like a brand name, but Rook quickly discerned the murderer had signed it.

Autographed it.

Cosmo assisted Rook with further chemical experiments, and they discovered that citric acid, such as is common in household cleaners, could hydrogenate the iron blue and render it toxic.

As long as it was mixed with scalding hot water.

Rook recalled parting the steam in the bathroom with his hands and the ghastly reddish gray blur of his father's corpse beyond.

Rook searched for handkerchief manufacturers and came across something unexpected: blue handkerchiefs were used in sadomasochistic clubs to indicate whether one was a top or a bottom and preferred oral or anal sex. Rook made a short list of underground sex clubs, and with a disturbed but excited Cosmo, they drove down into the city.

Later, when Rook found the murderer, the sadistic man was wearing black leather pants, a tight black leather jacket—and around his neck, like a braggart's trophy—a copy of the brilliantly blue murderous bandana.

***

The day following the solution, as Rook contemplated time and numerals in Cosmo's private clock museum, one hundred clocks synchronously clicked to 1:00 p.m. Rook decided he too was tired of being number one in the chess world. Knowing real detectives worked with brokers, he quickly negotiated a deal in which Cosmo would become his broker and provide the necessary financial backing for new forensic technology. The rapidity with which Rook had solved the crime profoundly impressed Cosmo, and Cosmo realized, this time with profound empathy, becoming his broker would ease Rook's mind by taking it off his father's murder.

There were numerous crimes Cosmo's wealthy pantheon of friends truly needed solved, mostly as revenge for money missing, stolen or lost. Most importantly, Cosmo and his friends at the Federal Reserve and The Wire needed the identity of The Machete. It was imperative that they stabilize the financial code. The Oroboros virus had not infected the Federal Reserve yet, but it was latching onto infected servers and brooding online at www.themachete.com, where The Machete blogged his threats, promising to become a literal information apocalypse. The Machete had posted a countdown timer on the website.

As if they were watching a televised stick of dynamite attached to a ticking clock, Cosmo and his associates knew they urgently needed a code bomb squad. Tracing the domain to a server proved impossible because The Machete had figured out how to piggyback his site on top of other servers. It was everywhere and nowhere at the same time.

Rook found The Machete a week later just the same. Cosmo was hooked.

9: Memories

As the evening drove toward midnight and the mysterious ball, Rook mulled his father's death. He and Angela, in tuxedo and gown, pushed across the bridge over the foreboding black Hudson River. He squinted abruptly as a Marco Polo towncar drifted in from where it had been lurking ahead on the bridge, and on either side two more cars shot in, closing in on them in a tight triangle. The arm on Rook's watch entrained to Millioni's limousine abruptly swung south. Rook pressed the gas, but the three cars brushed close, literally hugging the sedan steel to steel. The metal bodies scraped, and Rook slammed the brakes in an attempt to jar them free.

Millioni's limousine zoomed into the rear, making a quadrangle around them like the harlequin diamonds in Rook's vest.

His bumper pushed up against the rear of the sedan. Rook and Angela were locked in.

Rook knuckled his gun, and the memory of shadowing Millioni around his butterfly infinity loop hit him like bar fight baseball bat: one hard swing, hickory cracked.

No guns were brandished from the cars. As the five vehicles drove in unison toward the thief thick highways of Orange County, the metal auto bodies buckling but not crushing, Rook realized with bewildering relish, they were not going to kill him.

They were acting like a convoy.

Agent Orange, he thought, *wants me alive.*

***

And upstate the doctor tweaked the quantum-tuning console, finally successfully unblocking the interference that was disabling Rook's memories.

***

Rook's memories spilled like a waterfall, and in reaction his body began to vibrate with the onset of a seizure. Angela gently fished his gun from his trigger finger as he slumped over the wheel.

Outside the protective convoy eased the sedan into a right turn off the bridge, and while its driver succumbed to reliving the past week in an unconscious present stupor, the towncars and limousine guided him forward to his destiny and future.

The ink inside the book of tragedies began overwriting in spasms, spitting out across the open pages, metamorphosing into butterflies—and telling the story of Rook’s life.

CHAPTER EIGHT: Invasive Species

1. Hijacking the Butterfly

An invigorated Dr. Chess, clad in the darkest of his clothes, crept out of his lab into the night. His pockets were heavy, each packed with a plastic bag filled with pollen from the plant he had cultivated and named, *Assassin Chessus*. In a satchel he carried fresh living twigs from his latest creation. These he would graft into the trees of heaven, cutting like a surgeon into the rugged grayish-black bark and grafting beside the numerous leaves bursting along budding axes—the so-called pinnate fronds. And as the aggressive trees of heaven, an invasive species from China, sowed themselves, they would sow within them the seed of their own metamorphosis. The solution to the problem of the weeds invading the city, he had decided, was not through extermination but through grafting.

Hijacking, he thought, *the butterfly*.

He flicked a latch on a vented case, revealing his other latest graft. Tiny butterflies tilted on thin membranous and vividly crimson wings before looping into the air. When they tilted, their wings flashed with emerald. He had, as he had revealed to Dr. Cheng, successfully grafted plants, blood and crocodiles with lepidopterans, and he was very proud. His obsession with weeds had overwhelmed him for so long he could not recall its origin. His compulsions he merely chased like a dog after a car.

Embedded into the lustrous wings on the nanoscale, unbeknownst to him, scrolled the inky knocking passage from *Macbeth*.

As he approached his first tree of heaven, for a moment he thought he heard it thinking, *Come hither!*

***

At the Lucky Dead Pawn Shop, Jack the Butterfly twitched with the knowledge he was fulfilling his personal mission vicariously through Dr. Chess and others. He traced his fingers over the body of his prize synthetic knockoff—the synthetic Marco Millioni—and he laced his quantum essence into the quantum voodoo doll.

The Orange Woman had taken away the ones he had fabricated of the detective. Minutes following her departure the man he knew as The Pimp also returned and took away the volume of Shakespearean tragedies he had asked him to sample. Whatever these people were using those things for, it did not much matter to him. As long as he controlled Chinatown, they could have the rest of Manhattan. His prowess as a quantum botanist, sampled from Dr. Chess's immense knowledge, had given him everything he needed to graft in Chinatown.

He also did not tell The Orange Woman that the DNA she kept bringing him from Millioni had three different variations. They were minor but they were definitely real, and for some vague reason he decided she did not need to know. This minor secret he believed could in fact be major, and he filed it away in his shadowy memory, which lapped at the edges of his consciousness like waves against the shore.

Jack disentangled himself from the knockoff, caught his reflection in a mirror and realized he now had absolutely no idea who he once was. He had grafted himself into so many others, he could not for the life of him identify his ego separate from butterflies. *What the fuck is my name?* He peered into another room, where an unconscious and addicted Dr. Cheng was dreaming he was Dr. Chess. *Fool*, he thought, *you think I would let you go back to Ningbo just like that?* He yawned and, with his vague tongue, felt the edge of sharp teeth inside a mouth like a void. *The teeth*, he thought, *always the last to decompose.*

He picked up a vial, in which was stored the detective's DNA. Slowly he cooked it into nanographite ink, and as he injected the reality seed he thought, *Maybe I'll hire to you to figure out who I was.*

2: Marco Polo Motel

Five days prior.

After he had left the prostitute and her bitter cigarette ashes in the room above the crocodile wrestling club, Rook drove the cold concrete city avenues and streets in his black sedan. The untraceable gas-guzzler had been inherited from his father and keeping the tank full wasn't an option. Gas was gold. He carefully rationed the gas and kept a lock on the gas cap to keep siphoners away. In a drowsy pursuit of the limousine, made to not incite suspicion, the sedan sputtered and rumbled, driving side by side with the purring, compact solar cars manufactured by the Naranja Empire. Gas-guzzlers had become outlawed for a brief period when global warming had baked the Earth's deserts into dust storms and heated the humid climates into nonstop hurricanes, but when the economic depression trenched culture to new lows, anarchy skated in and plunged the internal combustion engine back between its wheels. The greening political parties had no choice but to back down from the gasoline empire's machine guns.

Rook possessed deep early memories of driving around with his father, the two of them playing blind chess without blindfolds and listening to classical music on the radio. He kept his emotions tucked away from these memories. The analog radio cloaking his sedan's quantum technology still worked, and he was able now and then to listen in to some renegade AM radio stations that pirates kept alive. Hidden inside the sedan's chassis was the quantum recording system he had developed with Cosmo at Tuxedo Park. The old mirrors and antenna hid tiny miniature cameras and microphones and even the hubcaps were cyclotrons. It was quantum surveillance sewn into the steel of 1962. With this technology Rook expected he would find out not just what Weedkiller had done but what he might potentially do. He would open his quantum tuner to parallel realities that shimmered like auras around what most agreed was classical reality. Where these parallel realities overlapped, he could plot both backwards and forwards in space and time. But first he would need to sample as much as he could in hard space and time from the man he was certain was Weedkiller.

Rook, driving away from the crocodile wrestling club, glanced at the compass arm in his watch: the arrow pointed almost straight North, but it was not magnetic. This compass arm was entrained to the global positioning code leaking from Millioni's limousine, and it led Rook to Midtown, to the Marco Polo Motel.

Rook observed the limousine parked in front of the motel's art deco stainless steel facade. The Marco Polo Motel, Rook noted, was not a motor hotel. It was a small tower with stepback art deco architecture, like a square wedding cake iced in metal. The facade's architectural ornamenting featured wheels and cogs like those contained inside Rook's watch, but in addition they were threaded with floral motifs. Rook glanced up and counted the ten stories. His gaze dropped back down to where Millioni was standing outside, laughing and talking with the doorman as Rook's sedan slid by. Millioni's cellphone rang, and Rook swept into motion as he answered.

Rook turned the radio on to a channel that broadcast his surveillance microphones. Millioni's voice jumped through the sedan's speakers, and Rook was surprised to discover him speaking in English and Italian. Rook only caught the tail end of the brief conversation—something about engraving or incising—and the word *intaglio*.

He pinged the cellphone server and immediately deciphered both Millioni's cell number and that of the calling party. The phone call had come from Marco Polo Precious Metals, and a database quickly revealed it was also located in Midtown, in the diamond district. Rook drove past it on his way back to his office and observed the décor of the sign above the entryway: even scales upon which coins were equally measured.

3: Intaglio

Back in his office, Rook's confidence he had made his man did little to slake the thirsty game.

Angela was out. She always went low during an investigation week, and she did not just go home to her apartment. She went away. A mere glance from her might fill Rook in on some part of the puzzle he didn't want to guess easily, and crossing paths with her was a possibility spelled out in their first chance meeting. The probability of it was too high.

He never asked where she went, and if she had other men, he didn't want to know. She always came back, enamored by his resolution of the case, and she would submit the evidence to Cosmo. She always drove it in, north to Tuxedo Park.

Rook settled to examining the hundred dollar bill he had lifted from the madam. It did seem to have been printed using the intaglio process, the standard for giving the print its weighted feel. The cotton and linen paper felt embossed, and under a microscope it proved to be so. The ink shifted from gold to green depending on the angle of the light, indicating it contained metallic flakes. The microprinting and fine-line engraving were clean at high resolution. There was no moiré, no strobing whatsoever in the circular reiterated patterns, indicating the bill's detail had not been scanned and counterfeited. The hundred dollar bill, he inferred, was real. *And*, he thought, *worthless*.

There was one other aspect to the bill Rook noted. The serial number: 1011010110. Rook tried to track its life cycle in a database and found only that the bill had left the Federal Reserve once. It had been sold in a large lot in a quantity of a million to Mr. Millioni at an auction. It was otherwise uncirculated and in mint condition except for some minor discoloring from a liquid. *Crocodile saliva*, Rook thought, remembering the snuff, *not tears*.

Crocodiles did not cry emotionally nor did the earth. Both were utterly emotionless. *Crocodile violence, not really violence*, Rook thought. *Instinct*.

Additional research proved to Rook that crocodile lachrymal glands well up while the beasts chomp and hiss through a meaty meal, just as the human eye weepd over a simple onion. He contemplated the phrase from *The Book of Job* about Leviathan being "the eyelids of morning." Crocodiles were as cold-blooded as the face of hell itself, and Rook already knew their brains were the size of a literal marble.

A spectroscopy test established the liquid stain on the bill was indeed salivary, and the saltiness of the stain indicated it came from the salty tongue of the crocodile, in turn indicating the bill had been in the mouth of the beast at least once before. From his event horizon experiences, Rook knew well the fear of being swallowed, of the curious lament drawing the fool near to the precipice, to the incision of the abyss. From a ritual he had sought out years prior, in which he had allowed himself to be symbolically swallowed, Rook also knew well the acute pain of bloodletting from symbolic, zippering teeth.

He had employed the straight razor that his father had been murdered with to scarify himself.

Rook's sleeves hid these scars, and there were none visible on his face. The scars on his head, in which the nanoelectrodes were embedded, were hidden under his black hair. In the muted light of his office he rolled up his sleeves and glanced over the scars crisscrossing his forearms, the scars he had come to take for granted. *How could*, he wondered, *the crocodile wrestling club have never been on my quantum radar?*

It was as if Millioni, a man with a lengthy history, was somehow brand new and had manifested in his world overnight. And the manifestation gnawed at Rook in a way that made him want to relive the night he let the anthropologist cut his body into slivers of skin and blood. He shut his eyes and witnessed only darkness, then the darkness shimmered into the edges of sapphires which became teeth. The tongue morphed into a hundred dollar bill and then the crocodilian darkness began to vomit pulpy money. The ink in the money swirled and formed the word: *listen.*

Weedkiller's case, like the crocodile mouth facing the orange-sapphire-encrusted enchantress, was wide open, and Rook wanted to jump right into it. He opened his eyes, set the bill into his fingerprint-lifting box and hit the on button. It promptly lifted five partial sets of latent prints from the bill: his, probably the madam's, the performer's and someone else's. The machine searched for matches in a database but found none. Clearly the bills added visual dramatic flair to the performance, but Rook was not satisfied that was all there was to it. *Fiat money*, he thought. It was money that once held value because the government had said it did. Then it had become valueless, and they had sold what was left at the mint in a widely publicized auction. Paper money had become as devalued as paper plates.

Rook sealed the hundred dollar bill inside a plastic case and placed the evidence inside a file.

Fiat was Latin for *let it be done*. Fiat money had destroyed the global economy, and when paper money value was finally exposed as a cultural hallucination, the cultural climate of what eventually became known as the Illegal System was born—like Weedkiller, Millioni, whoever he was—overnight. Rook reached for his jacket, thinking, *Let it be undone.*

Listen? To who—or what?

If snuff was a nightly affair crowning the evening at the wrestling club, Rook needed to know immediately who was being sacrificed. Rook strode toward his front door. The fresh off the boat smuggled and enslaved peasants who paid for their passage to New York through years of free labor—the FOBs as they were called—did not matter to anyone other than themselves, and Rook had to count them out of the possible victims he needed to research. His thoughts turned to the possibility someone prominent in the Chinese community had met their end at the club, and the next logical step was to discover who amongst them was missing. This was not so easy. His unfired gun was loaded, but he checked the chamber again out of habit and reached into his pocket for the keys to his sedan.

As the keys jangled, Rook felt he heard the sound for the first time. Jangle, the word, had to be an onomatopoeia. He jangled his keys, knowing his psychonaut subconscious was asking him to truly listen to everything—to hear acutely instead of substituting inference for what he thought he was hearing. The sound of the keys was more of a clinking, he decided as he prepared to leave.

The tightly-gang ruled Chinatown was comprised of intensely private tongs, and even during the days when justice prevailed, the Chinese subculture had been impenetrable. Murdering someone prominent by public snuff was so uncommon it was easy for Rook to marginalize the option. Rook also wondered, *If Weedkiller's real victim is Chinese, why would the Chinese hire a detective outside their culture to solve the murder?*

Rook did not have an answer. But he did want to know why Millioni preferred to speak in Italian when he had returned to the motel. Rook's mind slipped back to the word *intaglio.*

Briefly Rook contemplated death by *intaglio*, and as he stepped out into the night he imagined a scenario in which someone could be killed by being pressed between engraving plates and rollers. It was hardly impossible. Industrial accidents involving bone-crushing machinery had always been common. As he drove back toward the crocodile wrestling club, Rook commanded, "Search. Offline. Death. Intaglio."

The windshield computer monitor illuminated as a transparent screen within the glass and it positioned hits from the offline encyclopedia. Only a few seemed at all relevant and the rest trailed into irrelevance. Rook said, "Top three. Magnify."

The top three hits zoomed to four times their original size and Rook scanned them. "Read them to me, please. Short version."

The computer read aloud to him, and Rook listened intently. "The first reveals a newspaper article about an engraver who met an untimely death at the Federal Reserve when her hair became caught in the rolling presses. Subsequently, the gruesome article relates, her head was dragged into the machinery. But the case is two decades old. It's a cold lead."

Rook slid the information aside by darting his eyes sideways and focused on the next hit.

"This one is an old government article regarding death certificates and intaglio paper. Technical treatise on intaglio."

"Got it." He absorbed the information and slid his eyes to the final hit of interest. Rook regarded both it and the traffic outside as he quickly switched directions to head to Chrystie Street.

"This hit is about jewelry, rings that were for sale on an internet auction site, that is before the site was hacked by the Oroboros."

"Zoom a sample image," he commanded. As the lurid lights of Chinatown began to reflect on the black glossy hood of his sedan, the windshield loomed a ghostly magnification of the jewelry. The sample was of a clear ring in which a kind of intaglio engraving was set. On the surface around the ring circled a tiny engraved string of leaves, and indented in mirror writing that would correct itself in a wax seal, were the words, *In death I change only.*

Rook wrapped his mind around the phrase and thought, *Death I change only in, I change only in death, Change only in death I, Only in death I change.*

"Who bought this one?" Rook abruptly queried, and the computer jumped into the Federal Reserve database. Momentarily it tracked the seller.

"The owner is Lucky Dead Pawn shop, Pell Street, New York. There appears to be no buyer. It was, at least at the time, is unsold." With that, Rook heard a murmuring sound, then a clinking sound. It magnified from his watch. *Ing, ing, ing, ing, ink...*

"I hear you, ECHO. Loud and clear." Rook's hands tightened unexpectedly on the steering wheel, and he swerved around sunjuice vehicles toward the Bowery and Pell Street.

"Now, give me marriage licenses, thirty-five to forty years ago. New York. Chinese names. Italian names. Any variation on Millioni. Let me see them."

As the sedan crept into Chinatown, the ECHO windshield screen flipped through a database and imaged licenses of Chinese-Italian marriages. The first marriage certificate scrolled up and paused a moment, waiting for subtle interactive signals from Rook's eyes, waiting for a command to proceed with detail. Rook figured Millioni was close to his own age, so there was a chance legitimate papers could be found, and he needed to know right away what power the man held in Chinatown. He slid his eyes and scrolled for the next license. The traffic became too dense for him to focus on the monitor and his driving. He commanded, "Speak. Angela's voice. How many are there?"

It answered in a woman's voice, in Angela's, as he had programmed it to do, "Seventeen."

"That's all?" he asked.

"Yes," the computer answered, "Chinese-Italian marriages appear to be quite rare."

He hit the brakes and the sedan came to a sudden stop. "What about the name Millioni?" He shifted into reverse and squeezed the long sedan into a parking spot.

"I'm not finding anything," the computer answered in a voice so natural it was as if Angela was sitting next to him.

Rook turned off the ignition and rapidly scrutinized the remaining marriage documents. Little Italy had become swallowed by Chinatown years prior when the Italians had moved to the outer boroughs of Queens, Brooklyn and Staten Island. Rook decided Millioni had to be a local outsider and that neither of his parents was likely related to kingpins in either a prominent Chinese gang or the Italian mafia. Both strictly handed down the family business to purebreds.

Millioni could, Rook inferred, easily be the bastard child of a rape or a mistress. Whoever he was, Rook had the feeling he was a self-made man.

He stepped out of the sedan into the darkness and pulled his black hat low. Narrow Pell Street seemed to beckon him like a crooked finger.

4: Pell Street

At the corner he scanned from under the brim of his hat, and he found the narrow doorway marking the pawnshop. It was, he saw, adjacent to the Two Brothers Tong headquarters. He circled around the backside of the buildings but saw nothing that would lead him inside other than the front door. A sense of foreboding told him not to go in, and yet he was drawn toward it as if his will was slipping. He felt for his reassuring weapon and pushed down Pell Street toward the lonely dark door. When he hit the intercom button he had a déjà vu that he was home. The door lock buzzed and clicked open. He pushed inside. The shadow following behind as if it were cast from him by the lights of the street, as if it were his own, thickened as it trailed him in. Down the long hallway it stalked him, and when he reached the interior room of the shop it stopped and stood behind him.

The man behind the glass cases was the same man he had witnessed having coffee with Dr. Chess. The man politely said, "How may I help you?"

Rook knew he was deep inside the black market reality territory, and he knew at once the pawnshop was a front for it. He hid his face under the brim of his hat and glanced at the odd assortment of jewelry in a case. "I'm looking for a piece of intaglio." he said, "A ring."

The man flipped a small switch and illuminated another case, in which numerous pieces of jewelry were jumbled together like junk. "Here," the man said, and he pointed with a finger, slowly dragging his finger across the glass top, leaving a streak in the thick dust. Rook breathed in, wondering what it was Dr. Chess thought a dead pawn smelled like. As if reading his mind, the man said, "We thought your pawn dead. Been here a long time. Almost didn't recognize you." The man smiled. Rook was not sure what he was talking about, but he figured it was some sort of code talk to open the discussion to the reality seeds he was sure they traded in at this desolate and weird front.

Rook smelled must and the unmistakable odor of old paper. His eyes found the bins of old comic books before returning to the case filled with intaglio. He bent over it, and as he did the thick shadow behind him bent with him.

And he saw it. The unsold intaglio ring with the leaves. *Tree of heaven leaves,* he realized. "That one," he heard himself saying.

"Of course," the man answered, and he reached in and retrieved it. He set it on the counter and illuminated it with a light. "We sell your stupid ring and your DNA back to you for one million. We give your old detective comics back too!" The man waved to a bin of yellowed comics.

With that, the old paper smell overwhelmed Rook, and he fought the urge to vomit. His gun found its way into his hand. He pointed it at the man, who laughed heartily and chucked a comic book at Rook. It burst into yellow dust and made a weirdly lit halo.

Rook snatched the intaglio ring with his left hand, spun and ran down the dark hallway for the door. The thick shadow split from him and slowly limped back into the main store, where Dr. Cheng continued to laugh, his black mouth a gaping black hole sputtering yellow paper dust, "Not enough? Okay, we give you a new body too!"

"Shut up," Jack the Butterfly said. "Let him go."

Dr. Cheng calmed and obediently freed the lock on the front door by touching a button. As Rook burst into the bewildering lights of Pell Street he heard the pulsings of machine gunfire closing in. The crowded street tumbled into panic. Between the rolling bodies and suddenly slamming rattle of closing shutters Rook stumbled, gun in hand, toward his sedan.

He was driving away down a one-way street when he saw the source of the gunfire. From out of black Marco Polo towncars the muzzles of the guns protruded, igniting the night as they blasted away the storefront for the newspaper *Zhi*.

As a shower of glass spit into the night, the stench of old yellow paper overwhelmed him, and he leaned sideways, vomiting yellowy newspaper pulp. He saw within the vomited pulp swarming, living Chinese characters, and he knew he had made the very dangerous mistake of tainting himself with black market reality.

***

Jack the Butterfly pressed a button and steel walls three inches thick shot down outside the brick walls of the Two Brothers Tong headquarters, protecting his headquarters from the war outside. He had known the detective would make an appearance this night. Those who felt their essence slipping away through him always did try to find him, and when they were successful he always offered to sell them back their quantum DNA, which was essentially their quantum soul. He had no idea what The Orange Woman wanted with this detective man. When he first cooked up the detective's DNA into the quantum graphite ink and injected it into his nanoelectrodes, it was because he felt the strange curiosity to find out. As he nodded off that first time into a hallucinatory reliving of Rook's life, it began with a hurricane and a date.

April 23rd.

While the gunfire persisted outside, ricocheting off his steel enclosure, he cooked up another batch of Rook's DNA, injected it and lay down on his lohan. He hallucinated almost immediately that his blood was made of black ink and what skin he had left was paper turning to pulp. From it emerged a crocodilian darkness that swallowed him. He saw nothing more.

Later when he came to, he had the vague understanding of what The Orange Woman was up to and The Pimp as well. *War*, he thought, *an ink war*.

And even though the Two Brothers Tong building itself was not riddled with bullets, all of Chinatown was murmuring—even the pavement—about the towncar gang, Weedkiller and the violent extermination of *Zhi*.

Yes, he thought, *the solution to controlling Chinatown isn't in destroying Weedkiller, but by grafting myself into him. Who gives a damn about the Tong! It's all about control. You are more powerful than me? You think?* Jack the Butterfly wrapped his shadowy body around the quantum voodoo doll he had fabricated from Weedkiller's DNA. Inside the dark cocoon, he thought, *The solution is through metamorphosis.*

I become you!

5: Newspaper

Rook lifted his head up from the toilet and wiped his lips with a towel. He slowly pulled himself up, leaned onto the sink and stared at his face reflecting in the medicine cabinet mirror. It was pale and gummy. Dark circles, like half moons, etched under his eyes. He seemed suddenly weaker than he had ever imagined, his muscles flaccid and his skin loose. He ruminated on the event at the pawnshop, wondering why the man had addressed him as if he knew him. He lifted his left hand and rubbed at his bristling black stubble. The ring was cool and smooth and for some reason he had placed it on his wedding ring finger.

We sell your stupid ring and your DNA back to you. Give you a new body. For one million.

What does that mean?

Rook coughed and felt at last the violent illness was lifting. He drifted into his bedroom, confused as to whether the ring was keeping him ill or making him well. He slipped it off and placed it into a drawer. When he lay down, it was as if a curtain of darkness wrapped around him. Without another thought, he was out. His chest rose and fell and his limbs twitched all the dreamless night.

When he awoke in the morning under the dull steely light of a passing thunderstorm, it was, it seemed, to the sound of a newspaper thudding as it hit the front step. He rolled and raised himself. In the kitchen he filled a glass with tap water and drank deeply. He rubbed at his eyes and realized he was still clothed. The stench of vomit clutched at his loosened tie. He searched his memories and found only darkness. At his small wetbar he glanced over his bottle of whiskey. It was full as he remembered it. He thought of the only bar he frequented, and he checked his cloned currency to see if he had spent money there but no transactions appeared for the night prior. What had transpired he simply could not recall.

It bothered him.

He opened his front door and walked through the rain to where his sedan was parked, one tire awkwardly cranked onto the sidewalk. He did not recall driving back from wherever he had been. He peered in through the windows and spotted a sickly trail of dried vomit on the driver side door. He unlocked the door and the ghastly odor of gastric acid billowed out. Rook looked around, up and down the narrow street packed with brick tenement buildings, as if a window and maybe a stranger watching through it would be able to tell him how he had arrived home. He closed his eyes in a dizzy moment. As the rain saturated his black hair and rivulets of water ran down his cheeks to his jaw, he remembered with a curious tinge of guilt—as if he'd had sex without a condom—as if he had impregnated the very city, *Chinatown*.

Rook showered and shaved, all the while thinking about Chinatown and newspapers. A quick breakfast of eggs, toast and orange juice at the neighborhood diner settled his stomach, and his thoughts sharpened and focused around Marco Millioni. The Chinese possessed their own media, and Rook had not really penetrated it before. The Italians simply had their code of silence. As the illness faded, Rook shook off the guilt over not remembering what he assumed was a drunken romp. Back in his office he quickly discovered there were three kinds of Chinese newspapers: highbrow, middlebrow and tabloid lowbrow. The highbrow paper *Zhi* had ceased circulation and electronic back copies had been erased.

The night before.

A queasy Rook made another visit to Chinatown, looking to collect any paper copies of the suddenly dead *Zhi*, but he found the street newspaper containers emptied, tilted and beaten. There were no copies to be found at any newsstands, and Rook did not dare ask for one from any of the spooked merchants. Shutting down *Zhi* was clearly payback for something big. Rook tucked himself under his black brim hat and observed men and women scurrying, the bright orange translucent plastic bags of Chinatown markets clutched in their hands, leafy greens tufting out and newspaper-wrapped fish within.

Rook went shopping. After scouring the food stands for an hour, at a market on Grand Street, Rook spotted a stack of *Zhi* being used to wrap fish. It was typical Chinese thrift: use everything. Rook paid for two crocodile steaks and gestured by twirling his finger that they should be triple-wrapped in paper. The merchant resisted the man whose eyes he could not see behind the mirrored sunglasses, in which he saw his own warped face and the array of seafood behind him. He had no idea he was being looked at in black and white, and he stared at the cold man.

The merchant yielded when Rook opened his palm: inside was a gold coin the size of a dime. The merchant carefully wrapped the steaks in the now-forbidden newspaper without any concern for *Zhi*. It was well known in Chinatown what had gone down between the Italian-Chinese boss and the foolish journalists who worked for the Two Brothers Tong the night before, when the dark narrow streets had been punctured by gunfire. He was in the business of selling seafood, and when he had found the newspaper box battered, spilling its guts out onto the sidewalk in front of his shutters in the morning, he did what any smart businessman would and he salvaged the paper. He placed the wrapped steaks into an orange plastic bag and handed them to Rook with a rare smile, saying, "Good with lemon!"

Rook nodded in acknowledgement and, acting like a good sport, bought a lemon from the fruit market across the street.

Crocodile meat was pink-white, almost bloodless, like fish and fowl. In his kitchen Rook carefully unwrapped the newspapers, finding the pale meat lightly stained from the newspaper ink. *Like mirror writing*, Rook thought, *stenciled on the inside of flesh*. It only took a few minutes to broil through one. Rook ate it unseasoned while he brushed sulfide of ammonium on the newspapers to intensify the ink, and he pored over them through a translating scanner. The software compiled an index, and indeed there was one article lambasting the Marco Polo Crocodile Wrestling Club. It was an editorial and was numbered part one of four. Snuff, it decreed, was barbaric. Marco Millioni, it speculated, was inhumane to the Chinese because he hated his Chinese father and worshipped his Italian mother.

There was another article about a merchant from Ningbo getting caught in paper mill machinery in East Orange, New Jersey. Rook thought, *Intaglio*.

Rook wondered if Marco Millioni wasn't really so much an assassin as a snuff maestro, but he knew at the same time that he had not been hired to solve snuff ranted about in an international headline. Further offline encyclopedia research scoured back to the paper's earliest origin, when it had been a gazette devoted to fiction. Like most papers, Rook decided, it probably steered as clear of fact as it could and printed whatever headline would grab attention.

It made little sense to Rook that Millioni's father would be Chinese and his mother Italian, but if it was true it narrowed the background. It also meant the Chinese, if the tabloid could be trusted at all, had known of him for a long time.

Rook scanned copies of other Chinese newspapers. The sudden cessation of *Zhi*, the remaining middlebrow and lowbrow newspapers reported, was due to a family illness, and the editor had abruptly gone home to Hong Kong. There was a photo of the editor—a distinguished female—boarding a plane. There was no way to date the photo, and it easily could have been faked. Rook wondered if the editor was truly alive, but he discarded the notion Millioni would slaughter the editor at the wrestling club. A public slaughtering definitely would cast fear into the Chinatown population, and they might learn to keep their mouths shut fearing they would be dropped into the crocodile pool next. Still, it would be too easy to finger Millioni if that were the case, and revenge from a powerful Hong Kong family would be simple—and probably a lot more painful than being eaten alive by a crocodile.

They wouldn't need me to execute.

If Millioni was Weedkiller the assassin, it also would not make sense that he would kill just for revenge. He had to be paid. Rook decided the termination of *Zhi* was a warning to Chinatown to steer clear of Marco Millioni's business, a killing business he had yet to uncover.

Within the next hours, during day and night three of his investigation, Rook documented Millioni's travels from the motel in the morning and back in the evening: he took a morning swim at the Marco Polo Swimming Club, then ate lunch at the Marco Polo Noodle House, moved on to Marco Polo Silks and Marco Polo Tobacco in the afternoon before returning to the motel to freshen up. He briefly stopped in at the Asian Museum to look over a Marco Polo exhibit, then made a quick jaunt to Marco Polo Precious Metals in the diamond district before heading for dinner to the Marco Polo Lounge in what was left of Little Italy—a meal of ragout, red wine with an orange, a blood orange it seemed, for dessert. Then just before midnight he made his way back to the Marco Polo Crocodile Wrestling Club.

Rook did not follow him inside.

Behind the club, where he had previously observed freshly captured, wild saltwater crocodiles being wrangled into the building, Rook waited to see if human cargo arrived the same way. It did. A small van rolled up, and Chinese thugs unloaded a writhing, living body bag. Club workers received the human prey at the loading dock, and the van drove away. On the dock, a large saltwater crocodile was chained, its mouth constrained by a one-foot tall black bar on either end of which was a sharp spike that protruded through the top and bottom of its mouth. Four men returned and dragged the beast inside.

Rook followed the van less than ten blocks, where it parked outside an Off Track Betting storefront. It was a simple formula, Rook thought, *Snuff the losers*. Inside the storefront Chinese gamblers were crushed like drunken fish, and outside they inhaled tobacco, hacked and spit at the filthy sidewalks. Adjacent to it was a grimy methadone clinic.

***

Inside the wrestling club that night, Marco Millioni was motioned aside. An accountant informed him a one hundred dollar bill had gone missing a day earlier. The accountant apologized profusely—even shrieking—for not having caught the error sooner. The madam lined up the women and berated each in turn, scanning for a guilty face. The accountant started combing through profiles, furiously searching currency records and discovered the account of the man who had been sitting at table seven had vanished. He reported this to his boss, Marco Millioni. Millioni, all of whose staff operated in utter fear of him, calmlyscanned the security camera feeds in private but no images proved clear enough.

The only thing he could make out, even at intensive zoom, was a shape of darkness more shadow than man.

Marco called the prostitute in and asked for an in depth description. She opened her mouth to speak and only darkness tumbled from her tongue, "Shady." That was all she could remember.

Good, Marco thought, *they know nothing*.

Marco put the word out to his car service gang to throttle security. That night the last of the *Zhi* journalists foolishly following him around—the ones who hadn't gotten the clue the night before when he had ordered their newspaper destroyed—were cleanly gunned down by his armed drivers. It wasn't just his story he needed silenced. Marco's orders came from a godly way above.

In the back dressing room the performer straddled him and took him inside her. As she lowered her mouth to his, her jeweled breasts brushed his tattooed chest, exciting him. He whispered, "Soon, we will be liberated."

All of the lies he whispered to the women he fucked slipped away like river water, and his physical lust to orgasm inside this woman became inseparable from his lust to gain the freedom the coup promised.

His lips met hers and he pushed her tongue into his mouth. Her fingers found the fine chain around his neck and twisted into it like a serpent coiling to strike.

***

At the Lucky Dead Pawn shop, in tandem with their lovemaking, Jack the Butterfly writhed on his opium den lohan, the mahogany rattan platform digging into his crosshatched shadowy black back. Millioni's ruthless car service gang had killed his agents at *Zhi,* but with the man's DNA raging inside him, he cared less and less for destroying him and more and more addicted to becoming him. The orange bejeweled woman, he learned, had seduced Millioni. When she stole again his semen that very night—which she would later sell to Agent Orange—Jack the Butterfly vaguely realized she was stealing his as well.

Between his thighs there burned an inferno. Within his addiction he desired only more and more and more. When he came, the semen was gasoline. His quantum imagination lit a match, and he watched in imagination as New York City burned down.

CHAPTER NINE: Watch

1: Suckers

Inside the sedan Angela sat rigid with a knowing and watched Rook dream. She glanced from one window to another at the Marco Polo towncars tightly squeezing the sedan and guiding them, forcing them to their destination. The metal bodies of the cars scratched and scraped against one another as together they took a bend in the road down a hill. Cars coming at them veered around the quadrangle of steel, honking wildly as they did. From the towncars machine gun firing issued, scaring them off.

The convoy continued north. In the rear of the limousine Marco Millioni sat tall, gently fingering his .22 gun, his own titanium watch rapidly pulsing, synchronizing with Rook's. He remembered the tattooing session they had engineered for Rook, the one during which Rook thought he was watching him while in fact it was Rook who was being watched.

***

The Pimp, Jules Barbillon, gave his last instructions to the crew commandeering the submarine, and they obligingly raised the craft just to the water's surface. A small boat awaited him.

***

Dr. Naranja's surveillance flashed from a blank gray snow to an emerald green the moment Jules emerged from the submarine. The signal originating in Jules' grafted eyes momentarily blipped onto a live feed inside the blue room. The doctor pensively observed the imagery of the rolling harbor waves on a screen as Jules approached the island.

"I see you've made a swift recovery," the doctor spoke into his wire.

Jules smiled as thunderstorm wind gusted against the boat, excited the waves and pushed the papyrus fronds at the island rim to and fro like angry brooms. He responded, "I feel better than ever." He blinked and touched a button on the temple of his sunglasses, which intercepted the surveillance signal and sent it to Orange Security. In its place Orange Security streamed a carefully designed alternative view to Dr. Naranja.

After the boat delivered him to a dock under the Manhattan Bridge, Jules made his way swiftly by taxi toward Chinatown. What Dr. Naranja saw on surveillance was similar, except the streaming version of reality placed Jules inside his premier Blue Room club.

The machine gun pulsings had quieted and the streets were vacant. Everyone was home hiding, waiting for the gang war to quell. Jules wasn't worried about bullets. He had long ago grafted himself with the crocodile, and in his veins almost pure crocodilian blood flowed. Just like a crocodile he could lose a limb and easily survive.

It was not his reverence for fossil fuel inciting him to assist, in fact push, the reality revolution, but his reverence for Sobek. He directly worshipped the Egyptian god, kneeling in his home before the small temple pool inhabited by the live crocodile, and chanting, *Arise Sobek!* Suspended over the pool was a synthetic blue sky, a replica of the body of Sobek's mother: Nuit. The scientific parallels of the quantum sea and hard classical reality to the ancient myths of Nuit and her son Sobek, as far as Jules was concerned, were obvious millennial overwrites of the exact same ideas. Local interpretations of a nonlocal universe. Parallel realities were like butterflies, and a reality revolution was easily visualized as a butterfly ready to burst from a chrysalis. Only Jules, like many who worshipped Sobek, wanted reality to metamorphose into the cosmic crocodile, into the oroboros, into a feedback loop, into itself. Tapping that nonlocal yet formative energy was the key to what in the old days was called black magic. He believed firmly, if he could tap it, he could form any reality he wanted. His personal power would be, he believed, unlimited. He enjoyed his human form, and like many working with him, he never wanted to die.

From a special pocket sewn into the fatty flesh of his forearm, Jules pulled out a key, and he opened the door to the Lucky Dead Pawn shop. He seated himself on a box adjacent to the opium den lohan, upon which the shadowy Jack writhed. Jules utilized a small medical swab to collect a sample of gasoline-infused semen, and he held it up to the light. *Interesting. Very, very interesting!*

Naranja had invented the means to graft photons, and Jules, with some help from some unwitting Gasland patrons, had figured out how to engineer the grafting of gasoline. They needed a lot of it to burn Naranja's empire down. *Looks like the black hole butterflies are ready to ignite! From the inside*, he thought, *out.*

With a sweeping hand he slapped once at the darkness that was Jack. "Wake up, sucker!"

Jack's form writhed, and slowly he blinked, recognizing his client.

"Where's my ink?"

Jack fumbled for a minute then passed Jules a vial of quantum-sampled ink.

"Thanks, Jack!" He grinned, "And where is my sweet, sweet lollipop?"

Jack's shadowy shape raised up and he collected this for Jules as well. "Here."

"A mailman will be by to get it momentarily. And then of course, do what I told you to do with the money!"

"Fuck you."

Jules slit pupils narrowed. "I'd kill you if I knew how to."

"Huh! I've been dead long time."

"Hmm. Are you're absolutely certain, you never, ever said a word to Agent Orange?"

"Orange Woman knows jack shit."

"Jack shit? That will be your new name if you fail. The Jack Shit Tong. What do you think about that?"

Jack laughed. "Don't worry I do it. For this, believe me, I do it." He waved toward where his Millioni voodoo knockoff was bathed in quantum nanographite.

Jules retreated from the shop and watched from in front of the Two Brothers Tong as a mailman arrived and hit the buzzer at the Lucky Dead Pawn shop, then hit it again. The mailman carried a Majestic lingerie box, and Jules knew well that inside it were bundled one hundred dollar bills, each cloned, bearing the serial number 1011010110 and totaling one million dollars. He had sent it himself.

In exchange for it, a numb Jack handed the mailman a small box containing one engineered orange lollipop. The mailman dutifully plunked his muscled body into his mail truck, glanced at an address on his clipboard and headed toward the postal service's helipad headquarters. The address the new package had to be delivered to was simply, *Glass House, Tuxedo Park.*

Jules spoke into a wire to Agent Orange and Marco Millioni, "Mission, complete." *At least the mission you want me to complete, you fools! Don't you know what Sobekians want?*

Jules chuckled darkly, thinking, *Oh, dear Lord, my leviathanian Sobek! If you meet the Buddha on the road, ask him where the nearest gas station is, then blow him up!*

***

Dr. Naranja, not buying for a second the feed being issued through Orange Security into his blue room. Numbly realizing his guards were in revolt, he sipped at his scotch. At the stroke of midnight, space and time would enfold, and the new cycle of Seven—or some variation of it, they could never quite tell—would restart. Whatever they planned to achieve at Tuxedo Park prior to then, he knew well, either would or would not work exactly to plan. And when tomorrow came, it would in part enfold the night.

Dr. Naranja faced the terrarium spastic with his black hole butterflies. He walked purposefully to a closet. He drew open the mirrored door in which the starry night sky was reflecting, to a closet filled with bespoken tuxedos. He reached in, lifted one out and pensively dressed himself in it. He balled his right fist then relaxed it.

He peacefully strode to the terrarium, opened the glass door and stepped inside. Through the rushing of the black hole butterflies, merging with his tuxedo like digital snow, he made his way to a central chamber seemingly made only of harp-string-like tubes. The walls of the terrarium sealed hermetically with curtains of thick white paper. He thought, *Tomorrow and tomorrow and tomorrow,* and he prayed this phrase to his god Shakespeare during the last minutes counting down to midnight. As his prayers assumed command of the reality tuning chamber, through the tubes black ink flowed and wrote the word: *Tomorrow.*

***

Upstate at Tuxedo Park, Agent Orange prepared herself inside the Zodiac laboratory for Rook's imminent arrival. And inside his limousine, pushing Rook along in the magnetized sedan, Marco Millioni focused on the envelope of that imminence.

***

Inside the sedan ahead at the same time, Rook dreamed vivid memories of the week prior. Smothered over the memories appeared luminescent red pulsations like those in his wristwatch. It was a watch Cosmo has made for him per the requirements of the Naranja Empire, and now they wanted him desperately to know why.

Marco Millioni reached up to his neck, around which the fine golden chain spun, and as he touched it, ahead of him the dreaming Rook twitched, mad with memory. Millioni closed his eyes meditatively, and as he leafed through his memories of the past week, entrained through the special watch, Rook remembered his.

2. Golden Threads

During the tattooing session Rook had witnessed the glint of a golden chain so fine around Millioni's neck it seemed to be a mere thread, a golden moiré flash of a thread. Rook spent most of the sixth day of his investigation free-associating from this thread.

While Rook's currency trace had provided him with what seemed like years of electronic transactions, all placing Marco Millioni at the same establishments in predictable reiteration, no transactions surfaced from his visits to Marco Polo Precious Metals. He discovered the company was Italian and transparently allied, Rook inferred, with supplying deep mafia syndicates with gold currency. Gold had value because those who valued it believed it did. The precious metal was the Italian money of choice: fiat gold. However, Rook knew, none of the well-known *pater familias* in the city were named Millioni. It wasn't a standard family name, and it gave some credence to the possibility the man's father had not been Italian. *Millioni. Has to be a nickname*. Rook pondered the man's expensive attire, thinking, *Marco likes to look like a million bucks*.

Trade research listed the Marco Polo precious metallurgists as provider of bullion to legitimate jewelry manufacturers and private investors, but it was a thin cover, Rook decided, for accumulating privatized reserves. Gold and silver had been the constitution's named monetary standards from the beginning of American history, yet politics had altered the course of value around the same time Detroit gave birth to Rook's original sedan. The gold standard backing all paper subsequently became snuffed, and value became a form of pure confidence, a mere belief in the good word of the government: a cultural hallucination. Anarchically, shiny gold—and gold above all metals only—sustained both an emotional and monetary value despite the law. People valued gold regardless of the politics telling them they shouldn't.

Precious malleable metals, Rook thought. An ounce of gold could be beat into 300 square feet, with light able to shine through its transparency, or the ounce could be spun, like the thread around Millioni's neck, into a wire fifty miles long. In a world of controlled currency, there were many who created their own value systems. Money could be drugs, horses—anything. The actual quantity of gold was static. It could only be accumulated but never invested, and it was also untraceable. Precious metals could not be fabricated.

Rook wondered in a world where cloning was rampant, *Or could it?*

Back in his office Rook zoomed in on surveillance photos of Millioni, derived from The Wire's cameras, and he magnified the pattern in the black silk clothing the man habitually wore. Like the hundred dollar bill, the embroidery flashed with intaglio meets moiré.

Rook understood the nostalgic fantasy of gold's value, but he did not buy into it. In the post-inflationary period, after paper money crashed along with the global stock markets, the Federal Reserve auctioned off surplus cash to collectors at the value of the paper and ink only—real pennies to the virtual hundreds. Bills were now nothing but novelties, antiques: dinosaurs. Gold still glittered and had weight like guns. He imagined the tame club crocodile biting down onto a gold coin to mark it with its teeth, like a cowboy in a Western movie, thereby proving it was genuine due to its softness. *Yes*, Rook thought, like the steering wheel of his gas-guzzler and the ominously heavy turning of mechanically geared wheels, *Gold feels good in the hand or around the neck.*

Nothing more.

3: Tasteless

Rook returned his focus to the milliliter samples of hash and blood culled from Dr. Chess's lab, recalling it was the metallic atoms that gave both hash and blood their distinctive, tingling tastes. Rook opened up a safe in which he kept some of his own gold. He maintained a stash as a reserve in case he needed to pay for information on the gold market—for gasoline, for fire department protection, for *Zhi* wrapped crocodile steaks—for whenever it was needed. He withdrew a coin and licked it. He licked it again and again, and he thought of the crocodile club prostitute licking him. He placed the whole coin in his mouth and rolled it on his tongue: it tasted like nothing, if nothing had a taste. *Gold*, it struck Rook—the fashion taste of the rich—*Tasteless*.

Back out in the night he walked the narrow streets tall with slivery tenements, where Chinatown clutched old Little Italy like a heart ripped from the chest of a dying man. Little Italy still had a faint heartbeat, a faint muscle memory of the men who had been gunned down there while eating oyster primavera back in the days when the red and white checkered tablecloths anticipated blood spillage just like wine. Marco Millioni had face in the Chinese community and respect in the Italian. It meant he had something on somebody or a lot of somebodies, and he had held this power for seventeen transparent years.

That had appeared overnight.

Rook mulled: something about the crime stank and something else did not and was tasteless even. Chinatown had been nicknamed Gold Mountain, *Gum Shan*, but its collection of filthy row houses was just a shambling slum deteriorated further by the gangs. The Chinese had started to take over where the Italians had left off—with heroin, gambling, gun running—and their organization was less susceptible to law back in the day of law. Their languages and their customs were at extreme odds with the Europeans who had become Americans. The Chinese were even more ruthless with revenge, and the Chinese character for revenge, Rook knew, held the same meaning as the act of reporting a crime.

The Chinese did not report crimes. *They revenged.*

Zhi had been revenged.

Rook was also hired for revenge. Back out on the streets that night he paused at the intersection where sixteen people had been murdered years prior. They innocently dined on dim sum with a guilty gang leader, and all died, all during a firestorm when one Chinatown gang revenged the leader of another. Sixteen people—women, old men, children and an unborn child—all massacred. Rook's eyes swept the bright red, orange and white lights littering the storefronts and signage cross-hatched with the new Latin alphabet and Chinese characters. His eyes swept the rooflines and the brick boundaries where Chinatown ended and Little Italy began before dropping down and scanning the underground massage parlor stairwells. They were almost always located below the sidewalk. Foot reflexology charts invited the walker down into the cellar where the massage could include any conceivable sex act. It was possible also that Marco Millioni had been born to a prostitute, Rook thought, and that simply an Italian man, his would be father, had come to the bowels below the Bowery for a quick hard fuck.

At Marco Polo Tobacco, where Millioni stopped for his daily purchase,

Rook purchased a rolling machine, papers and tobacco. It was a means to entrain himself to Millioni, to loosen up his subconscious. At the Marco Polo Laundromat, where Millioni had his clothes laundered, dry cleaned and pressed, Rook watched a woman at the iron. He tailed a deliveryman from the laundromat and observed as the clothing was delivered to the motel. In exchange Millioni himself walked his latest daily soiled clothing out to the deliveryman. Rook noted Millioni's shoes: black stained crocodile, made perhaps from tannery skin.

Why doesn't such an auspicious man keep a servant? Where is his woman? His women?

Rook wondered indeed if there was not something going back and forth in the pockets of the suits. He decided he would buy his own silk clothing for further entraining.

But first he needed to investigate one other place Millioni ritualistically attended.

Completely unbeknownst to Rook, Marco Millioni was just as eager to entrain to him.

4: Silk Road

At the Asian Museum on evening five of Rook's investigation, Millioni, knowing fully he was being trailed, again paid his respects to a Silk Road exhibit. He spent his customary fifteen minutes inside the museum soaking in the details of the exhibit. He left curtly and slipped into his limousine, which ferried him uneventfully to his next destination.

Minutes later, his watch pinging the retreating solar powered limousine, Rook paid the entry fee with another dead man's currency and entered the marble foyer. Glass cases lit by small spotlights held artifacts: scrolls, jade, paper money, opium, hash, silk and the like. The real Marco Polo, Rook then learned, had traveled to Asia when he was seventeen and returned to Venice when he was forty-one. During his stay he had acted as a right hand to the Kublai Kahn.

Toward the end of the artifact displays featuring print, image, audio guides regarding Silk Road history, in a heavily guarded special archive room, came a trigger that shot Rook's mind in a new direction.

Inside a bulletproof glass case displaying an original, hand-written copy of Marco Polo's travels, an etched museum plaque politely suggested Christopher Columbus had owned the volume. Bending in to read the fine print, Rook read that the Silk Road stories Marco Polo had bragged about seemed so far fetched to the Venetians they had nicknamed him Marco *Millioni*. The plaque stated further that Marco Polo repeatedly, fatiguingly applied the word *million* to emphasize his elaborate tales with phrases such as *millions of pearls* and *millions of elephants*. It seemed to the Venetians who could not visually fathom such excess he must only be exaggerating. Subsequently, the scribe transliterating his tales had titled the book *Il Milione*—a book of a million lies. On his deathbed, after the scribe had taken down his tales, Marco Polo insisted that he could not replicate in words the half of the breathtaking magic that was reality on the Silk Road.

This is it, Rook thought. His heart pumped as the connection he had been trying to make kicked through him. Marco Millioni, an Asian-Italian millionaire and a man of leisure, a man obsessed with Marco Polo, was an exaggeration of himself. It was human nature to exaggerate, to reconstruct the personal past to vainglorious standards, and all of history as such was an exaggeration. As such nobody knew precisely what had really happened ever. At this point Rook still did not know how many people Weedkiller aka Marco Millioni had assassinated or how many he would. It was not a million, of that Rook was sure. *That's genocide.*

While the underbelly of the city murmured about an assassin named Weedkiller, a man rumored to have made a million hits, Rook's gut hunch closed in. *A million dollars*, he thought, *probably what he gets paid for a hit.*

Rook anxiously drove back to his office. "Search the financial databases for million dollar transactions in Millioni's quantum accounts."

"I'm not finding any."

"What's a million in gold?"

The ECHO computer churned through the database. "The equivalent of a million dollars in gold at current street value is one talent."

"Why talent? What does that mean? Speak."

In Angela's smooth voice the sedan computer answered, "Talent: the word derives from the weight of gold and is roughly equivalent to the weight of one human body."

"What's the origin?"

"Biblical. The word talent is a monetary weight and a human value."

"Cite the biblical passages," Rook requested as he swung his sedan toward Ludlow Street.

The computer purred in response, "*Matthew 25:14-30*. Summary: three servants were each left talents from their master, two invested and doubled the profit while one buried his and was punished."

"Read me the passage."

"'And I was afraid, and went and hid thy talent in the earth: lo, there thou hast that is thine. His lord answered and said unto him, Thou wicked and slothful servant, thou knewest that I reap where I sowed not, and gather where I have not strawed: Thou oughtest therefore to have put my money to the exchangers, and then at my coming I should have received mine own with usury. Take therefore the talent from him, and give it unto him which hath ten talents. For unto every one that hath shall be given, and he shall have abundance: but from him that hath not shall be taken away even that which he hath. And cast ye the unprofitable servant into outer darkness: there shall be weeping and gnashing of teeth.'"

What sort of crocodilian darkness weeps and gnashes teeth, Rook wondered, *other than hell?*

"Scholarly interpretations available?"

"Yes, the biblical interpretations differ. Scholar one: heavenly rewards double for those who invest in faith. Scholar two: the fearful but faithful will be stripped even of nothingness and rendered weightless in the digestive tract of purgatory."

"And what the hell is either one supposed to mean?"

"Do you want me to interpret?"

"Not now. What about his lack of transactions at Marco Polo Precious Metals?"

"He has many."

"Why didn't they surface before?"

"They're not quantum. They are...talents. They are recorded in gold as talents."

"How do you know? What are you looking at?

"I'm not looking at data, Rook."

"What do you mean?"

"In order to mine gold data, I have to flow through it. My energy talks to its energy."

"You *talk*?"

"Yes. I'm speaking with the gold itself. Let me image the conversation."

His screen filled with gold mesh, living gold mesh. It made a ringing sound.

"What is it saying?"

"It has nothing to say. Something is speaking through it."

"What?"

"It's the formula for Federal Reserve ink."

"No one uses that ink anymore."

"Someone is. In fact, it's quantum voice is everywhere. The entire city seems to be gold-plated with it."

"There's gold in this ink?"

"It's hammered so thin it's almost hard to trace, but yes, it's like a translucent veil."

"So when he spreads these hundred dollar bills around, they're like radios?"

"More like speaker cables, transmitting from one source to another."

"The hundred dollar bill from the club, in my office—"

"That's how I'm talking to the talents."

"Can it hear us?

"Abtractly, yes."

"Hush!"

"Acutely, no."

Rook pounded the vinyl dash as the ringing sound grew louder. "Hush!"

He parked quickly at a weird angle, took his memories of the Marco Polo museum exhibit into his office and pondered the meanings of million, talent and gold. He withdrew the hundred dollar bill from the evidence and turned it over and over as he held it up to the light.

The original Marco Polo returned to Venice with million dollar tales of paper money, hash, crocodiles, tattoos and assassins. And somehow Manhattan's talented Marco Millioni, worth his weight in gold, is doing the exact same thing.

His major dilemma was Marco Millioni, just like translucent gold, did not seem to be up to anything other than spreading word through his gold of his traceable wealth—his talent. Rook had only two more days to produce the evidence that would substantiate Millioni was guilty of assassinating someone, then if he got The Bonus, it was upon Rook to destroy him.

But if Millioni was listening to Rook through the hundred dollar bill, maybe it would be upon Millioni, he thought, *To destroy me.*

Rook picked up his feedback mask and went to his couch.

Later in a light dreamy feedback session, all that Rook's free-associating mind could focus on was a smoky golden string of ones and zeros imprinted in living ink on a one hundred dollar bill. He awakened with a start when the bill whispered to him, in Millioni's voice, "Do you hear me?"

5: Bulls-eye

During day six of his investigation Millioni's tattoo session ended while Rook sat in the bar up above. Rook calmly sipped his second whiskey and watched in his sunglasses viewer as the tattoo artist wrapped the man's pinkish swelling back in clear, clinging plastic and helped him put his black silk shirt on. The patterns in the shirt, Rook noticed, were similar to the tattoos. In his viewer they caused a moiré effect—a strobing interference pattern. In all of the security surveillance Rook had available to him, Millioni's image similarly washed fuzzy, as if he was there while he wasn't there. *Or as if*, Rook thought, *He's a quantum personality overlapping himself in feedback.* It was a phenomenon familiar to Rook from his feedback sessions but nothing he had ever witnessed in so-called classical reality.

The tattoo artist, the young attractive Chinese woman in the pink frilly Lolita skirt and towering black heels, gazed intimately at Millioni for a long moment while she buttoned his shirt. Afterward Millioni simply turned and left. Rook at this point awaited his exit. With the last finger of whiskey in his glass, Rook stood leaning against the rail of the deck up above the parlor, a bored affectation slumping his jaw. Millioni emerged from Marco Polo Tattoo and slipped nobly into the pedestrian traffic on St. Mark's Place. Rook knocked his whiskey back and placed a call to the parlor. The tattoo artist answered on the third ring, "Marco Polo Tattoo?"

"I was in your parlor about an hour ago. I think I may have left my sunglasses there?"

The tattoo artist apparently scanned and found them. Momentarily she said, "Oh, yes. I see them."

"I'm actually just upstairs. I can come right down." Rook paid with his cloned currency and walked down the steps to the sidewalk. As he did he zipped on a pair of microthin gloves made from a black synthetic material that looked like leather, and a moment later the tattoo artist was passing him his sunglasses. She was outside to meet him.

"They look expensive," she said.

"They are."

She handled them carefully, he could see, by the edges, and he thought, *A woman accustomed to etching fine line work on human skin would be careful with her hands.*

He took the cheap ones and threw them into a city trash can to make his point. She laughed, and as she did her surgically rounded, Americanized eyelids crimped over her one blue eye and one amber eye. The gems dotting her cheeks rose with her smile. Rook smiled in return and glanced at the emerald curtains.

She noticed, "The owner is done for the day." She stepped back inside to draw the curtains open, and Rook followed with both an investigative and a sexual curiosity.

"Did you decide on a tattoo?" she asked.

Rook didn't have any. He shrugged and feigned uncertainty, then joked, "How about a bulls-eye?"

"On your forehead?" she responded, "Or your back?" She smiled again and took up a bottle of disinfectant, "Both are painful areas to have tattooed. Maybe you know that already. Do you have any?" She was about to spray the tattooing chair down.

Rook noted the many colored vials of ink, and catalogued with special interest the crocodilian green ink. *Money ink.*

6: Practice Skin

On the headrest, where Marco Millioni's arms had crossed, his palms had been face down. It was the only location in the parlor Rook could be certain to lift a number of fingerprints from Millioni. The door handle—a metal bar across the glass—was not a good option as it would be muddled from all the other hands that had opened the door that day. Rook walked past her and pressed his gloved hands onto the headrest, his focus landing on the needles and ink. He leaned forward to examine them, and he directed her attention there as well.

"How did you get into this kind of art?"

"I was interested since I was a young teenager. I hung around St. Mark's and got to know the artists. I apprenticed here." She started spraying down the vinyl covering the chair, starting with the leg section. Rook leaned back and rolled his hands off the headrest as he did. The synthetic gloves were coated with the same adhesive as fingerprint lifting tape. Rook took a casual step back and let his hands dangle freely at his sides.

He asked, "But how does one practice?"

She sprayed down the rest of the chair and wiped it clean in methodical sways. "We use practice skin. It's synthetic. It used to be made out of some kind of rubber, but these days it really is skin. It's laboratory cloned." She looked up at him, sat in her chair and began sterilizing her needles. "If you want a tattoo, I can first ink it onto a piece of synthetic skin to prove to you both what it will look like and that I have the skills to do it. It costs extra."

"I trust you," he said.

"Is it a go then?" she asked, "Because honestly I don't see you being serious about a bulls-eye."

"I'm not," Rook answered. At that moment the door opened and a heavily tattooed couple entered.

"I have my next client," the artist told him, then asked, "Why did you come in?"

"It was the name of the parlor that brought me in," he told her.

She tossed the paper towels she had wiped the chair down with into a trash can. Inside it Rook noticed medical grade cotton fresh with blood dumped on top of used tattoo transfer stencil paper.

"Marco Polo?" she asked as she continued sterilizing. "Why?"

"Just a coincidence, I guess." Rook stepped back and let her make eye contact with the client. "I went to the Marco Polo exhibit at the Asian Museum yesterday, and I discovered he mentioned tattoos in his travel stories."

She nodded her head in understanding. "Yes," she said, "but there is more to the name of this parlor than that. This parlor is owned by a man named Marco Polo." She smiled innocently and waved her client in. The female in the couple handed her a drawing of a demonically barbed anchor.

Rook nodded in departing, "Thanks for your time."

At the front desk Rook peered at the company business cards. "If you change your mind about the bulls-eye, just call me."

"Thanks again," Rook said. The door opened as some new tattoo prospects entered, and Rook jammed his foot in the open door to exit without having to touch anything. Out on the street, before getting out his keys to open the sedan door, he carefully removed the gloves. They opened with tiny zippers along the edges so nothing would smudge. Inside the sedan Rook placed the gloves into a sterile plastic box.

7: Trash

As he drove away he contemplated emerald curtains and wallpaper, crocodiles and paper money, and knew he needed to get inside the Marco Polo Motel. Rook had studied the location of all of the last remaining payphones in the city—they stood like soldiers bullet-holed and unwilling to fall—and he utilized them to place anonymous phone calls. He drove to one, placed a call to the motel, applied a voice changer to the mouthpiece and asked in a baritone, "Dr. Chess, please. I'm not sure what suite he is in."

The concierge responded, "I have no record of Dr. Chess."

Rook asked, "Would you take a message? I'm sure Dr. Chess is staying there."

The concierge obliged.

Back in his office Rook commanded, "ECHO, on," and he placed the fingerprint gloves into his laser scanner box. As the scanner quietly hummed, the fingerprints digitized and projected wall-sized onto the mid-air monitor. Rook's first thought was the scanner had generated a moiré pattern, just like the surveillance images, because the fingerprint patterns themselves flickered, reminiscent of iridescent butterfly wings. This never happened with fingerprints. They simply weren't geometrically fine like print and did not lend themselves to the moiré phenomenon.

Rook scanned the gloves again, increasing the magnification and resolution by the power of two. He was correct: the scanner itself had generated the stripy, wavy moiré effect. The second scan stabilized the highly detailed fingerprint images.

But they were not human.

They were patterned, and the pattern was not organic: it was ornamental, just like Millioni's silks and just like his tattoos. Just like money.

Millioni's entire palms, grafted.

Rook was more than familiar with the process whereby new fingerprints were microscopically grafted, as it was a technique developed at the Tuxedo Park lab. The new process was so clean it was almost impossible to detect the graft lines. The graft skin was a synthesis of human skin sheets, shark cartilage, cowhide and silicone. The process involved acid burning the birth prints and laser resurfacing down through the layer below exposed skin, the dermis. Destroying the dermis meant destroying blood vessels, nerve endings and connective tissue. It also destroyed the papillary memory of the arches, loops and whorls that made the fingerprints unique. The early crude techniques historically had not succeeded, but they improved drastically after politics no longer minded the ethics of medicine. Subsequently skin grafting really did become political grafting.

While the graft skin, combined of dermis and epidermis, healed and accepted new skin, new fingerprint patterns were engraved by ultrasonics—soundwave etching. In order to ensure the original fingerprints did not return after healing, the new fingerprint patterns were laser etched daily into the synthetic epidermis. The synthetic skin was thicker than real human skin, so the organic ridge patterns of the original prints usually did not surface through it. Fingerprint grafting, however, had gone out of fashion due to the fact fingerprint value declined with the decline of crime scene investigation altogether. Altering one's fingerprints, like tattoos, piercings, cuttings and brandings, simply became body art.

Rook's synthetic gloves had picked up more than just fingerprints and contained some information from the palms. From this Rook could see Millioni's entire palms were incredibly unique signatures. His artful motive, Rook decided, was the antithesis of the rationale behind earlier grafting: he wasn't trying to hide, he was trying to be seen. Only a man who wanted someone to know exactly who had been where, would graft such a conspicuous rippling pattern into his skin. *Patterns,* Rook thought, *everything Marco Polo Millioni does is a pattern, down to his very skin.*

The artist had told him she had learned tattooing using practice skin and that she had apprenticed. *Under who?* Rook wondered, and in a brief feedback session he dreamed Marco Millioni's own hot running blood was swirling with ornamental silk.

***

Later that night he staked out the tattoo parlor trash in order to get the blood sample and the transfer paper. When the tattoo artist closed for the night she set the black plastic garbage bag on the curb and walked away down St. Mark's. After she blended into oblivion down the block, Rook drove up to the curb, opened the driver door and quickly pulling the garbage bag in. Nobody paid any attention. Everyone had their trash picked through, usually right on the street in front of everyone. Vagabonds and elderly people dug through trash constantly looking for recyclables or anything else they could find that seemed to have value. As Rook drove away he noticed a weathered, scrawny old lady bending over the bags cluttering a corner. She withdrew the sunglasses Rook had thrown away earlier and put them on.

In his office Rook opened the bag and sorted the contents into forensic clusters: there were fifteen bloody cottons, five tattoo transfer pages, five pairs of used black latex gloves, three tattooed practice skins, twenty-two paper towels that had been used to clean down the chair and one empty black ink bottle. Rook shined an ultraviolet light through the transfer papers to illuminate the tattoos, and he focused on the one that clearly had been Millioni's. The bloody cotton that had been on top of the transfer paper would likely be Millioni's also. Rook placed the cotton inside a saline solution, and as he did his mind drifted toward blood pattern analysis. Forensics had standardized the names for clusters of blood drops, blood splashes, blood pools, blood spurts, blood smears and blood trails. *If Millioni has blood on his hands*, he thought, *he has an eccentric way of showing it.*

Blood patterns from sniper assassination stretched out like seventeen foot long exclamation points, and blood patterns from up close shooting blasted like coronas, like crowns. Blood shadows were defined as the absence of blood patterns where one would expect to find them, and they indicated the movement or removal of evidence. Millioni's blood sample provided Rook with a DNA that matched nothing in his criminal database. Good or bad, innocent or guilty, if someone got arrested for anything their DNA was swabbed from the inner cheek and entered into the Illegal System database. Like the financial databases, it was two-tiered. The superficial code writhed with the Oroboros virus in the top public tier, but below it was the stabilized database Rook had helped create. Few knew about it.

The absence of a match in the stabilized database meant Millioni had no criminal record. Period.

Rook examined the pattern in the transfer paper. *Skewed hypotrochoids, meaningless reiterative circle geometry. Millioni's victim*, Rook thought, *is a blood shadow.*

More than anything for this case Rook needed a dead body.

***

"A bulls-eye? What did he look like?" Millioni purred into her ear.

The tattoo artist was drifting to sleep in Millioni's motel suite, her mind washing over the day and spastically replaying memories in fits. She woke briefly, opened her blue and amber eyes and tried to remember who had wanted a bulls-eye tattoo, tried to remember if he had paid for a practice skin version. Sleepily, she could not recall anything other than, "A silhouette."

The harder she tried to remember the darker the memory blackened until it towered over her, and slumber snuffed.

Millioni lay on his stomach next to her, the plastic removed from his back and his tattoo raised and scabbing. *Good*, he thought, *very good.*

In a private nook in his suite he made a direct call. Cradling an old landline, a blue colored plastic phone, he reported to Agent Orange, "He has almost found himself."

8: Seeing Stars

The package of silk pajamas arrived an hour later along with ornate silk sheets and almost simultaneously with the delivery of one ounce of gold, both from Marco Polo Silks and Marco Polo Precious Metals respectively. Rook spread the sheets over his psychologist couch and slipped into the pajamas. He only had one day left to solve the crime, and he would have to sleep on it for a while and let his subconscious mull in deeper feedback. He put the gold on his tongue, bit it, tasted it—tried to listen to it—and then pocketed it.

Rook had chosen violent reds and blacks for the pajamas and sheets, so he could in essence nestle himself into the blood shadow—the crime that was eluding him. As Rook played with his mind over the years he had found ways to manually shift his brainwave state to produce more than cognitive advantages: in addition to sleep induced lucid dreaming techniques, Rook had taught himself wake induced lucid hypnagogia. *Hypnagogia* was Greek for *sleep abductor.* Technically it signaled the brain's shifting from wakefulness to sleep, from the alpha state to the theta. Rook's subconscious had become so vibrant over the years, at will he could dream while awake or become awake while remaining in a dream, but ultimately he had come to realize the imagery surfacing in these states was quantum. It was during the dream states the ego mind slipped into the undifferentiated quantum sea. The nanoelectrodes implanted in his skin further aided his ability to tune into quantum realities. Rook was a quantum human machine.

All of the patterns imbuing Marco Millioni's world reminded him of one central, core psychological pattern: the light images the brain generates during hypnagogia. These images were peripherally pararealistic at best. People gifted with exploring the alien and shadowy territory of this in-between mind space, or who had discovered it through hallucinogens, frequently sought comfort in extraterrestrial or occult explanations. For Rook the images seemed sparks from a gearshift between brain-states, spastic releases of neuroelectricity through the optic nerves as the brain surfed quantum wormholes. He also believed they could be quantum bookmarks, visual placeholders for information that made a lot of sense to the brain but not to the personality in front of the brain. Rook removed himself mentally as fully as he could from all the religion and mythology associated with dreaming.

The neuroelectric images flashed as phosphenes, as light patterns generated by neuroelectrical stimulation. They were frequently quasi-geometric and implied that figurative patterning was essential to brain make-up. The phenomenon of seeing stars from cartoon blows to the head or the phenomenon of seeing flickering light in an utterly darkened room—the prisoner's cinema as it was called—were also phosphenic. When lacking external stimulation, the brain easily turned in on itself. Hypnagogia was a simple form of brainwave feedback.

Apophenia was the term relegated to the crackpots who made meaningful but psychotic connections out of random patterns. As a detective Rook's paranoia brushed up against apophenia like a black cat. It had to, for it was the truly psychotic who committed crimes and generated the crime patterns, and he had to be as borderline paranoid as them.

An exception, The Machete had found ways to ingeniously induce meaningful patterns out of what was otherwise a junkyard of human information.

Rook had cracked The Machete's code, and he desperately needed to crack Millioni's. Somehow there was a meaning inside all of Millioni's patterns, and by dreaming in deep feedback—near the event horizon where life was swallowed by death—Rook would let his subconscious connect the dots.

Rook had ordered the silk and had it delivered to Dr. Chess's earlier in the day. He had then intercepted the package at the sidewalk from a mailman and reshipped it two more times, thus scrambling the path of the package. He had done the same with the gold.

Rook sat on the edge of his couch, the cool silk warming against his body, and as part of his psychonaut entrainment, he smoked a blunt.

9: Astrolabe

Nestled in the silk and his psychonaut mask, as his hash heavy mind slipped toward sleep, it jumped alive with silken patterned light. The pajamas, sheets, currency and wallpaper patterns danced and writhed together seamlessly. Rook twitched as the inner light burst into a highly ornamented giant crocodile, and as Rook fell to the next level of sleep he felt as if he were literally falling headfirst. Falling asleep often arrived with the mind gear shifting out of gravity, inducing the free-fall sensation, and Rook inferred it was why the passage to sleep was known as *falling*.

The dreaming psychonaut Rook fell fast, and his dream self became the victim dropped into the crocodile pool at the club, but he did not scream. The giant beast, made of light itself, the source of the lightshow, opened up its jaws and swallowed Rook. Rook felt a profound suffocation, and inside the darkness Rook's mind dove into a deep black, silken quantum sea. The quantum dream crocodile wrestled with Rook's body, thrashing the pool as it jerked its neck with violent, murderous twisting. Spattering along the walls of the pool was Rook's own dream blood, and the dream blood transformed into ornamental, silken sheets. Flashing in red phosphenes like the red lights in his watch, the blood pattern ornament evolved into a portrait of the sapphire encrusted performer. The orange red sapphires exploded like internal fireworks, and Rook's body twitched in surprise. A shadow rose up from the thrashing crocodile and became a shadow cast from a man standing in the ring up above the pool. It was Millioni, and his entire body was woven of living, quantum black silk and liquid carbon ink. He extended his hand and released paper money into the pool. The ink on the bill was printed with the decor grafted onto his palms. His palms morphed into golden astrolabes, becoming two evenly poised judicial scales.

Rook's body jolted. He opened his eyes. He was inside a motel room. The sheets, wallpaper and curtains all shimmered: everything was alive with quantum phosphenes. Rook heaved himself out of the bed and walked past the desk, where even the stationary was ornamented. Next to the stationary was a piece of chalk. Rook picked up the chalk and wrote down three words—three essential clues—and when he looked up he was looking into a mirror. When he looked at his reflection, he merged with Marco Millioni. His eyes became gently Asian and his black beard a trim goatee.

The scene collapsed.

Rook fell into delta and slumbered deeply, undreamingly.

About an hour passed before Rook emerged from the delicious leaden weight of sleep. He rolled his legs out, sat up, unlocked a safe and withdrew a journal. The sound of the pen lightly etching the night, he quietly made notes in the dream journal.

He remembered all the details from the session but could not recall the three words he had chalked onto the motel stationary. They were on the tip of his memory, submerged.

Looking at himself in a mirror during lucid dreams was a repetitive theme, and it happened in almost every one. Rook knew it was the brain's way of subconsciously reflecting on the mirror boundary between ego and the collective unconscious. It was mind looking at itself through the wormhole. It was also common for Rook's dream ego to write something down in the dream, believing the words were very meaningful. Usually upon waking he did not remember them or else they were nonsensical, and he believed the act of writing in a dream was simply a symbolic act of bridging the rational, speaking consciousness to the fluid surrealism of lucid dreaming. It was also a repetitive theme in Rook's lucid dreams for him to find his reflection merged with the identity of a victim or a criminal. It meant he was closing in.

Still, like the servant who had buried his talent, the case still wrestled in nothingness.

CHAPTER TEN: Papyrus

1: Compass, Gunpowder, Print and Laundromat

Around the rims of seemingly boundless Manhattan, borne from the papyrus developed by the shadow man Jack the Butterfly, an inky stain was spreading. Even the fish darting in and out of the subaqueous rootings, nibbling away at the organisms scaling on the pale green stalks, were beginning to show signs of the invasion. Across their scales Chinese characters manifested and evolved with the living, organic language.

At a post midnight market Jules Barbillon bought a cluster of living, flopping, seven-inch blue snappers, their scales now riddled with ink. He asked the fisherman, from whom he frequently bought fish for his temple crocodile, what the writing meant.

"Not quite sure. Maybe, something about arch-villain, something about war."

"How auspicious."

The fisherman agreed by nodding and pointing at the papyrus choking the river's edge.

"Same here. See! Weed not here last week."

Back in his apartment, Jules dropped a fish into his temple pool. The crocodile opened its mouth, and Jules witnessed Chinese writing bleeding through a dark inky liquid from its tongue. As its jaws clamped down onto the fish, Jules unrolled a papyrus reed, the ink bleeding into his fingertips, and he thought with great enthusiasm, *How auspicious!*

***

There were three things the Chinese were most noted for inventing: the compass, gunpowder and printing. Of those things they were first to print was paper currency. *Djaou* meant the *lack of metal*—of coined metal; it was the Chinese word for paper money. *Djaou*. During his visit to the museum, Rook had learned these things and also had learned that the real Marco Polo was the first to bring word of paper money back to Europe.

Chinese culture had devolved inside its politics, and what the proud Chinese dynasties had brought to the urban American city was, ultimately the unproud laundromat. The majority of immigrant Chinese were poor, and on every city block they managed a laundromat where machines spun faithfully day and night. Within them the Chinese literally laundered their crime capital. Rook studied the monetary transactions of all the city businesses named after Marco Polo Millioni—even his laundromat—and it seemed the man was legitimately cycling quantum income through his tills, nothing more.

But the gold. What is he broadcasting? What is he listening to?

Early astrolabes directed travelers to Xian, Rook learned after his psychonaut session, to the origin of the Silk Road. They weren't exactly compasses. The appearance of the astrolabe in his dream struck him as the most significant key to unlocking the ornamental code inked into Millioni's skin and etched into his fingertips. Astrolabes—about six inches in diameter—were early simple brass tools that assisted with spherical geometry. They were engineered for predicting time, sunrise, astronomical positions and the spherical, geometrical movement of heavenly bodies. The main circular disc was called the *mater*—the mother. Stereographic projections were etched into the successive ring, the tympan, and flattened the spherical outlines onto a plane.

"ECHO, on. Search astrolabe."

On the hovering, tangible screen an image appeared from history: an etching of a godly man bearing on his shoulders an armillary sphere.

"What am I looking at?"

The computer, in its feminine voice, spoke back to him, "Keywords, atlas, armillary sphere."

"What's an armillary sphere?"

"A globe around which celestial paths are fabricated as metal hoops."

"Zoom."

In the etching, the shadows of the outlined celestial paths in the three dimensional sphere were cast onto the ground into two dimensions at the godly man's feet. Angels measured the arcs of the conformal two-dimensional shadows, transcribing the crisscrossing arcs and thus deriving them into two-dimensional angles.

Simply, the method scaled down the known cosmos to something that could fit into a pocketwatch. Rook knew the method well: it had been incorporated into his watch.

Rook retrieved the scanned paper transfer that held the design of Millioni's latest tattoo. If his hunch was correct, the seemingly meaningless whorls and scrolls were the two dimensional, stereographical shadows of three-dimensional locations. Included in the information, once extrapolated back to three dimensions, would be astronomical time.

Millioni was ink staining his body with either his exact location and time during a hit, Rook believed, the victim's or both. He thought, *If he's triangulating, means he making his hits by sniper fire.*

Rook sat back in awe at the luxurious beauty of it all, and he realized this man fascinated him.

2: Stereography

Since Millioni never seemed to leave the city, Rook decided whomever he was killing either also lived in the city or came into the city to meet their fate. With the hours ticking down on his deadline to solve, Rook knew he was finally hot on the case. His heart pounded in his ears.

Stereography was essential to cartography. Manhattan had long been laid out like a Cartesian grid, like a map of a map. Though still groggy from hash and feedback—and whatever he had done to himself the night before—Rook rapidly voice commanded the ECHO computer, "Map. Manhattan."

A map of the city filled the wall-sized monitor suspended in the center of the room. The computer was hypersmart, and even if it did not have a unique program it could quickly learn and generate one. Rook said, "Conformal map," and the ECHO wrapped the map of Manhattan onto a sphere.

"Render into three dimensions."

He walked around the digital projection as it hovered in his office, marveling at it.

"Render wireframe."

It did.

"Add buildings and animate into a twenty-four hour, 365 day and night sunlight and shadow simulation."

The globe spun like it was the Earth covered only by Manhattan, all of the city streets stretched around it and the buildings sticking up out of it like mountain ranges.

"Project a two-dimensional stereograph from the wireframe."

As if from above the simulator cast a light through the wireframed, spherized city. And, just as in the etching featuring Atlas and the angels, the city wireframe flattened onto a plane.

Rook scanned the tattoo transfer into the smart program he was generating and said, "Look for a match."

It took less than a second.

The matched tattoo pattern overlapped almost exactly a pattern in Rook's digitally morphed city, revealing a matched date, time and location by latitude and longitude.

Millioni's making a hit today, Rook realized, *at noon.*

Rook still needed to know if the location was the site of the assassin when firing the bullet or the site of the victim. "Triangulate to a prime sniper gunfire location. Infer a bullet speed of two thousand feet per second." Within moments the ECHO had isolated the best option, a rooftop at 27th and Broadway.

Confident and even excited, Rook commanded, "Wed the program with the photos I took of Millioni during the tattooing." The computer hummed as it churned data, but it found no further matches.

It explained, "The surveillance images are too oblique, and due to the moiré interferences, I'm unable to correct it. Only the transfer paper which cartographically projected the killing onto Millioni's shoulder is pristine enough to generate a match."

Rook responded, "But one match is more than enough."

Still, it did not mean that whoever was scheduled to die was a victim Rook had been hired to save. The information would allow Rook to place additional surveillance to monitor the act. He decided the latitude and longitude of a sniper would be fixed, and likely the victim's body would be in motion and only so predictable. He checked The Wire's security cameras and realized the ECHO's suggested rooftop at 27th and Broadway just above the Flatiron was not under surveillance. On the roof, Rook discovered, was New York City's largest rooftop bar, open from all night, seven days a week.

On the rooftop specified by the interpolated tattoo, around 3:00 a.m., Rook had a whiskey amidst an intoxicated crowd and stealthily planted a camera the size of a button.

When Millioni made the shot from that rooftop, Rook knew exactly where he himself would be: the motel. It was located a mere four blocks away from the rooftop location and the timing would provide him with an ideal period of time for a break-in. He quickly made a reservation and slipped back to the Lower East Side between for a quick nap.

Hard sleep hit him quickly, and he was deep in delta when a shadow, seemingly struck from car lights on Ludlow Street, rolled across his bed toward his phone. Simultaneously inside the Lucky Dead Pawn shop Jack the Butterfly, increasingly quantum entrained with Rook, though not exactly sleepwalking, placed a call. “Marco Polo Motel. Noon.”

The man on the other end made the arrangement, and minutes later another man got on a New York bound plane in Oklahoma City.

***

An hour later a millionized talent of gold was delivered to Marco Polo Precious Metals, and the shadow man Jack the Butterfly awoke on his opium den lohan in the Lucky Dead Pawn shop, his skin swimming with black ink, the ink in turn grafting war words into black silk pajamas. In a rare moment of near sobriety he tried to see his reflection in a mirror, but he saw again only blackish shadowy eyes with black slit pupils staring at him out of a cocoon of darkness.

Now, detective, he thought, *figure out who the fuck I am!*

3: Checking In

Rook woke up on his bed in the early morning with a grungy mental feeling like a hangover and a mental itch he could not quite fathom. He made his way to the kitchen faucet and drank deeply two glasses of cool, clean water.

As he showered, Rook remembered Dr. Chess making joking reference to the invasive species *Bromus tectorum* during the symposium. He remembered him laughing like a hyena, his lips gruesomely pulled back over purple gums, his shock of white hair waving, as he remarked that the grass was either named after him or he after it. The species was a winter annual in the grass family, Rook learned, with common names including cheat grass and chess grass. Rook noted the man made no reference to the game of chess and seemed utterly absorbed by the notion chess was nothing other than a weed.

After the symposium Rook had followed Dr. Chess and one of his Chinese collegial associates to a cafe. Rook had watched the man's mannerisms, the way he dropped four sugar cubes into his coffee cup, the way he lifted the porcelain cup to his hyena lips and sniffed his coffee studiously through long nostrils in a blue nose. He observed the way the man walked to the bathroom, leaving his leather satchel behind as if he had nothing to hide. Later Rook pinged the coffee house currency system and found the payments for the two cups of coffee under Dr. Chess's name.

Rook cloned the currency.

***

The Marco Polo Motel concierge ran the cloned currency and recognized the name of Dr. Chess when it popped up on a screen. The concierge said, "Oh, Dr.

Chess, you have a message from a Mr. Green. Could you please call him right away."

Rook pulled out a dummy cellphone and feigned disappointment, saying in a deepened voice, "The battery is dead."

The concierge offered up the house phone. Here Rook dialed Mr. Green. A computer answered after four rings and the digitized voice on the answering machine sounded like a human. While it played the voice recording, which was in fact Rook's own voice morphed within a sound editing program, the telephonic computer sent quiet code throughout the motel house phone system and bugged each and every room. As he stood near the column the house phone was mounted onto, Rook watched a machine gun armed mailman arrive with a small package. "For Mr. Millioni," the mailman said, "from the candyman." Rook observed as the concierge nodded dutifully and placed the candy box in the mailbox for Suite 1001.

Machine guns and candy, Rook mused darkly, *together at last.*

4: The Culture of Gardens

During the past days, Rook had not seen the assassin eating any candy, and knowing full well the killing hour was on the event horizon, he wondered if there really was candy inside the package or something else. Rook had purposely come early for his room, and he was told it would be ready in an hour. He used this time to sit at an open lounge reading an electronic copy of a rare book about the history and culture of gardens. He made certain to ponder a passage regarding a sacred grove and the god *Terminus*—the god of the boundary stone—while he drank a cup of coffee similar to the one he had seen Dr. Chess drink. He slowly dropped in four cubes of sugar and stirred them in. The sweetness was not to Rook's palate, and this made it even easier for him to drink slowly.

The Marco Polo lobby and bar reminded him of a garden. Gardens had been rarities on the city island for hundreds of years. He felt he hadn't seen one since he was a child, yet the greenery of the motel and memories of Dr. Chess's greenhouse nagged at him as if he had recently seen one. *Deja vu* and *jamais vu* were both, he had long considered, apophenic tracers of the quantum world. *Yes*, he thought, he was still groggy from the intensive feedback sessions he'd been utilizing to unearth Millioni's crime.

Groggy. The quantum world hung around Rook like a cloud of mental dust. *Quantum hangover*, he thought, *nothing more.*

He thought of hard edges to focus his mind, and he thought of the still existing Central Park. Ever since the city had sold it off to keep from going bankrupt, great walls had flung up around it, imprisoning it even as it was saved. The city rumors about the Park's destiny had become the fertile garden of mutual imagination, and it was growing within Rook as he read the book within the green lobby located a sniper bullet's distance from the walls of the park.

Rook pushed the book in front of himself, positioning it just so the lounge employees and security cameras could not see what he was reading. When he tilted the screen lightly the page switched to what looked like an index but was actually a live transliteration of all the phone conversations taking place at the motel. The phone in suite 1001 activated.

Millioni was talking to someone. The book screen translated the conversation in writing.

Marco Millioni: "Hello?"

Voice: "Mr. Millioni, I am calling to thank you for your order and to let you know the candy has been delivered."

Marco Millioni: "Thank you."

And that was it. The phone went quiet. Rook jiggled the electronic screen and shifted it back to the literature on gardens.

Rook observed the green walls of the lobby, a garish garden of silk in which emerald greens twisted with embroidered floral golds. Along one long wall an antiquated map stitched out the parent route of the Silk Road, from Xian in China across Afghanistan, Iran and Turkey. Rook observed it as elevator doors opened, and striding across the marble floor in front of the map came Millioni. He seemed for a moment, Rook thought, to be black ink as it bled from a pen, triangulating along the cartography of the Silk Road. In his characteristic black silk, in the glaring Edenic green of the lobby, the man seemed, Rook thought, *Satanic.*

As Millioni passed through the lobby Rook heard a concierge answer the phone with the word, "Marco" and before the concierge could finish Rook's tongue was struck with the response, "Polo."

Marco. Beat. Polo. It was a game Rook had played as a child—a game played while swimming, back in the day when people thought the water was safe and they found out it wasn't. Private pools had been built to replace wild water swimming, and at the Marco Polo Swimming Club, Rook knew, Millioni took a swim every morning.

Why, Rook wondered, *didn't I think of that game before?* And he realized he would have to investigate the origin of the game later.

Marco Millioni paused and collected his candy box. He opened the package, took out a small lollipop, unwrapped it and momentarily gazed inside the wrapper, then slipped the orange bulb into his mouth. As if nothing other than the taste of hard candy was on his mind, Marco Millioni slipped the wrapper into a pocket and made his way out the revolving doors with the candy box.

Rook paid for his coffee with his room number a casual minute after Millioni's exit. His room was ready. On his way up in the elevator Rook contemplated the exact nature of the water game. Did it have anything to do with water polo? In the past days Rook had been free-associating the words Marco and Polo, and he already knew *polo* was the word for *ball.* He closed his eyes and focused on memories of fractured, bright blue swimming pool waters from his childhood. *Why can't I see whether a ball is involved?*

Rook opened his eyes. *Because*, he remembered, *Marco Polo is a game played with eyes closed. It's a game of tag, a game of it.* The child who is *it* swims with eyes closed and calls out the word, *Marco.* The rest of the swimmers respond with, *Polo.* The *it* child swims as fast as possible toward the voices, and when *it* has finally succeeded in touching another swimmer, the tagged in turn becomes *it*.

Rook closed the motel door behind him. He had told the concierge his luggage was en route from a courier. Another memory popped, of an orange ball bouncing into traffic, of a lollipop ejecting from the young boy's lips.

Observing the queer room, Rook set the memory aside. He witnessed the curtains, bedspread and even the furniture ornately dancing with emerald threads in silken stereographic tranquility. It was a lurid trick of the eye, as ripe and bodacious as a garden in spring blossom. As his eyes adjusted to the near hallucinatory experience, he spied on top of the desk a standard yet beautifully antiquated folder holding, he inferred, envelopes and stationary marked with the name and address of the motel. Rook opened it with gloved hands. Sure enough, even the scrolled logo imprinted on the stationary paper was acutely ornamental. Next to it on the desk, instead of a Bible, was a copy of Marco Polo's travels.

Rook placed the stationary folder and book into a small black briefcase, and for a long moment he admired the room's wallpaper. It was made out of hundred dollar bills.

He walked up to a wall and peered hard at the bills. Each bore the same serial number: 1011010110.

5: It

With his briefcase, Rook made his way up to the tenth floor. He watched a maid pushing her cart toward Millioni's suite, where a "Please Service" sign hung on the door handle.

Rook thought of Millioni's back, of the stationary and the money. *Spirograph, also once upon a time a child's game. Spirographs made by spinning, wheels inside of wheels.*

If Rook had calculated correctly, Millioni was en route with his innocent, childish lollipop to the hit.

Rook strolled down the hallway and listened for the sounds of the maid's keys opening into the suite. There they were: the telltale jangles. He listened as she rolled her cart in, and he followed her like a shadow.

***

On the rooftop bar 2000 feet away, a man in a black overcoat stepped out of an elevator and walked right past a custodian vacuuming. The man's right hand flashed a diamond pinkie ring as he climbed the stairs to the roof and the ladders up toward the wooden water tower platform. He ducked unnoticed under it and pulled a black bag from his coat. He opened the bag and quickly, neatly snapped together three metal pieces. Lying on his belly, his cheek against the cold rest, he aimed for a window.

The curtains were closed.

***

Inside Millioni's suite Rook silently observed and photographed through his sunglasses while pulling duct tape out of a jacket pocket. It wasn't a roll—it was a flattened five feet wrapped around a small piece of cardboard—just compact enough to fit inside a wallet.

He did not reduce Millioni's colorful suite to black and white. Witnessing the blizzard of silk color, Rook knew, was necessary to unlocking the man's mind. The wallpaper in Millioni's suite was even more highly stylized, marked with patterns similar to his tattoos, and other walls were also papered with hundred dollar bills. The curtains, of the same green silk at the tattoo parlor, were closed. The maid set about to opening them.

Through the site the sniper watched the curtains part to the maid. He would wait for her to open them fully, to give him the greatest range. Behind the maid he saw at first a shadow. He squinted and brought the shadow into focus.

It stubbornly remained a shadow.

The abrupt rip of the duct tape startled the maid. She rotated toward the sound, but she couldn't make a full turn. He was already taping her mouth shut and ramming a pillowcase over her head. In the next moment, she was mute and blind, and she fought with her hands and legs.

The man with the rifle squinted and tried to keep the shadow in the crosshairs, but the maid was in the way. *It won't matter*, the man thought, *if the maid goes down too*. The .50 caliber bullet would easily take them both down along with a car if they were in it. *Better not though*, he thought, and for a long, uncomfortable second he waited for the maid to get out of the way. He had been told to kill the man in room 1001, and he was going to do it—the man and not the maid.

The sniper tightened his finger on the trigger, waiting patiently. The struggle with the maid was dying down as the shadowy man in room 1001 taped her wrists. *Got him*, the sniper thought, as the maid fell away and Rook came into sharp focus. The sniper smiled and squeezed the trigger just as the smell of hash hit his nostrils and a .22 caliber bullet entered his own brain. The sniper bullet sped at 2700 feet per second toward suite 1001, four long east-west blocks away as the sniper's cheek slid down the gun rest. The nudge he took when his life ended—so critically timed with the firing of his weapon—was not enough to challenge the trajectory of the bullet but just enough to alter its timing with the struggling maid and Rook's head. The sniper's bullet pierced the motel window, and it made a whizzing sound as it passed in front of Rook's eyes, between his face and the pillowcased head of the petrified maid. The bullet hit a mirror, shattering it and revealing behind it a safe.

As Rook dove, his thoughts bulleted, *It! It's a setup! Lollipop? I'm a sucker!*

6: A Water Tower

Beneath the water tower Marco Millioni stared down at the dead sniper. It seemed to Millioni that the sniper had fired at the exact same time he had killed him. In fact it seemed the firing had been a reflex. It was Millioni's job to assassinate assassins, hence his moniker *Weedkiller*, and he was very good at it. He had been tipped off as to the assassin's expected location the night prior, and he had the artist tattoo the imminent hit onto his body. The instructions for the kill were reiterated in the spirograph-stylized patterns etched into the lollipop wrapper.

These patterns were almost impossible to reproduce exactly. They were easy to generate but bastardous to solve, like solving the wave patterns on the surface of the seas—unless one was sailing in the patterns of Weedkiller.

Or one of his triplet brothers.

***

Inside the motel room in the moments following the solo gunshot, Rook lay on top of the maid. She was in shock. The sound of the bullet had come as an afterthought, ripping the atmosphere like a tiny, lethal jet. Rook peered up at the safe and wondered, *Was the gunman firing at me or at the safe?* Rook crawled on his belly and pulled shut the curtains. It wouldn't stop the shooting, but the shooter would give himself away with wild firing. More likely, Rook decided, the sniper would save the next shot for when someone or something was in dead aim.

***

As a child, Millioni and his brothers had codified their own alphabet. On rice paper, using India ink, they drew their own calligraphy: a private alphabet generated by circular motion within circular motion. Inside the Chinese and Italian mafias, the child Marco Millioni became a go-between, a messenger. He would transcribe coded oral instructions from mafia elders that made no literal sense to him into his circular alphabet that in turn made no literal sense to the elders. Only Marco Millioni and his brothers knew how to read the seemingly nonsensical code but they had no idea what it meant when they spoke it aloud. It was doubly encrypted, and carried by a child in lower Manhattan, the code looked like a child's elaborate daydreamy designs—nothing more. As a messenger, Marco would transport the text, then read the instructions off to the receiving party, and though the instructions were cryptic and incomprehensible to young Millioni, they were not to the party he delivered them to.

Marco Millioni kept all of his transcriptions in order in a memory book. As he became older and discovered the writings of Marco Polo, Marco Millioni felt a kinship to the great traveler and transcriber, and he began mapping the great tour of his own life onto his pale body. Since he did not want his body to be an open book, he had utilized the simple circular plastic wheels that came with the antiquated children's spirograph game to develop sophisticated, seemingly nonsensical patterns. From there he had turned to math, masterfully rendering the patterns astronomical.

At the Marco Polo Tattoo parlor on St. Mark's, Marco Millioni had his tales transcribed onto his body. His body had become a living map of all his deeds, be they though misdeeds. In time someone neither Italian nor Chinese, and powerful beyond his imagination, had contacted him and offered him a repeated opportunity. When it became time to move outside of the Chinese and Italian crime world, for this benefactor—as she called herself—they helped him generate the persona of Weedkiller overnight.

His brothers managed the contracts and the money. There wasn't a city street not under observation by them. The role the triplets played in New York City's cycle of Seven reiterated, and as key players of Seven, they acutely understood their weekly rebirthing in Jail.

Every seven days Weedkiller killed an assassin. The assassins came in from outside of the city. They were specialized loners who tried to make a quick New York City tour with a bullet, and it was because of who they were trying to kill, they never left the city alive. Weedkiller narrowed his eyes. He removed the rewrapped lollipop from a pocket and carefully, as if it was a flower being laid on a grave, placed it next to the rooftop water tower tank.

7: An Assassin

It had become Weedkiller's signature to kill them just as they were about to kill. The difference this time: a bullet had been fired. Pulling on his blunt, staring down at the dead man, he wondered if in fact he had failed and if the sniper's bullet had taken a victim. If so, it would be his first failure.

But the world was still hard and tangible around him, giving him confidence he had not failed. Weedkiller calmly squatted to his knees and peered through the gun sight in the direction the sniper had shot. He took a long drag on his blunt and contemplated the bullet-holed window he spied. *My window!*

The curtains were closed. Closed curtains meant one of two things to him: the assassin had fired by reflex with no target, or someone inside had survived and closed them. Weedkiller collapsed the rifle into its parts and returned it to its bag. He himself always used the standard assassin's weapon, the small .22 bullet meticulously fired at close range.

Weedkiller had quick work with the corpse, then he would have to connect with his brothers to discuss what was really happening. The hash calmed him, and whatever the circumstances, no matter how dire, *I'll face them.*

There were three water towers on the roof. Weedkiller's long fingers pulled a small strong rope and a set of pulleys from inside his jacket. In moments he was pulling the dead man up the side of one of the water towers with the effort needed only to pull the blunt from his lips. In his black suit, he looked more like a cosmopolitan owner of a chic midtown motel than a man disposing of a body.

***

Silence hummed with heartbeats and air conditioners. The maid was gasping and praying in Italian while Rook slithered to the safe and slowly raised himself. The bullet had ripped right through it, leaving a hole the size of an old penny. An electronic display hummed, indicating a biometric interface was still active. Rook quickly unzipped his case and slipped out gloves he had fabricated from latex and formed from Millioni's palm and fingerprints. He jammed his hands into the gloves and pressed his palms against the biometric reader. Swollen moments ticked in his imagination while the reader scanned and finally allowed the match. With a gentle pry, the door to the safe opened. Inside was a bundle of papers with dried hemp grass and a fine gold chain tying the sheaf together. Rook absorbed what he had found and decided quickly to take the book with him. When he lifted the chain, there was something to it beyond jewelry. The chain was made of fine filaments, of tiny golden string. It was concatenated with sequenced, miniature golden ones and zeros.

***

Weedkiller climbed the ladder on the side of the tower tank, opened a hatch and pushed the dead man in. He glanced across the city rooftops where water towers abounded. This water tower tank had an extra ingredient in it: lime. The pipes were connected not to fresh water but to the sewer system, and soon the corpse would be nothing but gel. The gel would flush through the drainage system down into the belly of the monster that was New York City. The thunderstorms would purge the blood.

***

Rook dropped the maid into the laundry cart and covered her. He ditched the cart by the elevator and fled via the interior stairwell just as the elevator doors opened. A motel security guard exited the elevator, and he heard a muffled cry issue from the laundry.

Rook was only three stories below, his feet pounding the stairs. By the time the guard had removed the pillowcase from the maid's head with a pocket-knife, Rook was six flights below with four to go. By the time the guard had removed the duct tape from her mouth, pulling some black lip hair with it, she was bleeding and whimpering. Rook was then nine flights down with one to go.

On the tenth floor the guard was wiping the blood from the maid's lips with the sheet that had covered her. “A man,” was all she was able to say, "like a shadow."

The guard relayed the security concern to the other guards. Marco Millioni, the owner of the motel and the resident of the tenth floor, was immediately called.

"Yes?" he answered. By the time the guard relayed the information about the maid, about an intruder and a bullet, Millioni was back at street level, shedding his Weedkiller persona by tossing the blunt to the sidewalk.

"I see."

Marco Millioni thought to himself about the shadow-like man in the motel room, *I just saved his life and he just saved mine.*

"Let him go. But keep an eye on him."

***

Rook wiped sweat from his brow and calmly stepped into the lobby. His hand was poised to pull his gun. He scanned and found the doorman making eye contact with him. The doorman pushed the glass door open, and with a swing of his arm he invited Rook to exit.

Out on the street Millioni's guards were waiting, ready to trail him. Though he could not see them, Rook felt the eyes.

Was the bullet meant for Millioni or for me? Did Millioni fire the bullet? Does Millioni have a contract on me?

The way the doorman had looked at him seemed a tell. *He's letting me go. Sort of.* Rook walked calmly out the door with the sheaf and chain tucked inside his briefcase. When he was a good fifty feet away from the motel, his back turned to his followers, Rook scanned the skyline for the shooting location.

Rook was making his way through what had been a park overrun by, of all things he realized, *Papyrus*, when four guards took the four corners of the park as points to close in on him.

And they never saw him again.

8: Shadowplay

The city's dissonant thunder choked by heavy humid air slammed the park with a sudden thunderstorm. Those prepared unleashed umbrellas. The baffled guards searched the park, the streets, the footsteps, and the longer they searched the harder it became for them to remember what he looked like. Black hair blended into darkness. None wanted to say to another, what did he look like? None wanted to admit.

Rook, his body increasingly transforming into a human shaped shadowy mist, was less than 2000 feet away, standing under the water tower, taking samples of the blood. This transformation did not affect him mentally, not immediately, just as a butterfly would not be troubled by its metamorphosis, nor that of a seed to a weed. He did sense an ecstasy, but this sensation typically accompanied the solution to a crime.

He spotted the wrapped lollipop near the water tower.

A telling red liquid line ran down the length of the grain in one of the grayed wood planks comprising the exterior of the water tower tank. Where the tower's small roof had kept the rain from washing the print away, on a metal band hooping the wooden tower, Rook found Weedkiller's ornamental fingerprints in blood. Rook climbed the ladder up the side of the tower, found the hatch in the roof and opened it. He flinched as he witnessed the corpse and smelled the stony lime. Rook quickly snapped on latex gloves over his shadowy hands, reached in and took hold of one of the man's hands, the one with the ring. He swiftly took DNA samples, fingerprints and the ring. The diamond design was simple, and it was the only artifact on the corpse. Rook rolled him, searching, but the man's pockets were empty. By the time Rook was done collecting evidence, the lime had eaten through the latex gloves and was burning his shadowy hands. A drenched Rook washed his stinging hands in a puddle on the roof. He saw now that his hands were becoming shadowy but for some reason his mind did not touch upon it as anything that mattered. Instead he felt tuned to a lust that choked him with the perfect sense accompanying the thoughtless quiescence of sex.

He vomited yellowy newspaper pulp and observed with dispassion as the thunderstorm washed it toward a roof drain. He dabbed a finger at a Chinese character printed in the pulp, the only one he could make out in full, and he placed it inside a small plastic vial.

He surveyed the skyline and the thousands of water towers he had taken for granted loomed like dark visual laughter. The taste of gastric acid and old paper, like a quantum ghost he was about to greet, haunted his breath.

He slipped back downtown to Ludlow Street in his sedan. "Rewind the footage from the surveillance camera I planted on the roof to 11:55 a.m." Rook watched in his sedan monitor as Weedkiller shot the man with the rifle. He was astonished that he did not sharpshoot and that he was in fact, Rook relished, *Avenging assassins.*

Back in his office Rook undressed from his wet clothing and observed his thinning shadowy frame with mild curiosity. He clothed himself in a clean dry suit and sat down in front of his black briefcase. As if he were unlocking the mystery of a god, with trepidation he opened up his case to the chain and to the sheaf. His shadowy fingers tingled with excitement as he tugged at the hemp binding the sheaf, and the pages, like an exhale, loosened. He lifted the top page with tweezers and gazed at the circular pattern inked onto it: it was, he realized, the original design of Millioni's—Weedkiller's—latest tattoo, of which the one he had collected from the trash was a copy. Slowly he backtracked through each cryptic, original tattoo pattern. Each original was drawn in an ink made of soot and gum on actual handmade papyrus. Rook puzzled at the inclusion of Egyptian culture into the man's already eclectic ethnic inclinations. Rook felt anonymous and safe in his office but at the same time there was a hunger to know exactly how Weedkiller was reacting to the violation of his motel haven and now the loss of his beloved, intricately occult sheaf.

His memory of vomiting after leaving the Lucky Dead Pawn shop vaguely shifted into soft focus as he sipped at a whiskey, the alcohol searing the vomit flavor from the tip of his tongue, clearing his senses. He knew somehow he had become contaminated, the parallel realities commingling in him and making him, he thought, *Quantum sea sick.* But as to why he would vomit pulp he did not know. He reached for the vial in which the Chinese character was sealed and opened it. He scanned it and commanded the ECHO, "Define."

The ECHO responded, "Bridge."

"Structure or music?"

"Structure."

Rook knew quantum bridges were nanodiodes long developed for the miniaturization of electronics, and he wondered if the conceptual quantum bridges he crossed sleuthing in feedback were folding in on themselves as he observed his shadowy hands. He thought also of musical bridges, of the pensive interlude that returns to the main melody. He closed his eyes and in his vivid imagination this internal music sprang taut with a visual of cables from the Brooklyn Bridge, a bridge that almost killed its chief engineer when he got the bends.

Rook felt as if he was jumping from a great height. His eyes flashed opened.

Not quantum sea sick, he thought, *quantum bends. I have the bends!*

Having self-diagnosed, Rook felt a relief, especially since he realized this had happened before. Many times. His shadowy nature dissipated, and his skin became grayish pink as he focused on his hands. He knocked back the whiskey, focused harder and contemplated water towers, using them as an anchor point to shift himself back into classical reality. He realized with a start perhaps the one in which he'd found the corpse was not the only one being used as a means to dispose bodies.

“Who is this man? Can you get his DNA from it?” Rook asked as he placed the dead man’s diamond ring into the scanner.

The ECHO flashed a grid of analytical lasers over the ring, “A Mr. John Smith. Petroleum Club affiliate. Lengthy record. The diamond is a Petroleum Club initiate ring.”

"And water towers. What are they?"

The ECHO responded, "The city code requires water towers. Water delivery by tower gravity is the standard in New York City. Ultimately the Landmarks Department demanded the towers be constructed on every building higher than six stories whether they were being used or not."

"Who builds them?"

"There have only been two companies building them traditionally, and they have been competing since they transformed themselves from barrel makers. Two rival families hold the water tower construction monopolies in the city. The companies are named The Tanks and Ulysses."

The one filled with lime and the dead sniper featured a small metal plaque giving the name and address of The Tanks, Incorporated, and subsequently Rook turned his attention to this monopoly.

"Tell me about The Tanks."

"The Tanks were founded by a man surnamed Paolo."

"Bingo. Tell me more about Mr. Paolo." Rooks hands were becoming pinkish beige, human fleshed, and he excitedly poured himself a victory drink.

"I'm searching. Found something. In his sons' birth announcement it's noted that the father had only came up with one name for his triplets. A later article states the father, in his despair over the mother's death in childbirth, could not come up with three names for three sons. He gave them all the same name, Marco, and further, he treated them all as if they were one. To him they were one son to the power of three. Following in his footsteps, a much later article states, the three Marcos became water tower coopers."

"But who owns The Tanks now?"

"Marco Millioni."

Rook leaned back, sipped his whiskey neat and contemplated how a young man who built water towers might have evolved into an assassin.

"This could be the only business not named after him that he owns."

"Apparently."

Rook thought also of his own mother, a woman he had never known, who had also died while giving birth.

Rook set aside the history lesson and the cold emotion he felt considering his own mother. Both were giving him context for Millioni-Weedkiller but not the crime he was hired to solve. He returned his thoughts to rooftop locations, and he inferred all killings had taken place on rooftops—not from them. Rook continued his line of reasoning, "Someone's prize assassin met their end today. Payback."

"The sudden cessation of *Zhi* under the bullets fired from the towncar gang ruled by Millioni also indicates a gang war."

"*Zhi* wrongly reported Millioni's father was Chinese."

"You sure you can't find anything else on the senior Paolo?"

"There's an old *Post* article."

"Yes?"

"Alleging Paolo had simply gone to an underground Chinese massage parlor and bought a cheap sexual time. The Chinese prostitute claimed Paolo was the father. Likely he would not have given a damn about a single child born to a hooker, the paper speculated, but the man had fallen in love with her because his Italian wife was barren and the triplets were ominous. The boys' mutual name is here listed as Marco Paolo."

"Marco Paolo? When did he change his last name?"

"Public databases establish it as yesterday. It's Oroboros infected."

"Of course. Yesterday."

Rook's evidence was enough to convict Marco of an assassination that day but not of any prior. Whoever had hired Rook through his broker, he figured, would already know who was dead and when they had gone missing. The evidence Rook had garnered thus far would simply be supplementary—the man was a killer—but not proof of whatever murder he had been hired to solve. Rook was compelled to substantiate further details. He summoned the ECHO, "Plot an electronic calendar from the tattoo scans and organize the killings on a city map."

The pattern that quickly emerged reflected gravely in his face, and his face literally flashed briefly into a shadowy wireframe. Rook backtracked by hand through Weedkiller's tattoo drawings, turning each semi-translucent paper over and contemplating them in his hands. There were thirty-seven in all. Rook opened his watch, inside of which his every personal quantum move was recorded.

"Sequence my calendar with the killings calendar."

A map of proximities, like electronic red thumbtacks, splattered across the monitor. Rook sat back, witnessing his increasingly shadowy hand, he contemplated his watch.

"You have been within two thousand feet of each of these locations at the exact same time as indicated in the tattoos."

As paranoid as he was, as much as he could still feel the rippling air from the bullet that had passed in front of his eyes earlier that day, he could not bring himself to believe he was himself the target.

"You mean…I'm the assassin's target?"

"Apparently."

"How would they know I would be in the motel? I did not even tell you."

"How would they know where you would be all of the other times?"

"My watch? Someone's tapped it?"

"I'm not able to locate any interfering code. The watch is clean."

"The gold? The wallpaper in the motel is made from money."

"Could be."

Rook contemplated, "Millioni—Weedkiller…He's assassinating assassins trying to kill…me."

"Affirmative."

It was not at all impossible to believe someone would want him dead. That was a given. *Who the hell*, he wondered, *is keeping me alive?*

Now he felt suckerpunched by a conundrum. A Fibonacci series of recursion, just like that in the golden chain found within the safe, flooded his imagination. Cosmo never told the client who Rook was. Rook always handed in the evidence clean—leaving no trace to himself. Handing over the evidence in this case could be, he thought, *Murder and suicide*.

Rook methodically set to scanning the thirty-seven tattoos from the sheaf.

"Composite these with the oblique image of Millioni lying on his back in the tattoo parlor."

The computer hummed and over the course of several minutes, it confirmed, "Composite complete."

The oblique photo sharpened fully as the tattoos morphed over the shape of his body into vivid ornamentation.

"Tilt the composite so I can see his back straight on."

ECHO projected an image that seemed almost tangible. Rook touched the light with his shadowy hand as it unfolded into the wall-sized monitor.

The tattoo patterns in overlap, reproduced in electronic light, rippled.

"Tilt another fifteen degrees. Another three. One. Good. Now, can you push the designs into three dimensions, like the armillary sphere?"

"Yes."

As the composite tattoo image tilted the image and extruded it, it spread, opening abruptly like an umbrella, into highly filigreed, three-dimensional angelic wings.

Awe coursed through Rook. *She's tattooing in three-dimensions!*

If he turned in the evidence, and he got The Bonus to execute, he thought, *I'll have to execute my own guardian angel.* Darkly he brooded, wondering somehow if that wasn't exactly what he wanted.

***

The motel guards and staff stared at their shoes that night while Millioni questioned them. The motel security cameras had no direct, clear shot of the man. The more they watched the footage, the harder it was to make anything of the man-shaped shadow. Like the night, their memories faded completely to black.

Marco Millioni became convinced that the man he had spent most of his adult life protecting from quantum overdose was going through withdrawals. In his suite he placed a call on the blue phone, and to Agent Orange he said, "Rook has the bends."

"Good. Thanks to you, Operation: Push the Envelope will succeed."

PART TWO: The Bridge

CHAPTER ELEVEN: Bespoken

1: The Tuxedo

Young Rook stood in Cosmo's library gazing at a book in a glass case. A year had passed since his father's death, and he had found himself spending more and more time at Tuxedo Park, pursuing his pilot's license at Cosmo's private airfield and studying forensics. The book he observed featured a skeletal hand fingering a tickertape, on which scrolled a mountainous terrain of brainwaves. This work of fiction was titled simply, *Brain Waves and Death*. There were only ever a few copies in existence. Research established to Rook the author had been a resident scientist at Tuxedo Park, and just as the book was published the author committed suicide by slitting his wrists in a bathtub. The book was barely fictive, and it revealed too much about what was secretively happening at the real and very private Tuxedo lab. The author's family had quashed the publication.

Rook was once again contemplating any possible connection the book could have to his father's death.

Like an expected chess move Cosmo quietly walked up behind Rook. The only sounds were the swish of his tweeds and the faint dull stop of his brown leather shoes on the wood parquet floor.

"Ah..." Cosmo said as he reached a hand out to Rook's shoulder, and he faltered, simultaneously remembering the author's suicide.

Rook turned to Cosmo, who quickly proffered a brown paper wrapped box.

"It came for you in the mail," Cosmo said quietly.

Rook received the package. It was his eighteenth birthday. "Who's it from?"

Cosmo shrugged, "Don't know."

"No one but you knows I'm here."

"Oh? The return address—"

"It's mine."

Rook held the box in his left hand and gently left his right index touch the quality of the paper. "This is butcher paper." He set the box onto the library table and carefully pulled the brown paper away, revealing a shiny black box within. He lifted the lid as if his own butchered heart might lie within. He lifted crisp white tissue paper. Under it was coddled a brand new tuxedo.

"Any idea who it could be from?" Cosmo asked.

"You or someone else. At any rate," Rook answered, "I am going to find out."

In the bedroom where he was staying—his few belongings thrift—he slowly clothed himself in the elaborate sleek tuxedo. At the age of eighteen Rook was his full six feet two tall. For a young man preoccupied with his inner life he still balanced it with an outer, quietly putting in his hours in the air toward his pilot license and lifting free weights on the ground. He had the firm sinewy build of a man.

As he gazed at himself in a mirror, the bespoken tuxedo sharpened him into an angular edge. *Randers me*, he thought, *black and white*. The bow tie was simple and lean. The shirt was standard and crisp. A ribbon of satin ran the length of the legs, stitched keenly into a cashmere wool blend. The jacket was spartan: the lapels were satin and eloquently masculine. Three button holes pulled the front cleanly together, and the buttonholes at the end of the sleeves worked. Reflecting the shiny box they came in, the black jacket lining and four button vest were sewn in lustrous jacquard silk and cotton. The lining and vest threads were woven into a harlequin pattern that looked like a microcosm of playing card diamonds.

Within the black label sewn inside the breast was stitched one word: *bespoken*.

Completing the tuxedo was an ominous custom stitched black leather shoulder holster for a gun.

It was utterly custom and fitted him excellently.

Rook Black took in his reflection and thought, *I've been sized up*.

In the evening he drove back into the city and cruised the streets, searching for his birthday party. And a gun. There was only one legal gun shop left, and it sold exclusively to cops. Rook wasn't about to sign up to the force for the sake of finding a means to buy a weapon. In his tuxedo Rook entered the gun shop and blankly demanded, "Sell me a gun."

2: Rex Rath

The proprietor eyed the overdressed young man and finally responded, "Gotta badge?"

Rook didn't respond. He just stared the man down.

"I take that as a no," said the proprietor.

"You sure," Rook pressed as he leaned in, "you don't have something to go with my suit?" Rook opened his wallet and flashed his currency, "Or something to go with my wallet?"

The gun shop owner gestured he should put his wallet away, "If you aren't a cop, no matter what kind of money you have, it ain't no good here." He spoke as if he was talking to a much larger audience than Rook. Rook inferred the man was showboating to a surveillance camera feeding directly into the police station across the street. Rook wasn't worried about it. He had already pirated the security feed. Across the street in a surveillance booth, a bored cop merely glanced at footage from inside the store, not realizing it was an edited mashup from the previous week.

"I like antiques," Rook said, and he lowered his voice to a grumble, "Know any antique dealers?"

"This is a gun store," the proprietor flinched and growled back, "You want antiques, go uptown." He began paperwork for closing.

Rook eyed a selection of holsters. He parted his tuxedo jacket, revealing his shoulder holster to the proprietor, and he said, "What make of gun fits this holster?"

The man's laughter was taut with insult, "No means no!"

Rook kept his jacket open, and the custom holster impressed the reluctant man.

He waved Rook closer, asking quietly, "Where did you get that?"

Rook did not say.

"Didn't whoever made it tell you what gun fits in there?"

Rook still did not say.

The proprietor pulled a few guns from a display and watched closely as Rook tried them. The pearl-handled Z-9 fit perfectly. Rook felt sexual the moment it slipped in.

"Modeled after the old detective specials," the proprietor said with something like reverie in his tone. He gestured Rook should hand it back.

Rook left the shop but did not leave the neighborhood. Fifteen minutes later the shop turned its open sign off, and the proprietor came out to shutter the storefront. Above him hung the gun shop sign: it featured a red and white bulls-eye, and below it dangled a large plastic replica of a pistol, about six feet long. Rook shadowed the man, who drove away in a brand new car—a post-hybrid that ran only on solar. Sliding behind him in his father's old gas-guzzling black sedan, Rook made his way to a broken down part of Brooklyn, to Crown Heights. He hit the gas, blurring past the man's compact brown vehicle into what would become their mutual future. When the gun proprietor parked in front of a brick building that bore a sign for the Rath antique shop, Rook had already been waiting several minutes. *This gun guy*, Rook thought, *is as transparent as they come.*

When the man stepped out of his car and paused to light a cigarette, Rook had a match out for him. The man looked up in wonder then feigned anger, but he still bent in and lit his cigarette with the flame. He took a drag and exhaled an impatient burst, “What the hell!"

"Rex," Rook said, "know any antique dealers?"

"So, you know my name," the man responded quietly. Rook didn't tell him he had already researched him, knew he drove straight home at the end of each work day—knew everything—but his coal black eyes indicated the unspoken.

After a tense moment Rook elaborated, "You're named after your uncle, who was found guilty of selling machine guns in the back of this antique shop. On the streets they called Rex Rath, *The Dinosaur*. Police gunned The Dinosaur down using the very weapons they had purchased from him in a sting."

"Look," Rex said, "I'm not my uncle. I don't sell guns to anyone but cops. I only sell them legally through the store. If you know the story about the antique store and The Dinosaur, you know gun sales out of this shop is history."

"How about a barter then."

3: Detective Work

Rook reached into his jacket, into the holster and withdrew a Z-9. Rex squinted.

"I forgot to pay," Rook answered.

Rex, a man who had dealt with rough and steely shooter personalities all his life, felt a flicker of fear in Rook's presence. Knowingly, under his breath, he said, "Where did you get that?"

Rook answered, "Let's go inside."

Rex was uncomfortable as he unlocked the door of the antique shop. It was no longer a business, and he used the building as his apartment. All of the furniture inside was antique, exploding with stuffing and elaborately patterned upholstery. It smelled of dust. Rook took a seat in a robust red leather armchair and gestured Rex should sit as well. Rex lowered himself, "Who the hell are you?"

Rook smiled an almost smile, "This gun exchange is simply between you and me."

"I got that," Rex answered gruffly as he lit another cigarette, "What payment are you offering?"

"I'll find the men who murdered your uncle."

"What good would that do?" he barked, but he already knew the answer. The police were bullies, men who hedged him in after his uncle's death. They had forced the family gun sale business to close to the public, and he could sell only to the police, to the most corrupt and vile people in the city. The identities of the men who had killed his uncle had been buried in bureaucracy and secrecy, but if he knew them, the family could take revenge.

Rook saw Rex mulling and finally answered, "It won't do any good at all." Rook stood and slipped the gun into his holster. It squeaked in tight.

"How do I know you will make good?" Rex asked.

Rook looked the man hard in the eye, and growled, "Because I already did." Rook nodded toward an envelope sitting on a glass display that held an extensive and ominous collection of guns. Rex stood and lifted up the envelope. He saw right away that beneath it, where he had kept his Z-9s, one was missing. He glanced over to Rook, who was emotionless. By the time Rex opened the envelope and found photos of the guilty cops posing over the dead body of his mercilessly bulleted uncle as if he was a game fish, Rook was gone.

Rook had taken interest in news of The Dinosaur's death when he had been fourteen, and he had keenly followed the development of the gun business thereafter. He had found the identities of the guilty police long before his own father's murder. He had in fact solved many cold cases.

That night, in his mysteriously gifted tuxedo with the accompanying gun holster, his Z-9 firm against his ribs, Rook knew detective work would consume his life from that moment on. Getting guns on the black market was not difficult but bullets were something else. He could have simply stolen the gun from Rex Rath, but he knew when he needed bullets, which were as difficult as an honest woman to come by, he would have no issues.

***

Later that night Rook waited for a man to exit a building, then he picked a lock on Ludlow Street in the Lower East Side. Into the basement of the speakeasy-like shop Rook descended. Even in the dim light he found public press photos of himself taken during chess competition. Some of them had been blown up to life-sized proportions. Rook hit the tailor's shop with a flashlight. Measurements were written in red pen on the photos at one inch intervals. It was from these images Rook realized, the tailor had taken numerous precise measurements of Rook's body. Rook stood in front of a life-sized photo and looked into his own photographed eyes. He turned.

Pinned to a mannequin were numerous pieces of hand drawn and cut pattern paper. He looked closer: it was the tuxedo pattern.

Rook found the tailor's cell number amongst some paperwork on the man's desk and called him from the tailor's own shop phone.

The tailor answered after the first ring with concern, "Hello?"

"I want you to make a blindfold."

There was a pause, and the tailor—knowing full well who he was talking to—asked, "What kind?"

Rook said, "A blind chess blindfold. Now!"

When the tailor arrived he said nothing. He was pale against his own simple black clothes. His head was shaved, and tattoos circled high on his neck, around which a blue bandanna was tied. Behind Rook, on a shelf in a glass container, a cloth was soaking in iron blue.

Rook aimed his gun at the man.

The tailor unbuttoned his shirt and pulled the cloth open, revealing his chest. Over his heart was tattooed a chess piece Rook as viewed from above. It looked like a crown and it was inked inside a tattooed bulls-eye. The sadistic bastard smiled and said, "Happy Birthday, Rook Black."

4: Jump

The headline screaming his father's apparent suicide turned murder had been: *END GAME!* Subsequent to his death the press was hungry for sensational news about Rook Black or at least who he had been. The paparazzi swarmed like killer bees, and the haranguing journalists pointed fingers of guilt at Rook in their press. While the headlines spun the story out of bounds, Rook decided he would have to find a way to control it. A week after he had solved his father's murder, the headlines hung him in nooses of accusations, claiming he only could solved the murder so quickly if his own hand had been in it along with the sadistic tailor's.

Rook's decision to decoy a story was quick and brutal. He let the paparazzi photograph him as he abandoned his father's house, walked halfway across the Manhattan Bridge and jumped. Rook's body disappeared in night, gravity and rain.

No one was seen entering or leaving his father's home for weeks thereafter. The paparazzi finally moved on to the other daily sensations surfacing in the city. Eventually Rook was all but forgotten, with only the rare blurb about the mysteriously public suicide finding print, and these blurbs sustained only due to the fact no body had ever been found. Saltwater crocodiles already inhabited the tidal straight, and it was assumed finally that the corpse had been consumed by the large beasts.

Rook's ruse had actually been quite simple to pull off. Manmade waterfalls designed by an artist had become permanent installs under many bridges in the city waterways. A salty spray hovered as a mist around each of the waterfalls before tumbling back down into the river, and the one tumbling from the Manhattan gave him a quick cloak of invisibility. Cables he had already installed gave him an elevator inside the waterfall. Underneath his clothing he wore water repellant lining to keep the chilly water from icing him. Once he was submerged he hit a remote, disengaging the cables from the top of the waterfall's mechanical frame. They sank quickly from the very weight that had held them down. A minute later Rook climbed onto a small raft placed by Cosmo, and in the deep blue night he simply motored away.

5: Desert

He spent a year in a desert, and not even Cosmo knew his whereabouts. He bought a silver trailer on an acre of hard bleak dirt from a nearly blind old woman. He paid her in gold. The exchange formed the last words he said to a person in his full year of solitude. With his pistol he spooked coyotes and occasionally killed them. He stocked up on staple food, and though meal after meal was exceedingly bland the simple nutrition leaned not only his body but mind. His father's murder had simply become what it was: a shadowy precursor to a long external silence. Everything Rook did that year was a meditation on life as a game of internal strategy spun into external control. His mind had hummed for too long, entertaining him within while disengaging him from others. A chess genius, he had never been known to be the life of the party, and though he was blatantly handsome, young women found him mechanical and cold. The roaring ache of his inner life was crushing him. He could have easily murdered the tailor, and he would have except he understood in that odd moment when the tailor exposed his chest, that was exactly what the man wanted. Rook had spared him and turned the evidence over to the police with the understanding the man would be brutally raped for the rest of his life in prison.

That was also, he knew, what the tailor wanted.

If Rook was going to avenge the tailor, and he had every intention of doing so, it could only succeed through neglecting the man, by completely forgetting him. Otherwise Rook knew he would forever be controlled by his hatred.

He focused on his future as a detective. He decided he needed at least a year to learn how to shadow, to become so mentally and physically still he could invade anyone or anything and leave no trace. He could only accomplish this if he could lose the pain, and he could only lose the pain if he could forget.

After the snows melted he took long runs in the desert, then the bloom of spring was quickly battered by desert heat waves. Rook quieted his mind one hot day and simply watched the shadows of the heat roll along the landscape. He witnessed for the first time the phenomenon of sky shadows: long thin folds in the atmosphere that were dense enough to cast shadows. Shadow watching became his meditation. From the peach bursts of dawn to the sulking blues of dusk, he observed shadows and charted their elongation and attenuation. On a cooler day he hiked to the top of stony black mountains in the west, and in the evening as coyote howling swirled the canyons, he watched the multi-layered mountain shadows overlap and filter the light out of desert to the east. He stood up and witnessed his own shadow stretch to the nethers of the rolling earth. It seemed to stretch for a hundred miles.

The fingers of darkness caressed the graying land before choking it to the black of night. Above the stars never known by city people coldly pulsated with the threatening wonder of the universe. The sight chilled him.

For the rest of the deadly hot summer Rook practiced shadowing shadows: he snuck across the dirt and hid his shadow inside other shadows. It took his mind off of everything, and soon he was adept at positioning himself so he seemed not to be there. When tarantula mating season arrived, he took a break, and through the windows of his silver bullet mobile home he observed hundreds of them stroking the land. *Tarantella*, he thought, *a wild erotic dance in ode to spider bite*. Rook's sexlessness caught up with his maturing body, and on his nineteenth birthday as he stood naked and shaving with his father's straight razor he felt the urge to masturbate.

But he wanted something more. The day after his nineteenth birthday he pulled the cover off the sedan, under which it had sat sheltered for the year, and he drove the thirty-eight miles to the nearest town. He was twenty some pounds lighter, and his limbs were strong sticks. In the local tavern he shadowed the sole barmaid and soundlessly sat on a stool. She jolted when she turned and discovered him sitting right across the bar from her. After a year of profound silence he said two words, "Whiskey, neat."

The words tumbled out of his throat like rocks.

6: Name

The barmaid chuckled and wondered, "What wind did you ride in on?"

Rook's coal colored eyes searched her. She was older than him, maybe early thirties. His deepened voice surprised him. It was rusty from disuse but maturing, and he did not answer her.

"Oh," she said, "the silent type."

For several minutes he sipped at the whiskey, and it seared his lips, tongue and throat. He had drunk nothing but water the whole year. He held the glass up and peered at her through the amber liquid. She wore a wedding ring.

"Are you lonely?" he asked her.

Her smile faded like the desert horizon.

"At night you lie next to your husband. Unlike the tarantula, you cannot devour him as your loneliness devours you."

Now she was the quiet one. Her eyes flickered over his. His very presence, his stare—his fathom deep voice—stroked her like fingers. His magnetism was overwhelming. He got up and locked the front door by a slide bolt then returned to the bar. He reached for her face, pulled her close and kissed her. His very smell, the essence of the dry desert, took her down. Fifteen minutes later the stranger was deep inside her, one nipple pinched in his fingers and his tongue in her mouth. He waited until he felt her pulsing and heard the peak of her unchecked moaning before he pulled out and came safely on her lower belly. It was crude, abrupt and a sexual prowess that remained with Rook for all the years ahead.

Rook buttoned up his jeans and helped her with hers. Both were sweaty, and she was blushing. Rook unlocked the door while she washed at the bar sink. He returned to his stool and his whiskey as if nothing had happened.

"Tell me your name," she asked.

During the year of his silence he had devoured himself and recreated himself. It was as if he could not remember the name given him by his father, just as he could not remember his father's name. Within the urgent silence, he had as good as forgotten.

"I don't have one." He finished his drink and drove away, leaving the dusty colors and lush skies for the violent storm warped world of New York City.

7: Revolution

Rook returned to Tuxedo Park, where he knew well quantum shadows were being isolated in Cosmo's secretive lab. Cosmo had agreed before Rook's disappearance to tap into his network of the ultra rich, who did not report crimes, and to develop himself as a broker. Rook was ready to learn all about the progress made the past year. Evading the guards that manned the fences, Rook entered the glass house by an underground tunnel and used keys to let himself into Cosmo's library. He let Cosmo find him in the library, exactly where he had found him over a year previously. Cosmo had kept his word and had not leaked anything to anyone about what had happened to Rook. Rook simply explained to him, "I had to get something out of my system."

"I understand," Cosmo responded, and he placed a comforting palm on Rook's chiseled frame.

Over the next week Cosmo grasped that Rook had revolutionized himself into the detective character role he had created. Sinewy in a freshly tailored tight black suit, Rook worked on the sedan in a lab, meticulously hiding the latest Tuxedo Park technology inside it. When the new surveillance sedan was complete, Cosmo handed him his first cold case. It was as old as Rook himself and involved securities, the Federal Reserve and a fistful of personalities who may or may not have conspired to the fraud that destroyed the economy and generated the anarchic aftermath of Rook's youth.

Rook drove his father's technologically enhanced sedan back into the city. There seemed nothing remarkable about it: it looked like thousands of other old black cars. He had driven it across the country and back into the city without plates, and no one had questioned it. No one, Rook was certain, would ever think of his father if they saw it. He bought an apartment in the Lower East Side and set up his office. Though he still owned his father's West Village brownstone, he never went near it. It was shuttered, cold, bequeathed to and maintained by Cosmo.

The case, uncovering who had knowingly though suicidally contributed to the end of capitalism, did not challenge Rook. Rook submitted his evidence to Cosmo a week later along with seven names. In turn, their client—a Nobel Prize winning billionaire who had lost ninety percent of his fortune—hired some hatchet men and finally found peace of mind when seven heads were staked on Wall Street. Their mouths were stuffed with hundred dollar bills.

Cosmo passed Rook his fee, seven hundred thousand in untraceable currency. Paranoid, Rook bought several currency readers on the black market, created several false businesses with accounts at standard banks—all of which reported to the central Federal Reserve—and ran charges for goods that did not exist. It was during this time he found a way to attack cloned currency with the Oroboros code, and reinvented Rook was able to exist without a trace.

Crime solved by crime solved Rook knew he was steepening the odds that one day he could similarly find his fate under a hatchet. As long as no one smarter than him came along though, he believed he would survive.

As the years passed he did survive, and the city food—coffee, eggs and bacon on a roll, whiskey—replaced the weight he had lost until once again the tailor made tuxedo gifted to him on his eighteenth birthday fit him just right.

CHAPTER TWELVE: Midnight

1: Radio

The convoy was a few miles from Tuxedo Park, with both midnight and the black and white ball nigh. Rook surfaced from the seizure in the driver's seat of the sedan. Through his thick black eyelashes he squinted out to the Marco Polo towncars hugging the sedan like a school of black metal sharks. He looked at his hands and realized he was not actually driving. *Being driven*, he thought.

The last mile and moments prolonged as if they were receding, as if space and time were approaching through a mirror. It was in part an effect from the windshield, entrained with Rook's neuroelectrodes. Angela watched as memory washed from him through the windshield to an external world he seemed only vaguely to recognize. He seemed like he was drunk on feedback and about to black out again.

She glanced furtively right, to the driver of a towncar, but the dark windows obscured. As she returned her gaze to Rook, fuzz rushed through the replicated old car speakers. Rook's ears jumped. Without manually turning the knob, Rook's brainwaves had turned the old AM radio on. The radio crackled and whinnied as words tossed into the airwaves. "Welcome," the radio said. And it said it in Agent Orange's voice.

Rook shot his eyes down to the simple clear plastic face covering a black radio tuner background. He focused on the white numerals and the moveable thick orange vertical line that marked the tuning over them. Instead of the old analog numerals—5,7,9,11,14 and 16—the call numerals were now 0,1,1,2,3 and 5. The orange tuning marker was aligned over the first 1 in the sequence.

Rook touched the radio face. It rippled. He jerked his hand back. The entire sedan, windshield, windows and mirrors—even Angela—rippled as if made of plasma.

Rook realized he was slipping again, and he squinted as he spotted the gated entry of Tuxedo Park. He focused on the hard edges of the gate to ground himself.

The trio of towncars drifted in retreat behind Millioni's limousine, which gently nosed the sedan through the Tuxedo Park gate. The gatekeeper's booth—usually manned around the clock—was utterly dark. Tuxedo Park seemed altogether both abandoned and hostage. The sedan slowed to a stop.

The radio said in Agent Orange's voice, "Finally."

2: Finally

End Game butterflies lifted from the knocking texts.

Rook bit down on his lip, teething the real stubble of his bristling black beard, fighting the dense feedback energy of the latest event horizon. Rook hung his mental anchor on his stubble, shouting inside his head, *Don't slip!*

"Remember?" the radio said in Agent Orange's voice.

Rook did not. Crime solving in the intravenously incestuous world of blue-blooded ultra rich had, he realized, finally poisoned him. He slipped his gun from his shoulder holster, cranked open the driver door and staggered into the thick night. He fell to his knees, vomiting Chinese newspaper pulp and gastric acid. Angela drew her gun and jumped out. She aimed the gun at Millioni's limousine. In response military style bulletproof armored zipped over the windows.

Thirty feet away the Marco Polo drivers got out of their cars and moved forward with guns. "Really Ms. Van Dyke? Get back into the car," Agent Orange said over the radio.

After a moment, Angela surrendered her gun back to her bosom, came to Rook's side and placed a cooling palm on his forehead.

"Rook, you're ill. Let me help you."

He hissed, "I have the bends."

"I know."

She guided him around the sedan and tucked him into the passenger seat just as he had tucked in the mannequin. That memory flashed to him.

Rook fought his bowing head. Angela opened the glove box, retrieved a flask and pushed it into his lips. The liquid tasted not like whiskey to him, like something refreshing, and on his lips it looked like blood.

"Now, Ms. Van Dyke drive. Do exactly as I say."

Angela was stoic as she took the driver's seat and drove toward Cosmo's infamous glass house. Millioni's armored limousine followed, and the three towncars moved forward to block the gate.

Cosmo owned the entire acreage of Tuxedo Park. There had been over three hundred houses developed on it at one time, but as the depression rankled the rich and generated a new breed of moneyless, Cosmo bought the houses one by one at slashed rates and ultimately ousted the other inhabitants. Friends came less and less to golf, the weather making the sport impermissible, and as his broker work developed Angela became his primary visitor.

His large staff of robots—humanoid things dressed in black and white hardened plastic and named Harlequins—maintained the Park, cooked and cleaned for him. And guarded it.

There was no sign of them.

Rook screwed the cap back onto the flask, returned it to the glove box and sat straight. Angela placed a loving hand on his thigh.

3: Glass House

She drove the curve of the main lake, also named Tuxedo. The black lake was an inverse opal under the cloak of night. Silence choked the land as they pulled up to the house made entirely of glass. A cold light bloomed. Beyond the soft glow lighting the glass door, the rest of the house was crushed in dark velvety shadows.

Agent Orange spoke through the radio, "Put on the masks, contacts first."

Angela killed the ignition, reached into the back seat and lifted up the orange box. She set it between them and parted the flaps invitingly. His hands shaky, Rook unscrewed the contact lens vial. She grabbed at his wrist to stabilize him, bowed his head back and one by one gently placed each lens on his corneas. Angela completed the same with her eyes. As their pupils widened, adjusting to the darkness, the bulls-eyes rings compressed and fine pink arteries threaded through them. Left behind were not lenses but iris grafts. His vision blurred, making jumpy wipes as if he was watching an old TV inside his head, surfing channels of black and white snow that kept changing. *The contact lenses*, he marveled, *are quantum receivers.*

Angela reached back into the box, pulled out the rubber rook mask and gently snugged it over his head and face. She palmed the Van Dyke beard and got out of the sedan. Rook found the energy to open the passenger door himself. On unsure legs, as he rose up from the sedan, he felt gravity force down on him. Each step toward the main glass door seemed a plowing through a thick darkness ripe with impending danger.

***

Inside the helicopter, hidden behind a pucker of chestnut trees strangled with the weedy trees of heaven, Dr. Kill van Kull struggled with the console. Rook's brainwaves did not respond. *I've lost him*, he thought.

It's a coup, Dr. Naranja answered.

Dr. Kull grunted and his emerald eyes gleamed, *I see. What should I do?*

***

Inside his terrarium, Dr. Naranja balled his fist and knocked at his thigh. *Some of what they are doing, I want them to do. It's still an intervention.*

Dr. Kull's thoughts answered, *And the rest of they want to do?*

Dr. Naranja faced his terrarium, *I won't give them that chance.*

You knew about this?

Of course.

***

Rook found the hard edges of the glass house walls with his hands, and he saw beyond the cold blooming light only darkness within. The silence suddenly lifted under a tent pole of rippling murmurs. Rook thought, *Crowd sounds.* The party, if it existed, seemed to be subterranean. The volume intensified along with a metallic thundering, some sort of beating of metal in the belly of a storm. Another light, from the center of the glass house, pulsed on.

Rook turned to Angela. "Do you see what I see," he asked, "the quantum world?"

"Yes," she answered.

"We're at the edge of an event horizon," he whispered. "A black hole."

She responded simply, "I know. *Remember?*"

Rook's brow tightened, and his watch pulsed slowly, its lit diode hands moving like a swimmer in a nightmare, limbs barely moving sluggishly to an unreachable shore of midnight. Everything slipped into slow-motion, and she handed him the Van Dyke in a space-time mud. Instinctually—as time splintered into nano-seconds—he peeled the fake Van Dyke facial hair from the paper backing and contemplated Angela before gently pressing it onto her face. The muddy experience was layered in *deja vu*, as if he had done it before or was just about to again. The rubber mask he adjusted over his head like his hat.

Agent Orange commanded seemingly from space-time itself, “Bring the book.”

From out of the shadows six of Agent’s Orange dozen strode toward them through the mud, wielding curious butterfly nets that seemed made of quantum netting. Marco Millioni emerged from the limousine wearing bulls-eye contact lenses and a small oxygen tank. Angela took the Shakespearean tragedies into her hands. The cover squirmed with quantum pulsings, and the face of Shakespeare merged briefly with Dr. Naranja’s face. He spoke quietly and urgently to her from the cover, “We’ll take care of Rook and the book. You, run!”

Angela turned protectively toward Rook. Her grafted irises dialed and synced with his, imploring. She threw the book high into the air, and as its pages exploded in slow-motion into a calamitous cloud of butterflies she ran, her heels plunged through the space-time mud. The darkness spirited her away.

Millioni shoved Rook through the mud into the glass house as the gang of six turned toward Angela.

Agent Orange commanded them through her wire, “Let the Harlequins get her! You, get the butterflies!”

In slow-motion they swept their nets and easily captured the sluggish butterflies.

***

Millioni pushed Rook through glass corridors and quantum shadow noise toward a navel, toward the source of the sound and the light. The sound was definitely coming from below, from underneath the house where in the secret Zodiac laboratory Cosmo's relatives had isolated quantum shadows—the archetypal forms behind classical reality.

A man stepped from the quantum shadows, a Harlequin guard. The robotic Harlequin's exterior—hardened combat gear—shifted colors like a swinging pendulum: what was black on him shifted to white and what was white shifted to black. His interior was humanoid, complete with beating heart and lungs. He was breathing through a small, portable stainless steel oxygen tank attached by rubber mouthpiece to a slick helmet. He peered at them through orange pupils. Abruptly the floor sank, and the three descended on a small elevator platform. Within a few moments they were twelve feet below the main floor level. A doorway slid open, and they were immediately thrust into—one word came to Rook's mind, *A bizarrerie.*

4: Bizarrerie

The crowd sound roared then lulled like a yawn. Harshly the sound of tick tocking clocks replaced it. There was something in the muddy air, *like a quantum nitrous oxide, laughing gas.* Rook smelled the sweetness and dumbly knew he was already affected.

"You walked into a trap, Rook. The last second before midnight." Millioni told him. "But we’ve all walked into this trap. A reality trap. Look." He pointed.

Cosmo, clad in his tuxedo, danced in slow motion, idiotically, inside a black hole butterfly glass terrarium as if he was a biological specimen. The terrarium was centered over an illuminated night sky floor patterned with an elaborate zodiacal circle. Rook blinked, the contact lenses ratcheted, and in turn the glass terrarium morphed, internalizing in his imagination into a quantum shadow of itself. Simultaneously it projected from his irises into a large quantum hologram. Through it Rook witnessed Cosmo twirling toward him with a humble recognition. The bald man wore a simple black domino mask rimmed with white velvet. His warm brown eyes were hidden behind bulls-eye contact lenses. Cosmo took Rook's hand and pulled him into the swarming quantum noise as if he were simply inviting him to waltz to the *Blue Danube*.

Like clockwork, from around the Zodiac laboratory the gang of Agent Orange's dozen churned in and unleashed the End Game butterflies from their nets. Rook staggered through the mud as if he was dragging a freight train. He reached for his gun, but he was too sluggish. Sober and no-nonsense, the dozen wore oxygen tanks, and they easily snatched Cosmo with the silly plastic handcuffs from Coney Island Fantasy. He placidly volunteered to be led off, out of the hologram. Millioni saluted Rook, “Have fun,” then he stepped out of the noise.

Rook stumbled in the increasingly dark internal room, a man whose body and mind were pummeled by the muddy event horizon.

Rook was again blacking out.

He lurched for his will and focused, shouting inside his mind, *Don't slip!*

He wanted to rip the contacts out, but he couldn't.

The Harlequin, through black and white concentric contact lenses and orange pupils, quietly eyed the man dressed in the rubber mask. He patiently breathed in through his mouthpiece and observed as Rook sank to his knees.

"Oxygen?" the Harlequin asked.

Rook expelled a precious breath, leaped toward the Harlequin, spun him and uselessly rammed his gun into the Harlequin's bulletproofed backside. The words crashed from Rook's tongue as if they would be his last ever, "Take me to the host."

"I will, but you will need to look me in the eyes."

Rook squinted, his lashes tightening over the grafted irises, and he slowly rotated the Harlequin to him. Their eyes locked, the corneas ratcheted and dialed them into a quantum channel. Around them emanated a black hole chamber.

5: The Host

The chamber hardened back into the Zodiac laboratory terrarium. Quintessentially composed, the Harlequin breathed easily through his apparatus. He pressed a button like a doorbell in a central cylindrical black wall and waited. Thunderous drumming carved into deep bass with sadomasochistic pulsing, into an audio feedback maze of people having lustful sex. The Zodiac laboratory shimmied with the pumping and looping soundscapes, diminishing into the sounds of just one woman gently moaning.

Rook's face ripened from pink to red.

"Oxygen?" asked the laconic Harlequin. Rook's response was to shove the butt of his gun deeper into the Harlequin's backside. Rook fought the drugged paralysis, battling the delirious desire to inhale and sleep. He clung to his gun so hard he felt a thought could pull the trigger.

The soundscape surged to silence so rapidly it pained Rook's ears. His equilibrium roiled.

The Harlequin inserted a key into a lock that appeared mid-air. He smiled wickedly, contorting his own slick hard mask like a piece of black and white taffy. From his face, the hologram unfolded into a black cylindrical room.

6: Latex

A woman was strapped to a stainless steel table and gagged. She was sheathed head to neck in orange latex. Her head was encased in a solid orange helmet. Nanoelectrodes were attached to the suit at symmetrical intervals. Thin wires connected the suit to the knocking text of *Macbeth*.

"Oxygen?" the Harlequin asked, waving his oxygen mouthpiece at Rook, inviting him. Rook didn't answer, couldn't answer. His tongue had become concrete, his thinking mugged. Rook collapsed to his knees, graying then blacking out as his lungs jerkily inflated, and he involuntarily breathed in the sweet nitrous oxide. The Harlequin collected Rook's gun and emptied it of bullets. He left Rook on the black floor, the gun replaced in his hand and he exited the hologram.

Outside the Harlequin adjusted the oxygen delivery until there was just enough in the room's mix to revive Rook a few minutes later. In his fuzzy haze Rook heard the woman's breathing. A small microphone amplified it, making it louder and louder. Rook opened his eyes and witnesses the black ceiling. He clambered up and leaned against the round black wall. His thighs, arms and stomach muscles ached. He was about to wipe at his eyes when he remembered the contacts.

"Remember?" It was Agent Orange's voice again, amplified.

Remember what! he screamed in his head.

There was a zipper in the latex suit, just between the woman's thighs.

Rook fell toward her, bracing himself against her body. He placed the zipper head between thumb and forefinger and yanked it. If an orange could be unzipped into a peach and a peach unzipped into a plum, that was the visual that rose in Rook's mind when he saw the mound and then the lips of her vagina. She moaned, and the moan was amplified, coiled inside itself, inside an audio feedback loop.

There was a lock on the orange helmet. Rook could only assume inside it was the faceless face of Agent Orange. His thoughts befuddled as he raised his Z-9.

"Happy Birthday," a voice—Agent Orange's—said. The words cycled through the audio feedback into a dizzying swarm of nonsense, jamming Rook's brain frequencies, and his ears heard only the sound of swarming of black hole butterflies. Rook slid to the floor.

The Harlequin adjusted the oxygen again. A minute passed, and Rook's eyes fluttered open, his grafted irises dialing wildly. His vision was a quantum blizzard of information. Somehow he knew he was lying down, and he felt the weight of something metal in his hand. He fumbled, found the wall and pushed himself up. Through the black and white quantum spatter he saw the orange outline. He weaved toward it, and as he got closer he could just make out the outline of a woman who looked like she was glistening in orange plastic light. The part of his brain that instinctively craved a sexual act slipped his fingers inside her. She was swollen and wet. She moaned, and the audio feedback rushed through his ears. He unzipped his pants and with his erection his mind surged with clarity.

I remember you.

Agent Orange!

***

Jack the Butterfly moaned as he spontaneously ejaculated gasoline, this time into a plastic tube. *Fossil fuel*, he thought. He made his way to his lab. The Orange Woman had taken the disassembled knockoff detective away that morning. *Or something like that.* He could not quite recall. He did not tell her he had sampled the detective's DNA himself. He opened up an aquarium and began lacing his essence into a copy of Rook Black.

"Tell me detective, am I so old, old as time itself? Am I a dinosaur?"

He wrapped his shadowy form around the knockoff Rook and in moments, sucking into Rook's nanoelectrodes, the shadow thinned and seemed to vanish.

***

Agent Orange, her face hidden in her helmet, her thighs still burning with sexual energy, left the Shakespearean End Game butterflies in the chamber. She retreated and closed the door. A vacuum lock sealed it shut. The pages transformed instantly into paper butterflies, their wings shuddering with veins coursing black ink. They wrapped around the interior of the chamber, making an endless pupa.

***

And Rook Black the knockoff, part plastic mannequin, part flesh, twitched and unconsciously vomited yellow Chinese newspaper pulp.

7: An Illusion

When consciousness possessed this Rook, it started in his mouth: a grassy alcohol meets blood aftertaste that felt like electric liquid velvet. He pushed his tongue around and opened his eyes. Rook sat in a chair. Before him spread an amorphous shadow, kicked from a dim light behind him. Rook couldn't quite make it out. He squinted and realized it was his own shadow folding up the stairs leading to the throne. It seemed, by a trick of the light, his shadow was in fact sitting on the throne.

The black circular wall was drawn tight around both Rook and the throne. It hummed with electricity, and in fact it was a black wall of energy, of quantum interference waves. It felt dense as the ocean and zapped him when he touched it.

A man's voice trenched from heavy metal, issued from nowhere and everywhere. It was Rook's own voice unearthly fatigued, and it said seductively, "Come closer."

Rook pondered the electric circle that imprisoned him, and he felt for his gun. As he did he saw his hands: they looked synthetic, almost like plastic, and as he peered harder he realized the joints were also synthetic. He touched his face and his hair: not quite plastic but synthetic.

Again, the voice said seductively, "Come closer."

Rook answered, "Rook, king's side?" and his voice was just as profoundly deep as the other. He stood slowly, warily, realizing he was somehow artificial, and he was talking to himself. He took a step higher, and he saw his shadow rise instead of shrink in the throne. The rubber mask he wore, rimmed like a stony Rook, cast up in shadow form became a crown.

This time the voice seemed to issue from the shadow, "Yes, I am indeed helpless. And I need your assistance."

Rook breathed slowly, gaining confidence, "You are the host." Rook climbed another step. His shadow stretched taller, thickening and refining in detail, like black electric glitter.

"I don't know," the darkness answered, "You tell me."

That strange sensation, that cold fear, licked Rook's spine. "What business do you have with Agent Orange?" Rook asked, ascending one more step. The shadow morphed from two dimensions to three, becoming harlequinned black diamonds like his vest, then becoming an electric wireframe of a man, of Rook.

"Your business," the shadowy Rook answered.

Rook rose another step. The air shimmered with the shadowy black energy, an event horizon forcefield such as Rook had never encountered. It emanated more densely from the shadow the closer Rook stepped. His vision was a black blur, yet he had his faculties. He could think, though he knew he was a mannequin.

"I have only business with you," the shadow said.

"What is this business?" Rook queried, unable to push upward another step. The air sweetened. The darkness dizzied. Vertigo knocked his knees out from under him, and his plastic limbs folded as if he had been dropped from a great height. He blinked and saw the shadow, his shadow, was not sitting on a throne. It was sitting on an ejection seat.

"The business of reality," the shadow rumbled, "It must come to an end. Only in death I change. In death I change only. Remember?"

Jack the Butterfly folded over this Rook like an umbrella wrecked in a thunderstorm. The event horizon energy gripped him, paralyzing him, and coursed through him like raging waterfalls.

"Tell me who I am!"

And with the sweeping quantum energy, this Rook went over the edge.

***

In the helicopter Dr. Kull struggled in the muddy space-time to cool Rook's brain through the console. Dr. Kull mulled his thought to Dr. Naranja. *Something is terribly amiss. Getting interference from Manhattan. Like there's two of him.*

He should be alright in about twenty-four hours, Dr. Naranja spoke quietly back through thought.

Dr. Kull sighed with relief, and a sense of austerity possessed his shoulders. *You mean we've gained twenty-four hours? Again?*

No, this is different.

How can you tell?

He's remembering.

The helicopter door opened. Two Harlequins appeared, wielding Angela—her white dress mucked. Angela looked at him, her grafted irises dialing rapidly and syncing with his. She feebly smiled. "Hello, Doctor."

She stepped up and in with the help of the two Harlequins, and she rapidly assumed a position of near militaristic command. "It's a midnight coup, Kull. They've seized the last second."

He sucked in his breath, "So, I hear."

"Sort of. The Harlequins can't resist me. Or the sound of my voice apparently. Now, what have the orange guards done to him?"

Dr. Kull answered, "I'm not sure. Something's going on in the Zodiac laboratory. I can't reach him with my equipment. Signal's jammed."

She stared at the Harlequins. "Go get him! Do not fail!" They turned and receded into the muddy darkness.

Through the nanotubes in the beard, Agent Orange heard her, and she smiled.

A hologram projected from Angela's eyes. Within it there appeared only dark black electronic noise. Her irises ratcheted, and a feed of Rook, or what seemed to be Rook, sitting in the small dark chamber appeared. He was slumped in a plain chair and apparently muttering, "In death I change only. I change only in death..."

"Can you reach him now?"

The doctor manipulated the console, and the two observed in the hologram as Rook's mouth stopped moving. His head dipped in slumber. "Delta waves," Dr. Kull said.

"Bring him to the helicopter," commanded Angela, her voice transmitting to the interior of all of the Harlequin's ears.

***

Through the trees came the sound of motorcycles revving and quickly receding. Only Millioni remained behind. He accepted the package from the postal office helicopter delivery and went back inside. He straddled a stool in the Zodiac laboratory wing housing Cosmo and smoked a blunt. Gagged with a plastic Van Dyke beard, Cosmo lay in an aquarium brimming with nanographite. Millioni pulled the adhered beard free, and Cosmo's face stretched and his skin snapped as he gasped for oxygen. As the nitrous episode waned, the hard edges of reality became as cool and slick as the aquarium glass.

"Do you have any last words to say to me, old man?"

"Why, Marco? Why!"

"Because we would rather be the authors of reality."

He pointed his .22 at Cosmo, "You people wove us together." He pulled the small lollipop made by Jack the Butterfly out of his pocket. As he twirled the stem, the spirographic pattern on the wrapper extruded as a hologram. Orange light spilled from it.

"Rook saved a boy's life. And now over and over again you force me to save Rook's life. You pay me in gold, in worthless, shiny, tasteless gold. However with this gold I have eavesdropped into your conversations with Naranja! You manipulate our lives! And you dare ask me, why? I ask *you*, why!"

"You know why!"

"Because if he dies, the eye of the storm dies, we all die? That's the line you've fed us over and over again." The blunt bobbed in his teeth, "Ever wonder why he is so attracted to the void? Ever wonder why he's *dying* to die!?" Marco's hand, as if moved by space-time and against his will, slowly turned the weapon round, lifted and placed the .22 to his own temple.

"No!" Cosmo shouted, his body contorting as he lamely fought to reach for the gun with his useless cuffed hands. "No! Don't do it!"

"I have to. I've just been hired to kill him by Jules Barbillon. So, as always, just as you've programmed me to, I have to kill the killer."

"It's not worth the risk! We desperately need you!"

Marco's finger tightened on the trigger, "Risk is all *we* have."

He dropped the lollipop and fired.

***

Inside the Lucky Dead Pawn shop, the sound and momentum of a fired bullet ricocheted in the quantum folds of the crusty laboratory. Nestled in an aquarium, the knockoff—or what seemed to be the knockoff—Marco Millioni startled, his limbs splaying and his hips bucking. Through the glass he stared at the dark ceiling, on which New York dust made the exposed steel beams look like matted black coral reefs. He blinked, his Asian eyes adapting to the muted gray light, and he slowly pushed up a hand and propped open the glass lid. He was naked, muscled with the body of a life long swimmer, and as fully tattooed as the original. His limbs were stiff but the tattoos rippled with rivulets of light and life. He felt invigorated, more alive than ever before.

By a pile of old phonebooks he found an analog telephone and called Agent Orange. As she drove away from Tuxedo Park, her dozen trailing, she answered promptly from inside her helmet, "Yes?"

"It worked."

He gazed at the adjacent aquarium in which the knockoff of Rook twitched, assimilating the shadow man, becoming one with it. *You think you are becoming me, when in fact I am becoming you!*

Now, he thought, *you will be the host! You're it!*

***

Through the muddy timeless space, the Harlequins carried the unconscious Rook on a stretcher to the helicopter. They gently placed him inside. As the helicopter lifted off Dr. Kull caressed Rook's brow with an antiseptic towel.

"This is not him," he said, and he lifted up a semi-plastic arm. It was wearing Rook's watch.

There is so much that could go wrong, he thought. *In 113.*

The energy of a returning quantum wave pounded them. It rode in on quantum soundwaves, on the thundering sound of a cosmic moment screeching in reverse. The sound battered his ears as it thundered through his nanoelectrodes.

The diodes in the watch blipped to midnight. Space-time receded like a tsunami tide then folded into a magnificent wave comprised of paper and ink End Game butterflies.

PART THREE: Extra!

CHAPTER THIRTEEN: In the Beginning

1: Good Morning

Bliss. As if sunshine itself emanated from a sun within, Rook felt calm, warm and peaceful. Morning sunlight touched his closed eyes like an artist's brush. He could bliss like this forever.

"Rook?" It was a woman's voice. He felt her hands touching him, and her lips kissed his eyelids. Slowly he opened them and squinted. The two were naked together in his bed, in his bedroom, in his apartment. She kissed his lips and said, "Good morning."

He blinked and wondered, *How did we get here?*

"Are you alright?" she asked. He felt it then, a dull pain in his head, "You've been sweating," she said, "a lot." He realized he was soaked as he sat up slowly, his mind waking from the cotton of a deep sleep. Her orange lingerie was scattered about along with his clothes, indicating wild foreplay and animal conclusion. His gun sat on the night table. He picked it up and looked it over: it was loaded, the bullets unspent. He picked up his watch. The time and date indicated it was noon and exactly twelve hours before the night he just went through.

She smiled at him as if everything in the world was perfect.

"Why the smile, Angela?" he asked, deadpan.

"Tonight," she responded without hesitation, "your birthday party will be out of control."

He visually searched her naked body for bruises and scratches, and he found some, but they were negligible. His face drew in concern.

"Don't worry," she purred into his ear. She glanced over his razed knuckles and kissed them. "Don't you ever feel pain?" Her smile wilted, and with concern she said, "Your head alright Rook? Made such a thwack."

Rook swung his legs off the mattress and observed acutely the haphazard puzzle of clothing on the bedroom floor. The black trousers, one leg inside out, the other crumpled like a closed accordion, were from a standard suit, not a tuxedo. The sheets he saw were ornamental: the black and red silk sheets he had purchased from Marco Polo Silks.

Rook quietly dragged himself into the bathroom and shut the door. His fingertips stroked his jaw where stubble spread high up to his cheekbones. Centered in it, his real Van Dyke beard remained as testimony to a night that had already been out of control. *We were heavily drugged*, he thought, *trapped inside a feedback event horizon accessible only through the contact lenses. Why would Agent Orange swing me back to normalcy? And how could Angela not remember anything? How could they have possibly erased so much in so little time? Or is she just acting?*

On impulse, he mentally severed from her.

He stared into his eyes. They were faintly bloodshot. He jerked open the medicine cabinet door, and after a quick ransack he did not find them—the bulls-eye contact lenses. On the white concrete floor he spotted small bloodstains. He bent over them and peered hard, examining eight squarish spots: *Knuckles, mine.* He bunched up his fists and matched them to the stains. There were a few pubic hairs on the floor nearby.

There wasn't a room, chair, counter or floor they hadn't had sex in or on, and he liked taking her on the brutally cold and hard tile.

Trouble was, he didn't remember this time.

He remembered acutely the woman in the orange latex. He remembered exactly what it felt like to have his cock inside her. He had not seen her face. He had assumed it was Agent Orange. *Who was she? What about the Harlequin? Who was he?*

Rook remembered in detail the climactic hallucination and the kingly shadow.

Remember?

He would have to separate fact from fiction, that is, if there was any difference. He would have to start at the beginning.

Outside the window, he heard a thud. He knew the sound: it was a morning paper being delivered. It did not make sense. Newsprint, like money, had long gone bankrupt. He peered out the window in search of the paperboy, but he saw no one.

2: In the Beginning

In the beginning, Rook thought, *a dark shadow lay upon the void. In an instant, time created itself.*

For millennia the human mind had vainly attempted to define how something could come out of nothing. But even nothingness, Rook pondered, was a subset of something—just as zero was a number—a number that could flatten all the others into becoming zero. He thought, *Zero times a million equals zero.*

He opened the bathroom door wearing boxers and snapped up a pair of trousers. He hastily dressed and jammed his gun into his holster. Angela witnessed the tension in his brow, and she looked worried. His coal black eyes shot at her.

His footsteps were rapid drum beats down the stairs, and he furtively searched his home for intruders and memories alike. He peered through a window and scanned the dirty street, finding pungent yellow blossoms scattering from a tree of heaven. *Trees of heaven*, he thought, *stink.* Rook flattened against a wall and rotated into his entry way, where he touched the video intercom and observed on screen more fully the street and the stinking sumacs someone had brazenly called trees of heaven.

He zoomed the intercom. On the doorstep screamed the newspaper, its headline positioned face up: *EXTRA!*

The newspaper triggered a rush of memories from the previous twenty-four hours—even of vomiting—and of the weird liquid Angela had made him drink. His body was sore, and it was not he knew from sex. He looked up and saw parked right in front of his apartment the black sedan. It was glossy in the morning light and unscathed. *Morning light?* he thought. Rook opened the door an inch and looked up into a pale blue sky.

He snapped on latex gloves, opened the door fully, bent and retrieved the newspaper by the edges. He opened the door with caution. The sub-headline read: *Naranja's Black and White Ball Tonight!* The date on it, Rook noted, was the day before tomorrow. The problem was, tomorrow was yesterday. *My birthday.*

In his office he unlocked a safe. From within he retrieved a catalog in which he carefully maintained the leads Angela had left him over the time they had worked together. The leads were paper-clipped into a black leather bound daily calendar. He kept them in strict linear order so that as he shifted in and out of quantum feedback he could keep track of the hard arrow of time—the arrow of classical reality most people agreed on was its only direction. He did not find the latest memo, the lead that had taken him to East Orange. He did find the one leading him to Dr. Chess—the man's phone number. As he saw it a memory surfaced, of the matchbook from Coney Island Fantasy.

Damn it, he thought. *I've slipped and am solving two cases at a time. Maybe even three.* They had become confused, entangled and tainted by quantum feedback.

Paper-clipped to the calendar page marking his birth date, April 23rd, was a black envelope. It was addressed to him, and it had already been opened. Inside he found an invitation to Dr. Naranja's Black and White Ball, for Rook Black and one guest.

This seemed impossible, and yet he had the faint memory of paper-clipping it into the calendar himself. He ran his fingers along the edges of the envelope, the edges of his desk, his gun, his face and the electrodes in his head: everything was hard and real. Outside in the strange spring day, he traced his fingers on the edges of the sedan, and he stomped the concrete.

Even hard reality, he thought, *has slipped? Means output is input.*

There was only one way to straighten it out.

Angela was showering and singing like a stupid bird. He parted the clear vinyl curtain with a jerk and grabbed her arms tight. "Get out!" he yelled. He shook her, and when he spoke again his words ripped with anger, "Get out of my life."

Her face went blank with shock. Shampoo suds ran into her brilliant blue lit eyes, and she winced. She finally muttered, "What's wrong?"

He stared at her emotionlessly, though the desire to slap her was potent. He fought it and dropped his hands to his sides. He had been too kind to her, and she had gotten the better of him. He motioned she should rinse. Impatiently he waited in the bedroom. When she came out in her robe, perplexed, he handed over her clothing and lingerie in a clump and said nothing.

Rook had not been an easy man, but she had not wanted an easy man. She knew his working habits were saturated with paranoia, but she had not seen him like this. She said tenderly, "Rook."

His eyes settled on hers with a chill.

She felt sickened. He was unparalleled, still she knew the stoic man had made up his mind. She had gotten too close too him, and he couldn't handle it. She thought, *It's over.* She put the ball of clothes into a small travel bag and slipped quickly into a simple black suit. He escorted her to the door.

"Keys?" he demanded.

The permanence of his gestures hushed her innumerable questions. She asked only one, "Why?"

He did not answer. She found the keys in her purse and dropped them into his open palm before turning toward the door, toward a life without him. She paused and asked one more, "Are you still going to the black and white ball?"

No answer.

Angela looked down the cold dirty street, into a future without him, and walked away. Rook watched her become a black spot in the distance, and as she did his thoughts saturated with shadows. In tandem the pale blue sky churned to feedback gray. *More like it*, he thought.

And he felt a curious power possess him. *The world*, he thought, *has become my windshield.*

He stared at the darkening sky and willed it to storm. An immediate wind rushed down the narrow avenues of the brightly lit city. Orange lightning shot down as thunder simultaneously boomed, shuddering the glass in sky rises throughout the city. *The whole city is entrained to my imagination*, he thought. *Much, much, much more like it!*

3: Slipknot

Rook sat at his desk, slipped his watch on and contemplated his razed knuckles. *Why?* He needed to isolate the games they had played with one another from real crime, from the crimes he had been hired to solve. Rook maintained a feedback session journal, a dream journal, the calendar, the hard forensic and clue catalogs and computer databases. Just as he remembered blind chess moves, he relied on memory to chart the rest of the viscous parallel realities that flowed in an out of themselves like metamorphosing plastic butterflies. Only reality was not so pretty. Some of his memories were definitely missing, and some had left no hard trace. There was no immediate hard trace that he could find leading him to Agent Orange—no acetate clue cards. He opened the calendar itemizing clues from the Weedkiller case. It was an artist style portfolio book comprised of clear plastic pages in which he inserted physical evidence. As he turned the pages, each was exactly as he recalled: from the leaflet overview of Dr. Chess's symposium to ECHO print outs of the armillary spherized Manhattan.

Rook flipped rapidly through the rest of the book. The contents indicated six days had passed since he had first gotten the lead to Dr. Chess and in turn Millioni. As if the pages might vanish after he turned them forward, he also flipped them rapidly in reverse. The information remained stable and linear, and he felt composed. In his safe he found the bound sheaf of Millioni's tattoo designs. *Linear*, he said to himself, *linear*. It gave him the grounding he needed in the shadowy occlusion of recent memory or lack thereof.

His thoughts turned once again to the editor of *Zhi*. Chinese newspapers —those had remained in print. Too many of the Chinese had never escaped the poverty they had come to America to leave. In their rubber sandals, in their laundromat black shoes, in their duct taped and infested tenement apartments—they smoked cigarettes, living emotionally off of Chinese pirate radio opera and paper copies of news.

A conversation with Angela arose in memory. He could almost hear it, a tangible sound, a sound he could hold in his hands. *Sounds like those from the radio*, he thought, *from the night before*. He closed his eyes and listened to a memory drifting up.

"And which of these crimes," he heard Angela ask, "were you hired to solve?"

"None," he heard himself answer, "I was hired to solve my own identity."

In memory he saw Angela smile as she said, "Well, then, just who are you, Rook Black?"

Rook opened his eyes and turned in the portfolio to the page holding the tattoo ink transfer paper, the one he had found in the trash outside Marco Polo Tattoo. He pulled it out with tweezers, and under ultraviolet light he examined the pattern again. He bristled as his memory felt the assassin's bullet zip past.

In the overture of remembrance, Rook frantically sought to piece together a week that had somehow been hit by a space-time sledgehammer, a quantum hammer so forceful it was beating hard tomorrow back into hard yesterday. Rook slammed a whiskey, then he closed his eyes, breathed deeply as he well knew how, and around his bucking mind he cinched, like a lariat, the slipknot of reason.

4: Unplugged

He tried to recall every detail of the drive up to Tuxedo Park, but as he touched memory with reason, it echoed with silence. *It seems*, Rook thought, *I had the conversation with Angela somewhere during a recent previous night, that I gave her a forensic package and that she drove alone to Tuxedo Park.*

He remembered in a rush he had gone out for a drink at a Blue Room bar, which he frequented when he desired to witness false starlight. He had returned to the office before dusk. That was when he had found the memo leading him to East Orange on his desk. When he returned, that was when he had received the Majestic lingerie package. It should have been filled with his payment, instead it had led him to the concussive gunfight with Agent Orange.

Rook tried to pry logic out of his memory but he found no fulcrum. As reason failed like a heavy dead horse, all he could think was, *My head hurts, I've slipped and have the bends.*

The rest of it—East Orange, Agent Orange, Cosmo and the oxygen starved ball, the shadowy king—all cluttered. The harder he tried to remember, to place specific memories in time, the more they turned sideways like thin men and paper edges, tattoos tilting off tangential backs, slanting and jamming in the quantum turnstile of time.

He knew how to control the onset of panic, to decrease his heart rate and limit the flow of adrenaline into his body during flight or fight. As long as he did not struggle against the rambling half-memories cloaking his own mind, he decided, *I'll be okay.*

He did not locate in his catalog the original black and white ball invitation he had found in his mailbox in what he recalled as another last night. He assumed that both the current one in his calendar and even the entire newspaper that had thudded on his doorstep were manufactured by both Agent Orange and Angela. He scanned the newspaper for prints and found only his. Agent Orange, he decided, had even mastered the art of placing fingerprints onto paper. *Not an easy thing to do. Or when I was drugged,* he thought, *they simply pressed my prints onto the paper and on anything else they were planting. Of course, that makes sense.*

There was no sign of the mannequin, and no sign of the bullets that had been fired into the wall. There was no five dollar bill, no *Age of Reptiles* stamp, no yellowed envelope, and no yellowed comic book clipping for fake beards. *Agent Orange,* he thought, *slipped away through a wormhole.*

In his closet hung his tuxedo, fresh and unworn, and adjacent to it was the white gown. He searched it for a bullet hole but found none. Rook bathed and retreated under the hot pulsing water massaging his aching muscles. He sat in the tub in clear water seeking clarity within it, but his mind slanted sinister, wrenching through ghostly memories from which he hoped to discern the macrocosmic engine that would render the world whole. He shaved neatly, trimming the stubble around the Van Dyke to his skin, and vaguely a notion lifted that he had some precise way of keeping track of time other than his watch. *That's right*, he remembered: he kept track by the length of the beard on his face. He shaved down to the skin at the start of each investigation, and he grew out the Van Dyke during the next investigation's duration. It was part ritual—an ode to his father—and part ritualistic timekeeping. His beard, he realized, was six days and nights long, but then again it always seemed to be six days long. He fought the strange urge to shave it off completely and start over.

Rook clothed himself in one of his standard black suits. His lightly mirrored sunglasses were in their neat titanium case, uncrushed. They were as they had been prior to the drive to East Orange, and they were empty of photos. Rook put them on, and with his gun firm under his shoulder he stepped out to the street. He walked once around the sedan and made a three hundred and sixty degree scan of his neighborhood. He approved of the menacing gray sky, and he slid into the driver's seat. He noted the mileage, which he always kept memorized: it was exactly as it had been before he had driven to East Orange in what seemed to be the past. As he started up the engine, the familiar rumble and the hard plastic wheel under his grazed knuckles made the present authentic and comforting. The radio was set to analog 990.

It was not implausible for him to be living a dual life. He essentially internally always had, but that this duality was rotating repeatedly around a single spatiotemporal axis—his birthday—was a leap his imagination but not his conviction could make. His head hurt, and that was a weirdly comforting constant. He felt hungover from the drugging, and he wondered if they had given him anti-seizure medication. He had tried it once, and he had hated how stupid it had made him.

He breathed in the dirty, humid city air and was relieved it was blessed with oxygen.

Rook cautiously uttered one word, "Knock," and was also relieved the word did not cascade across the city's illuminated facades that, even though it was daytime, still washed the city in bright colors. For the while at least he believed he was, from Agent Orange's Oroboros, unplugged.

Reality at best seemed to be on the tip of his tongue.

The business of reality, he thought, *who controls it?*

And suddenly he recalled the off-the-solar-empire-grid taxidermy. In contrast he remembered the very on-the-grid limousine owned by Marco Millioni.

***

A papermaker and bookbinder received a dozen crocodile skins in her Williamsburg studio from the Marco Polo Tannery, delivered by a Chinese man who spoke little English. The commission from this ongoing project made it easy for her to ignore other projects and relentlessly pursue the creation of what the patron called his crocodile skin library. She did not know his name. He had rung her studio buzzer in what now seemed long ago or yesterday. He had appeared in a mist of timeless time. The more of these books she created – twelve page skins folded and stitched into wallet size – the more she dreamed of vast libraries made of nothing but crocodile skin books. Nothing was written in them.

Jules Barbillon stood in his apartment and gazed over his mute library. He lifted up a pen nib, and with ink cloned from Federal Reserve ink and mated with ink cloned from the word *Leviathan*, in the center of each page he painstakingly stenciled an eye.

5: Tip of the Tongue

Rook took the Holland tunnel east, exactly as he remembered he had already done. He drove straight to the East Orange warehouse location by memory —he did not have to search the map—and he pulled up right next to the mailbox.

He recalled being dusted with glass when it had collapsed, but now it stood erect and undemolished, a taunting quiet giant of metal, concrete and the mirrored glass. A harlequin of a building, Rook thought, as he witnessed his warped reflection in it. The mailbox was rusted shut, just as it had been, and it seemed meticulously untouched by anything other than linear time. Rook pried it open. Inside: nothing. The front door was locked and seemed touched only by oxidation, just like the mailbox.

There had been one extra key on Angela's key ring, and he had noticed it immediately during the slow sluggish moment when it had dropped from her hand into his. *She wouldn't have given up this third key without reason*, he thought, and it was almost as if kicking her out was the trick to getting the key. She had meant for him to have it. The other four keys opened Cosmos' gate and glass house and the deadbolt and handle lock on Rook's own front door. They were basic keys, but this fifth had a curious circular ornamenting in the bow. The metal was orange-ish and the harder he peered at it, the more it seemed to glow like an orange sapphire. That tip of the tongue phenomenon assured him he knew what the key opened. He couldn't quite place it though, and instinct drove him back to this warehouse. He slipped the blade into the warehouse lock. It went in stiff, and when he applied torque to the bow sticking out, it did not budge. It was useless in this lock.

As he had done before, he shot out the lock and kicked open the door. He was angry, and it felt good. He glanced up at the steel carriage of the roof, expecting it to spontaneously destroy him and daring it to. Down a long hallway he stalked his memory in bitter daylight, his pale shadow passively trailing him like an afterthought. The door to Dept. A-165 was closed. He tried the key, but again it did not fit. It didn't matter: the cheap brass lock was unlocked. He slowly twisted the handle and pushed the door open as if the secret to the disassembling of space and time, like an executioner, sat within.

In the room where he had found the mannequin, Rook found only an old box of fake beards. They were to have shipped to Coney Island Fantasy—thirty-seven years ago—the year Rook was born. Scribbled on the shipping label in pen was the equation: $0 \times \infty$.

Rook placed the box of Van Dykes into the trunk of the sedan and solemnly gazed at the mysteriously simple warehouse before shutting the trunk. Driving back to the city his mind rolled over the equation, and at first he thought zero times infinity would simply also equal zero. After he put a few more miles under the hood, his subconscious loosening up within the alpha brainwaves common to driving, he began to think of the equation as a series: zero first multiplied by one, then two, then three and so on. Since no one lived into infinity, the equation could never be completed, he thought, *It's unsolvable.*

The equation penned onto the box was in his own handwriting. He decided, at least fleetingly, to wonder if he had left the clue for himself. On the tip of his tongue, he tasted with near certainty a memory that he had contemplated the equation long ago, but in what incarnation of himself—the chess player or detective—he could not quite recall.

6: Orange Street

Rook passed over the Brooklyn Bridge, and its rusting steel, harp string engineering flickered on his windshield and reflected like a spastic whipsaw in his mirrored lenses. Momentarily he slipped out of alpha, entrained into the light pattern, and he fought an oncoming seizure as his brain moved to lockdown. Usually he pulled over and waited for the aura to pass, but on the bridge he had no choice but to keep going. He jerked his eyes up, searching for any kind of visual constant to break the flickering, and when he did he found his focus pinned to a unique water tower. He was certain he had seen the water tower thousands of times but had never given it a thought. It was painted in alternate concentric orange and white rings and reminded him of the bulls-eye contact lenses. The water tower seemed to him a sign that he had somehow always known about the final orange, and he was soothed.

Time folded, enfolded and unfolded like paper money in crocodile skin leather wallets. *It is the hangover*, Rook decided, *and the seizures and the blow to the head, and was that blow actually some kind of seizure? Did I knock myself out?*

"Knock," he said, "out."

The words triggered nothing.

Behind him and in front of him black towncars drifted anonymously, and he gave them no thought.

A Kings County Kong soared over the water tower as it prowled for anyone or anything adversarial to Brooklyn. Certainly a derailed train would have caught pilot attention, and yet Rook could not recall seeing any planes when he had rescued Angela. That was why she had scrapes and bruises, not sex, he told himself. Rook pulled off the bridge—no towncars followed—and turned toward Orange Street in the Heights. It was the only neighborhood that remained fundamentally original, and it was Kings County pride. The sedan purred and rumbled past brick and brownstone row houses. *Fruit. Natural. Oranges, round, no*, he thought, *spherical.* He switched his gaze away from a green, yellow and gray house to a street sign up ahead. *Orange Street.* At the other end of the block ran Pineapple Street. *There is nothing more unnatural in Brooklyn*, Rook thought, *than a street named Pineapple*. Pineapples themselves were distinctly extraterrestrial, and neither oranges nor pineapples had grown in Brooklyn back in the days when they had named the street. Nobody could recall how the streets got their names either.

Nature, he remembered, was overtly fond of the Fibonacci series, in which the number one jumpstarted the series from zero, from nothingness, then conspired with itself again: 0,1,1, 2, 3, 5, 8 and so on. The series generated itself by simple recursive addition. *Just like last night's radio sequence*, he recalled abruptly. *Fibonacci channels? Could the quantum parallel realities similarly be sequenced?* he wondered. And of all his thoughts that day it seemed profoundly logical.

A towncar appeared ahead of him and one pulled in from behind, but they looked like any of the numerous towncars that filled the city streets, and he gave them no thought.

Vaguely he recalled that brainwaves also sequenced along the Fibonacci series, and he gazed briefly at his grazed knuckles on the steering wheel. Even fingers bore the mathematical ratio implicit in the series: the second bone was twice as long as the first bone (1 + 1 = 2), the third bone was the length of the first and second bones combined (1 + 2 = 3) and the fourth bone was the length of the third and second bones combined (2 + 3 = 5). The forearm was the length of the hand and the fourth bone (3 + 5 = 8).

And so on.

Nature loved those numbers, and all plant life—the pineapple especially —explicitly generated the series in growth patterns. A pineapple had 8 spirals going clockwise and 13 going counterclockwise. Flowers had 3, 5, 8, 13, 21, 34 or 55 petals. Each successive number simply being the sum of the two priors. Rook had wondered since he was a child why nature relied so heavily on simple recursive math. He was satisfied with the intuitive answer that the universe was a simple echo chamber and the mathematical equation for explaining its complexity really need be nothing other than stunningly elegant.

Rook was though forever stumped by the sequence's beginning with zero and the crass, impulsive jump to one. How did something come from nothing? How did zero spawn one?

As an orange is final. He rolled the phrase around in his mind and thought briefly that Agent Orange was scripting his reality over quantum scales and demanding his imagination be silenced. *She wants*, he thought, *to create that which has never been accomplished: like an orange, the perfect natural crime.*

Natural, he thought, *natural.* He had not let his mind touch the concept of crime as natural, and as he did a phrase peeled from the shadowy king's deep voice jumped into his mind as if it were speaking inside him: *You can't miss me.*

Rook jerked his eyes back to the skyline, to the obvious. Rook did not know how he would gain access to the spectacularly painted water tower, but his gut told him a major clue was within. The presence of the Kings County Kong, now obviously circling near the water tower, rendered access especially impossible.

He would have to undertake the stealth when shadows favored.

After his time in the desert, at Tuxedo Park Rook customized a real time, three-dimensional software shading program of New York City, in which numerous exacting details—down to the exact windows, were included. He was able to study acutely the light and shadow patterns of any location he needed to break into, and by studying the throw of darkness he knew exactly where, in his black suit, to hide his body in the shade. It was the technique he had mastered in the desert taken to its technical conclusion in the urban. First he would break into the tower through his imagination, through his vivid feedback daydreaming, then secondly via his software simulation program. Here he would hone his stealth strategy, making it realistic. Finally he would do it in person.

Naturally.

7: Hunter Orange

The sedan slid past the end of the tracks where the D train had derailed, but there was no evidence of it. A train packed with passengers rolled to the last stop on the orange line and opened its doors. The exodus of passengers was innocent, business as usual. Nothing whatsoever spoke of the crime. The wall where the sedan had crashed and ignited, just outside of Coney Island Fantasy, was also unscathed. The costume store itself was open and humming with activity. Rook parked and let his thoughts hum along.

He still did not believe the events as he remembered them had not conspired, and he refused to believe he would remain eternally confused. He did not believe he had an incurable concussion, and it was starting to make sense—that the blow to his head had been an abrupt seizure. The experience of event horizon density—that was also simultaneous with his auras. Superficially he was a man plagued with abnormal brainwave activity, and he had shared only with the most intimate that his seizures were a doorway to the so-called paranormal.

Angela Van Dyke was not one of them.

The strangeness, he was certain, would fade as he picked up linear pieces. When he entered the store, and the woman behind the counter turned to him—her plastic nametag pinned to her plastic skintight suit etched with the name *Ms. Hunter*—his world imploded.

Through the speaker in her helmet she said, "Looking for something in orange?" She turned to a counter, retrieved an orange box, and as she held it out to him, Rook smacked it out of her hands. He jammed his gun into her belly and dragged her to a back room. He kicked his way through a door while the woman struggled and screamed.

"Shut up!" he spat into her ear. He felt her breasts for her weapon and found none.

"Please, no!" the woman whimpered. He shoved her to the floor, kept his gun aimed at her and waited for her dozen to burst in. "No, no, no!" she begged.

"I admit," he said, "I am enjoying your game."

The back door opened, and a young man clad in black froze. Rook pistol-whipped the young man once, and he went crashing through a row of mannequins to the floor. In the sewing room adjacent, a tailor witnessed Rook brandishing his gun and dove under his sewing machine table. Rook spotted a male mannequin, upon which was draped a latex suit—a latex tuxedo. He aimed his gun at shadows, chasing down the saleswoman who had crawled away, as he realized he was in a sadomasochistic costume store.

He found her huddled behind a counter.

Rook grabbed the woman, virtually dragging her until pausing for a quick moment to pick her up. He yanked her along with him back into the showroom, where the shoppers were in no mood to be heroes: they were cowardly crawling behind mannequins as Rook burst through. He grabbed the orange box, shoved it into her hands and jabbed her by the butt of his gun out to the sedan.

Moments later he was roaring down the beltway, dazed, and the woman was in the trunk. He heard her screaming away like a siren, and he wanted nothing more than for her to shut up. *That*, he thought, *was all too easy. Against the complex mindfuck Agent Orange spun me through the night before, simply falling to the floor and whimpering in front of me just doesn't add up.* He remembered the mannequin head trophy.

She really wants me to lose my head.

Vaguely haunted by that tip of the tongue phenomenon again, he considered whether he was suicidally hunting himself or hunting her. *That theme again: hunting*, he thought. *Bulls-eyes. Hunter orange. I'm it again. The target. The game.*

He convinced himself she had let him capture her to give him that explicit choice: to kill or not to kill. He smiled and reached for the flask in the glove box. He sniffed it carefully, and inside was the scent of his whiskey. The bite of the alcohol calmed him.

He realized he had no idea what she looked like.

8: Ms. Hunter

In a desolate parking lot Rook pulled over and opened the trunk. Agent Orange, Ms. Hunter—whoever she was—writhed helplessly next to a gas can. Through the helmet her nostrils ached with gas fumes, and she tried to sit up, but he pushed her down and yanked down the zipper on her suit. She was wearing simple lace brassiere and panties. And they were also orange.

"No!" she howled. He put a finger under the crotch and pushed the cloth aside. Yes, it was exactly as he had remembered. He had definitely been inside her the night before. As he calmed, so did she.

"Rook," she said through the helmet, "What has come over you?"

The tender manner in which she pronounced his name was familiar, as if she had known him personally for a long time. That tip of the tongue phenomenon made him feel that in a way, she really had, but he couldn't place it. He wasn't into killing women, let alone hitting them.

"Rook—"

He grasped both hands around her helmet, and she was suddenly submissively quiet. He tried pulling free a latch on the eye-shield then he noticed it needed a key.

"Where's the key?"

"I don't have it."

"Who does?"

"You do."

Rook froze. He lowered his face down to her helmet and kissed it hard. A memory of kissing her pressed up into his mind, but it was timeless, unfocused, and it bent like a plastic limb.

"That's not quite it," she said. "Your voice is the key. Speak the code."

Rook's eyelashes tightened around his coal black eyes. "Knock knock?"

The eye-shield unlatched and the visor lifted hydraulically.

Rook looked into her eyes. The eyes that looked back at him in ultramarine blue told him one thing: she knew him well.

Agent Orange, he realized, *looks a lot like Angela Van Dyke*.

He jammed a hand inside his jacket for his duct tape.

"Rook, please! Please don't hurt me!"

She's a knockout, he thought, *and a knockoff*. He bound her wrists rapidly, then her feet, and he ran out of tape.

"This isn't a sex game I'm willing to play."

God, he thought, *she's really got me going*. His mind swarmed. He looked down at the cardboard the duct tape had been wrapped around, glanced hard at the Masculiner box and reached in. He peeled the backing off a deluxe Van Dyke and held it over her mouth.

"Orange!" she blurted out, "Orange!"

Rook sealed her mouth shut with the fake beard and slammed the trunk closed.

Sex game? She and her Harlequin had forced an exotic, sadistic breath play game onto him the night before. It was like a reverse rape, and now this was a reverse kidnap. It hit him like the blow to the head: she was making him guilty of kidnapping. *Where are her dozen?* Other than the thumping around in the trunk, it was all too quiet. Rook drove the long miles back to East Orange, to the warehouse. When he opened the trunk this time, Agent Orange clearly had been crying: her orange mascara ran down her cheeks, into the Van Dyke.

She started screaming again, and under the Van Dyke seal, the screams sounded inhuman.

A good actress, he thought. He slumped her over his shoulder and carried her into the warehouse. This real weight upon his shoulders made each step burdensome, as he remembered from before. *At least*, he thought, *this weight is tangible.* In the room where he had found the mannequin he dumped her onto a chair. He ripped her skirt into pieces and bound her legs to the chair while she kicked, scratched and screamed. Finally she was bound tight, and if she tried to move she would only drag the chair with her. He stood, a wild tower of a man, and glared at her. She shivered with what could be cold or fear, and she looked like she had something she wanted to say.

She said it, and it sounded like her throat was squirming over one word repeatedly.

"Making you talk would take the fun out of this," Rook said.

She began weeping again, and her head sagged. She gagged through the word once again as if it was going to make her vomit.

He mocked her, "That's not very sexy of you."

She gagged hard, and he was momentarily concerned she might spontaneously die. He ripped the fake beard off, and it tore skin from her lips. The upper bled, and the blood ran down the pouting lower, down her chin and dripped to the floor. She expired hard and gasped, spitting, "Orange!"

He did not know how to respond.

"No? Nothing? I trusted you," she said, "and now the safe word means nothing."

Safe word? He didn't want to hear any more. *Orange*, he realized, that was what she had been saying over and over. He peeled the wax paper backing from another Van Dyke, and she shouted, "Rook! I'm pregnant!"

Bewildered, he quickly sealed her mouth again. He adjusted his sunglasses, rendering the world black and white, and he placed them onto her face. This way he would be able to monitor exactly how long it took for her dozen to rescue her. The used fake beard he took with him: it had a blood sample on it he would test.

CHAPTER FOURTEEN: The Naranja Empire

1: Trust Fund

The city skyline, thrusting with towering glass, steel and stone necks, had long been choked then elongated ever upward by the money sweaty hands of developers. Skyscrapers had fallen under wrecking balls and been replaced by what were named *sky-rapers*. Around the spiking clusters of electrically lit glass towers a central nervous system of both subways and upways—train tracks suspended high above sea level—connected the city. Within it all illustrious Central Park remained, but what it had been under the guidance of Frederick Law Olmstead, a pastoral place for grassy knolls sculpted around outcroppings of glacial gneiss, was preserved in photographs only.

Global warming shifted the latitudes Rook's father had known as a child up into Canada. The cherry trees of New York City became replaced by citrus species: limes, lemons and oranges. Winter didn't exist anymore in New York City, where human beings, like living zeros with nothing but bad habits, were reducing the world back to chaotic nothingness. It did not matter if it was summer solstice or winter: hurricanes raged and the cycle of Seven rewrote over and over and over. Central Park became overwhelmed by drifters, and in the smaller parks, where scant grass and trees had grown, garbage piled upwards amidst the homeless. Soon after the government fell completely and mercilessly into the hands of big business oil, and in an effort to save the city from bankruptcy, the Petroleum Club put all of the parks onto the auction block.

Dr. Naranja, represented by phone at the Sotheby's auction, had his paddle raised electronically and bought them all.

Dr. Naranja was a philanthropist and beneficiary of the world's largest trust fund. The Central Park he owned and cultivated back to life was the last square of greenery on the island. He had purchased the park on the auction block with only a small percentage of whatever it was he was worth, and he protected the park vigilantly.

***

As Rook drove home from East Orange, the memory drifted up, that Marco Millioni's vehicle was powered by Naranja sunjuice. He remembered also that the man's taxidermy was not. It was off-grid for some reason he had not determined. *What doesn't he want the Naranja Empire to know? That he kills crocodiles?*

An irritating memory prickled but Rook could not quite place it. He saw in his mind's eye the crocodilian skin, and as he then thought of his own skin he felt a guilt, as if he knew quite well the answer to his question but that he was not willing—in some kind of psychopathic manner—to admit it. *Crocodiles,* he thought, *are guilt free.*

"Naranja," Rook commanded the ECHO in the sedan windshield. "What does Naranja mean?"

Momentarily the computer responded, "Spanish for orange."

Rook slid the sedan through the narrow street, thinking, *Of course.* He decided not to ask the sedan's computer any more questions.

12,992 of the exact sedan model had been manufactured in Detroit, and the one he had originally inherited from his father was numbered 3,128. The number was stenciled on a metal plate under the hood, a record of assembly line information. The sedan was a collector's item, and there had long been plenty of aftermarket parts available, including full quarter panels and radios on down to hubcaps. Rook had stocked up on parts and maintained a large inventory at a garage within Tuxedo Park. Repairing the car throughout the years has been easy until finally they simply replicated it as necessary. He wondered whether it was Agent Orange or Cosmo who had replicated the sedan in the hazy night prior. He parked.

Rook slipped into his apartment and swept each room with his gun. It had always been his custom—this paranoid search—but now the paranoia was no longer baseless. Agent Orange's violation, even as he had violated her, was overtly real. Until he figured out who Agent Orange was, why she was playing this game, and the game reached its logical conclusion he would remain on highest alert.

Nothing had changed this time. The apartment was as he had left it.

Looking down upon the anachronistic newspaper that had landed on his step that morning, Rook reluctantly sat at his desk. A memory surfaced as he read through it again. *Newspaper, classic thing people—especially detectives—hide behind.* Rook ran his fingertips down the newsprint, feeling its rough and flimsy texture. Paper newspapers had been replaced principally by small, flexible digital screens that streamed media. Like newspapers they could be rolled up, and the early digital newspapers that flowed through them had been stable even if highly propagandized—up until they were all hacked by the Oroboros.

Rook reached for his whiskey. It seemed, other than the pain in his head, to be the only other constant. He tried to read the article again, but he struggled. As the afternoon deepened, the words kept changing even as his eyes passed over a single sentence. He focused on a sentence indicating the ball guests were chosen at random through a lottery, but the word *lottery* became the word *letter* became the word *alliterate* became the word *alike.* Then all of the newspaper text scrambled and became Chinese. The effort was akin to reading something in a dream. He just could not make it out. He looked at his watch, where the lit diode hands moved both clockwise and counterclockwise.

"ECHO, on," he said, and his computer screen surged to life. He placed the newsprint into a computer scanner, sampling it to see if it was a hyperrealistic newsprint to the touch but digitally based.

A chemical sample proved the paper to be pure pulp.

It isn't just that tomorrow has been beaten back into yesterday, he thought, *the future has been jammed into the frequency of yesteryear.*

In the orange box Ms. Hunter had offered to Rook at Coney Island Fantasy, he found a mask for the black and white ball. It was different from the one he had worn the night before. It was a knockoff of his old blind chess mask, with a design exception: two eyeholes were cut into the leather. Rook tried it on, and into the void of his memory a thunderstorm of quantum static rushed.

Gasping, he ripped the mask off, and he wondered as he often had if classical reality was a hallucination. If quantum theory was correct, reality was just a cosmic radio station the feeble human mind was tuned to. The ego was a tunnel.

Whatever reality was, he had mistakenly thought he had mastered it. *I've taken it for granted.*

***

Agent Orange, who seemed adept at tuning reality, had not. As Ms. Hunter she sat slumped in the warehouse, physically uncomfortable but mentally soaring. She always did what the boss told her to do. She just didn't do it for the same reasons he asked her to. Dr. Naranja's medical staff had given her repeat gynecological exams and had kept track of her cycle. He wanted her pregnant more than she did.

Creepy bastard, she thought.

It wasn't just that for their primary operation she personally wanted a megadose of Rook's DNA—that was easy enough to harvest from the Blue Room bars, the brothels managed by Jules Barbillon. It was memory they were after. They wanted Rook to remember having sex with her. They wanted her to become pregnant with his child so he would have something to care for. In her diary that morning she had written again:

It will give him a reason to live.

And I am ever so willing to become pregnant with his child so I can graft with him. Grafts, that is what children are.

Human grafts. Reality grafts.

From our seeds, weeds.

***

Dr. Chess transfused another liter of crocodile blood into his cardiovascular system. His heart pumped vigorously. He caught his reflection in a mirror and noted that his skin was becoming yellowish-green-black and rough, like the stalk of a weed. He opened his lips in a weird smile and noticed his once purplish gums were blackening. The varicose veins in his long nose were also blackening and flaking. The date should have been April 23rd but it was, all of his computers suggested, once again April 22nd. He suited himself in his dark clothing and filled his pockets with pollen and butterflies. As the evening darkened, he crept back out into the night and nurtured the tree limbs he had grafted, had been grafting, it seemed, his entire life.

Near the walls of Central Park, he opened his shabby black overcoat, shook out his pockets and lifted his palms high to scatter his grafted creations. His closed his hands as if in prayer, then his blackening fingers pried open like a mouth and hundreds more butterflies, colored in crimson and emerald silk, flew out of the black skin of his very palms into the humid air.

I am now one, he thought, *with the butterfly!*

Thousands of them swarmed him, and his shabby wool coat along with the darkness encroaching upon him, fell like charcoal dust to the ground. Naked, he shrieked and clumsily ran back toward his brownstone, butterflies nipping meanly at his skin.

***

Millioni dressed himself in his black silk and adjusted his titanium watchband. He had also always done what the boss commanded. Just not for the same reasons. It had been his job to be at war with Jack the Butterfly, and in turn he always knew what the shadow man was up to. He was easy to spy on. He was always so high.

Didn't they ever think at least one of us might have mind of our own?

He turned, looked at a man identical to himself in every way and said, "Take the gold to the fire departments. Buy their protection. It's what the boss expects." He poured them each a shot of *bai jiu,* and they raised their glasses in a toast.

***

Jack the Butterfly gazed at his reflection, pleased that he had grafted himself into both Marco Millioni and Rook, pleased that he had some physical form. He appeared Rookish, but now entrained with Marco Millioni, his skin swarmed with ink. He exited the Lucky Dead Pawn shop carrying a Majestic box of cloned one hundred dollar bills he received from a mailman, wondering, *Where the hell did they come from and what the fuck are they for?*

He walked the crowded, mostly Chinese populated streets fully naked, his synthetic skin flashing with living neon tattoos. Around the neon illumination, dark lines of thickly sewn threads—the acupuncture meridians of his nanoelectrodes—coiled like bridge tension wires. The pedestrians veered away from him in mild shock and horror. Soon he found the tailor's storefront, above which hung a sign: Lower East Side Bespoken.

The nanoelectrodes embedded within his body were now somewhat attuned to Rook's. He had for the most part forgotten about his attempt to hijack Millioni. He was now, he believed, a detective.

Black, living ink seeped from fresh scars crisscrossing his body and at first displayed themselves as Chinese characters, then morphed into English, into Shakespearean phrases, before they dripped down the length of his limbs. Viewed from head to toe, he looked like a man-shaped map of Manhattan soiled in subway tunnel muck. He blinked and his coal black eyes became gently Asian. He lifted his left index finger and pressed the buzzer. In his right hand he held a gun, a pearl handled snub-nosed Z-9, one of many that had been sold to him at his pawnshop. Moment by moment, he was either brilliant, like a tropical fish, or gruesome, like something from primordial waters. His shadowy corona lifted up into a mockery of Rook's pea souper hat.

Inside on a monitor the tailor witnessed his client's telltale hat through what seemed to be hazy electronic snow, and he made haste to let him in. As the door cracked, he realized suddenly, like a boulder hitting the ground, this was not the Rook he knew.

The shadow slanting behind the grafted knockoff rose up around them like a cocoon. His breath stank of yellow paper. "I need a tuxedo. Now."

The tailor noticed the gun.

The knockoff slid inside followed by his kingly shadow. Submissively, the tailor snapped up his tape measure. An hour later, in a fundamentally lop-sided, hastily sewn tuxedo, the knockoff walked down Ludlow Street in his bare feet. He spied, *My front door!*

3: Nothing, Changed

Rook poured himself another whiskey neat and contemplated its harsh, antiseptic taste. He really had come to believe he was cold-blooded, and here were these women tearing his whole world apart in just a few days.

On the monitor he checked the live East Orange sunglass footage. He rewound, reviewing back to where he was able to see himself walking away from her in the warehouse. No dozen had come to Agent Orange's rescue as yet. The view, etched in harsh black and white, bobbed—indicating the sunglasses were still being worn. The live view altered from a 180 degree pan—she was looking around—to pointing down to her lap. She still seemed to be there, but Rook wasn't buying.

As he drank his whiskey and tested the blood on the fake Van Dyke, he wondered if he was thinking too hard.

"Blood type," he commanded the ECHO, and it flashed with the type AO. A-O was also a chess move, whereby the Rook moved to the king's knight's third square, but these chess moves, Rook knew, were not being played out on two-dimensional squares.

He closed his eyes, and the color ultramarine—the color of both Agent Orange's and Angela's irises—loomed. He opened his eyes and decided he should ground himself by visiting an oxygenated blue room bar: his past hours had been graffitied with too much orange. *Yes*, he thought, *I need equilibrium.* "Locate the DNA database," he ordered the ECHO, "and search for a match."

The database quickly matched a sample, only it wasn't just a random hit. It was cataloged as known, as in someone he knew personally. The name startled him: *Angela Hunter Black.*

It did not ring a bell.

He leaned back and mulled, then closed his eyes in meditation. Agent Orange had introduced something like the Oroboros into what had been his secure databases, but its behavior did not exhibit the intelligent rewriting of the Oroboros. Her code manipulated even further as if it had some kind of plan. He closed his eyes and let his mind wander in hypnagogia. Momentarily ultramarine images danced within Agent Orange's signature—the anarchic A inside the O. After a while the images became embroidered with ultramarine light and the O burst with brilliance. The composite image looked like a wedding ring in which diamonds alternated with black stones. The ring was chesslike. His mind went dark, and he opened his eyes.

In a public marriage license database, he searched for Angela Black. There were a number of them in the city.

But only one of them was married to a Rook Black, and the license gave the date as his birthday. Like zero times infinity Rook wondered it if his birthday would ever arrive.

He tested his own blood for drugs and found none.

He dimmed the lights, snapped on his feedback mask and breathed slowly in and out until his inner vision shimmered. He forced the shimmering to evolve into the ring again, and as he did the ring stretched, becoming the orange and white bulls-eye water tower illuminated from within. As he dropped deeper toward theta brainwave dreaming, the tower became a Chinese paper lantern and the concentric rings layered over one another like Millioni 's tattoo tracing paper. The water tower lamp cast light into the pitch black of his subconscious mind, and he saw himself, dressed in black, leaping from shadow to shadow and closing in on the water tower. The shadows, he realized, were all shaped like him, and even the black suit itself became dusky as it climbed the ladder on the side of the dream tower. When the shadowy detective opened the hatch, a kingly shadow rose up behind and pushed him in. There was no bottom to the water tower. As Rook's mind fell with it, the concentric rings became zeros and he plummeted endlessly down through them, morphing from a shadow of a man into the numeral one.

4: Blue Rooms

Only the wealthiest of wealthy possessed mile-high penthouse blue rooms in Manhattan. Above the constant layer of black clouds ushered in with global warming, the sky still existed as it had in young Rook's desert. In these blue rooms Manhattan zillionaires also invested in greenhouses that nurtured the foliage of new and old, and in these oxygen-balanced greenhouses they could watch the natural sunset and sunrise untouched by the filthy smog and roiling thunderstorms below.

Synthetic blue rooms below the clouds, usually near street level, were bars where people went to experience artificial and ultrarealistic dawn and dusk devoid of the industrial brown carbon emissions. Some blue room bars, like Jules Barbillon's highly successful chain, also sold hyperbaric chamber sex.

As he slowly, deliberately dressed in his tuxedo, Rook wondered why day seemed more real to the human than night. After the first major catastrophic New York storm subsided—the hurricane that had arrived simultaneously with Rook's birthday—day itself had in fact started to become more like night. Parties and balls had historically been thrown in the evening, when the mind allowed itself to flirt with make-believe. Bars were dark. Alcohol led the mind toward a kind of waking sleep in the blackout, when ugly became the cocoon of sexy. Rook opened a drawer where he kept his cufflinks, and he lifted out a small black box. Inside, there they were: two ebony and ivory inlaid squares.

And the clear intaglio ring from the Lucky Dead Pawn shop. He stared at it, suddenly remembering it.

Slowly he tried it on over his scraped knuckle, onto his wedding finger. It fit. It better than fit. The knuckle had been so razed he hadn't noticed the slight indentation further down at the finger's base, the kind that would only come from a long period of wearing a ring. There was a callous under it at the palm as well. *They must have had me drugged for a while*, he thought, *and grafted my skin to leave the impressions.*

Nothing added up.

That's it, he thought, *nothing—a zero is a nothing.* He flipped the phrase around, making it positive: *nothing does add up, multiplies, becomes something out of nothing, becomes the miracle of life, of reality—of parallel and multiple realities.*

A ring is like a zero, he thought, and somehow he was married to it.

Another circular thought popped: *In death I change only. I change only in death. Only in death I change.*

He checked the monitor again to see what Agent Orange, Ms. Hunter, Mrs. Black—was looking at. Nothing had really changed there either. She seemed to be stuck, though intuitively he knew she couldn't possibly be. *She is way too good at this game, better perhaps then Angela—Angela Van Dyke.* When Angela had come into his life at first there had been no game. *Maybe Agent Orange wants to replace her*, he thought, and he crooked his lips into something like a smile. Somehow he knew he could find the answer, at least partially, at the Lucky Dead Pawn shop.

***

Around the corner the grafted Jack the Butterfly leapt and caught the bottom rung of the fire escape. He pulled himself up and in the shadows made his way to Rook's rooftop. From there he watched as Rook opened the door of his sedan and got in. Jack's body collapsed into a wireframe, then as a bleak light from a car distant on the bridge touched the wireframe, it scattered the shadow of his shadowy outline to the dark roof below him. From there his flattened shadow slipped into the hairline cracks of the vented skylight and he sucked himself through this dark shapeless form into the house. His wireframe popped like an umbrella back into a man-like shape, and continued to extrude until once again he looked somewhat like a mannequin meets Rook, dressed in the haphazard tuxedo. He found the feedback mask right away as if it was singing to him, and he slowly attached it over his face, buckling it in the back. He leaned onto the psychologist couch, his grafted skin relaxing into tattoo practice skin, swarming with inky, living butterflies, and he demanded in thought, *Tell me who I am!*

5: Blue Room Bar

On his way to the Lucky Dead Pawn shop, Rook became overwhelmed by his desire to stop at a Lower East Side blue room. The joint was packed with synthetic sex addicts, from punks to Wall Street suits. Rook—equally strange in his tuxedo— bought a whiskey and elbowed his way to a nook, where the liquid light walls hummed with ultramarine blue. The technology was so illusive that the light itself seemed to be a sky, a sky within reach. Rook touched the light tenderly, and it rippled responsively. Not that anybody cared about suicide rates, but after blue rooms were invented the suicide rates plummeted. Rook's mind had been burning, and the blue room cooled him. He could go a long time without the artificial experience of blue sky, but he always appreciated the affect it had on him, especially when coupled with an orgasm.

He looked up. Another wall animated Nuit, the Egyptian goddess of night, into a realistic woman with skin like the starry night. She undulated and beckoned like a giant goddess of a whore.

The sex blue rooms sold was literally cosmic. The inventor of the blue room experience had combined actual astronaut memory of celestial awe with the hyperdimensional reach of new science to create the penultimate sexual experience: sex with god.

Rook made eye contact with the Nuit animation, and she immediately walked out of the wall of light, becoming a naked three dimensional woman made of liquid living night. Stars spangled her blue skin. She smiled at him and asked, "Where did you get this handsome tuxedo?"

He assumed the synthetic woman was sewn into Agent Orange's knockoff Oroboros, so he told her something she would probably already know, "The tailor who murdered my father made it for me."

"It was a birthday gift," she responded, and he knew he was correct about the knockoff infection. The synthetic Nuit was infected with the knockoff code entrained with Rook's brain. She lifted a black eyebrow, swished her black hair and was about to say something more when he put his fingers to her lips. He ran his untraceable currency through a slot in her palm, which quickly healed, disappearing into blue skin. She led him to a small hyperbaric chamber the size of a vertical closet. He pushed a button, choosing the non-exhibitionist soundproofing option, and the door shut behind them. In moments, her ultrarealistic synthetic tongue tangling with his, Rook's sexual adrenaline rushed, and he blissed, atemporally suspended in his own sexual galaxy.

The oxygen pressure increased, and he felt the quantum bends diminishing.

Her dark blue and starry hand unzipped his trousers and reached in. Her blue tongue licked him, and her blue lips swallowed him. He reached for her nipples: each was pouring out white light, each nipple a star. As he touched them white light washed over his hands, and an electric sensation coursed through him, making him even harder. She looked up at him, and her black lashes blinked over black eyes, the black holes to her black matter, to her reality and lack thereof. In her slick velvety blue thighs wet with white milk he explored her.

Back on the street his wounded memory did not weigh on him so much anymore. He walked in euphoria to his parked sedan, passing by a towering row of the ever-present advertisements and news that had become the windows of the Oroboros world.

His attention snagged on an article splaying across a giant screen about the weather. It was predicting, in courier lettering, a storm.

A reality storm.

That triggered.

In this storm chamber of future echoing past, of past echoing future, Rook dug his will into the spatiotemporal mud of the present. *The only way to survive this storm,* he thought, *is to become its calm private eye.*

He blinked, and a blue room Nuit advertising the blue room he had just left splashed across the screens, overwriting the storm prediction and growing rapidly until she was both six stories high and three-dimensional. She reached out of the screen to Rook, and her twelve foot wide palm opened up: inside was a pair of human-sized bulls-eye contact lenses. She said in Angela's voice, "Remember, Rook?"

Rook received them from her, and she vaporized in flickering digital snow as rain struck the city. No one seemed to have noticed. No one seemed to have cared. He looked around: in this city everyone always seemed to be self-absorbed, sucked into their own world.

Maybe, he thought, *we really are ego tunnels. If so, I am creating all of this. Every fucking detail.*

He looked down at his palm, at the bulls-eye contact lenses. His hands had become shadowy again, and even more so, the shadow lines crisscrossed at regular intervals like latitude and longitude lines, like a microcosmic city map, like scales of a crocodile. He looked back up to the city screens and found the Egyptian god Sobek—the crocodile headed man—splashed ten stories high above him but seemingly staring right into his eyes.

"In death I change only," Sobek said.

Rook blinked, and the godly crocodile was gone.

***

Inside Rook's office, on his psychologist style couch, the grafted Jack the Butterfly drifted in theta brainwaves, dreaming of fractured blue waters, of papyrus dripping into a living ink river. Receding down into them was the snout of a monstrous crocodile.

6: Safe Circular Word

Rook walked to Pell Street, which was located just down the Bowery from the blue room bar. His limbs seemed to be becoming increasingly shadowy, and he felt again strange guilt.

I'm pregnant.

That's what Agent Orange had yelled at him. *Is she really? Did I really leave a pregnant woman tied up in a desolate warehouse in East Orange?* The guilt deepened as he passed by the Buddhist temple and smelled the musky odor of the incense. *Masking*, he thought, *the stench of Chinatown.* At the entrance to the Lucky Dead Pawn shop he found the door locked. On instinct he tried the strange orangish key, and it popped in, a perfect fit.

He grabbed for his gun and pushed the door open. As he pushed into the darkness down the throat of the hallway, he smelled the odor again, of old yellowed paper. The bins of old comic books caught his eye and his nose. On one box was penned in magic marker the phrase, *detective comics*, and below it was marked something in Chinese characters. Rook inferred it also meant the same thing. He bent over it and remarked the thick tawny dust, indicating the box had not been touched in ages.

He scanned the glass cases, searching the cluttered gold and tarnished silver jewelry—all of the love affairs gone sour—and remembered finding the intaglio ring.

We sell your stupid ring and your DNA back to you for one million. And give you a new body.

Rook's heart beat, a steady pumping, and yet the silence in the shop seemed louder to him. *Where is everybody?* He made his way around the counter and parted a heavy black curtain to the back room. He observed, in great contrast to the funk of the pawnshop, the array of cryogenic chambers and the full medical-grade lab. Still, it looked something like a crystal meth lab: crusty coffee makers, duct tape, rubber hoses, glass tubes—all chained together through the cryogenic chambers. It was a lab definitely managed by a junky or addict of its own goods. Dark, dried blood streaked a bank of stainless refrigerators. Rook snapped on latex gloves and tugged the door of one open. It was filled with clear vials, in which DNA samples were collected and labeled by black pen on small white stickers.

There came a rushing sound and a thump, like a dead body hitting the ground. Rook scampered, crunched down to the floor and scanned for the thump.

His eyes met the papyrus pond and through the reeds he spotted a laundry chute. At the end was a bin, into which another laundry bag rushed from an overhead chute. After a thump the bag drop-off quietly concluded. Rook crept to the filthy canvas bin and glanced inside. Slowly he stood to his full height. Next to the bin was a table, upon which microscopic glass plates held fibers gleaned, he inferred, from the laundry. Then there came a creaking and the abrupt hoisting of a second bin up through an old dumbwaiter. Someone was retrieving another batch of laundry. Rook jumped behind the tall green papyrus, where the odor hit him like a suckerpunch.

DNA laundering, Rook's mind raced, *reality laundering!*

The stench of old paper overwhelmed him, and he vomited into the skanky and brackish papyrus waters. Incapable of moving, he watched his yellow vomit twirl in the muck that looked like old coffee grounds. The muck gurgled and convected the vomit through some kind of mechanical wave system, rippling the muck as if it was part of a real estuary system. After minutes of heaving he crawled to the opium den lohan and lay down. The room swam and swirled. After a while it calmed, and he raised his head to get his bearings. On a small table next to him was a biological ink syrup, a dirty black clotted needle and a DNA vial marked in tiny handwriting, *Rook Black*. His hands reached for the vial. Minutes later he was jackin' the butterfly, soaring high, high on his own DNA, high on his own life. Through hallucinogenic spatters his mind threw itself at a canvas of consciousness that was both memory and mirror. Rook's tongue moved and shoved a black hole of gravity aside. He said aloud, "Who the fuck am I?"

***

Inside Rook's apartment, the grafted Jack the Butterfly drifted out of deep delta sleep. He unbuckled the feedback mask and blinked at the pale light. In a mirror he caught his reflection, and as he stroked at his new modacrylic Van Dyke beard he said, "Who the fuck am I?"

***

Rook rinsed the vomit taste out of his mouth with whiskey from his flask as he drove toward Central Park in a state of euphoria, trying to remember why the circular death phrase on the ring made sense. *Circular. Circular thinking*, he thought. *Feedback. Logic stuck in feedback.* He slid the sedan near the sidewalk and turned off the engine. Great walls had been built around the park in black marble fortified with steel, and they were both slick and insurmountable. He stared at the walls and touched in his pocket the dirty DNA vial. He had taken with him the dozen copies of it bearing his name he found in its own refrigerator in the pawnshop. *Somebody sold me off. Somebody's letting me buy myself back.*

Rook glanced at his reflection in the rearview mirror, and he cautiously placed the bulls-eyes lenses onto his corneas. Through the contacts the soft, rainy world hurtled into sharp focus. There was a small red digital readout embedded in them, which he could see in the upper right corner of his vision both internally and in his entrained windshield monitor: it read simply, *CH 1. Channel one*, he thought. He focused hard on the readout, and in turn the lines of the readout sharpened in his vision. Instinctively he blinked.

The readout jumped to CH 2, and through the windshield he witnessed a wall-less Central Park gorged by a hurricane. A cherry tree, its branches stripping of petals, shot toward him. Rook ducked behind the steering wheel, then quickly concentrated, blinking his way back to the safety of CH 1.

He thought calmly: *bulls-eyes, reality storm.* His lips turned up into an almost smile, revealing purple gums and sharpened, rotting teeth. The desire for linearity faded away.

Circular logic was key to religious belief systems, and everything about the quantum realm was circular. *Why not*, he thought, *indulge in the conclusion of a circular reality*. That time was counting down to his birthday again made him curiously comfortable with the conclusion: *Reality is not just looping in feedback, it is consciously looping through me*. That he was born on Shakespeare's birthday made him chuckle. That he had become a private eye made him laugh heartily in a way he had never heard himself laugh. Emboldened, he concentrated and tried to tune to CH 0. His vision went black before slipping back to CH 1 without him trying to make it happen. He stared again at his reflection in the rearview mirror.

He slowly placed the leather mask over his face and fastened the buckles in the back. He snugged it, adjusting it. The resulting look, a diabolical black leather facemask stitched into decorative squares and framing the bulls-eye contacts, was startlingly mechanical meets sadistic. A streetlamp washed through the windshield and cast Rook's shadow behind him, splaying it as if it were a passenger. The shadow seemed once again textured and thick. Rook's eyes jumped focus to the shape, as he remembered the wireframe shadow from the druggy night before.

That is if there was a night before.

Rook surveyed the Park walls and the museum steps. All shadows seemed denser, tangible. *An effect*, he thought, *either from the contact lenses, the reality storm or both.* He laughed again. *The great storm I was born in on April 23rd a cosmic echo not just my birth, of my manifestation!*

Agent Orange had used the phrase *sex game*. He whiplashed. Reality was also her game. *I'm not her pawn*, he thought, *I am a Rook. Is she a queen? A queen of reality?* Whatever biotechnology she had her hands on, he understood, she had devastating plans with it.

She had used the phrase *safe word.*

She had shouted the word *orange* at him. Hunters, he remembered, wore orange so they would not shoot one another. *It is an excellent safe word*, he thought, and again he found himself laughing, delighted, as if he was just getting a cosmic joke.

As a safe word is final, he thought also. The safe word traditionally was a means for the sexually submissive to communicate to the dominant a line has been crossed. It was he, however, who was being manipulated by her. He was submissive to her dominance. She had stripped him of whatever he had believed was his free will, his world, his reality. He did seem to vaguely appreciate that she had flipped the energy, and he desired nothing more than to unambiguously dominate her mentally.

He glanced into a remote monitor built into the analog face of the sedan speedometer. Agent Orange still seemed to be sitting in the warehouse, pretending she was helpless. He knew she was anything but. He glanced at the radio. It had morphed again: the stations numerals were again comprised of the Fibonacci series. If she was channel surfing reality, storming it, creating the contacts that allowed him to see it the way he assumed she saw it, she was anywhere and everywhere and letting him in on it. *But she could also be a switch. After fucking with me, she wants me to fuck with her. A masochist.*

With that, automatically the sedan's ECHO spoke.

"Switch: in electronics, a device for making or breaking the connection of a circuit. Switch: in computers, a program variable that activates or deactivates a software function. Switch: a railroad junction. Switch: change, especially a radical one. Switch: a slender shoot cut from a tree. Switch: in sex, someone who could be on top or on bottom."

She seemed, like circular logic, to circumscribe every definition.

Rook stepped out of the sedan and strode up the wide stone stairs to the Park's museum. In his state of euphoria, it seemed he was floating. Tiny butterflies swarmed around glowing lamps that pooled light over the stairs, their wings glinting at once both green and red. Around Rook thickened a curious myriad of other black and white ball attendees, who anxiously swatted at the pretty but annoying butterflies. The air was static with real storm, and lightning flickered in pink bursts. Rook paused, witnessing two Harlequins manning the front doors. Their costumes were identical to what the oxygen bearing one had worn, with the black and white constantly shifting places: yet another technological feat. The butterflies were also attracted to the white light pulsing from their costumes, and the Harlequins stoically endured the irritating things as they swung from one side of their costume to the next.

He thought, *Switching. Is reality switching?*

Why not? The thought pleased him.

No Harlequin behaved as if they recognized Rook, and one of them checked the invitation, brushing at the butterflies with it, while another opened a grand glass door for him. The tiny butterflies rushed in and soared upward to the grand glass fixtures made of blown, opalescent glass, dangling and suspended like some kind of sea creatures stopped in motion.

More Harlequins inside manned thermal scanners—metal and object detectors—searching the guests for weapons through their minute orange pupils. One motioned to Rook with a crooked, black gloved finger, and though neither could see each others' eyes behind contact lenses Rook sensed their conspiracy. The Harlequin observed a small screen, on which rainbow colored images ignited alongside black and white renderings. He saw Rook's gun positioned at his left shoulder and with a welcoming almost knowing gesture allowed him entry with it.

Why? Rook wondered.

Inside, past a ten-foot thick stainless steel wall, a myriad of guests throttled the marble walls with cold, echoing chatter and laughter.

The ball had been announced months prior, Rook knew, and with each passing week the hype about it spun faster and faster. The public was desperate to see what Dr. Naranja had done to the park. That Rook clearly remembered. Long term memory seemed fairly intact, and it was only short term memory that seemed juxtaposed and splined. He felt, regardless of the dull pain and the confusion, confident in the euphoria, that somehow behind the screen of the contact lenses, he was going to be especially privy at the ball to the speed of Agent Orange's mind. *Mindwarp,* he thought, *that would certainly push a g-force pressure onto the mental landscape of quantum feedback. Would push the envelope of reality itself.*

If he had to go through an initiation as it were, he was all for it.

During Rook's routine meditations over the months, the black and white ball had loomed repeatedly, usually as a shifting chessboard. Rook quietly remembered the sex he had had with Agent Orange the murky nightless night previous, and he wondered if her mock, knockoff black and white ball at Tuxedo Park had been a controlling cue—a way to acclimate him to the power she held. *Maybe*, he thought, *she has given me a quick dose of hyperreality. Did I really impregnate her?*

Rook pushed into the folds of excited and loud partygoers, their elaborate black and white costumes catching on his sleeves, tugging at his trousers, as he submerged into a sea of silk and sequin. He pushed further to a wall and glanced at a pocket monitor to see if Agent Orange had been rescued, but the footage remained unchanged, indicating she had been sitting bound in the chair for roughly six linear hours.

Briefly Rook wondered what Angela Van Dyke was up to. He was somewhat surprised to realize he had almost completely forgotten about her. In fact the more he tried to remember her, the more the memories faded and merged with what seemed to be memories of Ms. Hunter. One memory popped and rattled through him: he pictured himself in the back room of Coney Island Fantasy having rough sex with Ms. Hunter. The harder he tried to remember having sex with Angela Van Dyke, the more the memories vanished. When he turned his mind to Ms. Hunter, they shot through one after the other, a violent montage of graphic, sadomasochistic sex. They spiraled backwards in what seemed like linear time to when the two had once sat across from one another in his office, over his chessboard, fully clothed and simply having a discussion.

In the sharp memory, and through the contact lenses, it was as if he was transported there. Ms. Hunter said to him, "Safe word? Because it is final, my safe word is *Orange*."

At the ball a Harlequin flourished a tray of white plastic tubes with black paper tongues. Rook almost didn't recognize them as he jumped mentally back to the museum. In a voice reminiscent of a waterfall, he said, "Favor, sir?"

Rook knew he had just wormholed. *This technology*, he thought as he reached for a noisemaker, *is mindblowing*.

Through the waterfall voice he heard: "We ask that you don't blow it until midnight." The Harlequin pointed to a giant clock hanging above them. It was a few minutes until.

7: Masquerade

Rook focused on the hard edges of the ball. He wondered also if there really had been a lottery. More likely each guest had been selected for some special reason, either because of status or lack thereof, but for some special reason nonetheless. He scanned the masked faces of the party-goers and was not able to recognize anyone behind them. Who were all these people? Many were buzzing about Dr. Naranja, trying to determine which costume he was hiding behind. A man in a tapering white clown hat, his cheeks rouged with large black circles, point blank asked Rook, "Are you, with your fantastic mask, Dr. Naranja?"

Rook shook his head in the negative and did not say a word. He plunged deeper into the crowd, taking his sterile identity with him. After he had lost the inquirer he stood with his back to a wall and observed the crowd. Unlike Agent Orange's *bizarrerie* this ball seemed to be an utterly traditional masquerade complete with the standard entertaining fare of music, drinks and dancing. A black velvet curtain some hundred feet long spanned the backside of the museum. It was a focal point of excitement, of some sort of hidden observatory, where guests murmured and paraded into a line behind it.

Those who came out the exit end were trilling, exalted and mesmerized. Black and white confetti burst into the air, giving Rook refuge as he made his way toward the end of the long line. A Harlequin allowed two guests behind the curtain at a time, and after several minutes, during which Rook analyzed the normalcy of the event, it was Rook's turn. The Harlequin made eye contact with him through his orange pupils and waved the guestless and knowingly armed Rook in solo.

"You have one minute," the Harlequin told him, in a now sharpened and masculine, human voice—the same voice Rook remembered hearing the night before. The way he emphasized his words alerted Rook there was something imperative in this one minute. Something he was required to do.

Rook passed through a dark hallway toward a flooding green light emanating from around the edges of black window screen. A dozen or so butterflies fluttered around it. He stepped deeper into an alcove, and the black electric screen barring the view of the Park slid up. The green light materialized.

It was not light. It was chlorophyll.

Rook beheld, *Eden.*

Lush orange trees, their leaves shiny deep green, were planted in concentric circles radiating out from the center of the Park. Moats clogged with papyrus surrounded each ring, and orange sapphire encrusted saltwater crocodiles slid in and out of them. Rook's eyes, accustomed to screening the world through black and white or naturally blending blue and red into the city grays, screamed with green. It was a vast garden such as he had never witnessed in anything other than a dream.

Beyond the curtain the crowd was chanting the seconds down to midnight. Many held the noisemakers close to their lips as they watched the clock.

Rook focused on CH 1 in his contact lenses and blinked to the fomenting and forbidding CH 2. The garden erased into visual static, and the raging hurricane ripped foliage from mud as a water wall rushed, flooding and gutting the park. Rook blinked hard, forcing his way back to the safety of CH 1, and he was just about to force his way to the ominous CH 0 again when, simultaneous with an awful cacophony of noisemakers, gunfire broke out.

He rapidly unlatched the safety on his gun and hid in a fold of the black curtain.

From out of the thousand or so noisemakers issued a cloud of orange dust, like a thick veil of pollen. A rolling wave of orange undulated through it and through in the black and white crowd. It was Agent Orange's dozen, clad in skintight orange jumpsuits and wearing orange motorcycle helmets and oxygen tanks. They raced toward the curtain firing shots in the air fron their orange metal guns. Panic surged and calamity sent guests ducking and rolling under tables. Whatever narcotic was inside the orange dust quickly immobilized the crowd. The music, *The Blue Danube*, stupidly continued.

The Harlequins, quintessentially composed, guarded their places at the curtain as the orange dozen closed in. Two of the orange gang forced their way at either end into the corridor behind the curtain, shoving the Harlequins in with them, and using the men as shields. The Harlequin's stiff full body armor-costumes, Rook realized, probably were meant to be fully bulletproof shields. The abrupt break in of the dozen, the fist in face absurdity of their skintight orange jumpsuits, impressed Rook. This heist they wanted well known. Tucked behind the curtain, the orange dust did not reach him, but the overpowering intense scent of citrus did. *My god*, Rook thought as the minute ticked along, *Agent Orange is going to steal Central Park*!

Realizing he had kidnapped their ringleader, and that she was not amongst them, Rook thought, *I've given Agent Orange an alibi.*

They had him surrounded, but Rook—gun drawn and anonymously masked—nevertheless seemed to be the epicenter of the unfolding crime. Rook was curiously thrilled to discover the dozen back at work. He was not afraid of them.

"Keys!" one demanded.

The Harlequins responded synchronously, addressing Rook, "In your pocket."

And Rook remembered the other strange spare key, the one that had opened the pawnshop. Whatever crime they were about to fulfill, the orange team had seamlessly orchestrated him into it. Rook reached into his jacket with his left hand and retrieved the key ring. They gestured with their weapons he should open the glass door leading to an elevator which was aligned with the park observation window. Rook slipped the orangish key into the lock, but it went in only a fraction. Rook examined the elevator lock, and the opening reminded him of his own front door lock. He pulled the orangish key out, and with a renewed wonder at the masterful plan he flipped the keyring to his own front door key. All eyes were on him as the key slipped into the lock without friction.

Inside the elevator chamber, at the insistence of their orange guns, he discovered that his own deadbolt key unlocked the elevator. The monolithic elevator, in stainless steel art deco, drew open with a silent stroke. The dozen streamed from around the curtain and pushed him in, and like a tight sunburst they surrounded him. The elevator doors shut, and outside the conspiratorial Harlequins guarded the elevator chamber. No guests were brave enough to spy on the violent activity behind the curtain.

The elevator ascended rapidly. Rook spun slowly and looked each of them, one by one, in the eye. All of them were wearing contact lenses with white and orange concentric bulls-eye rings. None of them said anything as they rose 440 stories, each story fleeting by in quick moments. Each of the orange gang members also had a gun on him. He did the only thing he could think of with his gun: he held it to his head. Surely he was instrumental to the crime—the instrument—and they would want him alive.

"I know you're not going to kill me," he said, "but you do want me to see whatever it is you are going to do to Dr. Naranja, who, I take it, hired me to find out who was going to commit a crime against him during his black and white ball. I take it I was hired to solve a crime you are masterfully pinning on me."

8: A Tree Grows

The dozen remained quiet. *Brilliant*, he thought. *Agent Orange managed to break into the museum and change the elevator lock to match my own front door key. All of a sudden I have all of the keys.* In the ball gossip it would seem as if he himself—the masked Rook Black—had assisted in committing the crime and had in fact masterminded it. All of the evidence Rook had been collecting would point to him, including the fictitious marriage.

When they reached the top floor, another key was necessary to open a door leading, he inferred, to Dr. Naranja's blue room. The door looked like a safe door: a massive steel slab arrayed with hundreds of bolts around a wheeled handle. The dozen pushed their guns into him, indicating again he was the one with the key. He wondered what would happen if he pulled the trigger, if he committed suicide, and then he wondered, with that tinge of guilt, if that was exactly what he wanted.

His curiosity peaked. He lowered his gun and flipped the key ring for the orangish one. This time it fit. It slipped in like his gun into his holster, sexually.

He turned the key and with a small pop, the latch gave. He cranked the wheel, and slowly the door groaned open. They pushed him in, quickly pulled the door shut behind him, and then he was almost alone.

Rook saw an aristocratic woman standing with her back to him. She wore a sophisticated, slim and nebulous black dress. He saw the shape of her body, but he couldn't quite make her out as the canopy of a tree obscured her. Large orange colored sapphires dangled from it like plump navel oranges, and they scintillated against dark bark and emerald leaves. Surrounding this woman and Rook was the night sky like he had never seen it. It was flush with thistly stars and twinkling like a living celestial Nuit.

The woman said, "Welcome home, Rook."

She turned toward him and stepped aside from the tree.

She was the woman he knew as Angela Van Dyke.

9: Naranja

"I am Anja Naranja," she told him, "My father invented synthetic reality and made our family very wealthy. He passed along his secrets to me, his only child. I was, given my position and wealth, unable to find a suitor in a traditional way. Through connections at Tuxedo Park, I discovered you. I did not, at the time, understand how deeply your addiction to feedback—to creating your own reality—ran. Bringing you back to linear reality and back to me, to the life we had, has taken years of effort, and we still have a long way to go."

Her voice was soothing, melodic and hypnotic. *The mindfuck ought to be giving me a headache,* he thought, but instead he felt seduced and overpowered.

"Kidnapping you in the atemporal eye of the quantum storm was a necessary intervention."

I only kicked this woman out today, this morning, and now she is telling me she managed to manipulate time itself and kidnap me?

She answered his thought, "It seems as though I have."

Rook stepped toward the tree and gazed hard at the living jewels.

"My father first brought orange sapphires to life by grafting them with a navel orange tree," she explained.

Rook wondered, *What else does he graft?*

She seemed to read his mind.

"Yes," she answered, "Time is graftable also. Time is the quantum inverse of space, and space is also graftable. Time allows space to occur as a series of synthesized events, like a mathematical series. Your past and future have been grafted into mine."

Rook asked, "Time contains the history of all other time within it?

"Yes," she said again, adding, "Time, like the navel orange, is feminine."

The dozen, he thought, *always surrounding me like clockwork.*

He said, "And cyclical."

"More like a spiral, feeding into itself, like the Fibonacci series," she answered, "Our two dimensional minds only view time as a piece of paper, as a page from a calendar. Time contains all original time within it, including the deep cosmic past and all potential future. Time functions as both a positive and a negative feedback loop—and the present is a quantum switch. When my father discovered this, he symbolically created this tree by selectively grafting the seedless navel orange, which is an ovary, with an orange sapphire and with time. The energy byproduct the graft emits is fundamentally solar. Instead of the tree regenerating itself through chlorophyll, it regenerates the sun."

"Sunjuice," Rook said, "You grafted light, photons!"

"Yes."

Rook reached up and touched an orange sapphire. Like an orange it was palpably soft, but like a gem it had a geometrical rigidity. Anja Naranja plucked it from the tree and peeled off the brittle outer layer of bright orange skin, and she explained further, "His invention was really a discovery that all time and space, like a snake swallowing itself, is in feedback. I know you don't believe me, yet.

But you used to. Time—in feedback—has memory, and it is starting to remember you just as you are starting to remember it."

"Remember," he said, "That's what you said to me last night."

She responded in her soothing voice, "I ask you to remember every night, for there is, despite the weekly cycle, existentially, only one."

"My birthday," he said, "Why my birthday and not yours? Aren't you some kind of queen while I'm only a Rook?"

"I am your queen."

He noticed she wore a wedding band that matched his intaglio ring. Cupped in both palms, she held the fruit up to him: inside the living orange sapphire blazed with what seemed to be a miniature sun, and she said again in the soothing and seductive tone that flowed like a peaceful river, "Remember?"

The brilliance of the light pouring out it in every direction blinded Rook, and against the blue backdrop of evening Rook felt swept into the center of the solar system itself. The orange energy flooded, consuming him, becoming a sea of deafening, roaring quantum orange in which he was drowning. Anja Naranja's wedding ring multiplied, brocading her skin, and like the sapphire encrusted crocodile entertainer at the Marco Polo club, her entire body scintillated. Her blue eyes became blue sapphires, and on her cheeks manifested a Van Dyke beard that looked exactly like his own. The weight of the energy crushed him, and at once Rook imploded.

CHAPTER FIFTEEN: Switching

1: Solving the Future

While Agent's Orange's dozen ushered the last of the guests out of the lobby with gunfire, in the blue room far above, Anja Naranja and the doctor looked down at the madly shivering Rook. Still clad in his tuxedo and the mask, he was strapped to a surgeon's table by a series of leather belts, his every muscle rampant with seizure. The doctor leaned over and inserted a stainless steel clamp into an eye-slit in the mask, forcing one of Rook's eyelids open. He peered in with a binocular microscope and shined a light into Rook's left pupil. Rook's bulls-eye ringed eyeball jumped around in a spastic dream state, making it difficult for the doctor to peer through the contact into the interior of the pupil. After a moment he gave up and bent straight.

"We've lost him again," he said.

Anja touched Rook's forehead and with an intellectual love at once cold and real said, "At least I have him here."

Nanoelectrodes and neurotransmitters stitched into the mask wirelessly transmitted Rook's brainwaves to a monitor, and on it the doctor examined a looping feedback report. The doctor turned what looked like an analog knob but which altered a digital amplitude. A software program in return emitted minor neuroelectric frequencies, adjusting and literally cooling Rook's brainwaves.

"I firmly believe if we keep cooling him, we will succeed in extinguishing this neural fire," the doctor announced.

On the monitor the brainwaves of a *petit mal* seizure reiterated into spastic red lines, scissoring the screen into a rapid red score of peaks and valleys. Anja pushed down on his chest as his body shivered and bucked. The doctor turned the knob on his machine again, sending back cooling amplitudes to Rook's brain until the red line faded to orange and his madly shivering muscles gently surrendered. Rook gasped for breath, and his arms and legs kicked under leather restraints. His clenched jaw, in which a large wooden reed had been placed to keep him from biting his tongue, relaxed.

"Good," Anja said.

She turned to another monitor suspended in the air, fabricated only of tangible light, and she touched it. It reviewed footage transmitted from Rook's contact lenses when he had been quantum channel surfing. She dialed into the channels he had visited neuroelectrically and visually when he had been sitting in the sedan prior to entering the museum.

"He wanted to go to channel zero," she said, "but he couldn't make it."

"It's more good news," the doctor said. "It means his willpower is taking him to the edge of the quantum abyss. Looking in but not diving."

They reviewed footage together quietly as Rook, his tuxedo sweat-drenched, passed into unconscious delta quietude in the aftermath of seizure. The feedback monitor lines drew cool rolling blue waves.

"He was attracted mostly to channel one, to linearity," the doctor said.

Anja looked down at her husband, took his hand and pressed her fingers around his wedding ring. She bent down and kissed his lips.

At ground level, the dozen orange gang members continued to disperse the black and white ball-goers with gunfire not meant to hit anyone. The guests, it had been well planned, were to be convinced they had witnessed a hostage taking, a break-in, some violent crime—anything other than a party. The last of them piled out of the front doors in hysterics and tumbled down the stairs, a frothing stream of calculated mass panic.

The doctor turned his attention from Rook and watched surveillance of the chaos down below. On the monitors feeding security surveillance footage they watched as the orange dozen escorted a mailman into the now secured building. Two of the dozen orange guards ushered him toward the central elevator. The doctor and Anja made eye contact. This was not part of the plan.

The monitors flickered and were overcome violently by digital orange snow. A recording of Agent Orange's voice pulsed in through loudspeakers, "We've always done what you've asked us to do. Just for different reasons."

The doctor quickly hit a button on a radio device, summoning into action his most elite jets, the Royal Rainmakers. Momentarily the supersonic jets shredded the sky with icy silver iodide, forcing the cumulonimbus clouds to moment into rain. The dark thunderstorm wrapping the city exploded with living, thinking, electrically charged ink.

Shakespeare, his mind raged, *think!*

Rainwater smeared the high windows of Naranja's towers and words etched over and over as gravity forced the thinking ink down the panes, coalescing into one: *Truth!*

This truth Anja desperately needed Rook to believe. She watched the black thinking ink running down the windows and thought, *If he doesn't, then there is no truth. No foundation to reality. And if there is no foundation to reality, then -*

"We are all a myth." The doctor stood behind her. They were all so close, those at the core of the Naranja Empire, they could frequently read each other's thoughts. "We are indeed a myth, a myth beholden to survival. He loves this world as much as we do. He clings to his life because somehow he knows if he goes, we go with it."

Rook's reality was the only reality they knew. They were only as real as he was or as real as he wanted to be.

The illuminated elevator panel flickered with floor numbers as the elevator quickly rose to the penthouse. It arrived at the blue room with a polite ding.

"Open the door," Agent Orange's recorded voice commanded.

The doctor hesitated before cranking the wheel and popping the seven latches that held it fast. Inside the elevator was a black envelope, sealed with the wax insignia of an A surrounded by An O.

"Open it. Now."

Doctor Naranja reached in and gently took the envelope into his fingers. The door sucked shut and the wheel cranked to the locked position on its own. The doctor tried the handle. It was fixed.

"Yes, doctor. You've been locked in. Kidnapped in your own penthouse. You are my hostage now!"

With a twist in his face he tugged at the triangular flap held by the wax and folded it back as if he might be opening into a black hole. A white card was tucked within. He took it between forefinger and thumb and gave it a smart tug.

The orange digital snow frothed and the loudspeakers hummed and screeched, as if the museum still echoed with the noise from black and white ball guests blowing through the party favors. The orange digital snow shimmered around a doughnut shape, an O.

His ears jumping anxiously, fighting the noise, the doctor flipped open the card. In twelve point Courier on the clean white cotton paper was printed, and it seemed even typed or perhaps hammered, one single word, in orange living ink:
WAR

At that, the noise overwhelmed them, and it seemed the very sky raged with orange static.

2: Orange Noise

Colors had long been attributed to kinds of noise: white noise, black noise, pink noise and so forth. The orange noise issuing from channel zero—the vacuum state of the event horizon—formed as bands of zero energy, the ground state of the quantum realm. These bands of zero essentially functioned as the concentric series around which the quantum parallel realities, like a spatiotemporal symphony of noise, scaled. Once the event horizon was reached, the vacuum state dispersed, leaving only what in his early research Dr. Naranja had come to understand was a jagged, quantum space-time edge. Many physicists experimenting with nanographite and nanodiamonds had already referred to this edge as *bearded.*

It was to this quantum beard reality clung.

***

In the East Orange warehouse the dozen arrived and released Agent Orange. She stood up from the chair and removed Rook's sunglasses. They passed her a jumpsuit, her holster and her orange metal gun. She unpeeled the Van Dyke from her mouth, and though her lips bled, she smiled. Everything was, she was certain, going according to her plan. *They took what I was*, she mused, *unwitting as to what I could become.*

She looked around to her dozen, each of who she had grafted her DNA into, each of whom was more and more so starting to look like her. "With Rook back in custody of the Naranja Empire, like a planet removed from the sky, my plan will arc like a destined comet to the heart of the sun."

She locked eye contact with each of them in turn. "What is our creed?" she commanded.

All chimed, "Royal Orange is never to be hunted! We are the hunters of the Royal Orange seed!"

And she felt Rook, like a sun, growing inside her.

The coup, she thought, *the reality coup, is officially war!*

***

The grafted knockoff Rook sat at the chessboard desk, shimmering and morphing, slipping back into Jack the Butterfly's ever evolving darkness. He looked down the length of his crocodilian snout and felt his sharp teeth with his thick tongue. That was the problem with the Chinese technology pirated from the mainland, which had in turn had been pirated from the Koreans. It was unstable as hell. He raised his once again shadowy form, still clothed in the haphazard tuxedo, and searched again for a mirror and his reflection. In the bathroom medicine cabinet mirror, he witnessed his crocodilian darkness. He limped closer to the mirror. In his pupils he thought he saw for a flickering moment, something like lightning and then only the void.

Maybe I am no one.

He stepped out into the night, his now clawish feet crammed into a pair of Rook's shoes and the Majestic box, clutched in a taloned darkness, drumming his thigh. As he drifted through the trendy throng of Lower East Side partiers his face contorted into a mannequin-like Rook. A man spilled onto the sidewalk from a club and called out to him, "Love the mask!"

He flagged a towncar and slipped inside. "Marco Polo Motel," he told the driver, not realizing that he was inside a Marco Polo service towncar that had been trailing him since he left the Lucky Dead Pawn. The driver sputtered Mandarin into his mouthpiece as the car slipped toward Allen Street and uptown. In a mild panic, forgetting that the creature in the backseat spoke Mandarin too, the driver did not realize what he was saying was being both heard and understood.

Jack's inner ear, roaring with darkness, understood, and Jack knew he was on his way to meet his nemesis.

***

The individual fire department companies willing to budge had all been paid off in gold, and each had been tipped off to the impending coup. Marco Millioni sat at his desk, etching with his spirograph the design for what he anticipated would be the last of this kind of tattoo. At what seemed to be an old radio—just like the one in Rook's old sedan—he tuned a knob and listened in to snippets of firehouse talk issuing through the gold coins he had paid them with. Inside each was a transmitter, and the gold was used as an amplifier.

When the blue phone rang, he answered right away, "Yes?"

Jules Barbillon asked, "Have you confirmed the shipment of the gasoline?"

"Yes. And something else."

"What?"

"Jack the Butterfly, or some variation of him, is on his way. Here."

"Thought he had sucked his way into Rook."

"So did I. My driver says one second he looks like Rook, the next like you, like a crocodile."

"Damn it. Do what you can to confine him."

***

"Mr. Millioni does not take spontaneous visitors," the concierge told him. But they very well couldn't let the black market reality kingpin loiter in the lobby.

They allowed Jack the Butterfly to wait in a suite.

Millioni thought, *You can wait for a million years.*

Millioni dressed himself in his black silks.

Meanwhile his brothers paid off the last of the fire department companies, except the ones who managed the Central Library.

They knew well what they were up against. As the guardians of the Naranja Empire—the reality empire—they understood more than anyone the power the family held. And as usual they did exactly what they were told to do.

Just for different reasons.

Millioni was slipping into his jacket when something caught his peripheral vision. His hand darted to his weapon and he turned to the window expecting a bullet to come through. But nothing. The curtains were closed. He crept to the window and pulled the curtain back an inch. Ink rain scrolled as it ran down the glass, briefly forming the very shape of the tattoo he had just been drawing. In tandem, the ink in his tattoos began to writhe. Millioni grit his teeth. He had but one last man to kill.

Shakespeare.

***

Jack set the Majestic box on the desk in the suite and lay down on the king size bed. He yawned and his crocodilian mouth made a Y shaped shadow before folding in on itself and melting back into the plasticity of a Rookish form, complete with a Van Dyke beard. Ink swam again on the surface of his skin as his shadowy form slipped into every crevice of darkness in the room. His darkness found shadows within shadows, swirled into the dark ink in the wallpaper, slipped between cracks in the windows and under the doors, spreading and thinning throughout the motel in an instant. Then into the darkness of the city he slipped, draining with the rain down to the gutters, spanning the lengths of the streets, rising up the spires of skyscrapers into the umbrella of dark clouds. Then back down he rained as ink into the weedy reeds of Manhattan until within moments he was the entire shadowy outline of New York City. Jack the Butterfly, more dead than alive, flowed into the tidal rivers surrounding Manhattan, and as he slept so did for a lull the inky waters that became him. As he dreamed of gasoline infused raindrops shaped like the Latin alphabet, so did the sea.

The Royal Rainmakers slashed through the quantum clouds and unleashed another storm, spattering the tops of umbrellas with the Shakespearean phrase, *knock knock!*

***

"With the collective city gossiping about this mysterious crime against Naranja, with Shakespearean ink-fire arch-villains spreading through black hole butterflies, the word of mouth on the streets will immediately find its way into the digital wires and should unleash enough force to engage the Oroboros infested news," Jules Barbillon whispered to his crocodile pool in his loft. The orange guards, Millioni and he were all conspired to erase Shakespeare through a baptism of fire, but he alone was obsessed with ushering in the age of Sobek. They knew he was a Sobekian, but he did not let them in on his obsession. The digital mural of Nuit above the tank, made of the same synthetic material in his clubs, reflected in the waters below, and from the ripples emerged one of his synthetic Nuits.

She heeded him dispassionately and listened as she always did to his confessions.

He knew as he spoke to her that she was connected to the fabric of the city's reality, and that by confiding in her, he was feeding reality the same gossip. He continued, "In turn the news will echo and echo and echo this *crime*. The heavy echoing of the spin will drum the city's collective unconscious. In the silence between the drumming, the black and white ball, the man in the mask, the women in orange—and the crime committed against the Naranja Empire—all of this carefully strategized disinformation-information will survive with enough quantum momentum and volume to bare some semblance to truth."

All around them the blue room walls installed in his loft pulsating with white stars suddenly twinkled orange. In tandem throughout his Blue Room bars, the same phenomenon took place.

This Nuit took Jules Barbillon's cold hand and inserted it into her chest. Where he should have felt a sensual, sexual sensation she was designed to relay, he found the edges of an orange sapphire the size of a heart. As it beat, crystalline orange blood flowed from it through arteries he had never seen. His skin swarmed, becoming blue and orange butterflies. With an orgasmic spasm he moaned and yanked himself backward. He collapsed against the tile floor.

"You're contaminated! In league with Naranja!"

"Of course."

"How dare you corrupt my altar!"

The Nuit spoke in Dr. Naranja's voice, "Come back to us, Jules. We can give you your Sobek!"

"Bullshit!" He crawled toward the detonating devices with which, *Sobek permitting*, he would incite war. The Nuit faded back into the fabric of his walls and ceiling. Clutching his detonators—a box of cigars infused with Jack's gasoline-semen—and his crocodile skin books inscribed with living ink, he slipped out his door into the night. While the Millionis had strategically built a pipeline into the city and paid off the fire departments, one puff on a cigar and Jack the Butterfly's quantum, gasoline fueled shadow would, in theory, spontaneously combust.

Fire in classical reality could be put out.

At the quantum level, Jules believed, it could not.

Sobek, rise!

***

Like a quantum lullaby, channel zero –the original black hole butterfly— still seduced Rook more than Anja did, and like a bee to a sexing flower he was always addictively hovering toward it, trying to figure it out, trying to feed off it in feedback. If he escaped from Anja again, she and her father also believed he would discover this addiction again. But they also believed the repetitive, alternating black and white noise unleashed via the ball into the Oroboros and into their carefully strategized knockoff realities, would keep Rook sane. And to some degree the black and white noise would stabilize him further both mentally and physically.

Now they were prisoners of their own plan. The orange noise incessantly hissed and fuzzed around them. Anja looked down at Rook, remembering the first time she had met him.

Rook had been a detective, and his father had been the greatest chess master in the world. Young Anja had followed the news of his bridge jump, and as the years passed, having fancied him a suitor, she had quietly investigated Rook's apparent suicide. She had approached Cosmo, wanting to hire the obscure detective he brokered to solve the mysterious disappearance of Rook's body.

Cosmo refused, stating, "I would myself hire my detective if I knew he could solve what was not a crime but a tragedy."

Anja responded, "Cosmo, wouldn't the detective need only to look in a mirror?"

She then handed him a mocked up version of *The Times*, on which the six-inch tall bold headline shouted: TUXEDO PARK BURNS! "Either put me in touch with Rook or the Naranja Empire will expose and destroy him, not to mention your beautiful park. Wouldn't it be better if we just became friends?"

Cosmo massaged his gummy brow, "You are leaving me no choice!"

"That's because I don't have one either. I must know him!"

Cosmo's brown eyes puzzled, "Why?"

"Let me sweeten the deal. We can become business partners. Reality business partners."

As money flooded into Tuxedo Park from the Naranjas, Cosmo became enchanted by her seductive powers. Though Tuxedo Park was enslaved to The Naranja Empire, every time her sapphire blue eyes made eye contact with his, he felt weak and helpless. In whispers over tea, he confided in her. It seemed to her he was desperate for a confidante. Eventually she even knew Rook had spent a year alone after the bridge jump.

“It’s time for me to meet him.”

At Tuxedo Park one quiet night, Cosmo arranged for her to cross paths with Rook at least virtually. He told Rook the truth, that Ms. Naranja was coming to offer insight into the new synthetic reality technology. Wired, Cosmo held a meeting with her. Rook observed them remotely from the Zodiac laboratory, and at once—glimpsing her blue eyes—he felt the need to possess both her and her technology. After the meeting, as she was stepping through long grass toward a Naranja helicopter, Rook shadowed her in darkness. From behind her he invited, "Please stay for a few more moments."

He was brutally intelligent, and within minutes as he took her to the Zodiac laboratory, Anja realized he was fiercely sexual.

"Do you know who I am?" he asked her, his coal black eyes piercing her blue eyes.

"Only the elite few could be allowed insight into my father's discoveries," she whispered, "and you, Rook Black, are one of them."

Within weeks they married in the blue room, exchanging vows in front of tuxedo clad Dr. Navaja Naranja and Cosmo Hamilton. Thereafter Rook only wore the wedding ring when they were together, and she knew damn well fidelity was never going to matter to him. As much as she enjoyed his body, she was in love with his mind. Over time his mental muscularity, hybrid with his desire to lift the quantum veil, resulted in lust, but a lust not for her: for escapism. Eventually his addiction to building his reality in feedback made him accidentally suicidal.

He hired assassins to kill him, thrilled by dodging bullets, thrilled by what he believed was his invincibility, and Anja in turn maintained a contract with Millioni to protect him.

***

Inside the Marco Polo Tattoo parlor Marco Millioni fucked the artist up against the tattoo chair. Parting her pink hair with his lips, he whispered into her ear, "Every crime the detective sleuthed was staged by the Naranja Empire. The

Empire grafted these crimes into the Fibonacci reality channels the Naranja's discovered using the technology the doctor had invented."

The artist moaned as he stroked in and out of her.

"The Naranja's grafted them one turn at a time, devolving the series through the quantum reality harmonics stabilized in channels 144, 89, 55, 34, 21, 13, 8, 5, 3, 2, 1 and 1. Channels 1 and 1 were mirrors, knockoffs—and the easiest channels to graft. The grafted crimes were all variations on a theme, a self-similar crime spiral pivoting around Rook's birthday and a kidnapping. The kidnapping is coded intervention."

The artist moaned again, "Marco, why are you telling me this now?" He stroked faster and faster until, with a deep groan, he came inside of her. After a moment, he pulled out and his glistening penis began to soften. He wiped himself clean and with a sigh sat down on the tattooing chair.

"Because I want our child to know who I was and what I did."

"Our child?"

"Depending on how tonight goes, you may never see me again. But you may see me in our child."

He motioned for the tattooing needle, "I have you tattoo me each time I've killed one of the assassins the detective hired to kill him. This time you will tattoo me before I kill."

"Who will you kill?"

"Shakespeare." He took up the tattoo transfer paper, held his penis up and gently pressed the tattoo around it. He gestured again to the needle, "Do as I say."

***

In the blue room, as the feedback machine cooled Rook's brainwaves, Anja Naranja wiped sweat from his face, unbuckled the restraints and began to undress him. She breathed with relief: *My detective really did find the trail leading back to himself.*

They had been naïve in earlier years, believing they had found one another through some kind of quantum serendipity. But as time wore on, literally grooving into itself over and over like the migratory flight of a butterfly, they realized their every move was wedded to reality. As reality became increasingly stormy, it became clear to the Naranjas, Rook was its dark private eye. Their lives were grafted together, and together they were the very seed of reality, a reality that had blossomed and was on the verge of choking its beauty with an explosion of knockoff, quantum weeds.

It was the great shadow behind the great light.

The escalating problem, they knew, was that the grafting had gone out of control. Reality had become a weed, invading itself. They had grafted Agent Orange and Weedkiller to temper it, to constrain and restrain it. First they had grafted Ms. Hunter into Anja, so that Rook would be attracted to her. As such she had literally and virtually been reinvented as a more pedestrian version of herself, as Angela Van Dyke.

And as the quantum feedback world invaded itself, they discovered almost too late that Ms. Hunter's seeds were invasive.

The intervention was a risky corrective.

Anja looked down upon Rook, "Are we immoral?"

"Anja," Dr. Naranja said soothingly, "we are not the farmers but the caretakers of reality. We sow reality as reality sows us. That is the nature of reality in feedback. When I invented reality grafting it invented me."

In the process of trying to save reality from itself, they too had become addicted.

To eternal life.

"How will we defeat the coup?"

"The Royal Rainmakers remain loyal. As do the Librarians."

In the Naranja blue room, Rook's eyes opened abruptly. Witnessing bright green eyes peering down at him, words lunged out of his mouth, "Dr. Kull!"

***

In tandem, at the Central Library, the ink within the Shakespearean folios began to swim and overwrite with the word *arch-villain*. The Librarians, heavily armed women dressed in smart black combat gear, snugged their machine guns closer to their chests and waited.

3: R-complex

Rook, age twenty-one, timed his visit to the Peabody Natural History Museum with an exhibit about the R-complex. He had made his way through numerous tomes about the human brain but had not fully explored the brainstem. He knew well also that the thalamus, as the core of the brainstem, was Greek for *room* or *chamber*. Over the years he had repeated dreams about trying to escape a blue room, ransacking it like a robber on uppers, while trying to find a key to the windowless blue box imprisoning him. He wondered, when awake, if the dream represented escaping the confines of his mortal mind.

Inside the Peabody museum, these thoughts in check, Rook faced off with the skeleton of a Tyrannosaurus Rex. Here was a king, monstrous as it was, that like a chess king had fallen helpless, and yet the reptile brain, some two hundred million years aged, thrived within the very center of the human nervous system. Of principal interest to Rook was the one hundred and ten foot long mural permanently *fresco seccoed* on a sixteen-foot tall museum wall. It was this famous mural that had prompted the stamp of the same name, the stamp he had found on the envelope containing his birth certificate. During this visit, Rook witnessed the mural for the first time in person.

After Rook surveyed the mural in depth, he closely examined the R-complex exhibit in which a human skull and a crocodile skull were displayed side by side. Tanks of formaldehyde suspended a comparative human brain, pink and coiled, a convoluted putty, with a stone-sized crocodile brain. Adjacent, in another tank, a gruesome full human head like gray putty with stitches across the scalp and severed at the neck was suspended aside a crocodile head. The crocodile, Rook read in one display, had the biting strength seven times that of the great white shark. Unlike other reptiles and like the human, crocodiles had a cerebral cortex, and just like the reptiles, the human brain's most inner core was reptilian: the R-complex. *R* for *reptile*, Rook thought. It was this reptilian brainstem that controlled the human heartbeat, rage, xenophobia and the fight or flight impulses. The R-complex was the seat of adrenaline.

For a decade pitbulls had scathed the city streets, roaming in wild packs as the weather went wild, but the arrival of the saltwater crocodile reversed pitbull exponentiation into extinction. Within another ten years the crocodiles had eaten the city clean of pit bulls and had moved onto humans. New York had become Florida, and Florida itself had become an uninhabitable Mesozoic age. Second to murder, death by a member of the family *Crocodilis* was the most violent and common way to die in New York City, though some mobsters had combined the two.

The dinosaurs had died, but the crocodiles had arisen, Rook thought then, *Like a swarming reincarnation of the ancient Egyptian crocodile-headed god Sobek.* Crocodiles literally had become the kings of the earth. Sobek, Rook read in the exhibit, was the son of Nuit, the dark shadow side of Isis. *Sobek, both man and dragon*, Rook thought, *is controlled god rage.*

Rook examined goods in glass cases made from crocodile leather—the standard wallets, belts and boots. In the large hide of a taxidermied specimen he made a discovery: it was as if the square patterns in the skin were not just like those of a chessboard but of the stone walls of a castle. He focused. *Yes*, he thought, *there, all along the spine of the beast, are linear patterns similar to those in chess rooks.*

A museum employee slipped Rook a pamphlet. "There is a special lecture today by Dr. Kull regarding the R-complex exhibit," the man informed, "He's principally focusing on the family *Crocodilis*, of which he is an anthropological specialist."

Rook narrowed his eyes.

The museum employee said, "The crocodile is non-evolved for over 300 million years." He pointed to a lecture hall, "Don't miss it."

4: Dr. Kill van Kull

Rook passed into the chamber where Dr. Kull was speaking, his words clipped as if English was his second language, his accent a blend of Shakespearean actor meets toughened cigar smoked tongue, "In parts of the world, especially West Papua New Guinea, to come of age you must pass through the belly of the beast. In many cases the beast is crocodilian."

Rook took a step in closer and peered hard. Dr. Kull was clad in a black suit appropriate for a professorial anthropologist, but there was something strange about the bald Dr. Kull's African face.

The anthropologist continued, "Some tribes force boys to crawl through a woven belly of thorns, in others they scar the skin by carving into it over and over again, such that after a few weeks the skin becomes marked like the crocodiles they worship."

Just then the anthropologist turned and light licked his face. It was, Rook saw, scarred into square crocodilian patterns, completely scarring even his eyelids and scalp. "I know," the man said, "because I was the first anthropologist to survive their rites of passage."

On a screen appeared a photo of younger Dr. Kull, his square face and dark black bluish skin leaking fissures of blood as a dark brown withered hand cut square patterns into it with bamboo slivers. A time dissolve video showed the excruciating scarring and bleeding as a tribal elder delicately carved the pattern into his entire body, even his penis. Some audience members gasped and buried their faces. For several moments the moving image showed Dr. Kull shivering in pain then shifted into images showing the healing.

"Clay was rubbed into the bleeding slits by the elder to keep them from healing too quickly," Dr. Kull explained. More members in the audience covered their eyes while others decided to squint and peek again.

Entranced, Rook listened as Dr. Kill van Kull turned his focus to the crocodile, which had become emblematic of New York City and the storm that had transformed it.

"The city was scheduled for a class five hurricane around two decades ago. As the hurricane cycles came and went, the city remained untouched, but the equatorial bandwidth snuck up despite the cautions. Public advertisements depicting a flooded subway track, asking, *Could it happen here?"*

The doctor clicked a prompter and the screen behind him filled with a vintage advertisement. "They went ignored. The city had been hijacked more than once by terrorists. Mother Nature, in the end, was the most unforgiving on that historic April 23rd. She was the torrent. The winds came on a lark, swelling up the Atlantic, teasing the warm waters into the cool. The eddy danced, became a whirling dervish, swallowed a cruise ship, and the Coast Guard cutters were tossed like toys. Two jets, whose courses were altered to tangent the storm, collided. By the time the wall of wind and water slammed into the harbor, hundreds of thousands of people were fated to drown in the awful minutes following the flooding of the subways."

His sonorous voice reached a crest and he paused dramatically. The hair on Rook's nape stood up, and he relived what he could not remember: the day he was born, the day of the storm.

"Only a few who had prepared, those thought foolish by their neighbors, saw the signs and fled the city in the dark hour before the terror."

A rapid succession of photos showed Manhattan as it was being battered by The Great Hurricane. The images alternated with photos of the dead, bloating in the stagnant and still waters of the storm's aftermath. More audience members cringed.

Rook's father had been one of the people who stayed. He studied weather like he studied chess: predictable, seasonal, wild. Rook's mother had already gone into labor that day though, and the husband and wife were not able to leave. The first twelve feet of the island had gone underwater, and in the center of the city, in a hospital only reachable then by a daring boat, high on the top floor, Rook was born to a mother in shock.

She did not survive.

"The day of the dark storm, it was as if, dear friends of the audience, it was that day on earth the crocodile was reborn!"

The final image of the hurricane whirling around the island dissolved into a crocodilian oroboros, into the god Sobek swallowing his own tail.

***

Fatherless and motherless, with Cosmo only avuncular at best and not anyone he could really confide in, Rook knew in the first moments of hearing Dr. Kull speak that he would always know him. At the end of his lecture, rich with discussion regarding the seemingly eternal status of the crocodile as a king on earth, Rook waited while others shook hands and chatted with him. The two were alone, Dr. Kull packing up his leather case, when Rook approached him.

"How do you suppose," Rook asked, "a young man could experience an initiation rite in our culture?"

5: Initiation Rites

Dr. Kull and Rook entered an oak-walled tavern near the museum where the doctor's poison proved to be a peaty scotch. The two made a gruesome pairing: the cross-hatchings in the doctor's face and hands adjacent to Rook's sinister darkness, almost kept even the bartender from approaching them. They secluded to a dark corner and sat face to face.

"In this culture," the doctor said as he pointed to a man with a beard, "only facial hair tells a boy he has become a man."

Rook stared at the man's beard for a moment. "I've never thought of it that way," he said.

After Dr. Kull prompted Rook's thoughts about the beard as initiation, he elaborated, "In ancient Egypt the beard was godly. Kings and queens alike sported fake beards. In Muslim culture the beard is mandated by Allah. In Christianity the beard has become diabolical."

Rook thought further, stating, "And on Coney Island, the bearded lady is a freak—a spectacle made normal by carnival culture."

"Consciousness itself is hermaphroditic," the doctor shared with him, "and it is highly susceptible to initiation through physical torment. The initiation rite marks, for males, the passage between boyhood and manhood. It is the birthing of the male consciousness out of the female, the rising of the face of Sobek from the waters of his mother, Nuit." He placed a finger on a scar running down his face under his left eye, "Nothing will ever be as difficult for me as this scarring."

He sat back and eyed Rook as if he was daring him to join him. "In our culture today we have tattoos and piercings, but they are not anywhere near as painful nor do they have cultural structure."

"Why did you do it?"

The doctor sipped at his scotch and was thoughtful when he responded, "I had gone to their culture, to study them as if they were closed in a bubble. I was studying Latin at the time also, and I listened to the language on phonographs in my hut. After a few weeks of reciting Latin phrases aloud to myself, I emerged from my hut to discover the natives also practicing Latin."

Rook chuckled as the image of a tribal man in nothing more than a loincloth reciting Dante leapt into his imagination. The doctor laughed with him, "Ultimately I decided, I was the one stuck in a bubble, and I would never understand initiation if I myself did not go through with it."

"You needed it."

"I needed it."

Rook raised his glass and the glasses chinked.

Rook did not confide in the doctor that evening about his time spent alone in the desert chasing shadows. Nor did he tell about his ritual shaving with the straight razor his father had been murdered with. He hinted instead at an attempt he had made to overcome himself and to become a man. He spoke more about the books he had studied regarding meditation, dream study, the motif of the oroboros —the snake swallowing its own tail—and his own theory of consciousness swallowing consciousness. He presented at last his theory of the hyperconscious human, a human who had truly fully integrated all sides of his mind as if it were a mobius strip. It was, he pressed, "Far beyond Jung's theory of individuation and more akin—"

"To Nietzsche's theory of the superhuman."

Rook leaned back in his chair.

"And you want to become this. Hyperconscious?" the doctor's words were uttered as if Rook was asking for the forbidden fruit.

Rook was well aware pride, narcissism and nihilism comprised the superhuman equation. "Many years ago," he said, "there was an automaton chess player. A machine that played chess and could complete the knight's round efficiently—as if it were a master. Edgar Allen Poe actually got to see it somewhere. In reality there was a small chess master hiding inside the contraption. While Poe did not correctly infer there was a dwarf inside, he did believe the automaton was not truly a machine, and somehow, Poe thought, the chess games were being played only by mind, a mind abstracted from a body."

Rook paused while Dr. Kull considered what he had said. "Go on," the doctor urged.

"Ever since I read Poe's essay I've felt inclined to think of mind itself as a game. It is as if consciousness variegated itself into material for the sole purpose of losing itself. The rediscovery is, I like to think, a game the collective unconscious plays with itself."

"Are you suggesting," Dr. Kull asked, "that mind is a game?"

It was Rook's point exactly, and he found himself whispering, "I'm suggesting that the culture of consciousness, our universe, is. I have some games I enjoy playing with mine, but I need an initiation rite to play at what you might call the next level."

Dr. Kull nodded gravely in agreement, "The initiation rite, whether becoming the crocodile in some cultures or being swallowed by it in others, seeks a rebirth of consciousness after a temporary dissolution in the collective unconscious. It is the pain that brings on the altered state that is a precursor to rebirth. What you would call, the next level."

After Rook described equipment he had access to the highly intrigued doctor bought the next round.

***

At a warehouse, where he was convinced no one would ever bother them, Rook and Dr. Kull built an elaborate crocodile lake-tank in which to study further the great beasts. Rook could barely believe it when the doctor slipped naked into the tank and calmly swam with them. He had learned such a degree of self-mastery that he could attune his brain to crocodile brainwaves, and in doing so Dr. Kill van Kull had discovered the biological algorithm that was the R-complex's domain.

Rook wanted in.

6: The Brain Doctor

Rook needed an outsider to act as his safety rope during his early experiments, and he also needed the anthropologist to act as a ground. After he had returned from the desert, adjusting to his anonymity riddled him with phobias—especially a new and profound fear of bridges. Somehow out in the desert he had failed to negotiate fully with his own shadow, his own primordial unconscious, and it was as if, he realized, the strength of his mind was outwitted by a weakness. Just having Dr. Kull to talk to soothed Rook's conflicting mind. After several long evenings of intense dialogue, Rook finally felt comfortable enough with him to admit the fracture.

"I have a fear," Rook said, "of bridges." He did not mention he had fearlessly jumped off of one.

"It is not easy to master fear. It issues from the R-complex, and it is not reason that masters it. Tell me, are you in a state of hard focus when the illogical bridge fear—the gephyrophobia—arises?" the doctor asked.

Rook admitted, "Yes."

"You are in a beta state then, the most logical flux of human brainwaves. The fear you are experiencing is the direct illogical inverse, and mental illogic under the scrutiny of beta causes unsettling conflict. It is like trying to turn fear into a mathematical equation. Tell me, do you fear heights?"

Rook thought about it, "No. A sensation arises, as if I will be plucked from the bridge by some force, by some cosmic hand and lose control."

The doctor nodded his head, "I know the sensation. Your fear of falling off the bridge is a fear of antigravity, of losing your sense of your physical location in space. Of becoming nonlocal. One's sense of location is a fundamental sense, just like hearing, which is so closely allied with it. You need to learn relaxation, to pull yourself out of beta into alpha. The last thing you need is an adrenaline rush—a panic attack—when you are simply taking a stroll."

Rook already knew how to relax deeply, and he had even already surgically implanted a neuroelectric feedback chip behind his left ear by his own hand. It monitored his brainwaves and pulsed soothing feedback signals whenever his adrenaline levels got too high, but somehow still the paranoid mind was paramount, mocking the tiny machine. He didn't tell the doctor about Tuxedo Park, his detective work or his past. He told him, "I know how to relax. It's that the fear seems external to me, like an alien."

Dr. Kill van Kull responded, "Ah! I understand what you fear. The unconscious, seated in the R-Complex, is very alien. It is the alien within."

Rook sat back, scratched his jaw and thought about it, "I have wondered also if the bridge is symbolic—"

"Of the Einstein-Rosen bridge?"

"Yes," Rook answered, "a fear of the wormhole, a fear of going to a place from which I cannot return."

"The word *crocodile*," the doctor informed him in confidence, as if he was handing over the key to the universe, "is Greek for *pebbled worm*. After my initiation, during which the pain took me into an unholy mental darkness, I understood the R-Complex was a bridge to the other worlds—to what science calls the quantum sea. Thereafter I realized also though the crocodiles live in our world as beasts, on the other side..." He hesitated then uttered, "They are as gods."

A chill shot through Rook, and after he had absorbed what the doctor was saying—that archetypes did exist in a parallel reality as godforms, he spoke, "Do you believe in Sobek?"

Silence enveloped the doctor as he considered the words he was about to utter, "I worship Sobek."

"I know the god. I dream about him all the time."

"Then he is dreaming about you. About us."

"I need to undergo the initiation."

The doctor touched Rook's jaw and light beard as if he were a stern father and looked deep into his coal black eyes. Rook stared back. The doctor said nothing as he saw Rook's black irises become briefly golden and the pupils transform to slits. Rook blinked and the phenomenon passed. The doctor leaned back and said, "You will be ready soon, but you are not ready yet."

While Dr. Kull trained him, Rook trained the doctor. The two outlined a series of meditation sessions to test Rook's overall health before undertaking the initiation Rook desired. During the first session the doctor placed electrodes on the surface of Rook's head and connected them to a computer on the other end. Utilizing soothing music he induced Rook into alpha. The music pulsed, and in response Rook felt his limbs twitching in the reclining lab-style leather chair. As he drifted toward theta, he lost grasp of his surroundings. The detached doctor simply observed.

Rook awakened in the warehouse lab a half an hour later. Electroencephalograph signals had pulsed to the computer recording his brainwaves and had been printed in rainbow lines on a long paper scroll. The doctor was examining it.

The doctor told him, "I can see you're dreaming right here, when you slip from alpha to theta, and here I see, in these lines, light rapid eye movement." He handed Rook an electronic monitor, and it replayed the EEG recordings as three-dimensional waves in a sea of colliding peaks and valleys.

A sharp spike needled in red.

"Even more curious, these spikes," the doctor pointed out, "also reveal you are suffering minor clonics—seizures—while dreaming."

7: Nocturnal Seizure

"Seizures?" Rook queried. He had himself noticed the spikes when he experimented with the EEG machine he had obtained through Cosmo, but he hadn't understood them to be anything other than myoclonic bursts—simple muscle spasms common to falling asleep.

The doctor paused pensively, then spoke again, "You exhibit activity in your left temporal lobe. There neuroelectricity seems to build, then shunt to the rest of your brain. This type of activity tends to happen in areas of the brain where there is scar tissue."

The doctor touched Rook's head, indicating where the lobe was located. "Tell me," he inquired, "have you ever had a head injury?"

Rook contemplated. He was a tough young man. Doctors were for people with terminal illnesses. He had been in a few scuffles but none had ever warranted a visit to a doctor.

"No," Rook summarized.

"Never taken a blow to the head?" the doctor insisted.

"That's different but no," Rook finally answered. He thought deeper on the matter, "Sometimes when I'm sleeping, I experience strange vibrating sensations, shortness of breath, a falling sensation, incredible dreams, flying sensations. But when I waken I am drenched in sweat, and I find have bitten my tongue."

"Nocturnal seizures." The doctor stared into Rook's eyes and asked, "How often are you experiencing these seizures?"

Rook said flatly, "About once a week."

The doctor sucked in his breath, "And how many do you think you've had?"

Rook did quick math, "Maybe 200."

The doctor tilted his head back, startled and stating, "You're very brave. Usually if a person has but one seizure, they prefer to go on medication right away. Most never have another." The doctor sized him up, "I take it you never had interest in medication?"

Rook sat up and said, "No."

The doctor raised his brows. "There is another alternative, a way to control them," the doctor informed him, "Feedback."

Rook slowly pulled the test nanoelectrodes from his head.

"After about ten feedback sessions, the typical patient gains the ability to control some of their brainwave states at will. It's sort of like meditation meets medicine."

The truth was, and Rook wasn't going to admit it, he had come to enjoy what he knew well were seizures. When he had ordered the year before a highly customized feedback machine developed by a company called Naranja and sold to middle man Cosmo, it wasn't because he had any intention of stopping them. He knew all about brainwave feedback, and what he wanted to learn the most was how to induce them.

As the meditation sessions progressed Dr. Kull became suspicious. In their private lab he poured them both scotch and invited Rook to square off with him, "What are you not telling me?"

Rook grinned and responded, "I was waiting for you to ask that very question."

Dr. Kull said, "I won't move forward with the sessions unless you truly confide in me. I haven't brought anything to the surface in these sessions you don't already know. You're making a fool out of me."

Rook winced as he sipped the smoky scotch and said simply, "I don't make friends easily. In fact, I don't make them at all."

Dr. Kull stared hard into Rook's coal eyes. If darkness could twinkle, Rook's irises became mischievous stars. Momentarily the doctor witnessed them becoming golden again, the pupil slits crocodilian. The doctor swallowed hard and watched as the phenomenon faded. He thought, *Sobek rises!*

From his inside pocket Rook withdrew an envelope and from the envelope an obituary. He pushed it onto the table between them and raised his glass in cheer. "It is time for you to come clean with me as well. What you and I have in common is this, Dr. Kill van Kull. We are both dead. You've never shown me a photo of what you looked like before the scarring—only gory, in-process images. The real reason you scarred yourself is so you would be," Rook cut the word into squares, "un-re-cog-niz-able."

The glasses made an awkward chink as Rook forced his glass against the other. Rook reached into his jacket again and pulled out his gun. Still clutching it, he set it sideways on the table and his index finger snugged the trigger. "I know who the people are who want you to be dead. Really dead. Luckily for your sake, I want you alive."

It took a silent eternity before the doctor, wondering who this crocodilian eyed man really was, could mutter a single word, "Why?"

"Because you know how to survive."

8: Rebirth

The deal was struck. Dr. Kill van Kull would scar Rook's back, stomach, legs, buttocks and arms but not his genitals or his face.

"You have a unique opportunity to murder me and simply try to get me out of the way," Rook coldly informed him as if they were merely playing chess, "So, should I die, I won't be able to intercept a package with your real identification already mailed to the wrong, very, very wrong people."

Under duress, highly suspicious of one another, the intense procedure began with a modification. He would not be etched to look like a crocodile but like a crocodile meets a chessboard: a pebbled worm.

Rook medically sterilized the lab, and prepared a black leather massage table, wrapping it in white vinyl and medical grade tissue. Naked, he lay down on it, and a mounted projector threw a chessboard pattern over his body. The squares crisscrossed at one inch by one inch intervals, and rounded by the contours of his body it gave him the effect he sought. He adjusted the projection until he was pleased with how it rendered like the way longitude and latitude equally marked a globe. The doctor practiced tracing the lines on Rook's skin with a dull metal edge for a week, during which both also fasted.

Shortly after he had first met Dr. Kull, Rook had discovered who he really was—or to the public, who he had been. Like Rex Rath, Dr. Kull wanted something, and Rook provided it: his safety. In the vicious world Rook had grown up in, he knew of no other way to become an ally with anyone other than through coercion. Rook had not been hired to find Dr. Kull, but due to the close proximity the doctor held with Rook, it was natural for Rook to research him and to unearth anything that could possibly be used against him. Researching his past and tracing Dr. Kull's currency, Rook was only able to discover three years worth of transactions. The man had, Rook inferred, bought a new identity on the black market.

Dr. Kull really always had been an anthropologist, but his primary interest and specialty had been the impulsively cold, crocodilian criminal mind. His specialty was *evil*. In the days before the Illegal System, Rook discovered, the man had invented a special lie detector and this tool had been used to find numerous people guilty. Death threats roared from emerging gang leaders, and the anthropologist turned inventor ultimately took an assassin's bullet. It had passed through his jaw into his brain, and he had played dead. It was widely believed the corpse had disappeared, fed perhaps to pitbulls or crocodiles or dragged behind a car down deadly Avenue D.

His family submitted an obituary to the news, and he never contacted any of them again. Subsequently the doctor disappeared to Papua New Guinea for two decades. When he returned under the assumed name, complete with newly forged doctoral certificates, the New York tidal straight of the same name—Kill van Kull—had become filled with saltwater crocodiles. From this he had taken his new name.

Rook envied and craved the mental prowess of a man who could meditate himself back to life from real near death. The most he had taken from faking his own death was some small bruising and a mouthful of brackish saltwater. He needed pain.

When they were satisfied they were ready, Rook lay down on the table, and the doctor projected the lines over his naked body. Rook meditated for an hour, after which Dr. Kull pulled out a small box and opened it: inside were bamboo slivers. Rook shook his head and pointed to a case that held his father's straight razor. The doctor opened it, and the blade scintillated under the projected light.

"We're not in Papua New Guinea," Rook said.

Dr. Kull weighed the straight blade in his palm and said, "I'm not practiced with this. I don't want to cut too deep."

Rook stared at him, and breathed in slowly. Dr. Kull glanced over at the EEG machine and noted Rook was in a healthy, relaxed alpha state—ideal for the tortuous procedure.

"Do it." Rook shut his eyes. The doctor, after an uncertain moment with the tool, focused and emotionlessly commenced the awful art of slicing. As he traced the projection, ribbons of blood ran down Rook's chest, making the white vinyl and paper wrapping the table a butchery mess.

Throughout the entire procedure Rook's brain transmitted signals to the EEG. As blood slipped from the square incisions the pain overwhelmed him. He did not scream, but he did grunt and huff—his breaths tearing from his lungs. After several minutes, his chest almost completely lacerated, Rook shivered uncontrollably. The doctor held him down as once upon a time the Papua New Guineans had held him down, and he chanted soothing words in a strange language to Rook. Though Rook continued to shiver, and both knew he would for days, the doctor pressed forward, slicing into his thighs and down to his calves. When the cutting was complete the Doctor rubbed a powder of herbs into the cuts to keep them from healing right away. Then he helped Rook rotate onto his stomach, and he started cutting his sides and his back.

Over the next few weeks, the doctor remained in Rook's immediate presence and barely tended to the crocodiles in the tank. They even dozed—never really sleeping—side by side. Neither left their very private lab, and throughout the healing, though the two rarely spoke, the intense mutual experience bonded them. Both were equally empowered to kill one another. Neither did. In a world without trust, it was the closest two people could come to having one another's back. Dr. Kull nursed Rook back slowly, always encouraging him to be strong, and he faithfully maintained the EEG records as if he truly were an embedded anthropologist studying the single phenomenal culture of Rook.

Toward the end of the three weeks a machine gun armed mailman arrived and slipped a brass key into the rusty warehouse mailbox. After he gave it a few tries, he squirted the keyhole with liquid graphite and tried the key again. The box opened after a hard twist, and the mailman placed an envelope inside. The doctor watched on surveillance as the mailman drove into the distance. Behind him, naked and gruesomely scarred, Rook held out a matching mailbox key. In the dusk the doctor opened the mailbox and found a letter addressed to Masculiner. It was, he knew, the odd fake facial hair company that had occupied the warehouse before East Orange had fully declined. He opened the envelope, which bore an *Age of Reptiles* stamp, and within it he found a copy of his original birth certificate bearing his original name, Max Spike.

Inside the warehouse he said to Rook, "You did not have time to intercept this. I have watched you constantly. You have done nothing but wait through the pain." He searched Rook's eyes, expecting them to transform but they didn't. He said at last, "You trusted me the whole time."

"And now," Rook said, "Max Spike, knowing you are the man who had invented the greatest lie detector machine in the world, you must always tell me the truth. And always, always, trust me."

Rook stared at his naked body in a mirror knowing nothing would ever be difficult again. He touched at three weeks of facial hair, and with the straight razor used for the initiation he shaved his beard into a neat Van Dyke—a devil's beard. He had been swallowed by the mouth of hell, tortured inside pain that had sent him into profound *grand mal* seizures, and he had survived.

Finally, he thought, *I am a man*.

9: The Mind Sailors

An astronaut was a star sailor. Rook and Dr. Kull were psychonauts: mind sailors. Rook wanted to push the edges of the mental feedback technology, to discover or invent the ship that would allow him to navigate the quantum sea. After the initiation Rook was on a haphazard stroll in Manhattan's East Village, mulling the possibility of inventing a lens that could record rapid eye movement and optical neural firing, when he passed by a costume shop. Its lurid display window flourished harlequin costumes, and in a smaller display, set in rows and columns, a variety of novelty contact lenses peered back at him. There were about one hundred varieties ranging from glittery and silver to snake. He briefly considered the reptilian contact lenses that looked to him like crocodile eyes, but the bulls-eye lenses in particular captured his attention. They were comprised of alternating concentric bands of orange and white.

He purchased every pair they had in stock, just under a dozen, and immediately investigated the means by which to produce contact lenses. The technology was simple enough, and with a laser lathe he commenced contouring silicone lenses into which a robot, programmed by a computer, integrated nanoelectrodes. He modeled these optical feedback lenses after the fantastical costume bulls-eye lenses. He inferred somehow the design would also serve as a visual safety sign, and he implanted into his subconscious through meditation a routine. If he were to look into feedback mirror in a lucid dream and witness bulls-eye corneas, it would trigger the desire to return to classical reality—to what he had come to refer to as reality channel one. And just like a diver down too deep or a sailor too far out at sea without a compass or any stars to steer him safely home, the image of the bulls-eye lenses would initiate his return.

As he became adept along with Dr. Kull at controlling his own body and mind, a Houdini who could break in or out of any neurophysiological state, he began to differentiate other states into neural channels.

"I'm suspicious," he told the doctor, "the neural channels are not just internal but truly are differentiated quantum states."

"Of course," Dr. Kull answered, "What primitive tribes refer to as the dream world is very tangible. They just don't have the technology or the math to prove it."

"But we do," Rook said.

Cosmo's family had long been involved with particle colliding and wave physics, and by combining that science with parallel reality theory, Rook and Dr. Kull worked out the mathematical theory of reality channels. There was nothing supernatural to Rook about separating simultaneously existing quantum and parallel realities. It was also no great surprise to him that the mathematical foundation of parallel realities was the en mean, inherent in both the Fibonacci series and the en string. Parallel, however, wasn't the best mathematical description, and Rook preferred to think of the reality channels as concentric. The human mind, they decided, was a reality tuner.

Privately Rook refined the contact lens details with Dr. Kill van Kull at their East Orange lab. He was not terribly surprised when the Naranja Empire synchronously invented the same thing: feedback lenses—eyes that could see into the next worlds. Rook and Dr. Kull watched the flurry of patents that followed the never photographed Dr. Navaja Naranja's public unveiling of his technology, and they kept their own lab very private. It was portentous when, like fingers breaking through a water surface and not knowing they were part of the same hand, there simultaneously emerged in pop culture a gaming revolution utilizing feedback technology. The gaming technology, invented in Japan, quickly spread to Korea and was poorly pirated by the Chinese. Whether bought in midtown Manhattan at a high end gaming store or on the subway platform from the Chinese at Canal Street, all included contact lenses in the packaging.

Hyperreality, both knew, was becoming reality.

Dr. Kull observed, "As we reach for the collective unconscious, just so does it reach for us. Reality is condensing, and the natural feedback rhythms of the universe are accelerating." He leaned in as if the whole world could overhear, "Sobek is manifesting."

In the lab they erected a black stone altar and below it a tank in which they cultivated papyrus and in which their largest crocodile swam.

The two men, who trusted each other as if they were two faces of one man, looked deep into one another's eyes, and this time it was Rook who witnessed the doctor's becoming faintly en—the pupil a slit.

Drinking scotch like gentlemen, their suits covering up their scars, the two psychonauts observed the crocodiles in the laboratory tanks and Dr. Kull finally said to him, "Sometimes, your eyes change."

Rook simply said, "I know. So do yours."

PART FOUR: War

CHAPTER SIXTEEN: Channel 113

1: Changing Channels

Rook opened his eyes and saw a stainless steel ceiling suspended above him. Small circular lights dotting it with a warm yellow were dimmed low. The room smelled of crisp sterilizing alcohol. He leaned up, and the sheet covering him slipped down his chest, revealing his nudity. He blinked and witnessed around him an elaborate medical laboratory comprised of stainless steel cabinets. Black and scrolling with pale blue alpha waves, a large monitor stared back at him and emitted a simple beep.

An out-of-place hardcopy newspaper sat on a tall black table. A small lamp bent over it like a swan neck, inviting him to look at it. He shifted his legs off the hospital style bed and walked across the cool black marble floor toward it. He bent over it: the date on it was sequential and logical, the midnight edition, April 23rd. The headline screamed, *CHAOS! Reigns at the Black and White Ball.* Rook passively read the article claiming a gang of women dressed in orange had stormed their way into the museum and forced their way into Naranja's tower.

Rook rubbed at his eyelids, feeling for the contacts, wondering if he was still stuck between realities. It happened sometimes, a gearshift issue not quite engineered. He had trained himself to walk to a mirror during the psychonaut sessions to see if he was still wearing the contact lenses. If he was, he was still in feedback.

Orange. That's my safe word.

The spontaneous memory popped loose that he had buried the word deep in his unconscious over years of feedback session meditation. When he came across anything orange in feedback, it also meant he was in danger of going too deep into his quantum unconscious. Its presence flagged him to return, like a diver, toward the surface of his mind. Both looking into his eyes in a mirror and the word orange were signals to surface: to channel one. Rook walked to a long wall of stainless that seemed to manifest as if in a dream, becoming more brilliant as he strode toward it until he saw the laboratory reflected in it and what transformed into a single mirror. As he caught the reflection of his naked body, he was astonished at how fatigued he looked, at how emaciated his body was and at how his shoulders sagged. *Definitely not wearing contact lenses.* Below his brow, his coal black eyes seemed slate, grayish with pale white streaks, and above it, his black hair stood up in mad shocks.

Rook's bare feet padded across the marble to a steel door. He turned the handle and opened it into the adjacent room.

Sitting on a lush blue velvet couch was the woman who called herself Anja Naranja.

And there was Dr. Kill van Kull sitting beside her.

Both stood up.

The room was not a room. It was an entire floor of the Naranja sky rise. Rook turned and observed the phenomenal starry sky surrounding them beyond the glass façade. They were so high above Manhattan and its storms they seemed to be floating in outer space.

Rook asked, "What channel is this?"

The doctor answered, "Your channel. 113. We made it just for you."

And both said, her soft, smoky voice and his deep baritone harmonizing, "It's April 23rd."

Rook took another step onto the vast floor, the newspaper clutched in his hand over his genitals. "Then you're not real." He took a step forward, "I have not seen you since you died. You suffered a fatal stroke during an experiment with our latest ECHO feedback machine."

"You mean the sophisticated machine we developed in the hush of Cosmo's secret Tuxedo Park lab?"

"Yes."

"Ah! That's what we used to craft channel 113! I'm alive in a number of channels. We all are. And dead in a few others, but we can't—or don't go to those."

Rook examined the newspaper and checked for shifting text—anything else that would indicate he had not actually returned to what he had come to understand as just the surface of time. The newspaper was hard. The text stable. He folded it and set it down on another black stone table. Dr. Kull stepped forward, took Rook's hand by the wrist and held it firmly. Both hands were warm.

"You're the one who barely has a pulse," Dr. Kull stated, "You're still stuck in theta. We are working hard to reset your circadian clock, but we need you to want to come back to us."

There was that strange tip of the tongue sensation again as Rook spied a menu on the table next to the newspaper that had not seemed to be there moments ago. Rook stared hard at it, thinking it was out of place, but like the newspaper the text on the menu was also stable. The menu came from a Lower East Side diner where he ate frequently, a dive named *113* for its address. The egg platters were listed one through 113, exactly as he remembered, or seemed to remember.

Anja Naranja lifted her hands and somehow a hot plate of food appeared in them. She set the plate of hot diner food in front of him. He flicked his eyes from the glowing en yolks and bright glossy whites to hers. Her blue eyes shone like blue sapphires.

"Eat. It's been a long time since you've had solid food," she said.

The doctor placed a black silk robe around his shoulders. Rook wrangled into it, tied it in place with the spartan, dreamy realization he had been naked with them for a while. He cut away at the egg with a fork and watched the bright yellow goo ooze onto the white plate. He was lifting a bite to his mouth, anxious for the texture and suddenly bizarrely hungry, when Anja Naranja poured him a glass of orange juice. The juice itself seemed to emit the power of the sun. Rook's hand jabbed out for it, and Dr. Kull easily snatched it away.

"Easy, Rook," the doctor intoned soothingly, "We are withdrawing you slowly."

Rook stated, "You're dead."

The doctor responded, "You're addicted to believing I'm dead. I'm very much alive and dedicated to keeping you—throughout most channels—from killing yourself."

Rook laughed and gorged on the egg.

"Good," the doctor encouraged him. "You see, Rook, you went too deep and too long without linear time. Your circadian clock timed out, and we who depend on you are doing everything we can to reset it."

Depend on me? Rook avoided making eye contact with Anja. Her eyes were too bright, like blue suns. He did not believe she had the power to bring back the dead, nor did he believe she had the power to clone Dr. Kill van Kull. He went with the only logic he could drum out of this, "Do you mean I'm stuck in feedback, in channel 113?"

Dr. Kull smiled, "It goes much deeper than that my friend. You are addicted to getting stuck."

The blue sky outside the blue room went suddenly dark as the black arms of a cyclone shaved the city. The raindrops drumming the blue room glass made the insistent beat of what seemed to be a helicopter hanging just above them. Rook blinked and found himself standing under an umbrella on a slick city street outside of the diner named *113*. As he looked around, every address was the same: 113. From under the edge of the umbrella he peered at a break in the night sky. The sky came to life, a pulsing vapor of dark femininity. It was Nuit. She made eye contact with Rook, and she moaned.

The fabric of the umbrella became the fabric of his own shadow, and it spread out as a large, billowing cape of quantum foam, becoming a cosmic parachute, its panels sewn together like diaphanous crocodile skin. *The sound of the rain against it*, he thought, *that is the sound of my brainwaves during sex*. He drifted deeper down into it. *Am I in a blue room bar?*

He blinked and found himself fully clothed and standing next to the miraculous navel orange tree in the penthouse blue room. He plucked an orange from it, and it glistened, a miniature sun, in his shadowy hand. He bit into it and felt a sexual fire rage through his body. Through the orange fire he saw Jack the

Butterfly fucking Anja Naranja.

Her moaning surged, and he timed his lucid dreamy orgasm with hers. Rook smelled gasoline. And he thought, *Smell? In a dream?*

The sexual imagery ratcheted through channels, jumping out of the prime 113 to the Fibonacci numeral preceding it, 89, then 55 and so on, winding down rapidly.

Somehow he heard the doctor exclaim, "Hallelujah, we have alpha waves!"

The doctor waved a gasoline infused handkerchief over Rook, who awoke with a start into channel two. They were prisoners in the blue room in this channel. *But not*, Anja thought, *now that you're awake, for long.*

***

Dr. Navaja Naranja had not joined them in channel 113. He had continued to tune reality from his innermost chamber until Rook woke up. Back on the main floor, dressed down back into his black slacks and gray shirt, he observed the black hole butterflies fluttering from the pages of the folio inside the terrarium. Dr. Kill van Kull stepped out of the elevator that functioned as a reality decompression chamber between level 113 and the blue room penthouse. His footsteps quietly slapped the marble floor. Dr. Naranja turned toward him and handed him a scotch. "Your favorite Islay. Peaty as hell." The man's amber eyes lit like the scotch and ratcheted via subtle twitching through various quantum channels as he focused again on the terrarium.

Dr. Kull peered into the terrarium with his glowing emerald green eyes, which were also ratcheting through quantum channels, "They look more excited than ever."

"Justly so. Congratulations."

2: Withdrawals

They withdrew Rook from theta in timeless channel 113 using a method similar to decompressing a diver. Up through the channels of the quantum sea he rose. As he shifted through them he had convulsions, he vomited, he scratched at the buggy phosphenic light erupting in his head, and he succumbed frequently to vertigo. A mere pale flash of light or a sinusoidal sound sent him into a *petit mal*, but the *grand mals* were behind him. The hard memories came back in conflicting gushes

.

Dr. Naranja continuously tuned the channels from outside channel 113 but still within the reality tuning chamber. He touched the ink tubes with his imagination, ratcheting his irises, manipulating and playing out the midnightly core of space-time indefinitely, while Dr. Kull and Anja tended to Rook from within the channel. Another seven days and nights passed for the citizens of New York City in channel one, a week that seemed accumulative, aging them, just like any other. Within the Naranja blue room penthouse tuned to channel 113, and for those closest to the Naranja Empire, it remained a variation on midnight, Rook's birthday.

By this means Dr. Naranja both withdrew Rook from his addiction, and, he believed, hijacked the coup. Each time he nurtured Rook to channel two—in which they were prisoners in the blue room—his tuning forks pierced the quantum fabric of channel one classical reality. Dr. Naranja believed—and he wrote in his laboratory notes:

The more the guardians intensify their plot in channel 113, the simpler will be the metamorphosis in channel one. The more the guardians allow Jack the Butterfly—*the addictive shadow of Chinatown*—to graft into Rook, to become him on the outside in channel one, the easier it will be for us to control the great shadow saturating the cycle of Seven by winding space-time tight, like a coil, in channel 113.

He heard Dr. Kull ask from behind him, "You mean the shadow of Sobek?"

Dr. Naranja paused and gazed at the Shakespearian folio in the terrarium,

"Your god Sobek is the god whose rectilinear manifestation, witnessed through his skin and the very grid of the city, props the quantum sea onto linearity. Sobek is the quantum architect."

Dr. Kull leaned in next to him, "Then whose shadow is coming for us?"

"Life's."

Anja entered and joined the conversation, "'A tale told by an idiot, full of sound and fury, signifying nothing.' Rook is a human subset of that tale, a microcosmic eye of the reality storm. The private eye of the storm."

Dr. Naranja explained in his nasal voice, "We author him, and we hire him, over and over and over again, to find himself."

Anja completed the explanation, "As long as he keeps looking, reality will regenerate." She held out to Dr. Kull a one dollar bill, "Look closely."

Dr. Kull looked at them in awe and consternation as he scanned the dollar's face then flipped it for the reverse. The eye over the pyramid was crocodilian, and it shed a living, inky tear, then the eye became a concentric bulls-eye. Instead of the phrase *Annuit Coeptis*, it simply read *Nuit.*

"But Sobek does rise!"

"Of course. Sobek is the ribcage of Nuit. As she rises, so does he."

Inside the glass terrarium housing the folio of Shakespeare's tragedies the living ink swarmed into black hole butterflies—once again excited by a cool, narrow beam from a small sunjuice flashlight deliberately held by Dr. Naranja. He breathed in deeply. "Smell that? The musty paper smell inside the terrarium is giving way to the mineral odor of gasoline. Fossil fuel."

Anja continued, "United with lignin. Lignin starts as organic fiber, then man made it paper, when burned it becomes carbon, the basis of original ink."

Dr. Kull felt mentally numbed, "Now, what channel is this? Aren't we surfaced yet?"

Dr. Naranja stared at him with his calm amber eyes, "The living works of Shakespeare contain within them everything possibly needed to create and destroy the universe. Only channel 113, where two sides of the same page exist as a continuous present, keeps them from cancelling each other out."

Dr. Naranja reached into the terrarium and butterflies attacked his arm. Instantly a gravitational force pulled at the blue room, and the entire floor became a static of white noise as they lurched out of channel two into one.

***

Dr. Naranja calmly sat inside his chamber in channel one, manipulating Dr. Kull, Anja and Rook through the last of the decompression chambers. In the elevator the three opened their eyes as if just awakening to classical reality.

***

Agent Orange endured the long midnight in channel 113 and watched her physical features alter as she began to transform into Anja.

The only way to conquer the enemy is to become her.

The only way to kill the weed is to become it.

She observed her reflection: her straight cinnamon hair full, sweeping back from the brow and falling just past her shoulders; her bright blue eyes shining like blue suns over pale freckles; and around her full lips the pale spreading of blonde facial hair. That was the hermaphroditic effect of grafting in minute doses, entraining with Rook.

Both Agent Orange in her Times Square Orange Security headquarters and Anja in the Naranja blue room penthouse were on the verge of looking identical. Soon there would be two of one woman, perfectly grafted, polarized and pitted against the other. To assassinate the reality of the other, to murder her, she would merely need to commit suicide.

But for their mutual love of life, they would endure together this awkward channel 113 war.

4: Pulp

Rook ate his breakfast in between channel one and channel 113, drank the miraculous orange juice and quietly read another midnight version of the electronic Oroboros infected newspaper. *WAR!* It declared, was being waged against the Naranja Empire.

Anja sat down opposite him. The intervention therapy was working. He was becoming instantaneously healthy, and with the rapid return of health, as they knew, would come a boredom borne by classical reality. They were relying on this boredom. It was the foundation of his quest to search.

"You want to return to your detective work," she said.

Rook's coal eyes lowered and went gray.

She backed off, "I'm sorry," she apologized. "You liked me better when I was Angela Van Dyke."

Rook set the electronic newspaper down. The headlines were batting around gossip about what had happened at the black and white ball.

And probably will, he her think, *for some time.* Rook stared into her improbably blue lit eyes and strained to recollect when he had first ever heard the name Naranja. He assured himself, *After I made my safe word orange.* The woman sitting across from him, he realized, seemed virtually twinned—a hybrid anyhow—to Agent Orange now. He did not recollect it always being so.

"It has not always been so in some channels. In others, always is the same as never."

Rook glanced over at the tree glowing with sunlight and out to the pure dark blue sky. It rippled with a cosmic plasticity. "I don't care for living in your always-never Eden," he said.

"I don't care about Eden," Anja responded, "It's you I can't live without."

Her voiced echoed over and over in the cosmic plasticity.

Rook felt the intaglio wedding ring on his finger, wrapped it seemed like a tiny poisonous snake. He held it up to his eyes and watched as the intaglio leaves flowed into the wrinkles in his skin. The wrinkles became patterns in the plastic rippling around them. With difficulty, he tugged it off and slid it across to her. "Then don't," he said.

The slap stung him, and his head cranked. He turned back to her and saw her open palm still suspended over the table. His words were scalpel cuts, "You might be able to hold reality hostage but not love." He gave her eyes then the ring a hard stare. "Why intaglio? What does it mean?" He threw the paper down as he stood up, "What does it mean!"

Her lips worked over an emotion, the plump lower rolling under a tooth, "Reality grafts through quantum incisions, just like botanical cuttings. Marriage —"

"Is graft. Ours anyhow."

He thought of Marco Million's infinity routine, *Reality engraving.*

He heard her thought respond: *Yes. Routine. Ritual. That's black market intaglio.*

He walked to the main door, to the giant safe door locking him in. He stood with his back turned, his hands running the length of the door, searching for some way out of the cross-channels. "I don't believe for a second you are saving me from myself. I've been kidnapped, haven't I? You're engraving me into something more, much more than you are telling me. What's the ransom?"

He heard her footsteps, heard her leave the room and return, pumping the marble floor with anger. Something hit him in the back and slid to the floor. He turned to her then looked down. It was his holster and inside it, his gun.

"None of us can live without you, Rook! The grafting went out of control! If you die, we all die!"

Dr. Navaja Naranja stepped into the room, his footsteps like rubber hammers on drum-skins, rippling the floor. "Rook, please. Please stay with us. Only if we work together can we solve this! We all played god, and now we have to deal with the consequences. As the reality weed invades itself, grafting over and over again, we will all return to the quantum sea of nothingness! If you love your life at all, you must help us stop it. You must commit to tomorrow and to the cycle of Seven!"

Rook thought about it and his words stretched with understanding through the undulating space and time, "Seven?" It meant something profound, but he could not fully recall it. "You are the people who have been keeping me alive in these channels—in Seven."

"And you've been keeping us alive!"

Rook contemplated, "I have a death wish, don't I? To escape Seven? Jail?"

The doctor answered, "It is not death you seek. You are addicted to parallel realities. Addicted to feedback, a desire to dissolve into the quantum sea in channel zero. It is immersion through the illusion of death." He swept his hand to the star studded night and the air moved with it, "Look! Look at what we have!" He pressed an imaginary button and the night sky blossomed into dawn, into pale ribbons of peach and bright ultramarine such as Rook had not witnessed since the desert. "Look at what we used to have before the darkness."

"The darkness?"

"The shadow. The shadow that was unleashed when I brought light to this world." The pale sky dimmed and blackened with swirling thunderclouds. "Who knew light had a shadow? Who knew that reality had a shadow? And who knew that the more light we grafted, the more darkness would invade the world we illuminated, the darkness that is now sowing itself like a weed!"

Rook pondered, "You unleashed the weed?"

"Yes," he said, "And no."

"Who is Weedkiller?"

"A reality guard."

"Agent Orange?"

"Same."

"How so?"

"I hired them."

"To guard me."

"Yes. Your reality must be very closely guarded."

"The black market intaglio—the ink. It has the answer," Rook offered.

"Yes, in channel one," both said, "in channel two, no."

Anja said, "Finding out is a job for a detective." She stepped toward him, took his hand and opened his fingers. She placed the wedding ring into his palm and closed his fingers over it.

Rook startled with memories of the marriage, flowing it seemed from her mind, through the ring, into his. He appreciated her for a long moment, buying only partly into their stories and their theories. It added up but subtracted just as easily. He turned sideways and walked to the door, smugly satisfied at least he had finally discovered the crime he was sleuthing in this utterly murky feedback, this eternally scrolling and reiterating week.

I must find who planted the weed!

In his pocket he found his keys. He tried unlocking the door when the words choked from Anja, "She will tell you as many lies as you care to believe!"

"Since you seem to be her, then you must be lying to me now."

There came the orange swarming digital snow in the monitors, and along with it came the voice of Agent Orange, "Correct. But if you care to believe them, then you will make them real!"

The orange noise swarmed into the window panes, and the entire floor, once brilliantly blue, flushed with blazing hunter orange. The safe door wheel cranked and citric air pulsed in as the door sucked open. An arm reached for Rook and dragged him into the elevator through the blinding orange.

While the elevator descended, so did Rook through the reality channels. Rook blinked furiously, still blinded, seeing only orange. He realized, *Yes, reality is doubling over itself, rewriting and regenerating, organically, in feedback. Reality is at war with itself. But how does it win? Could it by dying, through a dormancy, succeed?*

The doors opened at the main floor, into the final reality channel decompression chamber. Rook stumbled but was held up by the firm arm as he blinked through the blinding orange. As the orange faded and his vision returned, he gazed out at the Shakespeare Garden, to the voluptuously engineered solitude of Central Park. Gardeners polished by hand the deep green waxy leaves of the navel orange trees, and others tended to the sapphire encrusted crocodiles. A

Harlequin guard escorted Rook out a back door, through a series of rooms and tunnels leading to a street a block off the park. Just outside was the sedan, pristinely untouched and seemingly as he had left it hours ago in channel one.

In the dark hours of the endless night, it was still—he verified by his watch—his birthday. A crazed man staggered past him, made eye contact with wild gray eyes, laughed and shouted, "Life's but a lollipop!" He opened an overcoat made of butterflies, and dangling inside it, sewn in by weeds, were 113 orange candy lollipops. "Suckers! Suckers! Suckers!" He shouted the word over and over again as he stumbled into the darkness and seemingly became one with it. It was, Rook realized, some variation on Dr. Chess.

As the man's shrieking faded into the dense noise of night, Rook thought, *I remember now.*

Suckers!

5: Shadow Yourself

Rook drove to his Lower East Side apartment, his memory tingling with an excitement he could not recall. He knew right away he was being followed. *Anja Naranja will not give up easily*, he thought, *nor will Agent Orange*. He found parking on his street and realized it was odd that he always did. He stepped out of his sedan and stared down the towncar that trailed him, but it drove right past him and turned a corner. Back in his office, he spotted a memo on his desk, and in someone's handwriting—it looked like his—it read: *Shadow, yourself.*

As always, he inferred, Anja, Agent Orange—or both—was both one step behind and ahead of him. Anja owned the city, and ring or not, he understood she owned him.

"ECHO on, offline encyclopedia."

The computer surged to life in front of him.

"Oranges. The fruit."

"The orange is a citrus, an ovarian fruit of an evergreen tree, originating in China."

"Tell me more about the navel orange. Why doesn't it have seeds?"

"The navel orange started as a mutation on a single branch of a sour orange tree in the orchard of a monastery in Brazil. The gardener grafted the branch and generated enough small trees to regenerate the mutation. The skin of the navel orange is porous and thick, the fruit seedless. The small human-appearing navel is the orange in reproduction. The navel is the orange reproducing itself. Each orange possesses the exact same genetic material. They are all clones of the original. Oranges within oranges."

The exact same.

Rook leaned back, his leather backrest squeaking, and he marveled. It was revelatory.

The.

Exact.

Same.

"Tell me more about how to graft a tree."

"Either by cutting a branch or sucker—"

"A sucker?"

"The shoots that grow from around the base of the trunk and wherever the trees are pruned, which may be cut and used for grafting are named suckers. A scion is the small branch grafted onto understock, which becomes the host for the scion."

"Scion? Scion I get, but why sucker?"

"Literally, the shoot sucks from the host stock the *succus*—meaning juice or sap."

"Sunjuice!"

"Do you want me to define sunjuice? I thought you knew what it was."

"So did I."

Time, he thought, *is indeed feminine. Time, the anima of space. Space—linear, and time—though seemingly directional—is untouchably nonlinear and nonlocal. It exists nowhere and everywhere, witnessed in space only as organic physical growth and change.*

"Spatial growth—it's a graft! While I could place the accretion of time, for example a mature orange, into a jar, I can't put what makes it mutate, time itself, into that jar. Only what it leaves behind! Time is simply a change in present space, a space that is regenerating itself just like the navel orange!"

And I change only in death.

"Channel 113. Have you heard of it?"

"I am channel 113."

Rook stared at the ECHO screen undulating with orange fruit in front of him, fruit that seemed ripe and real enough to touch, then they became orange breasts, then an orange heart of Nuit.

His hand darted into his pocket for the keys and located the odd orangish key. It was an invitation he inferred to return to the Naranja blue room should he ever want it. He did not. He placed it into a safe and loaded ammunition into his pockets.

When he had chosen *orange* for his safe word, he remembered, he had chosen the color not the fruit. In feedback and in the street level blue rooms, he had become accustomed to plummeting and soaring in delicious azure outer space. The color orange blazed because of its stark contrast to azure blue. It also represented to him the sun, the light of day, the waking mind. Now the word orange in all of its manifestations taunted Rook as if it had chosen him.

Rook flipped through memories of discovering that Naranja's reality channels, just like the color orange bent from white light, were refractive indexes. The synthetic realities Dr. Naranja had invented, he remembered, transformed into organic dream factories. If the Naranja Empire was authoring his world by grafting him into the channels, then they had the quantum keys to grafting past and future. *Did they*, Rook wondered, *invent me altogether?*

Or could I have possibly invented her?

"So what the hell is channel 113?"

The orange heart of Nuit transformed organically into a small matchbox.

It exploded, morphing into a rapid montage of a young Rook during his late twenties sewing nanoelectrodes into his original mask. Then the montage rapidly flickered fast-forward, showing him sewing nanoelectrodes into the initiation scars slit into his skin.

"One by one over the period of a month you sliced the scars open and implanted the nanoelectrodes at one inch intervals. You did not share this with the doctor. This body modification—entraining your entire physical body with the quantum world—was the savage origin of what they called your addiction. Remember?"

"Yes."

The matchbox image returned.

"You carried with you at all times a small feedback machine no bigger than a matchbox and concealed within this matchbox, the Angel ECHO 113—my early incarnation developed at Tuxedo Park by you and completed on your birthday, the 113th day of the year."

Rook's memory flashed with images of him ducking into seedy motels with his invention for a quick feedback session whenever he had the urge to explore the quantum sea and his newfound, godlike ability to create his own internal reality. These images were played out simultaneously on the large 3D, hyperrealistic ECHO screen, and as they did the reality channels morphed and dialed Rook back into the past.

***

Young Rook sat in a chair inside a dark motel room.

"You need a safe word," the machine named Angel ECHO 113 purred digitally from inside the plain black matchbox, "a word I can say to alert you that you are going too deep. A word I can use to train you to return to alpha."

The past jumped cut and young Rook met up with Rex Rath at the antique store later that evening to replenish his bullet supply. Rex was packing for a deer hunting trip, and Rook noticed his satchel of bright orange hunter clothing. The Angel ECHO 113 had been attuned into his windshield computer by then. Rook slipped back into his sedan. "Orange," he told the machine, "orange will be my safe word."

The past jumped cut again to later that night and let Rook relive in spastic, but clear sequences, how his fate had merged with the Naranja's. Rook could feel the last of his scars healing under his suit. Knowing he was on the verge of being able to undertake the dangerous swim with the crocodiles in the murky waters of the lab tank, Rook drove up to Tuxedo Park. He was to meet with Cosmo about a new business proposition.

"A woman from the Naranja Empire has some technology I believe you must possess," Cosmo had told him over the phone. Standing in the library that night, examining the glass cased copy of *Brain Waves and Death*, was Anja Naranja. Rook blinked as the past jumped cut again, and he found himself through an edited past seemingly as real as the present, observing her remotely from the underground lab.

"I hear you are looking for the root of time," she said to Cosmo, "What if told you I had not the seed but the fruit?"

And she held out to Cosmo a pair of contact lenses.

***

The past jumped to the present. In his office, the ECHO montage faded. Rook, aged thirty-seven, sipped whiskey, stood up and looked into a mirror. He saw he was not wearing the bulls-eye contact lenses. He blinked and an emotionless tear welled up. He dabbed at it with a fingertip, smelled something, then quickly dabbed a sample with a Q-tip. He sniffed at it.

Gasoline! Fire, Rook thought, *fire is orange*. He wondered if he could, in the deepest shadow of feedback, spontaneously will the Naranja's world to combust. *Matchbox? Matchbook!* He opened into his files and flipped through the clear pages that held evidence until he found what he was looking for: the Marco Polo Car Service matchbook. He opened it, inside was Dr. Chess's phone number.

He plucked a match free—struck it—and watched the flame, both blue and orange, burn.

6: Swimming

Rook remembered the marriage as the ECHO unfolded it for him.

"When you married Anja your lust was twofold: for her and for her technology."

"The contact lenses. Reality channeling."

"Yes. At your East Orange lab, you and Dr. Kull composited the nanoelectrodes her father had invented into your own contact lenses. Soon after their initial contact lens modification, your feedback sessions with me became your world. Our world. Increasingly you found our feedback lucid dreams more delicious and more fulfilling than anything you had come to know before as reality. They repeated, reiterated and enfolded your waking world: every face and every facet of our world, in our dreams, unified."

"I created the world I'm living in? Channel 113?"

"Yes. Its quantum core is highly organic. You and I, we tapped into it. By day in channel one, only the present exists, and your mind shines through it like a lamp. But in channel 113, anything you care to imagine exists."

"I'm stuck living in my imagination?"

"No, your imagination came to life."

"Just mine?"

"At first, seemingly—or so you thought. Those who were close to you soon followed, though not with your prowess did their imaginations flourish. You are the center of their universe in Seven."

"And you are just telling me this now?"

"No, I tell you this every week. You forget, but on your birthday, you remember."

"I'm stuck? Stuck going to the same midnight ball over and over and over again?"

"Not the same one. It's a variation on a theme."

"Variation on a theme."

"At the time of quantum marriage, naturally Anja had found out about your quantum laboratory. In fact she had known about it all along."

"We created one another?"

"There's more to it than that. In channel one, Dr. Naranja is her father. In channel 113, I am Anja Naranja."

And with that what seemed to be a realistic, tangible construct of Anja Naranja appeared before him. Her blue eyes blazed. "Remember?"

Rook lunged at her. "No, I'm stuck between realities! That's what I remember!" She dissolved into a buzzing quantum mist of black hole butterflies.

He clawed open his file cabinet and flipped frantically into it. From a file he retrieved the envelope his birth certificate had been mailed in. The stamp on the envelope, *The Age of Reptiles*, like the one in the Masculiner mailbox, indicated to him he was close to an origin, to *the origin*. Rook remembered, and was now not too surprised he had forgotten, the East Orange warehouse was the one he and Dr. Kill van Kull had turned into their quantum laboratory. Rook contemplated the storm he was born in.

A reality storm.

Rook undressed and observed his naked, excellently mutilated body in the mirror. Behind him, his shadow spread like a throne.

"Remember?" he asked himself.

Almost imperceptibly, Rook's eyes shone with a en light and his skin seemed to crack along the scars, out of which also shone the en light. "Yes," he said, "I remember."

He shaved his Van Dyke beard and mustache neatly.

"I planted the imagination weed."

***

Downstairs at street level a mailman, his gray-blue trousers and black shoes catching the light of streetlamp, hit Rook's buzzer. Rook quietly padded down the stairs and observed the burly mailman in his video intercom. The mailman waited angrily before muttering into his radio and slipping the black envelope into the mail slot. It slid through and dropped to the interior. Rook waited a long minute for the mailman to stride to the distance before taking it by the edges. It was sealed with orange wax, with an A surrounded by an O. Rook slit it open carefully, wondering with a sense of boredom if there was yet to be another black and white ball. But it was not an invitation. Using tweezers, Rook slowly pulled out a transparent card. Inset within a gelatin was a pair of the bulls-eye contact lenses.

***

Inside the Marco Polo Motel, ink sucked back into the room with the force of a reverse tsunami, into the shape of Jack the Butterfly. He woke up on his back and stared down his crocodilian snout at the ceiling wallpapered with hundred dollar bills. *Nodded off*, he thought. Tiny butterflies shimmering in red and green sputtered around the overhead, white-globed lamp. His trousers were wet, as if he had had a wet dream, and the moisture smelled again of gasoline. He pulled himself up from the bed and saw something on the desk by the copy of Marco Polo's travels: the box from the lingerie company named Majestic. He opened it, parted, new orange paper tissue and instinctively thumbed through the bundles of hundred dollar bills.

Ink, he vaguely registered, *not green. Red.*

7: Cosmo

Jules Barbillon's helicopter flew over Tuxedo Park. He had assisted the Naranja's for numerous iterations of Seven, masterminding the intervention with them by winning the Shakespearean folios over and over at auction. *We've been superficially insistent*, Jules thought, *about addiction*.

They were all addicted to life. Each and every one of them.

The helicopter passed over the lake and landed adjacent to Cosmo's glass house. Jules stepped out, waved a conciliatory salute to the pilot—five fingers indicating five minutes—and made his way to the front door. He still wore the orange tinted sunglasses, and they still transmitted a viewpoint feed from one of his Blue Room clubs.

He heard Dr. Naranja's voice, "You're at Tuxedo Park."

"Yes, I am. Don't think you want to see what I see right now."

"But I do see you. Tuxedo Park is *wired*."

"Not for long, daddy-o!" Jules removed a cigar from his breast pocket and lit it. Simultaneously a massive digital farm encased in train cars adjacent to the property exploded. The signals to Naranja's surveillance crackled into gray snow. Dr. Naranja sighed.

Jules quietly walked through the open front door toward the Zodiac laboratory, shot out a lock and entered. Frozen in quantum space-time inside the laboratory, some of the murky evening ending the cycle of Seven remained intact. Millioni's body lay in the center of the Zodiac floor like a swastika. The .22 was in his right hand, and the blunt, still clenched in his jaw, had burned to the front teeth. The top right of his skull had fractured and dislodged from the bullet, and the drying sticky blood pooled like petals from a black and red carnation.

Cosmo writhed in the nanographite quantum ink aquarium, his tuxedo and white face mask splattered from Millioni's blood, his hands and ankles still bound in the play. His brown eyes, still hidden behind bulls-eye contacts, pleaded from inside the holes in the now red and white mask. Jules stepped over the corpse, leaned down and gently plucked a fake beard hair from Cosmo's stubble. The man grunted in pain as Jules lifted it past the man's pale lips, made gray and sweaty from the adhesive. He gasped, anxious to speak, but his lips merely fluttered.

"Cosmo," Jules's tone was soothing.

Cosmo's lips found the edge of a word, "What—What was that explosion?"

"Problem with Naranja."

"I knew—knew it was a trap, Jules! But not—not this kind of trap! I knew something was wrong—with the plan. The Naranjas told me Silk Road was an intervention—said it had to be done!"

Jules placed a calming hand on the man's bloody bald head. "Indeed it was an intervention."

"What do you mean?"

Jules pulled out a small tool. He snipped the nickel metal clumsily but effectively binding the wrist cuffs. Cosmo stared awkwardly at the corpse. His head fell immediately sideways and vomited. Jules held the man by the shoulders and soothed him by stroking the nape of his neck. The vomit was yellow and reeked of old paper. Cosmo wiped at his mouth. "I can't take it!"

"Drink." Jules turned a faucet handle in a stainless steel sink. There came not the biting scent of mineral water from the upstate aquifer but the vapors of gasoline. Jules observed orange tinted gasoline pouring from the sink faucet.

Without surprise Cosmo numbly stated, "That is not water."

"Yes, indeed it is a reality intervention and a reality trap, old man. But you trapped yourself when you grafted the Silk Road DNA into the intervention. You made the Millioni brothers your puppets. In Naranja's theater of reality, this didn't go over too well backstage. So, with the help of a reality trader, we made another Millioni. One we could use for our purposes. And the only way to get rid of this one, was to hire him to kill your precious Rook."

Jules picked up the orange lollipop from the floor, "Gets his instructions on this for the kill, right? Once he's licked it, your quantum magic kicks in. And he becomes programmed for the kill."

Cosmo's eyes widened, "But I -"

Jules backhanded him. "Shut up! Now listen, you robbed Millioni of his free will. And we robbed it back."

***

In his motel suite, the latest Marco Millioni rolled a blunt and answered the phone.

"Commence, Operation: Ignite."

"Yes." He tossed his book of matches into the air, caught it and lit his blunt. The guards knew well why Jack the Butterfly had been sampling his DNA, and they had let him. It meant his essential form had grafted into black market reality, the market place he and Agent Orange were about to seize. And with it, they could overthrow the Naranja Empire.

Millioni remembered the lollipop Cosmo had taken from the boy and how his entire life had been cultivated into the Silk Road intervention project as both a simultaneous beginning and a simultaneous ending. He thought of the reality war, *It will be like taking candy from a baby.*

He conference called his triplets. They answered at the same time, "Hello?"

"Prepare the tanks."

8: Period Doubling Route to Chaos

Jules flicked out a straight razor and slashed at Cosmo's jugular. The man slumped, and Jules pushed him down into the aquarium. "Sorry, old man." He quickly soaked a blue bandana in gasoline and wrapped it around the man's face. The indentations of the man's eye sockets, the protrusion of his large, hawk nose became discernable under the wet bandana. Jules screwed a small rubber hose onto the faucet and situated it into the aquarium. Cosmo's blood suspended like red milk as the nanographite solution twirled with gasoline.

At another sink Jules washed the razor blade in gasoline and watched the bloody gas swirl down the sterile stainless steel sink drain. From the corpse, a shadow rose up behind him. Jules watched it elongate and tower over him until it became a black crocodilian crown. Jules smiled, folded up the razor and placed it into a pocket, thinking, *Sobek rises!*

His fingers touched something else: a Shakespeare Company *arch-villain* matchbook.

Adrenaline roared through Jules, inciting him into vengeful rage. His footsteps spattered gasoline against the walls as he ran into the residential hallway.

Yanking open kitchen cabinets Jules found a jar of oily, dark brown coffee beans. He slammed a cast iron frying pan onto a burner and lit the blue gas flame to high. He poured all of the beans into the pan, and as they smoldered he threw the glass jar at a glass wall. The wall shivered and bounced the jar back toward him. It hit him, then the jar shattered as it hit the ground, angering him further. Jules cranked on the gas to the remaining three burners. Together they hissed like serpents with emotionless blue tongues.

"I'm sorry, Cosmo," he said, "I'm so sorry."

Smoke from the burning coffee beans was thick and along with the sweet natural gas filling the air the scents clamored. Jules turned on the kitchen faucet, and it too spewed gasoline. He dumped a bouquet of strange flowers from a vase, and twitched in surprise as what had seemed to be petals flew apart and became small End Game butterflies. He filled the vase and poured a trail of gas as he backed out of the glass house. Standing triumphant, he lit one match, touching the flame to the leading edge of gasoline on the doorstep. He pondered the primarily orange color of the fire as it instantly, viciously licked its course back inside the glass house.

He ran to his helicopter—jumped in and the pilot gunned the blades. He watched for a moment down below as the tailored and gated community of Tuxedo Park, where reality channels had been invented, exploded. Engulfed in flames reaching skyward, the past he had once believed in burned inevitably to the ground. In the corner of his eye welled a crocodilian tear.

Reality was synthetic, counterfeit, a knockoff, a dummy figure alibi. Jules Barbillon, a byproduct of Canal Street knockoff DNA, thought, *I love every fucked up minute of it.* He commanded the pilot to return to Manhattan, knowing fully that his Blue Room bars were about to become green rooms. In the walls of the clubs just then, the pulsating, cooling blues of Nuit spasmed with brocaded greenery, flashed into crocodile skin diamonds then exploded with scintillating triangular teeth. Then came a flood of opalescent tears timed with ambient music. All part of the show.

Jules Barbillon had one last visit to make before the endless night came to its endless end. In the heart of the Shakespeare Garden within Naranja's Central

Park, the most robust black hole butterflies had been grafted. While his other comrades in rebellion would focus on obliterating or protecting what was most in their interest—liberation from Naranja—he would perform some grafting of his own. It was not for nothing that once he had learned the prowess of the living ink he bought at auction each week in the reiteration of Seven, he had helped himself to every reference to Leviathan in the Bard's folios. It was with this sampled ink he had stenciled into the crocodile skins the eye of his God. His mission now culminating, he flew toward the Park with his crocodile skin books—each etched with living Leviathan ink.

Sobek rises, he thought, *rise Sobek!*

9: Sunjuice

Central Park had an estimated value of five hundred zillion dollars. It was no secret that the Naranja Empire owned it, nor was it a secret that any number of real estate developers wanted to find a way to pocket it. Only the guards knew that the principal Naranja product, sunjuice, was a solar power umbrella for the shadowy business of reality grafting. Central Park, the Shakespeare Garden its pumping heart—was a reality garden.

Those closest to the empire, like Rook, had evolved into quantum shapeshifters, gaming their imaginations against one another until Rook's channel 113 came to dominate.

It was Sobek, the Egyptian crocodile-headed god, who had emerged from the sea of chaos to create the world, and it was Dr. Naranja who had returned reality to the sea, to the quantum sea. There was nothing virtual about his reality. That Jules Barbillon would come to exist as a byproduct of Chinatown mutations of his own quantum DNA was no surprise to him at all. Inside his blue room penthouse, now held hostage by Agent Orange or so she believed, he waited for Jules Barbillon to make his not so clandestine after all visit to the main garden. The people closest to his empire were either grafts or knockoffs or shoots of grafts and knockoffs. But he was a trunk of the great reality tree. He sipped confidently at his scotch and observed the mutating black hole butterflies in the terrarium—now engorged with the Bard's ink—the same ink the Royal Rainmakers carried in the cargo holds of their planes. Both the Rainmaker pilots of his planes and the Librarians still remained loyal to him.

Through a trick of authored time, through the phrase *black hole butterfly*, they had been reborn yesterday.

In his youth, in his original incarnation as Navaja Naranja he had theorized that reality was modeled on the ancient archetype of the oroboros, that reality was in fact a quantum serpent swallowing its own tail. The black hole he considered a contemporary archetype. Later in Manhattan after he had invented sunjuice, he had theorized and mathematically proven reality was a feedback loop. He simply theorized that the Fibonacci series pervading the human skeleton, flower petals and even spiral arms of nebulae would apply to reality as well. Through meditation with his original ECHO, he learned to isolate the harmonics of his brainwaves, which scaled according to the Fibonacci sequence—the ratio of which was also the golden mean.

The contacts he invented allowed Naranja to see the different realities.

Classical reality, he theorized, was a normal fantasy that extruded the sea. It was the foolish human mind that plucked but one thread from the overripe undercurrents of reality, sewed it, tamed it and tailored it into the suit that best fitted it.

When his daughter had developed an interest in Rook Black, out of his paternal love for her, he had grafted their realities together. Or so at the time he had thought. He had not yet experienced the power of Rook's imagination, unhinged by the unholy channel 113. So he pirated it, cloned it, grafted it, believing he could wrestle it—like a crocodile—into submission.

He had failed. Stabilizing it into the cycle of Seven was the best he could do.

***

Dr. Naranja observed the monitors surrounding him and Anja, and they watched Tuxedo Park burn down. "Poor Cosmo," he said. He turned toward a glass-encased collection of books, to one in particular title "The Blue Room," by a lesser-known pulp author named Cosmo Hamilton. It had been a laboratory experiment, to sample this relatively unknown dead author's ink, that had resulted in backfire in Chinatown. The book and the author's mildly pornographic imagination had taken on a life of their own, wedded both into the lofty blue room penthouses and the lowly blue-room sex clubs, into the utter fabric of New York City. There was no tailor that could cut this backfired graft out. "Poor, poor Cosmo. But he lives on through his ink."

Dr. Naranja's plan to provide his daughter with eternal love was also backfiring in the most grotesque of ways. He had provided her with the quantum plastic reality surgery she had yearned for. He caught his own disfigured face reflected in a polished table surface, and when he looked up to behold his daughter, who was now the graft of two women into one body, he felt as much as a man could who lived vicariously through ink, at least her disfiguration made her a phenomenal lexicon of beauty.

***

Rook's hands were steady on the steering wheel, and he was relieved that no towncars followed him. Rook saw his eyes in the rearview again, and as he focused on a pupil through the new contact lenses, he thought, *blind-spot.* His sedan plowed through a heavy quantum mist. Herein he felt a euphoria, and if he surfed deeper into the mist, he remembered, he would feel narcotized. The high would become lethargic, and he would droop as he had when dragged down in Cosmo's lab, when sexing a seemingly vulnerable Agent Orange. The weight and the drowsy drugging, he realized with startling clarity, had been the weight of the quantum frequencies, of channels superimposed. He did not dare go there while driving. Rook surfed back to the safety of the first channel one, to the present.

Yes, he realized, *during sex we graft—over and over and over again.*

He was reasonably assured, however, as chaotic as reality was sharply becoming, it was still cohering, still sticky. Like the mannequin he could hang his hat on it as long as he had a head. Like the orange it was digestible. Like his beard it could be shaved.

And like murder, reality could be committed.

Agent Orange and Anja Naranja. They've become superpositions—overlapping waves—in the big business of reality. He mulled, wondering if that was what she had meant when she had told him he was making it difficult for her to be real. If Agent Orange would not kill him, it was because she couldn't.

If my reality ends, he though, *maybe her reality does end with it.*

At least that was, as he drove, his angel echo reasoning. Around him blazing sapphire blues rippled through the digitally clad glass towers of Chinatown and advertisements formed into swirling loops with the phrase: blue room.

10: Sunstations

Rook had been sixteen when he first drew his gaze up the skeletal satin steel and glass tower built by the mysterious Naranja Empire. Ninety some stories up the low hungry black clouds, like a hell-gate, swallowed it. The tower had gone up, so it was fabled, another 350 stories to a blue room where the inventor of sunjuice, a Dr. Naranja, lived. Rook's thoughts had then dismissed the brooding tower as he paid his entry fee to the sunjuice museum. The building was also fabled to be heavily guarded, and as Rook observed the grand vaulted lobby, he saw that it indeed was. The guards wore bright orange jumpsuits emblematic of sunjuice. They worked inside bulletproof glass chambers that circled the top of the three-story lobby like a running track. The floor of the runway was also glass, and the menacing guards glared down at the lobby crowds. Most curiously, Rook noted, the guards were all women.

Below ground through a heavily armored garage, the extensive sunjuice collection of energy revolution artifacts moved in and out. It was as if the history of sunjuice, Rook had thought, held more value than all of the city's fine art combined. Given the unbridled reach of the sunjuice empire, its monopoly on power reproduction truly was invaluable.

The ninety odd stories above the lobby comprised the global sunjuice headquarters, and above them no one really knew what occupied the floors. The elevators raising and lowering the employees faced the street and offered no glimpse of Naranja's prized Central Park. Narnja was awed, feared and unwitnessed in person. Press releases never revealed how the man had aged. Naranja's private elevator, which went from the lobby directly to the blue room, was the only one that faced the Park, and it gave him an ever-diminishing view as he rode the steel spire to the pinnacling blue room.

As young Rook strolled the exhibits, he recalled the first time he had dreamed about a blue room: within it the walls shone with blue light like living stained glass and inevitably he would find an orange key. Inside the surreal room the key to escaping did not, upon waking, make sense, but within it the key was native. Frequently along with the key, Rook would discover a sheet of dream paper and a chalky pencil of sorts. With these dream instruments he would inevitably write down clues regarding escaping the jailing room with the notion that when he woke, the itemized clues would still be tangible. Of course upon waking they never were. There was no dream paper and no hard written language that could pass through the two worlds of consciousness. Memory could only vaguely recall the hybrid neologisms his subconscious forged from words like key and lock, blue and ward. Dreams, like jokes, slurred meaning

Ultimately Rook knew the dreamy blue room could represent any room, and with the desire to persuade his subconscious to let him in on why it was obsessing over the blue room, he scrutinized the sunjuice museum and pondered passage up to Dr. Naranja's penthouse. For in reality, it was not that he could escape this real blue room but at that time in his life he had no way of getting in.

Young Rook eyed the menacing guards. They had orders to shoot to kill, and sometimes they did. Sometimes business people, long loyal to sunjuice, disappeared into the building and never came out—so the rumors went in *The Post*. Sunstations, which were basically solar gas stations where the energy consumer recharged, were heavily guarded also.

Dr. Naranja had discovered a way to harvest the power of the sun through satellite fleets junking the earth's atmosphere. Eco engineers working for Dr. Naranja followed the lead of silicon and invented means to coil the sun's energy into small chips. After the small fast moving rattlesnakes of North American deserts, these chips were named *sidewinders.* A dozen sidewinders connected in a series could power a small electronic vehicle for a day, and when the sunjuice, as the electricity was called, ran out, the consumer turned it in at a sunstation for a recharge. The sunstations received their daily dose of juice via satellite, and each sunstation was fed a daily ration equivalent to powering one hundred vehicles. Too much sunjuice in one place had led to grand theft and hostage situations, so by enforcing limits, the sunjuice empire was able to sell its power without becoming a victim of the self-same greed it subscribed to.

Still, gasoline's fire had not been put out.

CHAPTER SEVENTEEN: Gasoline

1: Black Market Gasoline

As Rook drove his gas-guzzler in the turbulent eternal midnight, Tuxedo Park burned in both real and imaginary time. *Remember?*

Rook's thoughts burst into flame.

Issuing from his imagination, projecting through the contact lenses—and still entrained still with the windshield—a hologram of orange flames rushed across the windshield. He realized through quantum whisperings, Cosmo had met his end.

In tandem, as the gas tank needle on the dash dipped toward empty, a visit to Gasland would have to transpire.

From Chinatown—away from the now incessant advertisements for blue room bars – he drove his sedan over the Manhattan Bridge, over the dark churning waters into the quantum mist thick night toward Gasland. Off to his right he saw Kings County Kong flirting the edge of Brooklyn, nosing near the exploded crown of the Petroleum Club tower.

When the hell did that happen?

Agent Orange isn't just trying to steal Central Park, Rook inferred darkly, *she's trying to steal reality.*

***

Beneath these waters Rocky Astor and the men of the Petroleum Club waited impatiently, imprisoned in the submarine named Leviathan. Simultaneously Millioni's brothers supervised the connection of natural gas pipes into the newly constructed gasoline pipelines running under the city. Of this Rook knew nothing but in the quantum sea a mirror of information, as yet not coherent, was just about to entangle his nanoelectrodes.

***

Global warming had prevailed despite carbon footprint reduction efforts, and gasoline, like drugs and feedback sex games, exchanged on the black market.

Gas was expensive, but it was still cheaper than the solar power cells harvesting sunlight above the clouds.

And all Rook had to do to find it was run out of gas. That's when the black market found him.

Rook circled around, pulling the sedan down under the bridge to the cobblestone streets below in DUMBO. Toward the water's edge an old black and red gas station haunted by rust was semi-submerged: only the top half of the old pumps, like sentries of a simpler time, were visible. Below the water level old steel automobiles that had been in the repair line when the first April 23rd storm ransacked the city, still hunkered like metal rocks. Rook watched a crocodile bellied on top of a car hood slip into the surly brackish waters of the East River.

Rook glanced at the gas gauge. The needle was now resting on empty. The sedan rolled to a stop, and Rook waited. The large tanks below the gas station had not been used for years, still this station and others in Brooklyn were meeting places for the exchange. Where the gas actually came from was as mysterious and shady as the origin of the sex and drug trades, though it was widely rumored the Texas cartel shipped it in small containers by truck. Rook did know the final delivery method, and though he did not know his name, he knew his dealer—his gasman—by shape. Rook got out of his sedan, and from the trunk he removed the empty gas can. It was a vintage zinc can with a wooden handle. The can was painted in alternating rings of orange and white. He did not remember this always being so. He set it on his hood. Another minute stretched in the cold darkness under the enormous steel ribcage of the blue bridge. Trains thundered above.

Against the rust streaked awning of the gas station, a dented and bullet-riddled black van rumbled down a steep incline into view. The side panel bore the remnant of a logo from an old American gasoline company, purposely sanded down and mated to steel and rust. The van stopped near the water's edge, and the driver, a man seemingly wrapped in darkness itself, stepped out. Rook scanned him: this was not the gasman he knew, usually a square shouldered side-of-beef of a man. Rook held up a small gold coin, saw the man recognize the payment, set the payment next to the can and retreated several steps.

The shadowy man advanced, lifted Rook's gas can and coin, pocketed the coin into a pocket of darkness, and returned to his van. He used a key to unlock the gas cap on his van, and he inserted a small hose into the van's tank. He slipped the hose into his mouth and sucked the end. The orange liquid siphoned through just as the man pushed the clear hose into Rook's five-gallon can. Regular leaded gasoline was always dyed orange to differentiate from clear pure gasoline and purple hi-test ethyl. Rook knew this but somehow it seemed like it was the first time he had ever seen it.

The shadowy gasman seemed at best to be a dense wireframe of a human, and he reminded Rook of the shade king. *Feedback junky*, he thought, *parallel reality junky?* Rook glanced down at his own hands, and in kind they thinned into wiry shadows. *We're all feedback junkies.*

The gasman wore mirrored sunglasses, and reflected in them was the orange color of fire—not just the color—they literally reflected fire. Rook knew one could buy these novelty sunglasses on St. Mark's, but what the gasman was using to cloak himself otherwise in quantum darkness, Rook did not know. The gas can was now full, and the gasman removed the siphon before walking right up to Rook and setting the heavy gas can down. He stared at Rook for long moments through the fiery sunglasses, then simply turned, strode back to his van and drove away.

Rook's thoughts returned to Dr. Chess as he tilted the gas can and inserted the nozzle into the sedan. While the tank swallowed a couple of gallons, Rook felt a strange sensation, as if he had just tapped himself on the shoulder. He turned to look in the direction the gasman had driven. Confident he was gone, Rook placed the gas can in his trunk and drove up toward where the behemoth bridge touched ground. He drove in darkness toward the ten-story building crowned by the bulls-eye painted water tower, and he parked under the monstrous blue steel skeleton, where the Manhattan and Brooklyn bridges met like knuckles.

Even as it spliced and grafted into itself, reality still had enough hard edges to give Rook choices. *Like the snout of the crocodile poised above the waters*, he thought. He looked out at the papyrus reeds clutching the riverbanks. Weeds had no real botanical definition. They were simply unwanted. *Reality*, he thought, *it's always been a weed. No human has ever wanted it. It's too hard, too ugly. Too crocodilian.* And even then the dark clouds above seem threaded with squares, becoming the face of Sobek peering through the quantum noise. Looking up into it, behind the contact lenses Rook's own pupils flashed with reptilian gold and his pupils narrowed into slits.

Face reality. That was what Agent Orange had said to him. As he looked up into the sky, he felt like he was finally, for the first time ever, accepting the consequences of a closed loop reality, a quantum reality in feedback. He desired to see his reflection in the liquid inside the tower tank.

I remember!

***

Marco Millioni and his brothers watched on surveillance as a cargo ship filled with grafted gasoline entered the harbor. "Right on time," Marco spoke into a radio.

Through camera feeds, Rocky Astor and the men of the Petroleum club watched in awe from their submarine. Rocky's rubbery lips twisted as he heard Jules Barbillon's voice, "Tonight, with the Shakespeare Company *arch-villain* matches, we burn Naranja's Manhattan down."

Jules Barbillon, flying over Manhattan, witnessed the island down below cut up by streets into its grid. It seemed to him it twitched, a great island becoming Sobek. As he headed for a landing inside Central Park he pulled out another cigar, checked the band on it for the code word Leviathan, and struck it with a match. Below the surface of the East River, the submarine exploded. Jules pulled on the cigar, inhaling smoke, them exhaling with spite, "Goodbye, Rocky."

2: Gasland

Rook witnessed the exploding waters as submarine shrapnel blew into the sky. He hid in the fire escape shadows, where one dark line after the other was a visual echo of steel step and rail, and he crept his way up the backside of the building. Biplanes hummed past, fleeing from the explosion. Rook flattened himself into dark creases as they swept by. On the roof he scuttled, crawled and slid until he was on his back in the belly of shade directly under the water tower. He didn't have to look inside to know what was in it: it smelled of gas.

It meant, he realized, the Kings County Kong had taken over some of the public works and were using water lines to pump fossil fuel into Brooklyn. Rook waited until the guarding plane looped away to investigate the explosion. He climbed the steel ladder on the outside of the tower and clung to it like a black ladder stripe as the plane looped back. The plane's lights wiped the tower and its black striped ladder. Spotting nothing out of joint, the plane swung away again.

Rook opened the hatch on the top of the tower, and after his eyes adjusted to the lack of light, he saw only his pale reflection like a white slick on the gently rippling dark gas surface. *No*, he thought, *something else*. Rook's neck whipped, and he found himself momentarily staring into his own shadow before it slowly slid down the side of the tower tank, washed away by the approaching lights of another plane. Rook dropped the hatch and swooped down into the darkness, where he lay on his back under the belly of the gas tower, utterly unseen by the pilot guards. The guards, he realized, were changing watch and steering clear from the tower as they gave one another breadth. Rook trickled like oil down a dipstick, down the fire escape to the street. He traced the plumbing pipes from the tower down to the old half-submerged garage where he had just bought gas, and from there he peered out across the river. His eyes followed the gas tower guard biplane as it toured the edge of Governor's Island, and he used a binocular zoom feature in his sunglasses to focus on the island. Inside a row of highrises two airfield landing strips hatched the island. Here the Kong squadron landed and took off inside its own densely protected territory.

Rook stroked at his beard and smelled the gasoline, a not unpleasant odor, on his fingertips. He was stabilized in macroreality channel one. It was dull and blunt. His mind jumped to the matchbook and to Dr. Chess, who did not own a car but did have a quart of petroleum ethanol in his lab. At first Rook had wondered how the doctor had procured it, and research revealed he had probably manufactured it: sulfuric acid and grass fermented into ethanol. Rook wondered laterally, aching with addiction, and he was partially convinced there was still a crime to be solved. As he turned back toward his sedan, he glanced at his watch, where the lit diode hands moved forward and back, closing in again to a midnight wherein all quantum time overlapped. It was just about his birthday again, he realized. Agent Orange, Weedkiller, Dr. Kill van Kull, and even the shadowy gasman—all overlapped as Rook closed in on his own origin.

Matches, why did they give me matches?

3: The Farmer

Rook drove from Brooklyn to the Parks Conservancy, where he had first witnessed Dr. Chess give his symposium in the haze of what had been, he was now convinced, the previous week. Dr. Naranja had grafted him into an intervention that seemed to have lasted for weeks, but Rook inferred from his watch a the lit diodes stuttered back and forth around the same hours, the intervention was likely a reality loophole.

Splashed across the city's lit screens the Oroboros funneled news about a black and white ball and a mysterious crime.

Rook recalled the feedback session where he had found himself inside Millioni's suite, when he had picked up a piece of chalk. It was also from chalk Rook had lifted Dr. Chess's fingerprints. *Chalk*, Rook thought, as he drove back over the bridge. Forensic detectives, tailors and teachers alike mutually used chalk to outline and define. *What else*, Rook wondered, *was Dr. Chess—the man seeking to bridge from chlorophyll to hemoglobin, from weed to blood—writing onto his blackboards?*

I need to start back at the beginning, retrace.

Rook picked the Parks Conservancy lock and entered the dark

auditorium, where he noticed someone had taken pains to sweep the chalkboards clean. He shined an ultraviolet light over the blackboard and photographed the superimposed chalkings that had not been fully erased. They were very much like the ghostly apparitions of superimposed quantum realities.

Rook surfed to where the two channel ones overlapped, and he reconsidered the chalky outlines. The chalk markings jiggled, and the quantum calculations came to life.

Sun, chlorophyll, blood and gas, Rook thought, and he surfed back to macroreality. He drove to Dr. Chess's Upper West Side brownstone, cruising in channel one, and on his way he scanned the tall walls surrounding Central Park. When Rook's father had been young, he had occasionally delighted in playing chess at the Chess and Checkers house within the old public Park. As a child his father played there for sport, and later in his life he played games there for the public as demonstrations and celebrations. Spectators gathered just to witness the grand master.

Rook had scant early memories of the park before the storm deteriorated it.

Why, he thought again, *was I given matches?*

Rook stealthily made his way into Dr. Chess's laboratory as he had before.

In the darkness he heard a heavy weight creaking, and he found the man's cold dead body hanging by a noose. The weedy corpse was growing a black modacrylic Masculiner, a stick on Van Dyke, and the noose was made of woven together chess weeds entangled and growing into his white hair. The stench of death suckerpunched him for the second time along with the gastric stench of vomit.

Dribbling down the man's chest and dabbling his feet was vomited paper pulp.

Rook shut his eyes and surfed into overlapped channels, where briefly he saw his own shadow like a demon committing every crime he had ever solved.

Rook saw his shadow wrapping Cosmo's head with the poisonous bandana, and he saw his shadow slicing the man's veins. Rook saw his shadow placing the noose around Dr. Chess's head, and Rook even saw his shadow murdering his father. *If my imagination has come to life, I'm responsible for every crime I am sleuthing.*

Rook wrenched himself back to macroreality and fell to his knees, where he gasped, huffing in the noxious rot of the corpse. *No,* Rook thought as his stomach settled from the vertigo, and the crocodile flies multiplied into a locust like haze around him. He smelled also a stinking sumac, a tree of heaven. When he lifted his eyes he saw something new in the greenhouse: a small, grafted tree of heaven with bark like crocodile skin, leaves veined with crimson blood and fruited with bloodberries that shone like rubies. Dr. Chess, Rook realized, had come to know too much, way too much. *The man's discovered,* he thought, *how to graft reality.*

Rook turned from the tree to the dead man's pale puffy skin and popping eyes and to the synthetic beard growing from the dead's mans face.

Next to a pile of off track betting forms, Rook found a suicide letter. It read, "I cannot endure the nature of my discovery. Maybe you can." The note gave the mathematical equation for grafting space and time, and it was signed *Dr. William Shakespeare Chess.*

A large dragon-like-fly with a lollipop stick spine and miniature crocodile snouted head sheared past him. Rook dodged it as another then another came zipping past, nipping at him.

Knock knock, Rook thought. *Who's there? Farmer. Farmer who?*

A Farmer who hanged himself on the expectation of plenty.

Behind Rook his shadow swelled, and when Rook turned toward the darkness, it turned and swarmed toward him. Rook fled the house, his feet pounding down the brownstone steps as the dark swarm exploded into a cloud of the dragonflies.

Agent Orange isn't trying to steal reality, Rook thought, *she is trying to steal it back!*

***

In the O-shaped Orange Security tower, its illuminated windows blazed, like they always did, alternating bands of white and bright hunter orange. It was the tower the Naranja's had built for her. *A jail*, Agent Orange thought, *about to break!*

Her voice pumped into the Naranja tower, "You've hidden me inside this helmet, obscuring my beauty and my power. I will hide no more!"

4: Blind Spot

Rook blinked, and his legs churned under him, wheeling him away from the stench of the body and the grafted tree. He tumbled out into the street, leaned against his sedan and looked back over his shoulder to his trailing shadow. He pivoted toward it quickly and swore there was a slight delay, as if his shadow had been studying him and had been caught off guard. The shadow slid on the sidewalk, adjusting its proportions according to the ambient light, which was a murk of night blasted with lights crisscrossing the vast skyline. Headlights, street lamps and advertisements washed over the shadow, thinning it. Rook turned away from his shadow, then whipped toward it again. His shadow was four-fold, and like a fingered hand, it splayed as light came in from a variety of directions in different colors.

Quadrupling, he thought.

In his sedan Rook jerked open the glove compartment and ransacked for his flask. He exhaled hard the stench of the dead body and the ghastly tree. He unscrewed the cap and shot the alcohol into his throat. He gasped and choked: it was not whiskey.

It was blood mixed with *bai jiu* mixed with gas.

His red saliva spattered the inside of the windshield, a mirror mockery of the raindrops that burst from the black clouds of a sudden thunderstorm. He hunched over and vomited paper pulp in which Chinese characters were visible amidst the yellow muck. He remembered the one he had saved before, upon which was written the character for bridge. *Einstein-Rosen bridge*, he thought, *reality bridge, fear of bridges, fear of jumping...*

He remembered he had never been afraid of bridges. Somehow they had grafted the fear into his early memories, *So that I will not jump!*

He gazed out to the city he knew so well, the city that was constantly reinventing itself in reality storms. Rod and cone cells comprised the human eye, with the rods distinguishing between light and dark contrast—enough simply to establish the sleep and wake cycle, the circadian rhythm. The cones were sensitive to three principal color wavelengths: red, green and blue. Orange was a combination of red and green. Rook contemplated for a moment the blind spot, that area in the eye that cannot see because it is where the nerve in the back of the eye connects to the brain. The human shadow, he thought, was another human blind spot, and there was something his private eye was not seeing. *Yes*, he thought further, recalling the bullets that had been fired directly into the mannequin eyes, *into the blind spots*. The bulls-eye contact lenses, they also framed the blind spot.

His mind turned from orange to garden green.

Rook drove to the Marco Polo Motel, witnessing the night through the dried blood spatters on the inside of his windshield, a blood pattern the storm could not wash away. In humid rain he crept up the fire escapes on the neighboring buildings, and he jumped from one adjoined rooftop to the next until he was across from Millioni's suite. The curtains were drawn, and the lights dimmed. Rook backed up fifteen feet, ran and leapt to the motel fire escape. He swam in the air, clutched for a rail and pulled himself up. In seconds he had picked the exterior fire door lock and opened the door.

The green walls were awash in pale green light. A Majestic lingerie box, like a birthday gift, was neatly shut at the foot of the king size bed. Rook snapped on latex gloves and opened it: inside were bundles of hundred dollar bills.

But they were not green. The intaglio print was perfect, but the ink was blood red.

The ink *was* blood. The serial numbers were all the same as those in the wallpaper.

Rook thought, *Blood money.*

***

Inside Orange Security, Agent Orange pulled a switch and orange light infectiously leaped from building to building in Times Square, then began to spread to the city beyond. She whipped her long hair as she walked in a circle, observing the infectious orange lighting overtaking the city once again. Her blue eyes burned, and inside these irises the Naranja Empire bulls-eye nanodigital implants flickered through a series of fiery quantum computations.

She reached for a nib.

***

In the Naranja tower blue room Anja's irises did the same but in the opposite reverse order. She pressed her fingers together as if in prayer. "Father, she's trying to cancel me out."

Dr. Naranja observed the black hole butterflies in his terrarium and said, "No. The metamorphosis of channel 113 is almost complete. Look here."

The butterflies coalesced into an ink fountain pen and pressed to a mottled paper page. Out of an intaglio etched nib, orange ink flowed in Agent Orange's handwriting:

Meet me in the Library.

***

Simultaneously, all across the city the phrase whiplashed through the lit glass. Through the motel suite windows Rook witnessed the orange light phenomenon, and he looked back to the Majestic box. It was, he decided, The Bonus: payment to execute.

Myself.

5: Dead On

Rook took the blood money with him and drove in silence down the muzzle of the city, wondering why the target had come to be known as the bulls-eye. He knew historically a coin had been nicknamed the bulls-eye, and gamblers had betted frequently with it, birthing the phrases *on the money* and *dead on*. The bullet holes in the mannequin head and the chalk outline connecting the twelve bullet holes he had awoken inside earlier were both dead on. Rook's crime solutions had always also been dead on—until, they claimed, he had smothered himself in addiction. He had not found Weedkiller's corpse at the Marco Polo Motel, but Rook was certain someone special had died for the ink.

He looked up. All along the city horizon, water towers installed by The Tanks only competitor had been painted to match the gas tower in Brooklyn. Crime coiled around the intervention, the concentric mouth of an oroborean snake about to strike.

Rook had a feeling people were betting on it.

Rook parked and observed an Off Track Betting franchise. Men and women toiled outside, sucking on cigarettes, drinking from bottles in paper bags as if it were still illegal to consume alcohol on the streets. The paper bag was a mere vestige of anonymity, and the deep addiction at these low-class betting joints was gambling. Rook hid the contact lenses behind his mirrored sunglasses, pulled his collar high, his hat low, and entered.

The gamblers stared hard at monitors flashing anything from horse racing to snuff. A group was riveted to the live snuff channel, Alpha TV, in which a victim was being stripped naked below the Brooklyn Bridge on the Manhattan side. The gamblers rushed to betting machines, where they slid their quantum currency and placed wagers against improbable wealth. They were so blinded by the hope of luck, they did not realize the whole system was rigged in favor of the house. The Alpha TV victim, a man now being pushed into the rogue waters of the East River, had negligible chance of making it to the Brooklyn side of the river, but he was stocky, almost muscular, and if alpha adrenaline kicked in he had the possibility of starting over on the other side.

All of the display monitors were three-dimensional and could be viewed from any angle. One group of gamblers hung on every combative move of a hyperrealistic war game, in which the sunjuice empire battled gas: it was a common game based on actual events. The players were remote, and they gamed through the computer networks. They were pinballers turned carpal tunnel joystickers turned gamesuiters. Gamesuits: low voltage, microchipped, latex suits that sent real body and brain signals to the central game hub. The gambling addicts bet away their own lives against the outcome of this fantasy game, barely realizing they could never win in Oroboros code infected games.

Agent Orange has placed a bet, he thought, *I'll either save Anja's empire or not*. Anja had said she could not live without him, and he had gruffly cared less. Rook slipped back outside and headed toward his sedan. He dressed well, he spoke well, he drank well, but like the lowlifes in the betting franchise, he was a jackin' the butterfly junky. Anja had cured him of his need but she had not even touched upon his lust.

EEGames Incorporated was the principal creator of three-dimensional games and interactive comics, and when they had refused to sell to Naranja, the takeover redefined the word hostile. A small private military had swarmed the company headquarters, executed the executives and replaced them overnight with Naranja's own management team. A misinformation press release was generated immediately, stating the business had exchanged hands legally, and the disinteresting story quickly faded in game and business news. The last thing Naranja wanted was his technology discovered by any competitor, not because he wanted to drop the virtual from reality, but because he knew reality was too dangerous. EEGames continued to generate the virtual realities gamers were addicted to without handing them the real key to reality feedback. The systems studied the players' strategies, and Naranja learned from them how to avoid any real war.

Only a handful of the select, people like Rook who were already discovering the golden chain of reality on their own, were allowed inside his inner circle. Dr. Naranja brought them in to keep them there. There was something about the dead center of being in that circle that was, Rook knew, a blind spot.

6: Comics

Rook's blind spot troubled him, and the thicker the curtain of night drew, the more it eclipsed his inner private eye. He was finding himself increasingly incapable of not thinking about his inner shadow, as if it were in fact thinking of him. Rook glimpsed behind himself, and he saw his shadow twitch in the pale light. It looked, he thought, more and more like the shadowy gasman. Past it, Rook noticed an old payphone that had not yellow pages but an orange-paged directory dangling below it. *The orange pages*, he thought. He flipped into it under the letter c and his fingers traced the words to *comics*. He found a peculiar advertisement, slapped the book shut and jumped back into his sedan.

Rook realized he had not discovered what comic book the beige advertisement for Van Dykes had been torn from. He wondered how he had missed it, why sometimes the obvious, like a bearded lady at the Coney Island freak show, hid itself from him as if it were the very meaning of life.

When Rook had been young, he had collected comic detective stories as well as detective pulp, and it had been many years since he had visited a comic book store. In the pooling illuminations of a nocturnal Times Square, Rook found the store advertised in the orange pages. Towering high above it was a circular high-rise blazing with hunter orange light. The logo in the sign hanging over the comic book store was a lineated eye, an iris and a pupil merged with a target. The sign was illuminated concentric rings of white and orange, and it read, *BlindSpot Comics*.

***

Up above Agent Orange observed Rook standing outside the store that served as the retail base of her headquarters.

***

Paper comics still existed but were collector's items alongside the current digital virtual reality comics. These interactive comics, in which one could take on the persona of the hero or villain, had evolved naturally from video games. Rook did not even need to enter the store to find what he was looking for. It was on display in the window.

It looked like an ordinary paper comic. The cover art merged a graphic design like that in the blood money he had found in the motel—alternating bold rays of black and red. In the center was a bulls-eye. Rook whipped again to his shadow. Mocking him, it slowly rolled away, pushed down by the lights coming from inside the comic book store. Rook tucked himself under his black pea super hat and went in on his own.

His shadow remained outside, watching him through the glass, through fiery sunglass lenses.

Once inside Rook turned, and he witnessed the living darkness, the gasman, standing outside. Not quite a trick of the light, it arched up into a kingly crown then dissipated.

Inside the store bustled with comic book and game fanatics, people who came from every ethnic background and whose ages spanned generations. Rook glanced around, trying to find more copies of the book.

The clerk, clad in punk black, told Rook, "The only copy we have is the one in the display. It was just released today but it went viral." The clerk explained, "The pages have addictive, narcotic qualities."

Rook waved he would buy it, saying, "Sell it to me," and he pulled out his currency.

The clerk retrieved it from the display, using mechanical pinchers and explaining while he did, "I can't afford to touch another copy. Even though I have one, I keep wanting another one. Once you touch it," he threatened, "it's next to impossible to let go."

He held it away from Rook, demanding payment first.

"Once you open it up," the clerk said, "the paper digitizes."

Rook was well aware from the *Extra!* newspaper he'd found on his doorstep in what he was now considering to be the exact same night of the self-same seemingly earlier day, that paper and electronic technologies truly had grafted, but he was impressed by the ultrarealistic look of the glossy exterior cover.

Since there was only one left, the kid taunted, the customer would have to name a high price. Rook became impatient but quickly dismissed the notion of buying it at the end of his gun. A stoic moment of standoff burst when the store's phone rang, and the clerk answered and listened while noisily chewing gum. The clerk hung up after terse dialogue about the exact same comic.

"Look," he said, "somebody just offered one thousand, and they will be here in five. So, are you serious or what?"

Rook pulled out his untraceable currency.

"There's one more thing I'm going to tell you about this issue," the clerk said as he nonchalantly rang up $1500, "This one is signed."

"By who?" Rook asked, his voice was deep and sinister.

"What do you mean, by who? By the artist!"

"How do you know?"

The clerk sputtered, "It's so cool. No one really knows who the artist is, but whoever made this wrote himself into the story, a guy named Shakespeare." The clerk held it closer. Rook saw scrawled on the cover the signature *Shakespeare* in synthetic black permanent marker. The signature was metallic meets testosterone: it looked like Rook's. He slid his currency over, and the clerk ran the transaction, passed Rook's currency back to him and placed the already clear plastic envelope in a bag marked with the store's logo. He pushed the envelope across the counter toward Rook.

"This is issue one in infinity," the clerk said, "but you never need to buy another issue. It's issued by a new company called Zeno, and it works like a mirror. It reads your fingerprints, scans your irises, IDs you from a database and interacts with your pulse and brainwaves through special contacts you punch out of the plastic first page. So, if you have a wild imagination, you can make up your own story. If not you can use the preset templates. Regardless, every time you read the story, it changes. Fucking cool."

When Rook left the store he felt his shadow join him again. When he slipped into his sedan, the shadow seemed to sit directly behind him. Rook chalked it all up to paranoia, and the need to have eyes in the back of his head. *Yes*, he thought, *paranoia is my blind spot.* Paranoia was Greek from *para*, meaning irregular, and *noos*, meaning mind. He thought of the noose that had hung the reality farmer, and from out of the bag he slowly pulled out the book. In another long moment his shadow reached around him and pulled the comic book out of the plastic sheath.

"Stop!" Rook demanded, and he blinked hard, thinking, *I'm slipping.*

The shadow withdrew and faded.

7: Zeno's Arrow

Rook painstakingly made his way into the story wearing latex gloves and his original contact lenses behind the sunglasses. He did not yet want to try Zeno's contacts—they would function like a human global positioning system feeding everything about him back to the company. Still, as he read each page and each cell strongly mirrored what he had been going through during the past overlapped days. The story was set in a city named Anycity, and within it crime was impossible to solve because time traveled the path of Zeno's arrow. In the comic he held in his hands, an Agent worked for a character named Zeno. The character Zeno was not shown, and whenever the Zeno character spoke it spoke only in a cell of complete darkness.

In its first appearance, the Zeno darkness told the Agent, "That which is in locomotion must arrive at the half-way stage before it arrives at the goal."

The next page in the comic illustrated the locomotion problem by showing an unnamed detective only getting halfway through solving a crime.

Rook was back to zero times infinity. He remembered he had left himself that notation on the box of Masculiners he had found in East Orange. On the next page the comic urged him to place the contact lenses on, and within the narrative the detective did. Rook refrained. In the series of story cells, the detective wore the comic contact lenses to a fictitious black and white ball. The illustrations transformed into point of view as Rook read, appearing as if the detective character was looking through concentric rings of zeros. The book narrated: blind spot—that which the detective could not see—was that which he could never see. The process of solving this crime, the comic book taunted, was infinite.

The detective could never solve that which could never be committed in a quantum feedback world: the end.

Even though he wore latex gloves, as Rook turned each page—just as the comic store clerk had forewarned—he found himself deliciously antagonized. And as he turned each page, the pages, like branches on a never-ending tree of heaven, bifurcated and multiplied. The further he read, the longer the book became. He thought, *Period doubling leads to chaos.* The comic was an event horizon, he realized, and it took all of his strength to close the book, flip it over and pull open the back page. In the last page he saw the last cells had been torn out. He closed the diabolical comic, and it resized itself from an encyclopedic tome back to the twenty-two page comic it had started as.

Rook opened to page one and began reading again.

In this second incarnation of the story, Zeno replicated reality grafting technology and wed it with fiction.

Whoever this author artist Shakespeare was, Rook was certain the water tower in Brooklyn and now the numerous newly painted ones all over the city were beacons to the paradox. *Zeno*, Rook thought, *someone who reached hyperconsciousness in this and Anycity. Was this who I was hired to find? Zeno?*

Rook flipped randomly into the comic book as if it was an oracle, and again the pages split into two for each one he read. No matter how the story forked, each page ushered Rook only halfway through the infinite story. As if wrestling a crocodile jaw, he slammed the book shut. He was going to have to force himself into Zeno's narrative, even if it meant it would make him look like the ringleader—the author. *But I'm no Shakespeare!*

Rook remembered the essential tenet of the original philosopher—the real

Zeno's *reductio ad absurdum: if everything when it occupies an equal space is at rest, and if that which is in locomotion is always occupying such a space at any moment, the flying arrow is therefore motionless.*

Rook drove back to his apartment with the blood money and the comic book. Inside his office he flipped open his crime portfolio and was relieved to find the hard copy of the yellowed comic book ad for the Van Dyke that had been ripped from a page and mailed to East Orange. He matched the old ad and its tear pattern to the tear in the new book. The torn edges fit magnetically like lovers separated by thirty-seven years. Immediately the quantum fibers, what scientists called ribbons and beards, wove together and healed.

On the back of the ad, which he had not focused on prior, was simply the word: "Next."

The clerk has it wrong, Rook thought. *Zeno and Shakespeare wrote themselves out of the story, into reality. Fiction's grafted with fact.*

On the suicide note Dr. Chess left behind, was the abbreviated code name he had attributed to his reinvented reality grafting. Z.E.N.O.: zero energy nano organics.

Rook heard the muffled sounds of a man being ill. He edged slowly to the room housing his psychologist couch, and with the butt of his gun he eased open the door. He witnessed the mannequin version of himself, now quite humanoid, wearing his feedback mask and vomiting yellow pulp onto the hardwood floor.

Good god. It's quantum feedback itself, like a weed, that's gone viral.

CHAPTER EIGHTEEN: Z.E.N.O.

1: Next

Next was another way of saying future. It was also a way of referring to the next world, either as parallel or ghostly or after death. If Zeno was right about space and time, the illusion of change appeared as next after next after next without end, without conclusion. This thought reminded Rook of the *it* games, in which someone was always next. Rook did wonder in the profound umbrage of the never-ending evening what was next.

Still, somehow the entire universe functions simultaneously.

With that thought his shadow leaned up against him and a preternatural early morning dawn broke. Pale yellow and orange light flooded the deep gray sky as if it seemed intent on reinventing itself as well. As light pulsed in, the comic book thinned and aged to a crumbly old yellow. The mannequin stiffened into plastic. *Quantum feedback*, he remembered, *principally nocturnal*. Its tides calmed by the sleeping moon and soothing, rebirthing sun. The sky trumpeted with golds as the morning lit like a fiery flower, but the Edenic momentary day quickly shattered back into the darkness of night, into what was becoming again his birthday. The mannequin became fleshy and twitched with life. It removed Rook's feedback mask, made eye contact with coal black eyes and lumbered past Rook. It took a seat in his office at his desk.

"Thank you for coming," it said in Jack the Butterfly's voice, and it lifted up the comic book then grunted with satisfaction. "This book was my greatest invention!"

Rook approached the thing with caution. The mannequin set the book down and held up the intaglio ring. Dim light caught it, making it glow like a pearl. Muttering, he set it inside Rook's scanner and he held up a jeweler's magnifying glass. The ECHO digital screen reflected the zoomed magnification, and the intricate intaglio carvings in the clear metal shimmered. "Nanometals. High quality quantum."

He rolled the ring along the indie of his arm. Ink and language spilled from it and wrote passages across his skin. “I embedded the interactive storyline into the intaglio. It’s American made. I give you one hundred dollars."

"What are you talking about? What the hell are you?"

The mannequin grabbed for the Majestic box of blood money sitting on the desk.

"I told you, I give you one million you figure out who the fuck I am!"

“Sell you your DNA back too.” The mannequin knockoff slammed the box down.

Blood erupted from it in money patterns, etching wireframe DNA quantum patterns all around them in crimson red. Jack’s shadowy essence issued from the mannequin, reached for Rook and wrapped around him, becoming Rook’s shadow. The two grappled with what seemed like gravity itself whirling down a space-time drain.

Rook yelled, "You're Zeno god damn it! Don't you know that!? Remember? You are Zeno!"

"I remember the damn butterfly guy from China! I’m not talking about him! I've been a lot of people detective. Who was I *before* I was Zeno?"

"The same we all were before we got trapped in your knockoff reality, Zeno! Everyone and no one!"

With a heavy rumbling the external sky crashed into thunderstorm. Jack the Butterfly spasmed into ink and exploded into nothingness. The sky wept a fury of black inky rain. The rain wrote phrases onto Rook's windows in Chinese writing, then transformed the letters into Shakespearean phrases as they slid down the glass. Rook stroked at his jaw, now heavy with six nights of Van Dyke beard growth, and his mental focus tightened on memory of his straight razor. He ran to his bathroom and rummaged in his medicine cabinet. He lifted the straight razor up, considered it, and thought, *This is what got me into this. This must get me out.*

Rook shaved what had become plastic: a plastic mustache and beard grafted into his face. He tried to remove the contacts and dug under the edge of them, but he could not: they had fully grafted into his irises.

He thought, *They are my irises.*

One by one through careful incisions and plucking of tweezers, he pulled the main nanoelectrodes from under the skin of his body. He parted his black hair in the center, raised the razor and made a clean slit about an inch long just above his brow. As a rivulet of blood ran between his eyebrows, across his lashes and blinked into his eyes set with the bulls-eye lenses, he plucked the main on-off nanoswitch from his scalp.

He cleaned his small, bleeding wounds and dressed.

Rook stepped out into the inky rain. It splattered into his white shirt as he slid into the sedan. The black marks, like long wet stitches, crosshatched with red blood leaking from under the shirt. They wrote into his clothing, *knock knock.* He drove past Pell Street, the windshield wipers splashing the black ink rain and the repeating inky phrases from the glass. He drove south.

2: The Triplets

In Alphabet City, below the main office to Ulysses—the only competitors to Millioni's Tanks—Marco Millioni sat smoking a blunt with his triplet brothers. They sat in a circle facing one another. On a monitor they observed a digitized network of all the water towers marking the tops of buildings throughout Manhattan. There were in fact thousands of them, their oak tanks mottled by oxygen and time into pale gray cylinders with roofs like small dunce caps. The monitor showed them as green dots flashing like fireflies over the grid-work of Manhattan streets.

"It's time," they said simultaneously.

Each blew a smoke ring. The rings wafted together and expanded, appearing momentarily like a bulls-eye ring before collapsing into white fumes.

Below the tumultuous waters, where the tidal straight of the East River met the Hudson in the bay triangulated by Governor's island, one of their men cruised the salty brown depths. The black submarine brushed past a muscular school of crocodiles and piloted to a stop. Robotic arms reached out and tooled a yellow pipe valve. With precise mechanical torque the valve opened. The underwater pipeline running from Governor's Island to lower Manhattan was now complete, and gasoline began pumping though it toward Manhattan with utmost pressure.

***

In the Orange Security garage Agent Orange monitored Rook's nanoelectrode transmission. He was, the monitor revealed, at home.

She commanded six of her dozen, "Find Rook. He's at home, dreaming. Bring him to me in one piece." She straddled her motorcycle, and as the parking garage gate lifted she gunned out toward the Central Library. Her dozen flanked her the first block, then six tore away toward the Lower East Side. The orange lights of her impending coup, blazing throughout the city's digitized towers, swirled as reflections in their convex helmet visors.

Through her own helmet Agent Orange dialed her irises, and immediately she was connected to the Naranja blue room. "Tonight your precious city will burn, and I will inherit the Earth."

Anja stood in the blue room wearing a black librarian full body armor suit complete with the Libra scales insignia. Her bright blue eyes moistening heavily as if she was about to cry, but she wasn't. She dropped nanographite lubricant into them—one, two, three, more drops—blinked and set the small bottle onto a table. She looked down to the black clouds smothering the city. Her eyes narrowed, and her irises dialed rapidly as her father escorted her into the butterfly terrarium.

***

Agent Orange's six burst into Rook's apartment. They found him on his psychologist couch unconscious, his limbs twitching in feedback.

That's not how he saw it. He observed remotely, his sedan parked near the harbor, as they grappled with the heavy, slumberly body of the knockoff mannequin Rook. He had planted the major nanoelectrodes into its skin and run an electrical current through it, which sent out signals he had programmed into the old Angel ECHO 113. The matchboxed machine was obediently tucked inside the mannequin's pocket. It had been the nanoelectrodes all along, he had realized, with which they were constantly able to track him and tune him to their reality, a reality Zeno had created and one they had come to lust for.

Agent Orange needed him alive, and she was trying to rescue him from himself, again.

On his desk he had left a memo in his own handwriting: it gave the word *Shadow* and the address, *Central Park.*

Rook stepped out of his sedan, which he had parked near the desolate South Street Seaport. One by one he removed his articles of clothing until he stood naked, his scarred and grafted skin mocking the refracted topography of sea.

In death I change only.

***

At The Towers headquarters, Marco Millioni pulled a lever. Those water towers still filled only with water in the city began to drain, and float switches within them popped up as the water level dropped a foot. Below street level pumps kicked on, pushing liquid up the flights, from six to sixty, to replenish the level, only this wasn't water pressuring its way up: it was gasoline. It was pumping in from Governor's island.

***

Recalling the moments he had first submerged during his faked suicide, Rook took one step into the brackish waters. Five hundred feet away, the unlucky man who would be the antihero of Alpha TVs nightly swim program was kicked into the nasty water with his heavy clothing on, and the broadcast crew shined spotlights down onto him, making him even easier prey. In the franchises, gamblers frantically began their betting—not on whether the swimmer would make it but on how far. Rook knew spotlights would stay focused on the easy victim trying to cross straight to Brooklyn and would avoid his own path to Governer's Island.

Rook's irises adapted to the saltwater as he submerged and swam into the heavy darkness.

Under ideal conditions Rook would be able to make it to Governor's Island in ten minutes, though there was nothing ideal about swimming in the deadly night with crocodiles slipping below and Kings County Kong sweeping lights from above. As Rook's arms stroked with the current and as his mouth pulled oxygen into his lungs, he switched channels. He amped up the feedback until the sea itself washed into quantum foam and the saltwater crocodiles transformed into shadowy, microcosmic Sobeks coldbloodedly at ease with the shadowy man. Rook's scars, like the Kong's own razzle-dazzle, made for quantum camouflage.

3: Dexter and Sinister

Agent Orange waited, her motorcycle positioned on the front Central Library steps between the two lions. She had everything in position—except Rook. She had made a bet, a wager he would suckle to his grafted addiction and retreat into his world—the world that was their world. For years she had known his every step, and now when it was most critical, he was missing. Reality had been fooling them for years. *Perhaps*, she thought, *now it is time to fool reality!*

She dialed her irises toward past memories, searching for a quantum anchor by which she could locate and restrain him now. After all, she'd had Jack the Butterfly make the mannequins for her purposes—to indicate to him he should look for himself. If Rook had implanted his nanoelectrodes into it, it might be enough, she felt, to fool channel 113.

She commanded the six, "Take the dummy to Pell Street. Put the damn thing into a nanographite solution, now!"

***

He really had discovered her at the costume shop years prior, and when he had walked in almost invisibly, she had heard only the bell at the swinging door. She had scanned, looking for someone, anyone. He abruptly stepped into view a mere foot from her, from behind a tuxedo-clad mannequin, and he inquired about the contact lenses in the window display. Each word he spoke was intently carved in a red mouth framed by a keenly shaped Van Dyke under coal black eyes. He was riveting.

She gave him an eye exam. In both his *oculus dexter* and *oculus sinister* he was better than 20/20.

"You've already had high definition surgery," she leaned back and said. The surgery was common, and while the visual powers it endowed were not hawk-like it did allow for intensely acute focusing—from within a few inches to half a mile. "You don't need these in prescription at all. Why didn't you tell me?" she asked.

Despite the optical test machine artificially separating them, they were really only about a foot from one another, face to face. In the backroom they had terse sex, and so it had gone on between them, with the sex increasingly verging toward violence. They created sadomasochistic safe words-words they could use to tell one another to stop because they did not feel safe. In fact, he had created hers: o*range.*

After many months of intensive sexual trysts, he invited her to try something different. He took measurements of her head with an antique tailor's tape: it was a brittle plastic yellow, much used. She asked him about it. He looked her in the eyes and declined to answer.

A week passed, and she met him at a motel. He closed the door behind her and gestured for her to sit. The motel was not squalid, but it was clandestine and seamy. He brought her an orange paper wrapped box, and slowly, assuming there was some toy or lingerie or sex thing inside, she opened it. The paper fell to the floor as she pried up the lid. Inside was a leather mask with nanoelectrodes sewn into it at regular intervals. She admired it. He raised a small gun-like tool to her brow, something that looked like it was meant to pierce a tiny piece of jewelry to skin. "You'll need a switch," he said.

"Thought I was a switch," she said, making a joke about someone who could be both a bottom or a top sexually.

He made that almost smile with his lips. “It’s an on button. Or an off button. It has to mate with the main switch in the feedback mask. I’m going to teach you feedback.”

She looked at the tool he raised in front of her face. She nodded her consent. Lightly he pressed the tool to her brow, pushed back her hair and clicked a button. She felt a strong sting, like that of a bee, and the sensation passed. She nodded she was okay.

He placed the mask over her face and snugged the buckles on the back. A thrill chased her spine as the switches mated, a tangible darkness rushed and light became a memory.

Sadomasochism had not been her thing, and she still did not consider it to be her thing. What they had done all those years together had no definition. What she had evolved into through their undefined process, their gaming, was to her natural. She had grown into the macrocosmic edges that circumscribed her, naturally.

That first night in the mask he talked her to orgasm, and it was as if his voice, like his cock, was inside her. Thereafter he took her to her increasingly novel sexual edges and brought her back safely over and over, entraining her to find her way back with him until he let her go and it was up to her finally to do it on her own. In time, as her mental prowess in feedback strengthened, she felt, as he did, an addiction to it. That was when he showed her what he had done with the contact lenses he had manufactured. He opened up his palm: cupped inside was a bulls-eye decorated pair customized for her. He tilted her head back and gently placed them onto her corneas with his own fingers, then he squeezed a nanographite solution onto her eyes. She blinked.

He held her hands firmly and said, "Imagine yourself standing on the tallest of buildings." Long moments slipped by while she breathed deeply. "You look down and you see the abyss," and when he knew she was there he simply said, "Now, leap."

Reality's horizon abruptly popped. It expanded deeper and farther than she had ever imagined, and the sex they had in this quantum free-fall was cosmic —far beyond the simulations in blue rooms.

"Because," he told her later, "it isn't a simulation. It's real."

4: The Guard

Rook had provided her with income, paying her as if she were an enslaved mistress even though she was essentially an enslaved volunteer. As the next year passed the games he wanted to play with her in feedback became truly violent, and curiously she found herself excelling. As she excelled his addiction raged. She became icy to him, to his feedback junk, and eventually out of boredom she began to trick him. He would be immersed in feedback during sex, and she would not. She discovered he was pathetically easy to control.

She understood then, he was easily addicted to her but she no longer not to him. His one enchanting, diabolically dark eyes were hidden behind contact lenses. His lust was a masquerade of misguided masculinity.

She had long noticed the indentation on his left finger, where a wedding ring claimed him, and she never inquired about it. The very last time she had seen him she played her final trick. While he thought he was having sex with her in feedback, she created an imaginary Marco Polo Motel lush with glowing green wallpaper made our of chlorophyll and living hundred dollar bills. Within this imaginary Eden an endless imaginary Silk Road of sorts manifested for him – a world of never ending mental pursuits.

She abandoned him in a suite at the Marco Polo Motel, a midtown dive with peeling green wallpaper. Unbathed, unshaved and mentally decomposing, he had become lost in feedback: a feedback junky.

Months passed, and she had no sign of him. Ennui rolled over to sheer boredom, and she visited sex clubs, dungeons and blue room bars, but even the lesbian sex with a synthetic Nuit was incomparable. She supplanted lust with detest and anger at him for blowing it, for becoming weak. One night she headed toward midtown to investigate and was astonished the motel had become even more than she had fantasized for him. Through the glass she peered at the grand lobby. It was a spectacle of opulence. She almost dared not enter, wondering if somehow she had been tricked and it was in fact she who was lost in feedback. The rotating doors pushed open by a man in a black silk suit. He glanced at her knowingly, his titanium eyes like clocks for a brief second, and he nodded for her to enter as he exited. She watched him get into a limousine, then she entered the lobby. The very air was palpable with charge, a charge that thrilled her. Concerned she had been sucked into a new game with Rook – one that she wanted to win – she quickly retreated back into the night. But even the night now was charged, and the entire city seemed to have transformed in mere moments. Across the expansive light emitting diode screens of skyscrapers, there whirled tuxedo-like black and white images and simple masquerade masks. Emblazoned intermittently was the phrase, "Tonight! The Black and White Ball! Are you ready?"

She was hit with an instantaneous memory, of a grand black and white ball to take place that very midnight. Her mind flooded with tangible memories of selling many costumes during the past weeks. Later as she was locking up the costume shop she noticed a grayish customer holding up a harlequin costume as if to size himself into it. She approached him and realized he was in fact cloaked in a harlequin costume. He held a rook chess piece, like a finger to lips, to silence her. He handed her a bag that cloaked a suit of some sorts. She unzipped it and saw bright orange latex inside. She sparked, darkly hopeful. The man pointed to his wrist as if to indicate a watch, then held up five fingers, indicating five minutes.

In the changing room she pulled out the skintight suit and slipped into it. It was indiscreetly slick, forming to her naked curves, and the hood fully encased her head. The eye holes were customized and exactly traced her eyelids, conforming perfectly to her face. Two small nostril holes were cut out for breath play. Sealed inside the orange latex suit she admired the curves of her body in the mirror, and in the mirror she saw her full red lips and bright blue eyes only. A few minutes later she stood out in front of the costume shop as the shutter automatically rolled down behind her. A limousine ushered up, and the Harlequin man opened up the door for her. He slipped back inside onto the driver seat and pulled into traffic.

"Where are we going?" she inquired.

The Harlequin emotionlessly answered, "The black and white ball."

She remembered more fully the costume shop had been busy with people who had won this year's Naranja lottery. She herself had not and had never. She felt a brief rush of excitement, thinking that perhaps Rook had cranked a twist into their games, that something really extraordinary was about to take place.

And it did.

"One problem," she had said to the Harlequin, "I'm dressed in bright orange."

The Harlequin quietly steered them toward the blazing sky rise lights, glimpsed her in the rear view mirror through his orange pupils, and momentarily answered, "Your role is not as a guest."

When they reached the opening to the Naranja tower the Harlequin driver slipped past it, drove around a block and gunned the gas. Fearing sudden death, her heart jumped into her throat, her arms crossed over her face, and the scream was on its way as the limousine seemingly shot off the street into a mired muckish fountain in front of a shuttered building. The image of the fountain fractured into a storm of interference energy. They had not left ground at all, and the limousine pulled up to an impenetrable and secret gate, which yawned open. The limousine shot through it and into the subterranean bowels of the Naranja tower.

She lowered her arms, grateful the scream had not left her throat.

They pulled onto a platform—a car elevator—encircled in darkness. Automatically the platform descended further, hundreds of feet, until the car elevator slowed and stopped at some uncoded level. Lights flashed on, and surrounding them a dozen women similarly dressed in orange, all armed, were positioned like the markings of the clock. The Harlequin got out, opened her door and gestured her to follow. She stepped out and observed the stoic women. The Harlequin wordlessly handed her an orange metal gun. Inside the bosom of the suit she had noticed the holster, and she had thought of the always-armed Rook. She unzipped the top of the suit and slipped the heavy metallic weapon into its place. The Harlequin handed her a small earring of sorts. She clipped it on, and right away she heard the voice of a woman.

The woman said, "You're smart. You'll catch on quickly. Keep an eye on my husband, and you will be rewarded. The twelve guards surrounding you answer to you. Forget all about Ms. Hunter. You are now an elite member of the orange agents, and you will be known as Agent Orange. And never forget, Agent Orange, you answer always to me."

There was nothing more.

Agent Orange, as she was becoming, realized she had just become a Naranja guard. It took a few more days before she fully realized she was *the* guard.

It wasn't Central Park—the reality garden—that was the Naranja Empire's most valuable possession: it was Rook. He was the eye of the reality storm, and without him none of them would or could exist.

It was easy to babysit him. They simply spied on his probable futures.

But their job was to ensure he always had at least one.

***

Agent Orange, emboldened, stared out at the Manhattan skyline up to the Naranja tower. It glittered with orange lights. She knew the other side of her, the one who loved Rook, was imprisoned inside the doomed tower. And she knew it was love that had gotten in the way of the big business of reality.

Rook was missing. Whether as foe or friend she did not yet risk a guess.

But risk was all she had. All she had ever had.

She pulled a Shakespeare Company matchbook from a pocket the size of an incision. She flipped open the cover. The neologism inside was *arch-villain.* She tore a match free and struck against the switch in her brow. As she did instantly, simultaneously, remote detonators sparked wicks running the length of underground power lines throughout the city. The electrical wicks tensed as current shot through them, reaching into the foundations and mechanical systems of 113 high-rises spread at angles, like a chessboard, across the grid of Manhattan. With delicate, precision timing, the electrical currents tripped master breakers, each of which had been turned into a detonation switch. Simultaneously the gas towers throughout lower Manhattan ignited. The wind tunnel avenues of the city rushed with grit and fire as all 113 buildings exploded, and the city transformed into an inferno.

***

In reaction the Central Librarians ran toward the vaults protecting the Shakespearean folios. The vaults were comprised of giant ice-chambers—freezers protecting the aging pages. Surrounding the chambers were pools of liquid nitrogen. They circled the vault and raised their guns in preparation for a different kind of firefight.

5: Ring Leader

Rook's arms swept through the water. He was a hundred yards from the shore of Governor's Island when a quantum Sobekian crocodile brushed close, its snout poised just above the water. Beast and R-complex man swam side by side. Rook rolled gently once onto his back then over onto his belly, settling on top of the crocodile. Positioned behind the massive head of the beast, Rook's mouth and eyes blended into the scaly back. At the rocky shore edge a fleet of adult saltwater crocodiles suspended, their snouts held just above the water. As harsh lights from the Kings County Kong swept over Rook and his crocodile, it seemed only a saltwater giant was slithering close to the shore. Rook rolled off the crocodile and pulled himself to the rocks. Through a barbed wire fence he watched as the Kong guarded a row of biplanes and a row of drones. The drone squadron was aligning for quick takeoff.

Rook crawled out of the brackish waters on his belly and crawled like a crocodile through the shadows toward the barbed wire fence. He observed a fuel maintenance technician straddling a ladder and filling a plane tank up with avgas. Momentarily suspicious, the man whipped around, but he saw only the snouts of the vicious crocodiles. The suspicion passed, and he began to whistle a dark unthreaded tune. In the foreground, Manhattan blazed.

Rook stared at the main avgas tank, and as if Rook's mind itself ignited it just then the tank exploded—an unexpected back flash from the burning city.

The man jerked the nozzle out of the plane, but he could not disengage the pump in time, As fire raced toward him, shooting out of the hose, he dropped it, and fire sprayed like a fountain around him. He ran in horror as combusted gasoline showered down, and one by one each avgas tank exploded in a daisy chain of backfire.

Rook turned to the city spectacle. He had been clued in the whole time, he realized, to the smell of hash burning, the smell of gas burning, to *bai jiu*—to the matches.

The drone squadron, one by one, shot into the sky. War against Naranja already had been declared by Agent Orange, but now war was upon the city of New York.

A pilot ran toward the abandoned plane but a wall of fire halted him. Over the tops of the flames he watched as Rook stood slowly and reached up into the razor wire fence. The razor edges slashed Rook's skin, opening the fresh wounds, and to Rook, whose chilled body could barely feel pain, whose brain was a quantum reality storm, the fence might as well not be there at all. Rook crawled over it. Naked and bleeding he approached the wall of fire and walked through it. The stunned pilot stared at him, and in darkness Rook vanished.

Behind him, standing in the man's shadow, Rook clocked him cold hard with the butt of the man's own gun, and he rolled the pilot behind barrels. At the biplane, he wound the propeller, and momentarily it whipped, cranking the engine to life. As the piston's pumped, a bleeding Rook promptly scrambled into the cockpit of the man's plane. He flipped toggle switches, and the engines sputtered, warming, then he taxied the biplane through the fire toward the runway. Down at the end a man holding two bright orange cones signaled it was safe for takeoff. Rook focused on the orange cones as he gunned down the runway and eased the nose of the plane into the humid air.

The lower Manhattan inferno clotted the sky with thick soot under the blazing rooflines. Doors to fire engine houses all over the city rolled open to bullet hail from low flying drones. An Engine on Naranja's payroll blared to the closest scene, and the firemen screwed a hose to a hydrant. Instantly and unexpectedly they spread the fire by a thousand fold. The flames shot back toward them and engulfed screaming men.

One screamed, “It’s gasoline! *Gasland!*”

Around them citizens ran in panic as the entire city reduced to mayhem.

High above it all in her blue room, Anja Naranja breathed fresh air pumped in from above the thunderstorm clouds, but already the urgent pungency of fire was pushing into the upper atmosphere. Her Rainmaker jets were exterminating Kong drones by simple radar locating and laser fire, but her city, as Agent Orange had promised, was burning down. The console dedicated to tracking Rook through the nanoelectrodes embedded under his skin established he’d been jackin’ the butterfly in his home and was now swiftly moving toward Pell St. Dr. Kull made sympathetic eye contact with her, “Once again, it’s not him.”

Dr. Naranja balled his fist. His cheeks crinkled his salt and pepper stubble as his lips expanded into a grin. He commanded his fighter pilots, "Don't shoot plane seven."

Don't, Anja thought, *then don't.*

That was what Rook had said to her.

Clad in the Librarian combat suit, Anja stared at her Z-9. As the made-up Angela van Dyke, at a time when Rook no longer remembered her as Anja, she had met him in the library. Her library. If channel 113 rebooted, like it always did during the cycle of Seven, she would come to in time a week prior to this nightless night. She would awaken as Angela van Dyke. She would receive a clue from Cosmo, and she would leave it for Rook.

Only this time in the cycle of Seven, Agent Orange had become a double agent and had crossed her as she became one with her. She looked into the eyes of her father and her irises dialed wildly, syncing with his. Getting the old gasoline empire tycoons riled up in the classical reality Petroleum Club of Fort Worth, Texas and then in Brooklyn's Gasland had been so easy. *Hell, like taking candy from a baby,* the doctor thought. *New York City's been burned down before by the people who loved it the most.*

What other better way to preserve his empire than to destroy it before it could be taken over by others? He knew they were coming to get the quantum book of channels, but they did not know he had planned all along on surrendering it to them in a code too complex for them to decipher. He had secretly nicknamed the code *Shakespeare* during his early studies, and cleverly embedded it into literature long known. He had programmed the code so that once tampered with, it would catch fire.

After all fire had long been a way to exterminate weeds, and weeds—especially the dominantly invasive *bromus* genus—had long been the planet's fuel for fire.

The quantum book of life, he decided, *is about ready to self-combust.*

His corneas reflected the inferno raging around their tower. He reached out to Anja and handed her a vial of ink and a miniature nib.

"This will take you straight to the Library."

Anja jabbed the miniature nib into the vial, positioned a small tube into the crook of her arm and connected it to her nanoelectrodes.

Agent Orange, meet me in my library!

***

Outside the Library Agent Orange's six drove their motorcycle past steel fire doors and tossed sticks of dynamite toward the blocked entry. They retreated down the front steps and joined Agent Orange across the street. She lit another match, and the entry exploded and collapsed. The fire bore her insignia, of the A surrounded by an O.

Outside the Royal Rainmakers shaved the city skyline, spraying their cargo loads of ink onto surrounding flames, preserving the Naranja tower, Central

Park and the Central Library.

Agent Orange stormed into the Central Library with her orange metal gun drawn, her six surrounding her. In the antique vault section she was met by the armed Librarians

Agent Orange demanded, “I have Rook, so you know shooting me is forbidden! Now, open the vault!”

The Librarians answered fearlessly, in unison, “We don’t have access.”

Agent Orange scanned the antique vault, and knowing it had direct connection to the Naranjas, she shouted, “Open the vault!”

A stoic Anja appeared in front of her, at first in hologram, then in flesh. “With pleasure.” She stared into an iris recognition scanner, and as her irises dialed it verified her. The wheel handle of the vault turned, and the great door yawned open.

Together they approached a vacuum chambered glass case. Inside it a swampy soup of pulp was encased.

“What the hell is this? Where are the Shakespearean folios?” Agent Orange demanded.

“I don’t know.”

Her face went white. Her skin transformed into paper and her features into ink. She uncoiled, a giant ream of paper exploding from her spine. Space-time mottled into pulp inside the Library. Within the paper and ink storm, Agent Orange struggled to retain her human form.

Through the storm, they heard the voice of Naranja, “You were grafted, authored into an imaginary reality, and little by little, over time, you began to realize you are as characters in a book, authored by a god as mysterious as Shakespeare and as chaotic as Jack the Butterfly. Take my magical paper. Take my magical ink. With it you may write your way into reality in anyway you please. You are slaves to this author no more.”

They heard Anja’s voice, "You are the authors now. But not of the cycle of Seven. We will hold onto that. You may have midnight, channel 113."

Through the maelstrom—a pupa transforming into a butterfly of paper and ink—Agent Orange lit an *arch-villain* match and touched it to the rest of the remaining 113 *arch-villain* matchbooks Jack the Butterfly had grafted, then hurled the burning books into the quantum vault.

***

In the Central Park sunjuice tower, simultaneously, Dr. Naranja's amber eyes flinched as his Shakespeare code, embedded in his personal library of glass tubes, spontaneously combusted. The Royal Rainmakers sheared the sky, unleashing torrential ink from the fabric of space and time.

6: Eject

Down below in the city swarms of dragonflies with lollipop stick spines nipped at the papyrus fronds choking the island—the fronds that had become critical for holding hurricane surges at bay. The inky rain saturated their paper spines, and they became as pen nibs, writing Shakespearean knocking phrases into the sky.

Rook circled in the biplane upward. A black cloud manifest at first as an edge, then it flipped sideways and became a half-mile shroud of the dragonflies. Rook grit his teeth as they pelted the biplane window, cracking it with their tense spines.

The Kong's small delta shaped drones were using the smokescreen to fly north, riddling with bullets water towers that had been turned into deadly gasoline bombs. The Kings County Kong, like a spasm of hornets, turned south and then east, fleeing the island. Rook aimed the Vickers machine gun at them and hailed the Kong squadron with bullets. Biplanes flipped and rolled back in response, rushing in on him. He was already halfway across the East River with five Kong following in chase. As he had expected they veered sharply back toward Brooklyn the closer he got to Manhattan, and he wailed into lower Manhattan through the brutally dark smoke, clutched at the radio and uttered into it, "Plane seven speaking. I am not with Gasland."

Over the airwaves Agent Orange and Anja Naranja heard the words.

Rook jumped the plane upward, climbing it up high as if he was chasing the lightning rod on Naranja's tower. Slowly he circled the tower in a spiral, climbing ever upward toward the top. He was closing in on the black clouds when he saw a flash of mirror, and he braced for gunfire, but there was none. The mirrored Naranja jet, so difficult to exactly place, reflected the razzle-dazzle paint of the biplane he had stolen and zoomed past him safely. Everything went darker as he flew through the blanket of coal colored clouds, and the sky darkened into a pitching black thunderstorm.

Rook burst through the cloud cover, and the cosmic blue sky above it rushed him like a drug. He found himself alone, lost in the awe of night—closing in on midnight. He slowly leveled the wings, and he said, "I am with Zeno."

He turned the plane vertically up past the blue room toward the eye of the storm issuing from its lightning rod pinnacle. As he rushed close he saw the room was filled with the lush, grafted orange tree. He remembered it, and he spoke again, "I remember everything—from the beginning of time to the end! I want to rest!"

The lightning spire needled up another several stories like a mighty orchestral art deco baton. Some dare devil Kong rose through the clouds further east, and as two jetted toward him Naranja's fabled mirrored jets blazed past, fired lasers and dropped them like zeros from the sky. Rook turned back toward the tower, and set the course of the plane to fly straight over it. When he was almost directly over it, he reached between his legs, found the lever and pulled for eject. Leg restraints snapped him tight, and the top wing of the biplane snapped in half, jettisoning away from the craft. A momentous bang from the seat gutting itself was followed by a zipping rush of rocket explosion. Rook catapulted out and up. The g force was five times his body, and his stomach filled his mouth. The secondary ejection rocket fired, propelling him another hundred feet or so up, and a gunlike blast shot out the small drogue parachute. It unfolded into a five foot canopy, slowing him down considerably, and within seconds the drogue yanked the larger, full parachute out. It shot open like an umbrella.

The last step in the ejection sequence, of the ejection motor separating man from seat, gave a yowl, a grind, and it halted, failing. Nine seconds had passed. Slowly in the magnificent heavens, Rook drifted down while seated.

The unpiloted biplane buzzed forth toward New Jersey, the mirrored jets zapped it. It plummeted toward the Hudson like silver dust.

Rook whipped through the night, down past the clear glass walls of the blue room.

Rook in response clawed at the grafted contact lenses as he drifted slowly down.

The dark clouds swallowed him and whipped him, then wound him like a clock as the spiral arms of hurricane whirled. Amidst sheets of spastic lightning, Rook peeled the contacts free, revealing his golden eyes and crocodilian slitted pupils. His skin was transforming, and the bleeding lacerations emitted a golden light. The ejection seat transformed into an amorphous throne, and swathing above him his shadow transformed into a diabolical umbrage.

Rook, pinned to the eye of the storm, remembered exactly who he was. More importantly, in his imagination, who and what he wanted to be.

He focused and dialed into channel zero.

With talons shaped like his father's straight razor blades, he slashed at the parachute cords. As the throne dumped below the clouds into the harsh theta pounding of quantum thundering rain, Rook's head transformed into a crocodile's. Below him concentric rings of orange trees made a bulls-eye in Central Park's most central grove. Ringing trees alternated with concentric moats, and in the very center was a pond in which lived the largest saltwater crocodile in captivity. It was fifty-five feet long, and it arched up, wielding open its massive jaws. Standing on its back, Jules Barbillon wore a suit stitched from his crocodile books, and he upheld his auction paddle emblazoned with numerals 113. It morphed, swarming into a black hole butterfly folio. He shrieked with joy, "Sobek rise!"

The crocodile's skin erupted into embroidered emerald fire as it simultaneously swallowed Rook and its own tail. New York City exploded into quantum butterfly mist.

The explosion reversed, and the quantum black hole butterflies swallowed into themselves, sucking the Park, the city, the world and the universe into nothingness the size of a quantum pinhead.

The imploded dot simultaneously exploded, expanding cosmically into nascent stardust, into Nuit. Her pregnant belly glowed with an orange sun. An array of planets orbited the sun.

Sobek the quantum oroboros slept inside her, his own belly an infinitely looping quantum supercell storm. Full of self-knowledge, his transitory journey as a human psychonaut lulling, he rested on both the moment of his creation and his death, the seventh day and night. Around the supercell eye of the storm, on his birth and death day, an ominously eternal quantum echo, like a beckoning finger, like a barb in a universe, hooked.

CHAPTER NINETEEN: The Beginning

Agent Orange sat in her office at Orange Security and faced an antique typewriter. A ribbon saturated with ink took the hammering impressions from the typefaces. She smiled as she wrote.

***

As the evening waned and Seven rolled over into a newish Sunday, detective Rook Black awakened to the sound of a newspaper hitting his front step. Black ink splashed from it like blood, wrote wriggling, wormy passages into rain, then slipped down into the gutter. Black inky rain etched the entire city.

Rook slowly pulled himself out of bed and massaged the sleep out of his face, noticing the stubble in the shape of a Van Dyke beard along his jaw. In his bathroom he brushed his teeth, blinked at his coal black eyes and shaved his fresh, prickly modacryclic stubble into a Van Dyke. The scars crisscrossing his semi-plastic body he barely noticed. In his office he turned on a lamp, flooding light over his chessboard table. Set upon it was a matchbook he did not recognize. The cardboard was some sort of fake crocodile skin. His nanoretinas scanned it. He touched it by the edges and carefully opened it; inside in a woman's floral handwriting, in mirror writing it read, *Shadow: Genesis Avenue.*

Rook sat down and fingered open a small humidor he also did not recognize. He extracted a cigar, and with a match, he lit it and inhaled. *The problem with resting*, he thought, i*s we are not aware when we are there.*

Rook showered, dressed into his black suit, set his black pea souper over his shocks of black hair and headed out into the inky rainstorm toward Cafe 113 for his usual breakfast.

Genesis Avenue, he thought, *Genesis Avenue can wait until after breakfast.*

***

Agent Orange leaned back from the typewriter and gazed out over the majestic orange lights bathing the parallel reality city she was now the author of. *My city*, she thought. She scrolled the paper out of the typewriter, dipped a quill into a vial of orange ink and signed her insignia into the paper, an A surrounded by an O.

***

The same pattern rippled momentarily through the egg yolk under Rook's fork. He finished his breakfast, pushed out into the inky rain and saw the same pattern rippling in the gutters. His lips pulled into an almost smile. He fingered the matches he held in one pocket and his gun in the other. *Genesis*, he thought, *Genesis Avenue*.

He knew there was no such street name in Manhattan. He folded into the driver's seat of his sedan. He thought of mirror writing.

"ECHO on. Map," he commanded. "Dead ends."

Made in the USA
Charleston, SC
22 November 2013